"I hate you." She hissed. But she turned to him and held
him tight, shuddering in his arms and weeping against his
neck. "I hate you so much, Ben Pipestone."

"What can I do?" The fires of hell burned in his throat.
"Just tell me, honey, what can I do?"

"Tell me it isn't true." She sobbed. "Tell me you didn't
really ..."

"I can't." And it was killing him. "I won't lie to you
anymore. All I can say is I'm sorry."

"Why doesn't that help?"

"Because it doesn't make it go away. If you want me
to go—"

"I don't." The embrace of the man who'd betrayed her
seemed an improbable place to find comfort, but there it was.
"I don't want to hurt alone. And I don't want to hurt with
anyone else."

"Jesus," he whispered, "we make a hell of a pair."

Other Avon Books by
Kathleen Eagle

FIRE AND RAIN
THIS TIME FOREVER

KATHLEEN EAGLE

REASON TO BELIEVE

AVON BOOKS ◆ NEW YORK

REASON TO BELIEVE is an original publication of Avon Books. This work has never before appeared in book form. This work is a novel. Any similarity to actual persons or events is purely coincidental.

AVON BOOKS
A division of
The Hearst Corporation
1350 Avenue of the Americas
New York, New York 10019

Copyright © 1995 by Kathleen Eagle
Inside cover author photo by Robert Knutson
Published by arrangement with the author
Library of Congress Catalog Card Number: 94-96256
ISBN: 0-380-77633-2

First Avon Books Printing: February 1995

AVON TRADEMARK REG. U.S. PAT. OFF. AND IN OTHER COUNTRIES, MARCA REGISTRADA, HECHO EN U.S.A.

Printed in the U.S.A.

RA 10 9 8 7 6 5 4 3 2 1

For the runners and the riders, and for all those who offered support. May the sacrifices be known, the injustices be rectified, and may the healing touch battered hearts everywhere.

PROLOGUE

Mid-October 1990

Anna Pipestone tucked the bottle of Obsession for Men beneath the pile of stuffed animals that served as sentries in the dark corner of her closet. It was a safe place to store all the booty she'd stolen since her friend Jennifer had introduced her to the thrills and skills of shoplifting two months ago. As long as the closet didn't look too messy, she knew her mother wouldn't bother it.

Each small item in her stash was like a trophy, snatched right out from under the nose of a certain bigheaded clerk who manned the cosmetics counter at Dalton's. Sadly, Anna had lost out on the last trophy—an umbrella offered free with any fifteen-dollar purchase—when a skinny guy in a black leather jacket had stopped her the second she'd stepped over the line into the mall. "Store security," he'd mumbled past a lip full of chew. At first she'd thought he was just some horny kid trying to hit on her. People always found it hard to believe, just looking at her, that she was only thirteen. But he'd been careful not to touch her, and it was a good thing. She'd have popped him a good one. She'd seen a show on TV about bogus strip searches by guys who looked just about as sleazy as this one. Besides, cops weren't supposed to chew snuff.

But this one did. And in her defensive mode Anna had almost forgotten about the damned umbrella. At her hearing she'd tried to tell the juvenile court referee that she'd just taken the giveaway sign at its word and missed the fine print about having to buy something, but he hadn't bought it.

Neither had her mother. The best part of it was, Dalton's was her mother's favorite store. Anna sat back on her haunches and smiled at the white bear her dad had given her for her eighth birthday. She still remembered these things. Who'd given her what for which birthday. Her dad was always saying she wasn't getting any more stuffed animals, but then her birthday would come around, and he'd be the one to give her another bear. Her mother favored clothes and maybe something for her room, like the new yellow comforter on her bed.

Anna didn't like the room's yellow and white decor anymore. She'd tried to tell her mother she wanted to change it to red and black, but Miss Clean and Straight wouldn't listen. As soon as the furor over this crappy probation she was temporarily chained to blew over, she was going to get herself a few cans of black paint and put the daisy wallpaper out of its perky misery.

She pushed herself up off the floor, then flopped on the bed and snatched the morning paper off the alarm clock that sat on her nightstand. According to Daisy Duck's white-gloved fingers, it was almost two o'clock. She was skipping fifth period. She'd have to get moving if she was going to make it to sixth. She didn't skip class very often—detention was a pain in the ass—but somebody had asked her if that Pipestone guy in this morning's paper was related to her. Even though she hadn't looked at the paper, she'd said he wasn't. She didn't ask what it was about, and she didn't want to check out the story in the school library. If it was something about her dad—if he'd fallen off the wagon and gotten picked up by the cops or gotten in a wreck—she'd wanted to be alone when she read about it. She'd gotten a ride home with Jennifer and her scuzzy boyfriend.

But the story wasn't about Ben Pipestone. It was about the upcoming annual Big Foot Memorial Ride. The article quoted Dewey Pipestone, Anna's grandfather, as saying that he was getting too old to be the spiritual leader for the Lakota on such an arduous venture, but there was no one to take his place. Anna knew that the remark was an oblique reference to her father. Dewey Pipestone was determined to live to see his son succeed him as carrier of the Sacred Pipe. Ben's standard reply was, "Guess the ol' man's bound to outlive me, then." *Outwait*, Dewey would say. And round and round it went.

Round and round, Anna thought. Just like her and her mom. The ol' lady had only one person left to rag on, now that she'd kicked Daddy out, and that was Anna. Well, if the woman was going to bitch anyway, might as well give her something to bitch about. And as long as Anna was already skipping school, she figured she might as well have some fun. Jennifer Hardin wasn't exactly deep, but she was good for a few laughs. Maybe a little party or something.

Anna reached for the white Princess phone beside the bed. The *Tribune* snagged her drifting attention, and she dropped the receiver back in place.

It had been a while since she'd seen her grandfather. He'd had a crappy-sounding cough ever since she could remember. An old man's way of hacking. She couldn't imagine he'd gotten any younger. Two weeks was a long time to spend in the saddle, especially in December, *especially* in *South Dakota* in December.

Of course, it would have to be a lot easier nowadays than it had been the first time around. Anna had read something about it in school—about a paragraph's worth in the eighth grade history book about the "Battle of Wounded Knee"—but she'd also heard it from the Indian

side. A century ago, back in 1890, most of the people
had walked those two hundred and some-odd miles, and
they'd done it because they had no choice. They were
being hounded by the U.S. Army.

But Anna's grandfather *did* have a choice. He didn't
have to risk his health, not in this day and age. He could
turn the pipe over to someone else. He was too old to be
spending eight or ten hours a day on horseback for two
weeks and camping out in the winter.

But Anna could do it. She had a long Christmas
vacation coming. Her father wasn't interested, and she
could just about imagine what her mother would say.
But so what? Those two were so screwed up, it wasn't
funny. She'd told them once that if they ever split up, she
wasn't going to stay with either one of them. She wasn't
going to visit them or let them come to her wedding or
baby-sit their grandchildren, nothing. When she'd said
it, she wasn't thinking it would actually happen.

It had happened to Jennifer Hardin and a bunch of
other kids she knew, but it would never happen to her.
Her parents had had a hard enough time getting together,
what with her dad being an Indian, her mom being white.
They'd had a few problems, big deal. Her dad was
working on his problem. As for her mom's problem,
well . . . being too damn good probably wasn't curable.
The woman just couldn't be wrong, couldn't cross over
the line, couldn't make a mistake.

But Anna could do it. She could do anything she
damn well pleased. Who would stop her? Near as she
could tell, her dad hadn't even tried to stand up to
her mom. He'd just tucked his tail between his legs
and moved out. And now her mom couldn't look at
a picture of him or find one of his socks in the back
of the drawer or even make a pot of goulash without
getting all teary-eyed. If she thought she was hiding
all that sniffling from Anna, she was definitely mistak-
en.

What had he done? Anna wanted to know. She got no answers. She'd stopped asking. She had her own life, her own friends, her own stuff to do. Great stuff, too. Just ask her, and she was ready. Just *dare* her, and she'd try it. Like this ride, for instance. Just let somebody say the word *no*, and she'd tell them just where they could go.

Anna could do it.

I

It was the song playing on the radio that made Ben Pipestone tighten his two-fisted grip on the big steering wheel of his old red and white Chevy pickup. Somebody up there had to be orchestrating moments like this, putting "Me and Bobbie McGee" in the DJ's hands just as Ben was approaching the newly resurfaced driveway of his former home. Some all-seeing body who had nothing better to do than to mess with a man's head just when the sorry bastard thought he was finally getting it on straight.

He doubted that Tunkasila had much time for him these days. Probably not Jesus, either, or the Virgin Mary or anybody in the upper echelon of the Spirit World. He'd bet on his old buddy, Iktome. It was just like the wily Lakota Trickster to play on the sentimental bone a guy could have sworn he didn't have in his body.

Clara was the one who was always getting sentimental over songs, but there Ben sat, staring at the house and letting his throat tighten up over foolish memories. It hurt to swallow, but he actually savored the fleeting twinge. Yeah, pour on the pain, he told himself. Pain was good. Physical pain was the kind of a challenge a guy could really sink his teeth into and hope to beat.

The best way to kill it—well, maybe the second best— was to get busy and concentrate on the here and now.

Forget the past and face the present. Deal with the condition of the driveway right in front of him. Take note that the guy who had sold him on the asphalt had done a nice job, which was good to know since Ben had paid the bill simply on Clara's terse approval. No detailed report, no "Thanks, we needed that." All she'd said was, "Yes, it's fine." So he'd taken what satisfaction could be had in writing a check for the balance owed on the job. After all, it was still his house, at least partly, if not his home.

The yard needed some work, though. Clara was a great one for putting in flowers in the spring, but after the first frost, she'd always left the dead stuff for him to take care of. Not that he'd minded much. This was the first house he'd owned, and he'd never had a yard before. Probably never would again, not one like this. He figured he might as well drive back up to Bismarck and take care of the fall cleanup next week, sometime when no one would be home.

The thing he'd liked most about the house was the view of the river bluffs from the big window in the front room. Clara had had her list of requirements, but he'd mortgaged his soul so that he could see forever on a clear day. And in North Dakota you could count on plenty of cloudless sky. Someday he was going to buy the adjacent farmland, he'd told Clara. Plenty of room to keep a couple of horses. Some primal part of his brain still measured his personal worth in horses.

The late afternoon sunlight slanted across the field behind the house like long fingers reaching for the last biscuit on the table. *Don't reach*, Ben could hear Clara saying in that soft, crisp tone she took when she was being the authoritative mother. *Ask, and it shall be passed.*

Ask, and it shall be passed.

How about, ask and it shall be *past*?

Not likely. Not after what he'd done.

He set the brake and draped his wrists over the top of the steering wheel, rubbing his chin on the shoulder of his denim jacket. Softly, absently, he added his deep voice to the song's final refrain as he gazed out the pickup's side window. The backyard had faded to yellow-green, but the autumn sun had turned the alfalfa stubble to pure gold. The hollow echo of one single yesterday was all he had to hang on to most nights. It wasn't always the same one, but he tried to stick to the good ones. The days when the troubles were still far away and the nights when he'd slept nearly guilt-free. Those were the yesterdays he believed in.

Today Clara wanted to talk to him about Annie. She'd said so over the phone, taking refuge in a tone she'd once reserved for salespeople and bill collectors. He should have just said, "Talk. I'm listening." That was usually the way it was anyway these days. She'd talk. He'd listen. It was always about Annie. Clara wouldn't talk to him about much else.

By now she'd have seen his pickup in the driveway, and would be waiting for him to come to the door. He didn't have time for a cigarette, but he sure could have used one.

It wasn't that he didn't want to see her. He did. He always did. Even when he knew he wasn't going to enjoy seeing the look that inevitably crept into her autumn-colored eyes whenever she saw him these days. She always managed to coat that sad look with something harder—a cool glaze, an angry sheen—but at the core of it he could see the hurt. It was always there for him to see, which was as it should have been, for he had been the one to put it there.

The last time he'd mounted the front steps, all hell had broken loose when he'd walked right on in and announced his presence. In the interest of trying to keep the peace, he slowly extended one finger toward the doorbell, but he couldn't quite bring himself to punch the button. Granted, she'd been making most of the house payments since she'd kicked him out, but before that it had always been "we," "us," and "ours." He couldn't see ringing his own doorbell unless he was locked out.

Which, he discovered, he was. The door opened just as he'd thrust his hand into the pocket of his jeans in search of his key. He was greeted by enthusiastic paws, nose, tongue, and wagging tail.

"Hey, Pancho. You still remember me, huh?" Ben plunged both hands into the shepherd's plush ruff and squatted to greet his old pal, eye to eye. "How's the mutt?" he crooned, playfully shaking the dog's head. "How's the ol' bruiser?"

"Pleased to see you, obviously."

Straightening slowly as the smile slid from his face, he tried to remember how her voice had sounded when she'd been pleased to see him. He dusted off the warm, soft echo from the annals in his head and let it light a spark in his eyes. "Hello, Clara."

Once caught, she couldn't look away, but her tone didn't change. "Thank you for coming. I know how busy you are."

The stiff greeting rankled. How in the hell could she possibly know whether he was busy?

But he shrugged it off. "You said the magic word," he reminded her as he patted Pancho again, who was whining and wagging to beat the band. "Annie."

"Yes. The magic word." A word that was slightly different for her than it was for him, much like most of the magic they'd shared over the years. "*Anna* is going through a difficult time, and I'm at my wits' end."

"Your wits' end," he repeated thoughtfully. "Can't imagine anybody goin' quite that far, Clara."

"Of course you can. You've driven me there many times." She gave him a sharp glare as she stepped aside to let him in. "You and this dog. Go on out, now, Pancho."

"Driven you or taken you?" He couldn't help smiling a little when Pancho had to be shooed along. "Are we thinking about the same place? Clara Pipestone's wits' end, where thinking leaves off and—"

"Stupidity takes over."

There it was. The bruised look. Her parti-colored eyes reflected it perfectly, and whenever he saw it, that small but troublesome good thing that dwelled deep in his gut got to feeling a little sick. It was the kind of morning-after sick that made the drinking man head straight for the refrigerator or the liquor store or the bar—wherever he had to go to find a can of beer. Ben knew the procedure only too well.

"Wrong subject," he admitted, stepping into the living room as Clara closed the door. "Is Annie here?"

"No, and she should be." She checked her watch. It was a gesture she used often to convey any number of messages. Ben recognized the worry-nuance when she glanced at the mantel clock for a second opinion. "I thought she would be. I had a call at work from one of her teachers who had trouble with her in class today, and that's when I called you."

He could tell the call had been a last resort.

Clara sighed. "But she didn't come home on the bus. I've searched both malls. I've called everyone I can think of. All her friends."

"The police?"

"No," she said quietly. "Not yet. If they pick her up, they'll take her to the police station again." She hit him with one of her meaningful looks. "Yes, *again*."

Annie and the police? His brain refused to put the two together. "What's goin' on?"

"Her parents have split up; that's what's going on. Not to mention the fact that she's a thirteen-year-old female, and she can't decide whether that particular fate or her mother is the worse bitch." She challenged him with a cold stare. "I'm sure you can set her straight."

He saw her stare and raised her one cocked eyebrow. "I'd only be guessing."

"Yes, well . . ."

She folded, sinking slowly into an overstuffed brocade chair. Her fluttery gesture invited him to occupy the matching one, so he took a tentative seat on the chair's front edge. They'd called them the mama and papa chairs. He wondered when she'd had them reupholstered.

"She's so much like you, it's scary, Ben. She's reckless. She takes awful chances just to prove . . ." The small, pale hand made another powerless gesture. "Whatever it is she's trying to prove. Independence, maybe."

There was something a little scary about Clara's apparent undoing, even if it was only temporary. She was not easily undone.

"Maybe she's not trying to prove anything. Maybe she's not thinking all that straight. Did you check with security at the malls?"

"No. I checked all the fast-food places and searched the stores she goes to. I looked all over."

"All over?" She probably believed her own bullshit, too, but the fact was, he'd never known Clara to look carefully for anything. He gave a knowing smile. "What you did was, you marched up one side and down the other, blinders cuttin' off your view and smoke rollin' out your ears so you couldn't hear a damn freight train howling at your heels."

"That's not true at all, but I'll tell you what is true." She wagged a finger at him, and he silently congratulated himself for getting her back up so quickly, with added starch. "You have no idea what it's like to worry about someone else's safety and well-being, to be angry because they don't have sense enough to call home, and then to feel scared because—" Her finger came down, and her gaze drifted to the clock on the mantel. "Because there's always the remote chance that something terrible might have happened."

"If it's so damned remote, why is it always the first thing that comes into your head? Can't you just . . ."

She slashed at his throat with her eyes.

He surrendered with a sigh. "Jesus, here we go." He closed his eyes briefly, regrouping. "Look, I'm sorry. I don't want to argue."

"Then let's just stick to the problem at hand, which is finding our daughter."

"I'll make the rounds again while you stay by the phone. Maybe she saw you coming, and she just ducked out of sight."

"And I suppose if she sees you, she'll come running."

"She's just a kid, Clara. Who knows what kind of a game she's playing?"

Her smile was slight and smug. "Her father wouldn't, that's for sure."

"Looks like she's got her mother buffaloed, too."

"Like father, like daughter."

"You wanna back off, just a little?" Her eyes said no. He braced his hands on his knees and pushed to his feet. "Forget it. I'm outta here. I'll call you if I find her. If I don't . . ."

"Call me anyway."

The soft plea drew his head around. Her eyes pleaded, too, and he nodded.

"If I have to go to the police . . ."

He was sure she'd never so much as pocketed a pen at a cash register. *The policeman is your friend,* she used to tell Annie. But now she seemed to have some misgivings about that. That, too, he could see in her eyes. "If it comes to that, I'll do it," he said.

"She's already on probation," she said sadly, then added, "Sort of."

"Sort of?"

She shrugged. She looked devastated, on the verge of tears. It wasn't the time to ask for more details.

"You just stay by the phone."

He stopped at each of the places Clara had already covered, made himself clearly visible for a time, then moved on. He knew his best hope was not *finding* but being found, assuming Annie really did want to see him. That was the case he chose to presume, even though he was probably stretching it to suit his own needs.

He figured Annie was probably having a good time somewhere, and since she was on her own turf, she wasn't going to turn up until she was ready. He knew the game well. He'd played it a lot himself. The futility of the search frustrated him, but he didn't know what else to do. He was a relative newcomer to the role of being "the responsible one" in this kind of situation, and he was spinning his wheels, running in circles.

He'd been doing that a lot lately. His father was always expounding about the sacredness of the circle, but this was more like spinning his wheels in the clay ruts of his own private hell. His father was a holy man, a pipe carrier—*the* pipe carrier, to hear him tell it. Not all the Lakota agreed that Dewey Pipestone was rightfully the keeper of the pipe given to the people by the White Buffalo Calf Woman during a time that lived, at least in Ben's mind, only in legend and lore. Ben would have been hard-pressed to think of *anything* that all the Lakota were likely to agree on, but the "traditionals" upheld Dewey's claim to the title, and that was all that mattered to the old man. He took his calling seriously, even though the ravages of age made it more difficult all the time.

Ben respected his father, and he didn't discount tradition, but he couldn't see himself as pipe-carrier material. The fact that he'd screwed up his marriage notwithstanding, he just wasn't big on ceremony. Besides that, he himself had been a shitty father. His daughter was thirteen, and he'd been out of the house for almost two years. He didn't know what she was taking in school this year or what kind of music she was listening to on the radio these days, whether she had a boyfriend yet or wanted one.

Or where she was. Goddamn, he had no idea where she was or where else to look, and it was getting cold, and it was already darker than hell.

He drove the length and breadth of Bismarck, dragging Main like a youth on the prowl, scouting out cars, scanning the sidewalks. But the Main he'd once dragged had been a hell of a lot shorter than this one. Fewer corners. Fewer white kids. More Indians.

And it sure was a whole lot different when a man was looking for his daughter.

Every carload of boys raised his hackles. Take a good look at these young bucks, he told himself. Cruising for tail. Horny as hell, every last one of them. Annie was thirteen, but she looked older, especially now that she was using makeup. What was her mother thinking about, anyway, letting her put that stuff on her face?

Christ, he hoped she hadn't met up with a load of testosterone on wheels like the one in the slick red Mustang he'd just passed. A guy oughta carry a shotgun loaded for teenage boys, just in case. Blast his ass with saltpeter if he comes sniffin' around your daughter. Especially if he wears a cowboy hat and a pair of sharp-toed Tony Lamas with worn-down riding heels.

Which was exactly what he'd been wearing the day he'd met Clara . . .

Actually, his father had met her first. The minute he saw the little white Escort turn off the blacktop and come bouncing along the rutted dirt road toward the house, Ben knew somebody from off the rez was looking for an "Indian expert." Anybody local would have skimmed the ruts and created a wing-shaped dust wake. Long before she drove into the yard, he'd figured the driver for a woman with a mission, and he also guessed she didn't know a hell of a lot about cars.

She stepped out, closed the door, straightened her nice white skirt, and approached him without giving her poor gasping car a second glance. She carried a folded piece of paper. Clearly she had business to attend to.

She also had great legs.

"Is this where Dewey Pipestone lives?"

Ben nodded.

She shaded her eyes with a cupped hand. The warm breeze lifted her dark blond hair like a billowing cape. "Is he home?"

Ben sat back against the hood of the car he'd been working on all afternoon. He'd gotten it started, but it wasn't going far without a whole bunch of parts he didn't have. He tipped his straw cowboy hat back with one finger. Let her get a better look.

"Who wants to know? You a social worker?"

"I'm a student, actually."

Ahh. "*Studying* to be a social worker?"

"Studying the history of the indigenous people of North America, particularly the Great Plains." She smiled, accepting his low, ostensibly appreciative whistle as an indication that he was duly impressed.

He was, but not necessarily with her academic pursuits. She had several assets going for her besides the legs. He liked the way her lips were shaped like a dime-store valentine. And he was glad she wasn't a social worker. They could be damn meddlesome.

She offered a handshake. "I'm Clara Whiting. Mr. Pipestone's expecting me." She glanced briefly over her shoulder, reconsidering the distant two-lane highway. Not a car in sight. "Maybe I took a wrong turn somewhere. The directions were—"

"Where you comin' from?"

"Bismarck."

"Not too many turns between here and Bismarck," he drawled, deliberately reeling out the words as though he couldn't spare too many. "Pretty hard to get lost."

"But it's a long drive. I hope I don't have to . . ." She unfolded the paper and quickly scanned its contents. "If you could just tell me . . ."

"If *you* could just tell *me* why Clara Whiting would be lookin' for Dewey Pipestone, I might be able to help you." She looked at him expectantly. "The name's Ben Pipestone. You're lookin' for my dad."

"Oh." She acknowledged her relief with another pleasant smile. "Good. I didn't think I could've missed the turn. There was only—"

"Dewey's away from his desk right now," he said, tucking his thumbs into his belt as he eyed the wispy steam rising from her car hood.

"Pardon me?"

He chuckled. "He's not home."

"He must have forgotten, then." Her gold wristwatch glinted in the sun. While she checked the time, he glanced at her car, which was still running. Barely. "Of course, I am a few minutes early. Maybe he . . ." *Changed his mind* didn't seem to be a possibility. "Do you know when he'll be back?"

"When he's done what he set out to do, I guess. Have you met him, face-to-face, or did somebody point you in his direction?"

He wondered if she realized that the steam wasn't a real good sign.

"I met him at a powwow," she said absently as she glanced down the road again. "I hope I've got the right day. I'm sure I do."

"You hope you do, you're sure you do." Ben smiled. Just because Dewey Pipestone was well beyond prime didn't mean he didn't enjoy looking. And Clara Whiting was a damn sweet eyeful, from the curve of her lips to the curve of her hips. The ol' man would have her thinking he was the be-all and end-all of Indian wisdom. "He'll be here."

"You're sure?"

"Oh, yeah." He tipped his head to the side as he stepped back and checked out the puddle gathering between the dry clay ruts under the front of her car. "If you're gonna wait around for him, you might think about shuttin' your engine off. Looks like you're runnin' pretty hot."

"Hot?"

He indicated the telltale steam with a chin jerk, and she finally turned to look. "I'm also sure you're overheating, Clara Whiting."

"Oh." She said it as though he'd told her she'd dropped a nickel. "You know, I *thought* there was something funny going on, but I wasn't sure."

"Sure enough. Funny as hell."

"Not funny ha-ha. Funny *strange*." Accordingly, she approached the car with caution, checking to make sure Ben wasn't far behind. "And something really is going on. It's steaming, isn't it? I thought maybe it was a mirage." She shook her head and gave a merry little laugh that tickled his ears and made him smile outright. "I'm afraid I don't know much about cars except how to get places in them."

"And this one got you all the way here without its gauges going nuts? It must love you." He nodded toward the driver's side. "You wanna pop the hood once? I've gotta see what's under there." His sly grin was meant to tease. "An engine or a bleeding heart."

"I always forget about those gauges," she muttered as she opened the door and reached inside to shut the ignition off. She bent down a little more to pull the release latch, accentuating yet another of her assets.

He took his time about retrieving an oily rag from his toolbox. He didn't want to miss any of her cute moves as he ambled back over to lift the hood.

Using the rag and a deft touch, he released the pressure on the radiator cap without scalding himself. Once the steam had dissipated, he was quickly able to locate the problem.

"You've got a busted hose."

She looked at him skeptically. He wasn't sure whether she was maintaining that safe distance from the engine, its trouble, or him. "How bad is that?"

"Bad enough." The assessment pretty much covered all three. "This is as far as this baby can take you until *somebody* takes care of *her*."

"Oh."

"But it could be worse. If the pump was busted, that somebody wouldn't be me." He walked away. He could feel her eyes on his back as he tossed the rag into the open toolbox. "Not that I couldn't fix it. I just wouldn't have the parts."

"You *can* fix a hose?"

"I can rig something up. Come on in." He jerked a nod in the direction of his father's three-room house. It wasn't much, but it was shade. "I'll make us some coffee. I'd offer you a beer, but the ol' man won't have it in the house."

"I'd really prefer a glass of water, if it's not too much trouble."

"That's exactly what your car wants, and you're both in luck." He sneaked another peek at those legs. "But I just might be in deep trouble."

"We'll be out of your hair before you know it." She smiled sweetly. "Promise."

As far as he knew, that was the only promise she'd ever gone back on. She'd taken root in his hair and permeated every nook and cranny in his brain. Not that she was part of his every conscious thought. Far from it. He worked hard at excluding her most of the time.

He did think about Annie a lot. He thought about his father once in a while, his friends occasionally, and his business was always right there in his face. He thought about himself. Hell, he thought about himself the most. But no matter what else he might be thinking about, Clara was still there, always there, firmly embedded in his head, thoroughly rooted in his hair. And she probably always would be.

He didn't want to go back to her now, tonight, not without Annie in tow, but his search wasn't getting him anywhere but edgy. It would have been nice to be able to save the day, to bring his daughter home safely, see the old my-hero sparkle in Clara's eyes. He liked that much better than that damned raging wounded look. But when he got back to the house and walked in empty-handed, he saw worse. He caught Clara crying.

Tucking her chin into the cowl of a soft blue sweater, she did her damnedest to hide the evidence behind the fall of her side-parted hair. Hanging her head was so unlike Clara that it unnerved him.

Ben greeted Pancho with a passing pat on the head as he strode into the living room. "Did . . . did somebody call?"

Her hair shimmied with her stiff headshake. "No."

"Is Annie—"

"She's not back yet, no." She dragged the heel of her hand quickly over the high curve of her cheek and sighed deeply. "I guess we'll have to call the police."

"I hate to do that." He peeled off his jacket and tossed it over the wing back of the "papa" chair.

"You don't have to." She snatched up the jacket before it had a chance to settle into place. *Let her hang it up if it bothers her that much*, he thought, but she seemed to have forgotten what she'd had in mind for it. She folded her arms around the black poplin and confronted him, hugging his jacket fiercely beneath her breasts. "You don't have to go with her when she has an appointment with a probation officer. You don't have to listen to her teachers' complaints."

"I will. Be glad to. She can stay with me, too, you just say the word."

"The word is no." Moving as though the weight of that small word exerted a terrible pressure, she eased herself into the chair, the mama chair, the smaller one, the one that fit her. Even so, it seemed to swallow her up when she sighed. "But just don't tell me what you hate to do, Ben, because you don't know the half of it. You don't know what it's like. Every day it's something else. She lies. She talks back to me. She—"

"Teenagers," he said sympathetically, seating himself in the chair that felt as though it could be his again, even with its sissy new disguise. "We always said she was gonna be a handful, remember? She always had a mind of her own, even when she was just a little squirt."

"She's not a little squirt now," she firmly reminded him, folding his jacket in her lap as though it were part of her laundry. "And it's certainly not cute anymore."

"Having a mind of your own isn't supposed to be cute. It's supposed to happen that way if you're gonna grow up to be your own person."

"Well, it's not happening that way. She isn't her own person. She's hanging around with a different bunch of kids lately. I don't know them. I don't know their parents. This Jennifer Hardin has a much older boyfriend, I know that. And she *smokes*."

"Annie?"

"No, Jennifer." She shrugged, now seemingly intent on aggravating a hangnail on her right thumb. He noticed that she'd been biting her nails again. He noticed, too, with a rush of relief, that she still wore her wedding band.

Her voice thickened as the list of concerns mounted. "Maybe Anna does, too. I don't know. I hardly know her anymore. It's something new every day. It's . . . it's just . . ."

"It's what, Clara?" The threat of her tears always made him feel clumsy, especially when they were basically on the outs with each other. He didn't know whether to try to touch her, or how to comfort her without touching her. "Tell me what it is. Tell me all of it."

She glanced at the ceiling, blinking furiously. "She pretends to be sick."

"Pretends?"

"I *think* she's pretending. I don't know for sure. It's so awful to have to take her to the doctor when she has symptoms nobody can seem to explain."

"Why?"

She shook her head, again furiously. "I don't know. They've done all kinds of tests. They keep asking the same questions, and she's—"

"No, I mean why is it awful to take her to the doctor? She says she's sick, you take her to the doctor, right?"

"Yes, of course." She squared her shoulders and glared at him. "Of course I do."

"It's not an inconvenience, is it?"

"Never!"

"Or an embarrassment to you?"

The fury in her eyes pinned him still, and the quickness of her lunge caught him off guard. She slapped him, hard enough to sting them both. They glared at one another some more, but neither could turn away because the hurt was so strong. And it was better than nothing.

Finally he closed his eyes, willing the fading sting to thicken his skin. It was such an unusual move coming from Clara, and so charged with emotion that he almost took pleasure from it.

"How can you suggest such a thing?" she hissed.

"How can it be awful to take her to the doctor?" he asked again, quietly this time.

"You said to tell you. You said to tell you all of it, but you don't really want to know, because you don't have to deal with this . . . this . . ." She gestured helplessly. Her cheeks blazed with the rosy color of chaotic emotions.

"How can it be *hard* to take her—"

"They don't have any answers," she wailed softly. "She has stomachaches, headaches, sometimes nausea, and nobody seems to know whether it has something to do with her menstrual cycle, or . . ."

His jaw dropped slightly. He managed to lock it right back into place, but not soon enough. She saw that he'd been unprepared for the news. His male ignorance steadied her. Suddenly she had that earth-mother look in her eye, designed to convince him that she knew the secret of all life and he hadn't a clue.

"Well, naturally," he muttered. He tried to ward off the memory of the day he'd taught a flat-chested little beanpole with knobby knees and skinned elbows how to ride a bike. Annie was his little girl, wasn't she? She could have any bike she wanted, he'd told her, and she'd picked a little racing bike that he couldn't afford. But he'd bought it anyway. For his little girl.

"She's thirteen. She's, um . . ."

"She started almost a year ago."

"Really?" He cleared the frog from his throat. "So that probably has a lot to do with it. I mean . . . wouldn't it?"

"She says it doesn't."

"What does the doctor say?"

"We've seen three doctors. They say . . ." She shook her head and sighed. "They say a lot of things, but they haven't solved the problem. And I want it solved. I *want* the problem solved. I want Anna to be able to concentrate on school and get her grades back up to where they should be. I don't want her to be sick."

She glanced away quickly, and it took her two tries to get out the last heartfelt gasp. "I don't want her to be unhappy."

"I don't either."

"So . . . so where do we go from here?" She needed a concrete plan. Knowing Clara, she would find her salvation in some sort of plan. "We're going to have to call the police soon, and I just *hate* to . . ."

They exchanged a look. He cocked one eyebrow, and she acknowledged his prior claim to that statement with another terrible sigh. "Because she's already in so much trouble."

"For what?"

"Shoplifting for one thing."

"Shoplifting? Annie?" The surprises were coming in droves now. "Jesus. When did she start that?"

"All I know is when she got caught." As if to forestall another loss of control, she folded her hands tightly in her lap before she leaned closer. "I couldn't believe it. I try not to spoil her with a lot of stuff, but anything she needs or really wants . . ." Clara bit her lower lip, checking the flow of assertions that were not news to him. She looked him in the eye. "She took an umbrella. Can you imagine?"

"Christ." He shook his head. Under different circumstances, he would have been tempted to laugh. Annie? An *umbrella*?

"Oh, Ben, we have to find her. I should have called you long before this, because we needed to talk, you know, all three of us, but I couldn't . . ." She didn't seem to realize she'd clamped her hand around his wrist. "We have to decide."

His throat went dry. He glanced away, studied the clock on the mantel and registered, not the hour, but the minutes, as though he were anticipating his execution. Five more, and it would be straight up. He nodded once, although he wasn't sure what he was agreeing to.

"It's cold out there, isn't it?"

Her question was almost as surprising as the fragile, teetering-near-the-edge tone of her voice. He nodded again, heavily. His neck felt stiff. "Gettin' that way."

"She's not wearing a very warm . . . She was just wearing a thin little . . ." She closed her eyes, lips atremble, and a single tear slipped down her cheek.

He moved instinctively, planting one knee on the floor next to her feet as he reached for her. He could feel every muscle in her body coil up in her defense, but he was prepared to ignore any rejection. He needed to hold her now, and she needed to be held. She looked at him, tears rolling, and he could feel her resistance softening, melting like candle wax as he pulled her against his chest, absorbing her tremors into his own body. Her tears dampened the side of his neck. Her quick, ragged breaths warmed his chin.

Too soon she came to her senses and drew away. "I don't want to call the police. They'll think she's . . ."

"They'll think she's what?" He felt a little awkward reversing the motion of his rescue attempt as he backed into his chair.

"A troublemaker or something. But she's not. She's not." She hammered his folded jacket with her fists. "I hate it when they assume . . ."

He knew what they assumed, but unlike Clara, he knew from his own experience. He knew what biases his features triggered, what the color of his skin meant to the bankers, the sales clerks, and the cops who'd been brought up on Hollywood illusions. He had the classic Indian face, and he'd passed it on, with a few feminine refinements and a lighter complexion, to his daughter.

"Sometimes I just want to punch somebody," Clara said.

He smiled indulgently. "Who?"

"*Anybody*. Except Anna. I wouldn't . . ."

"I know you wouldn't."

He nodded.

She nodded.

For a long, gentle moment they looked into each other's eyes, acknowledging that they had that much faith in each other. Where Annie was concerned, neither wanted the pain they caused each other to spill over. But it did. They both knew it did.

She glanced away first. "I'm sorry I slapped you. I don't know why I . . ." Yes, she did, and so did he. But she turned to him again, her apologetic eyes glistening like sweet, warm maple syrup. "It's not like me. I don't do that sort of thing."

Granted. He smiled, giving her credit for holding off this long. "Bet it felt good, though."

"No, it didn't." Convincing herself required something physical, a firm shake of her own head. "It really didn't feel good."

"Then how did it feel?"

"It didn't feel like anything."

He knew better.

"It didn't feel like me, and it was stupid," she insisted. "A stupid waste of time and energy. We have to find Anna, and then we have to sit down and have a quiet, sensible talk about—"

He interrupted her with a crossing-guard gesture as he cocked an ear toward the back door. "There's somebody outside."

Clara closed her eyes and blew a deep sigh. "Thank God."

Pancho scrambled across the kitchen floor, barking his head off. Ben followed as far as the hallway, avoiding light switches, listening in the dark. "Two somebodies," he reported quietly.

Pancho made a growling beeline down the hall, tracking the movement outside.

Wide-eyed, Clara sprang to her feet. "Her bedroom window."

"I'll go around," he proposed, heading for the front door. She handed him his jacket on his way by. "You go back there to her room, but don't turn any lights on."

He felt a little like a thief in the night, even though he was sneaking around his own bushes. When he rounded the corner to his own backyard he spotted two shadowy figures. He couldn't tell much about the one on the bottom, but he recognized the one who was getting the boost up to the bedroom window. The braided ponytail, the impossibly long hands, and the smaller version of his hawk's-beak nose belonged to his daughter.

The tipsy giggle did not.

He squared his shoulders, stepped out of the shadows, and took a Matt Dillon stance. "What's goin' on here?"

"It's my dad!"

"Shit." The booster took two stumbling steps back, nearly dropping his burden on the ground. "I mean—"

"If you guys are playin' camel, you need a pool," Ben said, wishing for the days when he would simply be blowing the whistle on an innocent game.

"We're not playing camel. We're playing spyyyy," Annie intoned drunkenly. "Spy and see if Mom's back is turned."

Ben shut his eyes briefly, steadying himself. "But since Dad's back isn't turned, you might as well get down, Annie."

The boy took pains to extricate himself without letting her fall. He left her hanging on to the window ledge, turned, and faced the paternal music. "I was just tryin' to help her out, Mr. Pipestone."

"Who are you?"

"This is Larry Prit—" reaching for the boy's shoulder, Anna leaned away from the house like a windblown willow "—chhhert. I was gonna give him an Indian name. Larry Pret-ty Churt. Chit. Shit. Priddy Shit." She gave in to the giggles as Ben edged closer. "Larry Pretty

Shirt," she corrected, enunciating with exaggerated care. "Whuduhya think?"

"It's Pritchert," the boy said tightly.

The pungent smell of beer hit Ben in the face like a sack of cement. The crisp night air suddenly felt surrealistically thick and heavy. "Are you driving, Pritchert?"

"I just gave her a ride. That's all."

"I'm asking, should you be driving," Ben explained, summoning patience in the face of a strong urge to wring the boy's scrawny neck. "Are you okay?"

"I didn't have nuthin' to do with this," the boy said, backing away. "She's a friend of a friend, and I'm just tryin' to help her out."

"Yeah, Dad, he's jus' a fren, jus' sorta helpin' me out. So what's yer excuse for buttin' in, Dad? Jus' passin' through?"

"I got a distress call from your mom." He spared the retreating boy a quick wave. "Thanks, Pritchert. Take it easy, now."

"Yeah."

Larry Pritchert backpedaled a few steps, then turned and ran, disappearing around the corner of the house.

Anna grabbed her father's arm, dragging his attention back to her sad state of affairs. "What's she so 'stressed about? I wuz out wi' sum frens. Don'cha want me to have any frens?"

"There's friends, and then there's drinkin' buddies," he said, reaching out to steady her. "Which kind was that guy?"

"He's nuthin'. Jus' a way to get places." The statement, Ben realized, echoed her mother's cavalier attitude toward cars. Nothing important. Just a way to get around.

Anna giggled. "Ol' Larry Pretty Shit," she repeated, enjoying the fruits of her liquored-up wit. She started slipping toward the ground.

Ben caught her by the shoulders and hauled her up on tiptoe. But her legs had gone rubbery. She giggled and went limp again. "Cut it out, now, Annie, we're goin' in the house."

"Can't say Pretty Shit in th' house, ya know. *She'll* have a damn piss fit over it."

His little girl slumped against his side. Tucked under his arm, she dragged the toes of her tennis shoes in the grass, the way she had years ago when she didn't want to quit playing and go inside for supper, a bath, homework, or any number of other fun-killing demands parents were wont to make. Silently Ben cursed Iktome for punishing him with the vilest trick imaginable. Of all the lessons his child might have learned from him . . .

"Is she mad?"

"You had her worried."

Anna tipped her chin to look up at him, and her head fell back like a hinged lid. "How 'bout you? Were you worried?"

"Yeah." *Worried* would do for starters.

"Never thought you'd see th' day," Anna mocked with a child's knack for hitting the nail on the parental head. "Course, I've seen you a whole lot worse off."

Drunk as she was, her aim was true. But he'd never felt any worse than he did right now, supporting his thirteen-year-old daughter while she tried to find her balance on flat, solid ground. God, how he wished he could do it for her.

"So how do you like it so far?"

"Got your attention, din' I? Jus' like you use ta get ours whenever you . . ." She pressed her face into the open front of his jacket.

He paused, knowing how rocky the motion made her feel at this point. He brushed his palm over her forehead, as though he thought his baby might have something easily treatable, like a fever.

She groaned. "I don' guess I feel so good, though. I think I'm gonna—"

She jerked away from him and vomited behind a rosebush.

He was glad he was there to keep her from falling in it face-first, even though the stench was, an unwelcome reminder of a past that still nipped too closely at his heels.

"I'm sorry, Daddy," she muttered as he wiped her chin with a wool glove from his pocket.

"Me, too." He lifted her into his arms. Still his baby, he thought. Still his long, lanky little bit of a thing who needed her daddy to pick her up and put her to bed tonight.

"I promise I . . ." Her head lolled against his shoulder. "I won't do it anymore. Don't tell Mom."

"Don't have to." He glanced up at Clara, who was standing on the doorstep holding the door open for them. "She knows."

"She always knows . . . everything."

Not quite, he thought. Clara worried, but she also hoped for the best. And she was trusting. At least, she had been, once upon a time.

"We're going to put you to bed," he told his little girl, laying his chin against her forehead as he stepped past his wife. They exchanged a look, sharing the bittersweet heartache. "Me and Mom, the way we used to. We're going to tuck you in."

"You're going to stay?" Anna's arms tightened around his neck, her innocent hopes tormenting his ear.

"I'll come back tomorrow."

"No, don't go." She wedged her head beneath his chin, pressing hard against his Adam's apple. He could hear the dog panting at his heels as he made his way down the hall, sidestepping to keep her shoes from touching Clara's wallpaper. "Daddy, I wanna go on that ride. Want you to take me."

"What ride?"

"The one Grandpa's going on. Wanna see my Lala."

"Tomorrow," he promised as he bent to lay her on her bed. He held off until Clara had pulled the covers back, then settled her down in the nest of ruffled pillows.

"No, you stay home, Daddy." Suddenly almost lucid and nearly desperate, Anna gripped his jacket sleeves. "Sleep here tonight. Stay . . . stay home with us, Daddy."

2

"I'll make up the spare bedroom."

He stared, his disbelief fairly bulging out his eye sockets. He hadn't spent the night under the same roof with her in almost two years. He wasn't sure he ought to now, especially with the offer couched in such a duty-ridden tone.

"I can come back tomorrow."

"It's too far to drive."

"I've been drivin' it, haven't I?" Something about the way she'd dismissed his offer sounded like one of her indirect reprimands, the kind that set his teeth on edge. "Maybe not often enough, but I always try to get up here whenever—"

"I think you ought to be here when she wakes up. I've dealt with you in that morning-after state often enough. *You* can deal with *her*."

He scowled. "Fine."

"Fine." She smiled, tentatively satisfied. "Are you hungry?"

He shook his head, wondering how a referee might have scored that round. She'd gotten her digs in, but he'd gained more than a foot in the door, plus a free bed for the night. He didn't feel like making that hundred-mile drive.

"My stomach's not too steady," he explained. "She

threw up all over the side of the house."

Despite the strain at the core of his remark, Clara expected, almost hoped for, a little Indian humor at this point, some ironic comment about him being sober and still feeling sick. Then she'd get after him for making light of a serious situation, and he'd tell her the problem was only temporary. Part of her would believe him, and the other part would be consigned to ready-reserve status, in case she needed to worry some more.

In this case, of course, she did, and he wasn't attempting to persuade her otherwise, nor was he granting her an excuse to distract herself with some fussy little hospitality chore. He felt sick, and so did she, even though she had let him deal with the worst of tonight's incident, telling herself it was long past his turn.

But that, too, worried her. She knew she had shirked her motherly duty.

"I went to the window when I heard you talking, but then . . ." *Then I backed away. Then I chickened out.*

She dismissed the notion with a curt gesture. A father had his duty, too. "I didn't want to interfere. You handled it well. Anna, the boy, the whole thing. I would have been—" Paralyzed and utterly useless, probably, but she refused to say such a thing aloud. With a nervous laugh she shrugged off candor in favor of hyperbole. "—a raving madwoman, no doubt."

"She's safe now. She's home."

And yes, that was a relief. The simple act of assenting with a nod instantly engorged her throat with embarrassing, burning emotion. God, more stupid tears. She turned away from him quickly, but he caught her shoulders and pulled them back against the wall of his chest.

Which felt, for the moment, like blessed support.

"I'm not ready for this." She closed her eyes and drew a deep breath. *This*, she guessed, referred to more things than she cared to recognize. "It scares me."

"It scares me just as much," he said quietly.

It was hard for Clara to imagine what he meant by the word. He never *sounded* scared.

But he always seemed to know when she doubted him.

"Maybe more," he professed. "I thought Annie would stay away from it. She hated it so much when I was boozin'."

"It's one thing after another." She wanted to delineate each and every one for him and let him carry at least half their weight. "I can't even catch my breath. It's like she wants to try everything all at once. Everything dangerous. Everything . . ."

"Bad?"

"If *I* say it's bad, it's on her list to try."

"Have you tried any reverse psychology? Tell her milk is bad and sugar's good."

"You already told her that. I lost the battle against sugar when you dumped it all over her cereal and gave it your stamp of approval. Reverse psychology would never work on any child of ours, Ben." She sighed and tipped her head back, letting it rest briefly against his shoulder. She'd missed his strong shoulder, the warmth of his body, the spicy scent that was his alone. Some things hadn't changed. Particularly the bottom line. "We *are* reverse psychology, you and I."

His low chuckle rumbled close to her ear. "You're everything I'm not, that's for sure."

"How do I differ from thee?" She stiffened and shook her head, dismissing her moment of weakness as she drew away from him. "Let's not count the ways just now. I'll get you some bedding."

"I'll do that myself. Later." He grabbed her arm and made her turn around and face him. "I make my own bed these days, and then I lie in it. Sometimes for hours before I can finally fall asleep."

"That's not surprising." It was easy to steel herself against any attempt he could possibly make to gain sympathy on *that* particular account, if that was what he had in mind. All she had to do was look him straight in the eye and remember. And let the chill claim her body. "You used to lie a lot when you slept in my bed."

He didn't flinch. "*Our* bed."

"It's mine now. And I don't have any trouble sleeping, except . . ."

"Except?"

Except when the dreams come.

Forget dreams, she told herself. Stick to the cold, hard facts, the unfair reality.

"Except when Anna's had a day like this one."

He released her, and she turned away, taking quick refuge in tangible worries. "We have to see the probation officer tomorrow. I don't know whether I should tell her about this incident." She wandered into the kitchen, and he followed, trailing the bits and pieces as she parceled them out. The new adventures of Anna Pipestone, complete with new players. "The probation officer, I mean. I hate the look that woman gives me sometimes. It's like, 'What's the matter with you? Can't you handle your own daughter?' "

She lowered the dishwasher door, opened a cupboard, and started putting plates away.

Poor Clara, Ben thought. She always claimed not to care what other people thought. But she did. She cared plenty. At the very least she wanted them to respect her for her ability to keep all her ducks in a row. She had never quite understood that most people didn't give a damn about the order, as long as all the ducks were the same color. And Clara, for all her fastidiousness and all her ability to organize, was genuinely, guilelessly color-blind.

He opened the cupboard next to his shoulder and signaled for her to start handing him the glasses. "Maybe it's time this cop met Annie's father. She'll be so busy givin' me the evil eye, she won't have time to look down on you."

"Really." She slapped the bottom of a juice glass into his palm. "Knowing you, you'll win her over before we even get through the introductions."

"Naw, I gave that up." He held out his other hand. "I used to buy charm in a bottle. Now I'm just wingin' it through life on straight talk and hard work." With two glasses shelved, he turned, smiling, offering his hands for more. "Following your fine example, Clara."

She refused to crack even a slight smile. "Too bad you didn't start out with that philosophy fifteen years ago."

"Sixteen years, four months, and some odd days," he averred, and her puzzled expression was his reward. "That's how long we've known each other. Thing is, Clara, most of us don't start right out knowin' it all."

He smiled boyishly.

She glared and handed him two more glasses.

He shrugged. "Besides, I'd 'a never won you over without a little of the cowboy charm that comes in that bottle."

"Like fun." She took out the silverware basket, then swatted the dishwasher door shut.

"Like fun is right." He could tell he was making some headway. She was putting the knives into the drawer without giving him any purposeful looks. "C'mon, now, be honest with yourself. We did have fun."

"Really? When?"

"Right from the start." He smiled wistfully. "You always liked to get out on the dance floor and make all the other cowboys wish, and I couldn't dance worth a damn unless I had a couple shots under my belt."

"That isn't true. You're a wonderful dancer. You always were."

"I've never danced sober." She looked incredulous. "You didn't realize that?"

"I think you're exaggerating." She glanced away, her

lips pressed tightly together. Then the words came in a quiet rush. "You must be doing it now."

"Doing what?"

She lifted one shoulder. "Dancing sober."

"You're the last person I danced with." He caught her chin with his workingman's fingertips and turned her head until their eyes met. "Like I said, straight talk and hard work is all I've got time for these days."

She closed her eyes and held her breath for a moment, as though the smell of his hand offended her.

The hand pained him suddenly. Its joints seemed suddenly aged. He withdrew it slowly, awkwardly clearing his throat.

"And Annie," he said quietly. "I've always got time for Annie."

Her eyes expressed doubt, which didn't surprise him. And a trace of regret, which did.

"Why didn't you call me about this sooner?"

"I didn't want to call you at all."

"You've been cashing my checks."

"Only for Anna. When we . . ." She braced her arm on the edge of the counter, steadying herself. "When this is all settled, there'll be some sort of child support anyway." She risked another glance, but it ricocheted off his. "It's kind of remarkable that you're so good about providing that without—"

"She's my daughter." He wondered if *settled* meant the same as *over*. Again he cleared his throat as he patted his breast pocket, searching for cigarettes. Even if he couldn't smoke in the house, it was a comfort to know he had a pack on him. "Have you, uh . . . filed for—"

"No. Not yet. I haven't had time." Then, quietly, "Did you want me to . . . ?"

"I'm in no hurry."

"Well, right now I think we need to concentrate on Anna's problems," she said with a sigh.

He sighed, too. And they stood there, close, but not too close. Disjointed, but not completely severed.

Then, unexpectedly, Clara brightened. "There was a nice piece in today's paper about the Wounded Knee ride. Did you see it?"

Ben shook his head.

"They interviewed your father." She started toward the living room doorway, then stopped, disconcerted by a change in the order of things. "I think I saw the paper in Anna's room, come to think of it."

"She'll probably show it to me tomorrow," he said, and she nodded, dutifully deferring to her daughter. He thought he detected a little disappointment in her eyes, as though she actually liked the idea of showing him something that might please him. Which pleased him more than she knew.

More than reading about that damned ride would.

"Must be what started her thinking about making the ride herself. The ol' man's been after me to go, but I don't . . ." He shook his head again. "That's not for me."

"He still wants you to become a pipe bearer?"

"*The* pipe bearer. I don't know where it's written that the next one has to be his son."

"It probably isn't. If it's in print somewhere, then it's dubious, according to your father."

"Probably made up by some white anthropologist," he said, imitating his father. "And if we don't watch out, the sacred pipe's gonna end up in a museum somewhere."

"He was always willing to share his stories with me, though. I learned so much from him." She shrugged the whole matter off. "Until we were married. After that . . ."

Some small guilt brought him to his father's defense as he followed her into the living room. "In the old way, it's not right for him to talk directly to his daughter-in-law. Hell, you know all that better than I do. It's his way of showing you respect."

"I liked it better when he'd tell me stories by the hour."

He flopped into his chair and smiled, remembering. "With you filling up notebook after notebook, and me sittin' outside, goin' through half a pack of cigarettes while I waited to take you out riding."

She took a seat on the sofa and set about straightening magazines—a perfectly neat stack of three—on the coffee table. "Have you been riding a lot lately? I mean, now that you're . . ."

"Some. I've got a couple of horses out at Dad's place. Took 'em in trade for some work I did. You fix cars for a living down on the rez, you never know what you might get paid with."

"I remember."

But not happily, he thought. They had lived there for a while after they were married. She'd taught high school history, and he'd rodeoed in the summer and fixed cars all year long.

"But you're your own boss again." She made the observation ungrudgingly. "You always preferred it that way."

"Yeah." He'd gotten a job as a mechanic at a car dealership after the Historical Society had offered Clara her dream job and they had moved to Bismarck. He hadn't minded the work so much, but he'd hated punching someone else's time clock. "I've even got a guy working for me now. He's got a lot to learn, but . . ."

But it felt good to be able to put Darrell Takes The Hat on his payroll, if you could call paying yourself and one other guy a payroll. Darrell had a wife and kid, too. Only he lived in the same house with them.

"How's your job going?"

"Fine. I'm curator of the Indian collection now."

"That sounds real good. You're takin' good care of our stuff for us, huh? The ol' man'll be glad to hear it's in good hands."

She winced at that.

"I ain't kiddin' you. He will. He always said I got the best end of the deal when we got married."

"I'm glad *he* thought so."

Ben thought so, too, even if he hadn't always shown it. Not that she was a princess and he was a total bum, but she'd always had a lot going for her. And she'd loved him once. The silence between them felt heavy, and he knew it was the weight of regret over the loss of that love. Maybe she'd stopped grieving over it by now, but he hadn't.

And there was nothing to break the silence but talk of the most important concern they had left to share. Their child.

"That ride goes on for two weeks, and it can get damn cold during those two weeks." He could feel it now, just as surely as he felt the heat and the goddamn pressure gradually being turned up on him. He was one cowboy who did not ride well under pressure. "I don't think Annie could hack it, do you?"

"I doubt if she's serious," Clara said absently, intent on brushing something hardly visible off her wool trousers. "Just a whim. A test, maybe, to see what we'd say."

"A test," he echoed hollowly.

Now, there was a word he didn't much like, unless he was the one doing the testing. He tended to fail them, sometimes for lack of interest, others maybe for lack of purity.

Like the time he'd sat up on the hill for three nights and two days, doing the *hanble ceya* his father said would help him find direction in his life. Thirteen years old, and all he wanted to know was, which way to the place where they keep the horses? But he'd gone up there, and he'd done what his father had told him to do. He'd tested his endurance. He'd gone without food or water, and he'd seen his first big pink elephant.

Only it wasn't an elephant; it was a stout red roan horse.

His father had said that the horse would come back to him one day, in the flesh. And it had. Twice. He'd gotten bucked off once. Broke his goddamn arm. Another time he'd bet on a red roan in a Calcutta team roping and lost fifty bucks. Since then he'd stopped looking for that damn horse. So much for tests and foolhardy vision quests.

Ben shook his head. "I don't have time. I keep tellin' the ol' man, I can't take that kinda time."

"What does he say?"

"He says I sound like a white man." A no-win notion that made Ben chuckle. Like trying to pass a Mustang off as a Thoroughbred.

Not that he had any use for a damn hay-burning Thoroughbred.

"Auto repair business is good this time of year. I can't just take off for two weeks." But he felt pressed to add, "I guess I have been gettin' back into the, uh . . . some of the old ways a little more lately."

"Really?"

Oh, yeah, she liked that all over. "The sweats are good," he allowed, figuring at this point he had to milk whatever interest he could drag out of her. "I thought I'd forgotten how to talk Indian, but it comes back. You hang around the ol' man, it all comes back. Some things easier than others, but I figure I'll hang in there, you know, for something to do." He glanced away and added, unbidden, "Helps me stay away from the bottle."

"That's good," Clara said, and she meant it, but her crisp tone invited no further discussion.

And so the weighty silence took over again.

It *was* a good thing he'd stopped drinking. But she didn't want to talk about it. The sweat lodge, yes; his first language, certainly. His bout with alcohol, not really. It made her feel stupid, knowing that in all the time they'd lived together, she'd never considered that he might actually be an alcoholic. It had never seemed that bad. Maybe once or twice a year he'd go off on a half-hour errand that became an all-nighter, or he wouldn't come home from work until Sunday morning. But usually she'd been able to find him and coax him home. In fact, she'd thought *she* was doing a pretty good job of keeping him away from the bottle. He'd only slipped when *she* wasn't looking.

His DUI had come as a total surprise to her, mainly because she didn't find out about it until six months after the fact, when their insurance rates had skyrocketed. She couldn't believe he hadn't told her. More than once she had confidently made the claim that she and her husband never kept secrets from each other.

God, she'd been blind.

And she'd failed. She didn't want to think about it any more than she wanted to discuss it. Failures of that magnitude could not be erased.

"I'd better get that bed made up. You must be tired, and tomorrow promises to be—"

"It's early yet," he said, touching her knee to forestall her flight. "Annie doesn't have to miss school for this probation appointment, does she? She's already missed—"

"There's no school tomorrow. Teachers' Convention. I can only take part of the day off." She settled back down, albeit tentatively. "I have to put the finishing touches on an exhibit," she explained as he withdrew his hand. Its warmth lingered, like a melancholy memory.

She smiled wistfully. "Remember when Anna used to love to go to the museum with me, especially at night when I was preparing an exhibit? She thought it was wonderful that we had a special key. She'd tell her teachers that she could be in the museum when it was closed to 'regular' people."

"She liked being around all that old stuff as much as you did."

"She doesn't anymore." Her smile faded. "And I can't believe she got a deficiency report in history. She knows this stuff. She won't do her assignments, that's all."

"I'll talk to her about it."

"Oh, like that's going to turn her around."

"What do you want me to do?"

Good question. What *did* she want from him now? Not his touch, surely. Answers—sensible ones, at least—were harder to come by whenever he touched her.

"Talk to her, I guess. Maybe she'll listen to you. She thinks it's all my fault." She shot him an accusatory glance. "*Everything* is my fault."

"You want me to tell her it's my fault? I've told her that."

"You haven't told her . . ."

About the other thing Clara refused to discuss. He waited expectantly for her to name it, but be *damned* if she would. It was his juice, and he could go right on stewing in it.

"She doesn't need to know any of the gory details, Ben. She's a child. *My* feeling is that we have to spare her as much of that as . . . as we possibly can."

She paused, daring him with a cold look to come up with any more feeble objections. But of course, he didn't. Why should he? He knew she wasn't about to discuss his sins with anybody, especially not Anna. She was trapped in her own code of ethics, which was just the way he liked it. Damn him. He always came out looking like the good guy. How in the hell did he manage that?

"When you come up to see her . . . what do you two talk about?"

"Whatever she wants to talk about, which usually isn't anything earth-shattering. Just, you know . . ." He shrugged, clearly at a loss for memorable examples. "She asks about different ones she remembers. Some of her cousins. My sisters."

"How are they?"

He gave her a dubious look.

"I want to know," she conceded. "I'm asking, too."

"They're all about the same." He eyed her speculatively. "Annie always asks how I'm doin'. Like she really wants to know."

"And what do you say?"

"Depends on how I'm doin'. Usually I'm doin' okay." They shared a quiet moment, an unintentional exchange of soft looks. Then he asked, "How are *you* doing?"

"Me, personally? I'm fine. I'm taking an exercise class. I just had my annual—" She forgot herself and readily reported everything to him, the way she used to. "You know, *that* checkup. The one I hate. But everything's fine. I think I've even lost a few pounds."

"I think you've lost more than a few." He smiled. "But you look good. You look . . ."

"Are you sure you don't want something to eat? There's plenty of—"

"I'm not hungry. I'm not tired." He laid his hand over her knee, warming up the same spot he'd touched before—and disturbingly more—with a reassuring squeeze. "I'm doin' okay."

She avoided his eyes as she stood quickly, shedding his hand. "I'll get the sheets on, so the bed will be ready whenever you are."

She grabbed a set of sheets from the top shelf of the linen closet. She wished she had some new ones. They'd slept together on all the sheets she had for that bed. She wondered whether he'd recognize the old blue and white tulips.

When she bent to the bed-making task, she felt his presence, even though he hadn't made a sound coming to the doorway. He stood there watching her, and she was certain she could hear his thoughts about the sheets. Sissy sheets, he'd called them, predicting the flowers would wilt the night they broke them in.

But if the memory was truly in his thoughts, he kept it to himself.

"You put more bookshelves in here, huh? Feels cozy."

The room had been almost bare for a long time. When they'd bought the house it was going to be the baby's room. None was immediately on the way, not then, but they'd planned for it to be a bedroom for the second child they were going to have someday. It had, in the end, become the "spare" bedroom.

"It's a *guest* room," she reminded him, putting him in his place, as though he'd said otherwise. "I wanted it to feel cozy. But it serves more purposes, with the desk and a place to put more books."

"You get much company?"

"No." She opened a dresser drawer—the dresser they had refinished themselves, making it almost a match for the bed, but not quite—and took out an extra blanket. "My mother was here last spring."

"How did it go?"

"It was fine. I took her to work with me. She wasn't very interested in the museum itself, but she enjoyed meeting people. She's good at that." Ben had always been most tolerant of her mother, who was at times quite difficult to tolerate. "Anna was on her best behavior. Her grandmother kept buying her things, playing the bestower of gifts."

"Annie ate that up, huh?"

"I think she accepted it for what it was worth. She's not easily fooled. Unlike her mother."

She refused to look up when he came into the room, stationing himself on the other side of the bed. If she looked up, he would look into her eyes and see what she wanted him to say. That *he* was the fool. Not she. But he wouldn't say it because they both knew it wasn't true. Still, that was what she wanted to hear, and he would see it and know it for sure if she looked up at him. And he'd have something else over her. Another power.

She unfolded the flowered sheet, then flipped it across the bed. He caught it by the corner, and together they tucked it under the corners of the mattress. It was their original bed and the first piece of furniture they'd bought. It seemed small now, but they'd had a small room then, and he'd assured her that anything bigger than full size would be a waste, as close as they slept together. When they'd moved to Bismarck, they'd bought a new set of bedroom furniture, four matching pieces with a queen-size bed, so that his feet wouldn't hang so far over the end. But the new bed had given them more width than they'd needed. Most of the time.

She smoothed out the top sheet, worn soft by their bodies during so many nights that were so long past. He followed her lead. She watched his hand, inches from hers, caressing the cotton as though in his mind it covered a woman's thigh. Hers, maybe. Or maybe not. Maybe his fantasies were less specific than hers, or, rather, more specific and less pure.

Stop it, Clara. Either way, you absolutely could not care one whit less.

But she took a martyr's pleasure in testing herself, letting her hand linger close to his. His wide gold wedding band looked almost delicate on his big brown hand. He had marvelous hands. Skilled in so many things. Masculine. Incredibly masculine. It gave her pleasure to see hers next to his and think of them as partners.

It *had once* given her pleasure, but enough was, surely, enough. She snatched the top sheet off the dresser and snapped it open, letting it fly across the bed, hoping to catch him off guard and make him flinch. But she didn't. He caught it, smiling as though he'd heard her silly thoughts. She glanced away quickly, her face hot.

"I can get a room somewhere if it bothers you."

"If what bothers me?"

"Havin' me sleep here."

"It doesn't bother me at all." It wasn't a lie if she

willed it hard enough to be true. She tossed him a pillowcase and decided to let him finish the job himself. She jerked the cord on the blinds and made them *thwack* shut. The plant she'd hung in the window captured a hank of her hair in its droopy leaves. She reached for its greenhouse hook.

"You takin' that out?" He chuckled softly. "I promise not to breathe on it or anything."

"You always complained about too many plants. It's getting to be a jungle in this house, you said."

"I was just teasin' you, mostly." He moved closer, eyeing the plant with newfound fondness. "I kinda got used to having them around. Bought myself one of those spider things like you've got in the living room, but I must not've watered it enough or something. Finally threw it out."

"You might have given it too much water. Most people make that mistake."

"Yeah, maybe."

"This one doesn't seem to be getting enough light here." She made a production of studying wilted leaves and steadfastly ignoring his warm proximity as she prattled on. "Anna gave me this years ago. It was just a tiny thing. So was she. Her teacher gave her some cuttings, and she started it herself." She pinched off a sad-looking stalk. "Every time it gets spindly like this, I start to throw it out, but then I just cut it back. It always comes back to life."

"You always had a way with plants. You still got the kind you used to put on all the cuts and insect bites?"

"Aloe?" She nodded. A glimpse of the bulge in the pocket of his blue chambray shirt reminded her of the time she'd used aloe juice to soothe a cigarette burn on his arm. He'd been a little drunk, a little silly, as she recalled. "I still have aloe. Maybe I was an herbalist in a past life. A simpler life. Maybe I was a cook, or maybe I used herbs to doctor people up."

"Maybe you were an Indian. You like all that old Indian stuff so much."

She looked up and found his eyes doting on her. She felt warm in the face.

"The ol' man says you have an Indian heart," he told her.

"He said that?"

"Not an Indian *head*, mind you. You do think different."

"From you? I wouldn't say that's all bad."

"You wouldn't say *I'm* all bad? Which part of me isn't?" He challenged her with a look, then tempted her with the light sweep of his knuckles along her jaw. "Hmm? Can't you just give some little part of me a break? Just one small . . ." He offered a gentle smile. "My hair, maybe? You always liked my hair, and it never got me into any trouble. I never did anything bad with my—"

"Stop it, Ben." She closed her eyes and stepped back in desperate defense of her fragile balance. "I don't want to know anything else about what you've done, or where you've been, or who you've been—"

"The hell you don't. You always wanna know what I've been doin'. Not *how* I'm doin'. *What* I've been doin'. Where I've been and who I've been with." He glanced toward the dark hallway beyond the bedroom door and lowered his voice. "I've been working. I set up shop in a gas station that had been shut down for years, down in McLaughlin. The place is like an oven in the summer and colder'n hell in the winter, but it's got walls, a roof, and a lift, so I'm in business."

"Good for you," she said smoothly.

"Yeah, good for me, so that's what I've been doin' with myself, day after day. And where have I been? I've been livin' in a room about this size, maybe a little smaller. I've been out to my dad's place a lot. Keep my horses there. Go to his sweats once in a while."

He took a step closer, claiming her breathing space. "And who have I been with, you ask? Nobody. I'm alone. I eat alone. I sleep alone. Every night. In a bed just like this one." He turned to take its measure with a practiced eye. "No, I guess it's smaller. But it doesn't matter. I sleep alone." On that note he cocked an expectant eyebrow her way. "Aren't you gonna say, 'Good for you'?"

"Is it?" She stared fiercely. "Is it good for you, Ben?"

He sighed and turned away.

"I don't think about those things anymore." She tried not to, anyway, which was close enough.

After a moment, he turned his head, presenting her a strong profile. "Never?"

"Never." She avoided making eye contact. It wasn't *much* of a lie if she willed it to be true. "It's a relief not to go through all those mental acrobatics, trying to figure out how much of what you're telling me is honest. I don't care anymore." Saying it often and with real conviction helped. "So I can just take it at face value. It's no skin off my nose simply to say . . ." She smiled and recited carefully, "If you say so, Ben."

"I say so."

She nodded. "And you're not drinking *at all* anymore?"

"Not even a little."

"But then, you never drank a *little*, isn't that right?"

He laughed, moving in closer. "The ol' Clara-bow *touché*."

"You were wide open for it."

"I know." A warm smile danced in his eyes as he backed her up against the dresser. "Don't you know by now, Clara-bow . . ."

Whatever it was, she would not betray any surprise. She put her resolve even further to the test by permitting him to trace the curve of her lower lip with his fingertip. *Steady. Show him you don't feel anything. While you're at it*, don't *feel anything*. Oh, God. She hated it when he smiled that way.

And dropped his voice barely above a whisper. "Don't you know that I open up on purpose once in a while, just to let you *touché* me?"

"Do you, really?" Relieved to find her voice, she continued to look him directly in the eye as she calmly sidled away. The move felt like an achievement of sorts.

She returned his smile. "Make yourself at home in the kitchen if you get hungry."

"I think I'll do some reading." He turned to the bookshelves. "What would you recommend?"

She reached past him, plucked a book off the top shelf, and presented it to him with a flourish.

Strange Sex Lives in the Animal Kingdom.

"Be careful, babe," he warned with an appreciative chuckle. "You don't wanna be toyin' with the tiger's tail."

The tiger. What a ridiculous term for a woman ever to apply to a man. Clara shuddered to recall the coy smile she'd given him along with the name intended, yes, thoroughly *meant* to give his male ego a mercurial boost. Lord, what fools these women be. The tiger, indeed.

The cowboy, the warrior, the stallion, the stud—*her* stud—and all the rest, she'd called him all those things. What utter foolishness. She fancied herself an intelligent woman, but the phrase and the sound of his voice along with that cocky-bastard smile had her brain going gushy all over again. He knew it, too, damn him. He'd always known it, and he'd always been able to work her with the same old routine.

But she'd christened him herself, hadn't she? He *had* once been her tiger, her now gushy brain insisted upon recalling. Once upon a time she had thrilled to the idea that Ben was different and dangerous, that he was quite possibly the wildest male animal she'd ever met. A long time ago, when sentimentality and idealism had run strong in her, while she had scoffed at the notion that might made right, she had truly believed in an idea that was equally simplistic. She had once been thoroughly convinced that love was all the power she needed to tame the tiger. She had really believed that her love would make him behave.

But, then, he would not have been the tiger, would he?

And she would not have been . . . Oh, the memory of it made her face burn! How could she, a perfectly intelligent, self-sufficient woman, ever have been his "kitten"?

Or worse, his "little elephant."

Ben had often teased her about her unflagging memory, the way she recalled every milestone. Well, *of course* she remembered exactly what he was wearing when they first met, she would say proudly. A battered straw cowboy hat and worn, oil-stained jeans with a cowboy fit, allowing for an easy swing into the saddle, but never, never baggy.

When she'd pressed him, he could recall her short white skirt and her "funny ol' shoes" with the thick wedges she'd thought quite chic at the time. What he remembered about them was the open heel, where the run had started in the panty hose that hadn't survived the buckbrush and buffalo grass that covered his dad's yard. He could tell her exactly how that run had zipped straight up the back of her leg and disappeared under her skirt. That was one trail's end he'd promised himself he would one day investigate, he would say just as proudly.

Not that she didn't make him wait. It was more than a week before their second meeting. But that was the day he'd first kissed her. And that kiss was no tentative get-acquainted offer, either. It had been the longest, slowest, deepest kiss Clara had permitted herself to experience up to that moment.

After that, her interviews with Dewey Pipestone became a summerlong project. She was soon thoroughly enamored of Indian culture. She was also hopelessly enchanted by that irresistible oxymoron, the Indian cowboy, and namely, Ben Pipestone. The four-week course she'd been taking in Bismarck ended too soon, and rather than return to Wisconsin, she took the boldest step she'd ever made in her short, sheltered life. She'd called her parents, told them a half-truth—that she was going to take an extra couple of weeks to see more of the West with some of her new friends—then left with Ben to follow the amateur Indian rodeo circuit and sample with him those "cowboy days and Indian nights."

They'd left her air-conditioned car behind in favor of his pickup. The cowboy days were hot and dusty, but Clara had loved watching him ride those broncs. Whenever he finished in the money, they'd rent a motel room, and they'd share a bed, kissing and touching each other and finding deliciously frustrating ways to bring each other to climax without actually coupling.

Because she'd fully intended to keep saying *no*.

Because he'd prided himself on being able to coax a woman to say, *Yes, Ben, please*.

And the chase had been a merry one, the denouement made sweeter by the protracted buildup. Ever after he'd delighted in teasing her about parting with her virginity in an old pickup bed. Her comeback had usually been a reminder of how pathetic he'd looked with the black eye and bruised knuckles he'd earned defending her honor and how humbly he'd confessed his need for her.

He'd never let her teasing bother him that much. He always got the semifinal word in. "You know you loved it."

He knew her final word would be his triumph. "I know I loved *you*."

It happened somewhere west of Faith, South Dakota, after he'd lost two go-rounds. Only one of them had been with a horse. It was the first time Clara had seen him miss his horse out on the first jump, and even though he'd spurred high and scratched the bronc out like a pro, the judges had declared "no time" because Ben's bootheels were off the mark when the horse shot out of the chute.

He didn't even want to stick around for the rest of the show. It wasn't that he disputed the decision, he explained to Clara as they headed for the nearest saloon. When a horse sprang through the gate like a bat out of hell, a cowboy couldn't positively *swear* the rowels of his spurs hadn't slipped off the animal's shoulders before it landed the first jump, not without seeing himself from the ground. But he'd rather get his ass kicked by the horse than stick with him all the way to the whistle and find out he'd scored a goose egg right out of the chute.

"I don't know why you're so down about this, Ben," she said as she sipped the Coke he'd just paid a premium for. "You don't expect to place every time, do you?"

He drained two-thirds of his beer, set the glass down, and eyed her carefully. "Don't you expect me to?"

"Of course not." She answered him with an easy smile. It was just a sport, after all. There were too many elements beyond the rider's control. Why anyone would want to ride a wild horse was really beyond her.

"It's what I do best. You do know that, don't you?"

She gave him the anticipated nod, but she assumed there was some overstatement intended. There were too many other more important things he did well, and at his age, he'd only scratched the surface.

He nodded, too.

Their nods went right past each other.

"And I only do it for a few months out of the year, so I have to win most of the time just to break even."

"You're lucky you don't break your neck."

"No, *you're* lucky I don't break my neck," he shouted as the jukebox pumped out the first few bars of a Willie Nelson tune. He leaned closer. "You wouldn't like to see that, would you?"

She leaned closer, too. "I'm not even sure I like seeing you get down in that chute."

"Sure you do. I've heard you cheerin' me on. You get all excited, watchin' me ride."

He lifted his glass in a mock toast, but she stilled his hand. "I get excited and scared, too. What if you get hurt?"

Lips close to her ear, he teased, "Then check my billfold. If it's empty, then be sure and take me to the nearest Indian hospital." He gave her a wink as he sipped his beer. "Otherwise, you take me to some white hospital, you'll have to hock the pickup to bail me out. Then how would you get home?"

"I'd cash a check."

"That's right. You've got that funny money." He drained his glass, then tipped his chair back and shoved his thumbs in his belt.

The cowboy posture. She loved it.

"Feel like dancin'?" He had that fun-loving gleam in his eye again.

The one she could not resist. "Don't I always?"

The black eye came later, when a sandy-haired cowboy with a farmer tan stopped her on her way back from the ladies' room and asked for a dance. She saw Ben talking to someone at the bar, and she wasn't sure how he would react if she danced with someone else. But she didn't like the feel of the man's sweaty palm on her forearm or the lustful look he had no business turning on her, so she tersely declined.

The man was indignant. "Why not? You danced with *him*. He's a damn redskin."

Clara's eyes fired a quick volley of arrows as she tried to pull away.

"Hey!" The sweaty grip tightened. "I'm the one who beat him out in the saddle bronc."

Half a beat off his cue, Ben closed in. "You askin' my girl for a dance?"

"She don't got no brand on her."

"She's got a mouth on her, and she said no."

"She's got a nice ass on her, too, and I just thought she oughta shake it one time for a white—"

Ben landed a solid right that effectively shut the man's mouth and sent him sprawling in the dance floor dust like a turtle on its back.

But the sandy-haired cowboy was not without friends, and Clara was lucky to get Ben out of the bar with relatively minor damage.

He assured her the damage was hardly insignificant and definitely rated her attention since it had been sustained mostly in her honor. Using his bucking saddle for a pillow, they bundled up together with an army blanket on a bed of hay in the back of the pickup. She made a fuss over his eye, treating the swelling with the bag of ice she'd picked up at the gas station on the way out of town. And kisses. He kept wanting more kisses. She leaned over him and applied them liberally.

"You know what *really* takes the swelling away?"

She smiled as he loosened the button on her jeans and pulled her shirt free. "What?"

"A nice, pink, boneless . . ." He smiled in response to her smile as he touched her through the single layer of cup-shaped cotton. "What's this?"

"Underwire."

"I said *boneless* breast of—" he pinched the hook and eye apart, then replaced the wiry cup with his warm palm "—mmmm, woman." And he fondled her, then hungrily suckled her until she groaned his name.

"You like that, too, huh?"

Oh, yes. "Is it helping your eye?"

"You wouldn't believe how much."

"Then I like it, too." So much, she could hardly breathe. He smiled, pleased with himself, watching the signs of rapture spread over her face as he slipped his pleasure-making fingers past the no-contest barrier of her panties.

"How about this? How does this feel, Clara?" He didn't have to ask. He knew exactly where and how to touch her. A quick, deep shot of liquid fire made her shiver. "That good?"

"Mmmm-hmmm."

He moved her hand from his waist to the rigid bulge in his jeans. "Then be fair, darlin'," he whispered. "Touch me, too."

She returned his favor, caressing him the way he'd taught her to, but this was to be the time they couldn't make do with touching.

"I really need you, Clara. Please don't turn me away tonight."

"Ben, we can't take . . . the chance of . . ."

"I'll be careful. I promise." He brushed scant kisses over her lips and cheeks, probing her portal with gentle fingers and eager penis, desperately trying to make her ready. "Tell me you want me, Clara."

"I do." There it was. And there he was. And there they were, coming together. "Oh . . . Ben . . . yes . . ."

It was a forever vow for Clara.

For Ben, it was the consummate conquest. She belonged to him now. He was her first, and he decided, then and there, that he would be her only man. Ever. He told her how beautiful she looked in the starlight, how much he loved her, how much he would always love her.

She believed every word. She kissed his sore eye and called him her tiger.

" ' . . . burning bright, in the forest of the night,' " she quoted as she licked his bruised knuckles with a pointed tongue.

"No forest out here, honey, but I'll find you one if that's what you want."

His words made the stars in the South Dakota sky burn brighter. Oh, yes, indeed, he had the power. In her ears, his promises were more lyrical than any other man's poetry.

"Just tell me what you want, Clara. Anything. I'll find it, buy it, steal it, whatever it takes to make you happy."

"You make me happy," she told him. "You're all I want."

"You got it, baby." He smoothed her hair back and traced her eyebrow with a reverent forefinger. "Comes the time when I'm not enough—"

"Never," she said, and she took his face in her hands and kissed that silly notion right off his lips. "That time will never come."

Remembering in the solitude of their bedroom—yes, *theirs*, she couldn't help but think of it that way—made her cry for the loss of something. Innocence, she told herself. All she'd lost was her innocence, and good riddance. For an intelligent woman, it had taken her too damn long to wise up.

3

They were all in the car before Clara gave the first thought to where she was sitting and why Ben had his hand out. She'd automatically headed for the passenger's side and let him take the wheel. He had turned the keys over to her in the same manner more than a few times when he'd been drinking, but otherwise, Ben had always been the driver. He knew cars inside and out. He couldn't stand to ride in a car with someone else driving. Clara didn't like to drive, so it had always worked out well.

Until now. There was an awkward moment, a wordless power struggle. But they were already in the car, she told herself as she turned the keys over to him.

No one had spoken much this morning. Clara had said quiet good-mornings and made a perfunctory inquiry as to whether Ben had slept well.

"Sleeping is one thing I do better than most people." He'd handed her a cup of the coffee he had made—just like old times—before she'd gotten up. "Even better than you," he'd added softly. "Your eyes always give you away, Clara-bow."

She had glared at him—snapped her eyes, as he used to say. Words generally made the better darts for Clara, but *kiss off* was hard for a woman to say effectively when she had puffy eyes.

She'd noticed that Anna was treading lightly this morning on the delicate balance between physical misery and mental elation. Her father had stayed, and she wasn't about to upset any apple carts if she could possibly help it. She offered no excuses, asked no questions, invited no lies.

Clara was half expecting Ben to impart some words of warning or wisdom to his daughter, but all he'd acknowledged so far was sympathy for her aching head. "Nothing to do but ride it out," he'd said with a sad smile. "Wish I could do it for you, Annie girl, but I'm afraid you're on your own."

It galled Clara to think that if *she* had made a remark like that, Anna would have offered some bitter retort instead of the wan smile she'd given her father. But Clara realized that coming from her, it wouldn't have sounded the same. It wouldn't have carried the same meaning. Ben was speaking from experience.

With Ben it was all empathy and no judgment. Clara stared past the intersection at the state's only skyscraper, the seat of its government. The capitol building stood next door to the Heritage Center, where she worked, where she did what she did best and did it very, very well. Clara knew her stuff. She also knew right from wrong, and *that* was something worth sharing with the daughter she loved. Why should she resent the famous sympathetic ear of Ben Pipestone? The one thing she could not deny was that he loved Anna, too.

Under any other circumstances, Ben would have considered probation officer Margaret Turnbull to be a reasonably attractive woman. Her blazer and slacks suited her stocky stature, and she had a nice, soft hairstyle, manicured nails, friendly handshake—all qualities he thought pleasant. But her office was down the hall from the room where he'd been booked for driving under the influence, and unless his nose was playing tricks on him, she smelled of fingerprinting ink.

"We meet at last, Mr. Pipestone," Officer Turnbull declared. With an expansive gesture she offered chairs all around.

"I should have come sooner." He wasn't sure what she'd been told, so he glanced Clara's way for some hint. None seemed forthcoming. "I'm stayin' down in McLaughlin now, so it's hard for me to—"

"No problem; I understand. But it is good to meet you. It is definitely in Anna's best interest to have everyone in the family involved with her program." Ms. Turnbull led the way in the taking of seats. "We don't always get that kind of cooperation, but we do try."

"You'll get it from me," Ben assured her. "You just tell me how."

She offered a perfunctory smile. "You're taking the first step right now."

"Yeah, well, I don't know what you've heard, but my wife and I . . ." Staring at his bootheel, he resisted the urge to try again for some clue from Clara. "Look, I haven't always been the best father, and I guess that's part of the reason my daughter's in trouble now. Mistakes have a way of—" he gave an open-handed gesture, groping for the right words "—sneakin' up on a guy in unexpected places, messing with the wrong people." He cast his daughter an apologetic look. "Annie's always been a good kid."

"Still is, right, Anna?" The woman's quick smile dipped to a frown. "Or Annie? Which do you prefer?"

"Most people call me 'Anna,' but my dad always calls me 'Annie.' So I answer to either one, if people say it right. I don't answer when they say it, like, *An-na Pipe?* Pipe*stone*?" She feigned an exaggerated struggle over each syllable. "Like they think I just dropped in from another planet, and even though it looks simple enough, there must be some weird way to say it, so it goes with my face better."

"Your face isn't weird," Officer Turnbull said in all seriousness.

"No kidding," Anna aped.

"So . . . where do you want to start today, Anna?" Turnbull planted her elbows on the arms of her desk chair and steepled her fingers, preparing to be regaled by her charge. "Good news? Bad news?"

"My grandfather was in the news," Anna was surprisingly eager to report. "Yesterday's paper. Did you see it? About the Big Foot Memorial Ride? They have it, like, every year—or at least for the last couple of years—and my grandfather is the pipe carrier for the whole Sioux Nation. Right, Dad? The whole Sioux—"

Ben gave a curt nod, hoping Annie would take the hint and just tell the woman whatever was required.

"So, anyway, it's coming up again, and they interviewed my grandfather about it. He said some real good stuff."

"I'll have to dig out yesterday's paper," the officer said as she jotted a note on a legal pad. "Does your grandfather live . . . close by?"

"He lives out in the country, down on the rez. He's very traditional. Right, Dad?"

"Oh, yeah, he's traditional, all right."

"What does that mean? Does he . . ."

"He practices traditional Indian ways," Anna explained. "He speaks the language, tells a lot of good stories, does all the ceremonies and, you know, like . . ." A glance at her father elicited no encouragement. "Well, he's in charge of spiritual stuff. And he's my real grandfather."

"How interesting." Turnbull made another note, turned briefly to Clara—silently inviting her to jump in anytime—then to Anna again. "How's school going?"

"It's okay." Dead silence. Anna shrugged. "Okay, so the bad news is that I skipped two classes yesterday because I had to go home and look at the paper right away." She glanced at Clara, who tacitly took issue with her choice of words. "Well, what happened was, somebody asked me if the Pipestone guy that was in the newspaper was any relation to me. So I had to find out what they were talking about."

Turnbull bounced the eraser end of her pencil on the legal pad as she eyed Anna. "The school library doesn't get the newspaper?"

"I didn't have time to go to the library. And besides, I was scared it might be—" Anna slouched in her chair, slipping her father a furtive glance "—something bad."

"You couldn't have gotten more information from the person who mentioned the article?"

Anna shook her head.

"Anna, that's not a good reason to skip class," Officer Turnbull concluded.

"There are no good reasons for skipping class," Clara added quietly.

"I finished my work in Kraus's class, turned it in, and asked if I could go get a drink. He told me to sit down. I asked if I could go to the bathroom. He told me to sit down and be quiet. I asked him why he let Amy Trask go, and he gave me some bullshit about—" Anna threw up her hands in disgust. "I don't know what. So I just left."

Turnbull leaned back in her chair, contemplative, distant. "Why didn't you *ask* to go to the library?"

"If he's not gonna let me go to the bathroom, do you think he's gonna let me go look at the newspaper? Anyway, with guys like Kraus, it's always why, why, why. I don't see why they have to know everything. And Kraus hates my guts anyway, so why should I tell him anything?"

"Mr. Kraus called me at work," Clara volunteered. "I must say, I didn't appreciate his attitude. I didn't like the way he spoke to me. I found his . . . his suggestions to be totally inappropriate."

Her carefully controlled tone set off an alarm inside Ben's head. "What kind of suggestions?"

"Well, he—" Clara cast a quick glance Anna's way. "I really don't want to get into it now, but suffice it to say that I think Anna may have a point about . . . about her math teacher." She uncrossed her legs and leaned forward in her chair, looking Ms. Turnbull in the eye as though the probation officer and the teacher came from the same camp. "But I made it perfectly clear to him, as I have to Anna, that I don't condone rudeness, and that I expect my daughter to afford him due respect . . . *and* vice versa."

"He needed to be told this?" Ben asked, trying not to sound too menacing, not in Turnbull's office, anyway.

"We probably should have discussed this matter before we . . ." Resentment drew Clara's tone in tight. Dirty or not, this was laundry she was opposed, simply on principle, to airing. She gave a deep sigh. "Well, I guess Anna will know soon enough. I've asked that she be removed from Mr. Kraus's math class. The situation has become untenable, and I've come to realize that it isn't altogether Anna's fault. But that doesn't mean—"

"Ha, see?" Anna clapped gleefully, as though she'd beaten Clara's hand. "He even gave *you* some kinda bullshit on the phone, didn't he?"

Clara rolled her eyes heavenward. "Anna, please don't use that kind of language."

"I tried to tell you, but you wouldn't believe me about him. Nobody likes him. He's always got this miserable look on his face, like he ran out of Preparation H or something. He can't control the class, and if I just barely crack a joke or something, he's all over my case like the Gestapo."

"I never met a math teacher yet who had a sense of humor," Ben said with a deferential smile. "This one maybe doesn't appreciate"— he arched an eyebrow— "Indian humor?"

"He did make a comment that . . ." Clara's frustrated gesture and the guarded look in her eyes reflected a struggle that left her no room for humor. "Actually his rather rude remark led me to think . . ."

"But you've asked for a different class for her, so that should solve that problem," Officer Turnbull determined, turning abruptly to Anna. "The important thing now, Anna, is that you must not skip school. You've had a serious run-in with the law, and you don't want to add truancy to your record. Or anything else, for that matter." She flipped through the pages of her *Anna Pipestone* file. "Has there been anything else?"

"Skipping class was the major problem we've had this week," Clara said quietly as she, too, turned to her daughter. "I'm really pleased that you told Mrs. Turnbull about that yourself, Anna."

"Might as well," Anna said with a shrug. Then she turned wide, innocent eyes on her probation officer. "I've got a question."

"Ask away."

"If I wanna go out of town, or even a little ways out of state, like, to see my grandfather, can I do that without getting arrested or something?"

"I think it's a good idea for you to visit your grandfather. Your parents can certainly take you . . ." Turnbull glanced from one parent to the other. "Or a *parent*, either one."

"Yeah, but what if I just wanna, like, go on the ride with my grandfather? It lasts two weeks. But it'll be during Christmas vacation."

"A two-week trail ride in December?" Turnbull did a little shoulder shimmy and set her cheeks ajiggle with a mock shiver. "Brrr."

"Anna . . ."

Anna shot her mother a warning glance. "No, I'm serious. I really wanna go."

"That's up to your parents. I would need to be notified, and I would want one or preferably both of them to accompany you." The probation officer gave a self-satisfied smile as she closed the file on her desk. "It sounds like quite a trip. I'd love to go with you if they were doing it in the summer."

"Trouble is, it's a *memorial* ride." Ben looked the woman right in the eye and affected a charming smile in a halfhearted attempt to sweeten the sarcasm. "The army didn't chase the Sioux down to Wounded Knee Creek and shoot them in the summer. You're gonna do something like that, you do it in the winter, right?"

"I guess so," Turnbull allowed gingerly. "But is it safe? What happens if the weather gets bad?"

"Then the Indians stay put, and the massacre gets put off a few days." Shifting in his chair, he caught Clara stifling a chuckle. But Turnbull clearly didn't know how to take it, so he just shrugged. "I don't do the ride myself. It was started by a group of guys from down on Cheyenne River Reservation, younger guys, and my dad can't get it through his head that he's not as young as he used to be."

"That's why I'm going with him," Anna declared.

"Let me know what you decide. Anna's going to need to check in with me." Officer Turnbull rose from her chair. "You have four more months, Anna. You want to get through this, get it behind you, and get back on track. I do think a visit with your grandfather would be good for you." She bestowed a smile on her charge's parents. "Family is so important."

"I agree," Clara said tightly.

"How do you feel about that, Mr. Pipestone?"

"I'm all for family," Ben said, extending his hand. "You've got my vote, Officer."

"How come nobody told her what I did last night?" Anna wondered aloud when they were finally back in the car and on their way home.

Ben knew why he hadn't mentioned it. Paying a visit to the police station was unappealing enough, but being there on his daughter's behalf was like leading her through a jungle without a map. He wanted to put her in a steel crate and carry her on his back, but he figured that wasn't the way these things were supposed to be handled by the conscientious mainstream parent. Annie had gotten herself into this mess. He wasn't sure how much of a mess it was, or what was expected of him, which left him watching for clues, trying to follow Clara's lead. She was the epitome of the conscientious mainstream parent.

"You told her you'd skipped school, and I thought that was enough for now," Clara said. "I thought we should talk privately about the other part."

"So how about the three of us going out for lunch and hashing it over?" Anna suggested, cheerful now that she had her parents right where she wanted them—together, for the moment, anyway.

"I'd rather hash it over at home," Ben said. Basically he was with Annie on this. He wanted to stretch the moment out as long as he could, and since he'd moved out of the house, he and his daughter had discovered that when they hadn't seen each other in a while and they didn't know how long it would be before they'd share another meal out of fast-food boxes, it could take an hour to consume an extra-large order of French fries.

But today he was trying to satisfy everybody. He slid Clara a quick glance. "I'd rather go . . . like Mom said, someplace private."

"Yeah, but . . ." Anna's tone readily took a downturn toward the child side. "Can't we just glide past a drive-through window?"

Can't we just buy a little more time?

Clara heard the plea in Anna's voice.

It was the same plea she saw in Ben's eyes. They looked at each other, kept looking at each other, as though neither one remembered how to make a decision. She was tired of saying no, couldn't remember how to give a simple yes. *Yes* was the happy answer, the one people wanted to hear. But it was an answer that required stipulations these days. Parameters. Safety nets. Only if you behave, be careful, be trustworthy. Suddenly Anna couldn't manage any of those things. And Clara was very much afraid that she had no answers anymore. No way to steer her daughter on the right, the correct, the *safe* and proper course.

And Anna's father, damn him, was looking to Clara for an answer, too. Or an invitation. *Is it okay if I buy us a little more time?*

From the backseat Anna seized the moment. "Turn right at the Golden Arches, Dad. C'mon, I haven't had anything to eat today."

"Yeah, well, wonder why." Ben glanced out the window as he signaled for the turn she'd suggested.

"We can take the food home," Clara said quietly, feeling strangely relieved.

Anna and Ben ordered their usual favorites, but Clara wanted nothing more than hot tea. She knew her stomach wouldn't tolerate anything else. Not when she'd worked so hard to build an ark to save herself and her daughter, and it had started listing again. One damn rocky shoal after another. She hated it when things went so badly awry that she couldn't fend off that awful little-girl-lost feeling. She hadn't been able to fend it off the day the police had called her to come to the station.

She'd cursed her exiled husband's hands for not being on the steering wheel that day, of all days. Hers had felt shaky. They hadn't *looked* shaky. But beneath her orderly surface, chaos reigned. The words on the sign in front of that building would never again look quite the same to her. *Police* . . . God, the police had arrested her child . . .

*   *   *

Anna was waiting, chin in hands, elbows planted on the long white table, when Clara was ushered into the barren, windowless room. Her dark eyes met her mother's immediately, but they betrayed nothing. No guilt or remorse. No fear or confusion. Nothing but *here I am*.

And here Clara was, every inch of her Anna's mother. She took a deep breath and spoke quietly. "Is this true, Anna? Did you take something from a store without paying?" She couldn't quite say the word *shoplift*. She didn't want to imagine her daughter actually doing the deed.

Anna glanced at the female officer sitting across the table from her, then at the young man in street clothes sitting at the far end.

"You've made a mistake," Clara said to the woman in uniform. "Anna wouldn't—"

"*I* made the mistake, Mom. By getting caught."

"Oh, Anna." It was all Clara could say, and even that much came hard. The man who'd brought her to the room wheeled a chair in her direction, and she melted into it like snow hit by a March wind. She barely heard the introductions. The younger man was from Dalton's security. Clara would have taken him for a high school kid, and if he'd approached her daughter on the street, she would have kept strict maternal vigilance. He looked greasy.

He was writing up an incident report on Anna's crime. "Native American?" he asked without looking up from his clipboard. A brown wad of chew peeked over his fat lower lip. He glanced up, and Anna gave a curt nod. He put a check mark on his report.

"What does that have to do with it?" Clara asked, a mental red light suddenly galvanizing her.

She and Anna both grimaced as the security man spat into a paper cup.

He curled his forefinger and carefully wiped his lower

lip with his knuckle. "These are just routine questions I gotta ask. You the biological mother?"

"Is that on there, too?" Clara demanded, her voice gaining defensive strength. "Is there a space marked '*biological* mother'?"

"Legal parent, then?"

"Yes." Looking the man in the eye, Clara straightened slowly, gaining her full, regal stature like Phoenix rising. She enunciated each syllable purposefully. "I am Anna's mother in every way, shape, and form."

"That's all I gotta know." The little man shrank back from his report once he'd marked the box. "See, she's a minor."

"I realize that. And she's not a criminal. She's never done . . . anything like this—"

"Before, yeah, I know. Your first name?"

And so it had gone. Clara had recovered her poise in defense of her daughter. There was something about the bits of chew stuck between the security officer's teeth that had taken away his power to intimidate her. Anna had done something wrong, and the man had a job to do. So did Clara. But she had something over on him, she decided. She had class. She always managed to pull herself together on the inside and take care of business on the outside with a good deal of reason and some measure of dignity.

She had done the right thing when she'd finally called Ben, she assured herself as she led the way into the house. It was the reasonable, sensible . . . it was the *classy* thing to do. It just proved that now that Ben was getting his own life in order, she was going to be able to handle this awkward separate-household parenting in a civilized manner, which meant acknowledging that Anna needed her father. The two of them needed to have a good talk, and it was perfectly all right to let him come home for that. *Someplace private.* She wasn't backing down. She was simply being civilized.

She set the dining room table with place mats and dinnerware, even forks she knew they wouldn't use. Neither Ben nor Anna said anything as they sat down to their burgers and fries, but Clara read their amusement in the glance they exchanged. She resolved to keep quiet. She knew that if she waited until the food was at least halfway digested, Ben would eventually launch the requisite discussion.

And he did, leaning back in his chair, staring at his empty plate in his old familiar way. "Tell you one thing I learned when I was in treatment, Annie." No lead-in, no tell-us-why-you-did-it, just *boom.* "The younger you are when you start hittin' the bottle, the more likely you are to get hooked."

"How old were you?" Anna asked innocently, clearly hoping to divert her father into a storytelling mood.

Ben rubbed his chin for a moment, as though he were sifting through memories, trying to decide just how much of his vast experience he ought to reveal. Clara watched him, anticipating his approach. He was bound to say he was even younger than Anna was, thinking something like *twelve* would really shock her.

He frowned slightly as he stared at his plate and ran his thumb back and forth over the rim. "Some older kids got me really drunk—and really sick—when I was about five. Made a strong impression on me, and I swore off."

"Five?" Anna gasped. "You swore off when you were *five?*"

"Hey, I was smart back then." He glanced up, smiling ruefully. Then he reached for the quart-size paper cup full of pop he'd been nursing through a straw. "But I started flirtin' around with it again when I was about your age."

"You never told me that story," Clara said, unconsciously taking a new interest.

"It's not the kind of information a guy likes to volunteer. Even a drunk knows it doesn't sound too good."

"I still don't believe you were ever a *drunk*, not—" Clara shook her head quickly and slid a reassuring glance at Anna "—not in the *true* sense of the word."

"Whatever the hell that is," Ben said with a dry chuckle. He looked at her across the table, smiled patiently. "You mean I didn't spend a lot of time passed out in the gutter. Well, the truth is, I had a few good friends and a lovin' wife, kept pickin' me up when I was down."

"I don't understand," Anna said to her mother. "If you still don't believe he's got a problem, why did you kick him out? I mean—"

"I didn't say there weren't problems." She didn't like being put on the spot like this, either. "I simply said I wouldn't call your father a *drunk*."

Clara glared pointedly, but Ben ignored the message as he gazed into her eyes and smiled knowingly. "She'd like to call me a lot of other things, but she doesn't have the vocabulary for it."

"We're discussing Anna's problem, Ben. Not yours."

"Okay." The smile faded. He turned to Anna. "Your mom tells me she thinks it's mostly your friends' fault."

"And *you* think it's *your* fault," Anna assumed.

"I think I made my problems, and you're makin' yours. I wish you could just take my word for it, Annie." He shook his head sadly. "It'll cost you, Annie-girl, and it's not worth the price."

The wounded-bear look in her father's eyes clearly cut deep. Anna hung her head. "I didn't know you'd be here. I knew you'd find out, but I didn't know you'd see me. I didn't want you to. Not like *that*, God."

Father and daughter exchanged a look of pain and empathy. Clara saw it and read it, but she understood only that she was not included in what they shared. She had missed something, and she felt a surprisingly deep stab of regret.

"I saw what you went through in treatment, Dad. Some of it, anyway. I didn't mean to . . ."

She'd missed that by choice, Clara reminded herself. The right choice, the only choice. Watching them now, wondering what this wordless memory was, she felt like an intruder. She turned and stared sightlessly out the window.

She wanted to kick herself for feeling left out.

"Hey," Ben said softly, laying his hand on Anna's shoulder. "You're the only kid I got. I find out you're in trouble, you think I'm gonna ignore it and hope it goes away? You think what I don't see with my own eyes doesn't bother me?" He lifted her chin on the edge of his hand, tracing its curve with his thumb. "Doesn't hurt me?"

"I didn't do it to hurt you." She turned her face from him, and Clara felt the threat of Anna's tears creep into her own throat. "I just wanted to try it," Anna whispered. "I just wanted to see what it was like."

Clara cleared her throat. "Anna, you don't have to try everything right now, and *surely* you know enough about the effects of alcohol without sneaking off and—"

Ben gave Clara the covert signal for a change of tack. "So what was it like for you, Annie-girl?"

"No big deal." She stared hard out the window, focusing on a bare tree in the backyard. "I gotta admit the aftermath is a real bitch."

"Uh-huh. I'd say you've met Iktome, the Trickster. One way or another we all get to meet him, but you don't wanna get too friendly." Ben patted his daughter's knee. "We'll get your grandfather to tell you some Iktome stories."

Anna fairly whirled in her chair, turning her mood around just as fast. "When?"

"Well . . ." Ben slid Clara a lopsided smile. "*Toksa*. Pretty soon."

"Don't *toksa* me." Anna grabbed her dad's brawny

arm and shook it as though she expected apples to fall. "Let's go on that ride, Daddy."

He laughed. "Don't *Daddy* me, you little weasel. You know how cold it can get that time of year. You want your butt to freeze to the saddle and your toes to turn to ice cubes?" He gave her earlobe a playful two-fingered flick. "You want your ears to turn black and fall off?"

"I'll dress warm."

"You wanna spend Christmas camped out in some icy pasture? How's Santa Claus gonna find you?"

"Don't *Santa Claus* me," she returned, pulling on his arm again.

"Tell you what, Annie-girl, that has to be one miserable way to spend your holidays. Your teeth won't stop chattering until spring."

Anna shoved his shoulder with the heel of her hand.

Still laughing, he shook his head in protest. "I ain't kiddin' you, they do some hard ridin'. I'm hopin' your grandfather'll come to his senses and take his pickup instead of a horse."

"*You've* got horses," Anna reminded, resorting to a little whining. Which, unlike crying at her age, was still okay.

It wasn't his way to say no to her. He was inclined to let her make her own choice, even at thirteen.

But Clara had not been raised the same way, and when she spoke, she echoed her own parents.

"I'm not going to let you go off on a two-week ride, Anna. At this point you're just as unpredictable as the weather. I'm not about to let you out of my sight for that long."

Anna grinned. "Then you come, too."

"Me? I'm sure they wouldn't want *me* along."

"Why not?" Anna demanded. "The paper said there would be some women going. Kids, too."

"I know, but—"

"And you're always telling me stories about you and

your wonderful bay mare, Misty," Anna recited. "You *used* to tell me how you and Dad would take long rides and how he looked so great on a horse, you could hardly control yourself, just watching him handle the reins."

"Oh, for heaven's sake, Anna." Clara shot her daughter the grimace of the sorely betrayed.

"And if you can't ride, you could at least drive along so I could go," Anna insisted. "So I could at least give it a try and see if I could make it all the way."

"Listen, Annie, I'll . . ." In a glance Ben sought alliance with Clara. "I'll take you down to see your grandfather, okay?"

"When?"

"This weekend. If that's okay." He turned to Clara. "You wanna come?"

"I think we should talk," she said quietly, instantly regretting the pall she'd suddenly thrown over the conversation. But she wasn't prepared. This was all going too fast for her.

Ben nodded and pushed his chair back from the table. "There's some stuff I wanna get done outside before I head back."

He figured raking the yard was about all he had time for after he'd thrown the ball for Pancho a few times, hosed off the mess Annie had made at the side of the house, and watered the shrubbery. "Put 'em to bed wet," he remembered the guy at the nursery advising when he'd bought the first bushes for fall planting. The expression had struck him funny. Still did. *Put 'em to bed wet.*

In his zeal to establish a nice yard, he'd learned about a lot of things the hard way. Like "putting them to bed wet" was a good idea, but you had to take the hose off before the first hard freeze, or you'd have busted pipes. Hell of a mess, busted pipes. But he was going to have a nice yard, come hell or high water, and he'd gotten himself up to his neck in both. He didn't want the neighbors saying anything about his presence devaluing their property.

So he'd learned this stuff the hard way. Before he met Clara, he'd thought buckbrush and buffalo grass made a perfectly good yard. A guy didn't have to worry about busting his pipes—didn't need any pipes. Prickly pear cactus took whatever water the heavens could spare and produced pretty yellow flowers in the spring. The taproot on a yucca plant could grow twenty feet deep if you left it alone. But roses and Kentucky bluegrass had to be watered constantly, and even then, a good, hot Dakota summer or a normal Dakota winter could kill them.

But he'd had those Joneses to keep up with, and by damn, he wasn't going to give them anything to complain about. Except when they wanted him to get rid of the cottonwoods that grew in his backyard. The cotton was blowing into their yard, they'd said. They'd cited an ordinance against planting cottonwoods in the city.

Ben had to point out that he hadn't planted them. As far as he knew, those trees had been stuck in the same plot of ground since before Lewis and Clark had come nosing around. And they were staying put. They belonged in this country. They were *native*. That Russian olive in Jones's front yard was an import, for crissake. Even Ben Pipestone, who didn't know a goddamn thing about trees, could figure out why some plants grew better on the prairie than others. To hear his father tell it, the cottonwood was sacred. But Ben wasn't going to try to convince his neighbors of that. They'd probably start a rumor that he was practicing some kind of satanic tree worship in his backyard.

He didn't mind raking up after the cottonwoods. He was determined to have his nice yard, but if he'd ever bought that little piece of land behind it, he would have let it go back to prairie. No damn cornfields for Ben

Pipestone. He wanted to be able to look out his window and see a few acres of prairie and a couple of broomtails.

He had most of the leaves raked up when Clara came outside. She'd changed into a soft print skirt and a blazer that matched her eyes. Fall colors. And he could tell by the spring in her penny loafers that she was ready for their talk. He knew it had to come, sooner or later. But later was fine with him.

He picked up the blue rubber ball and flung it toward the horizon. "Go get it, boy."

Clara took a seat on the tree bench he'd built at the base of one of the cottonwoods. "I had planned to spend the afternoon at the office," she began, "but it's getting to the point where I can't trust Anna on her own."

"Go ahead. I can hang around until you get back." He smiled as the lively border collie came bounding up the slope carrying the ball in its mouth. "There's plenty for me to do around here."

"I can hire someone."

"To watch Annie?" He gave her a get-real look as he pitched the ball again. "You'd be treating her like a kid. That would only make things worse."

She brushed a brittle brown leaf off the bench and crossed her ivory-stockinged legs at the ankles. "I meant I could hire someone to do the yard work. I don't expect you to come all the way up here to rake the yard."

"I don't mind workin' outside," he assured her as he reached inside his jacket for a cigarette. "Besides, the house is still in my name, too."

She squinted up at him, watching his every move. His glance ricocheted off hers as he planted one boot on the bench. He could just feel it, the way she was looking at him, judging him for some damn thing. All he was doing was lighting a cigarette.

"When are you going to stop smoking, Ben? It's not good for you."

"So I've heard." He spat a stream of smoke past the drooping cottonwood branches. "When are you gonna quit naggin' me about it?"

"Force of habit, I guess. Anna will probably take that up next."

"Oh, for crissake." He took one more deep drag before he ground the cigarette out against his bootheel and flipped it into a pile of yard debris. "There. Happy?"

The disconsolate look in her eyes said no. There was no way he could make her happy. Not anymore.

A terrible sadness drifted over him, like the cloud of gray smoke he'd just forfeited. He tried to shrug it off. "They don't advise tryin' to give up all the vices at once."

"Who's *they*?"

"The vice doctors," he said absently. "Guess they figure if they drive out all the devils at once, there might not be much left."

"It's just . . . for your own good."

"Tellin' the truth was supposed to be for my own good, too. Part of the cure." He looked down at her, sitting there primly on the bench he'd had one hell of a time putting together before he'd invested in a table saw. "Is this what you wanted to talk about?"

She shook her head tightly and spared him a glance, then wrapped her arms around her middle as though her stomach hurt her. "I think Anna needs more stability in her life, Ben."

Here it comes, he thought. She was about to tell him she'd finally met the right man. The Rock of Gibraltar who would give her what she needed and love her daughter like his own. He'd thought he'd prepared himself for it, but he was ready neither to hear it nor to step aside without a fight. Two years ago when he'd hit bottom he probably would have, but not now. He'd come too far.

"Stability?" He reached up and snapped off a brittle twig. "That's why we moved up here. And I guess that's why Annie's staying with you. You've always been perfectly steady."

"But I'm only one person. And I'm not . . ."

Not what? Could she say it? *Not perfect?*

She sighed. "There are some things I just can't be. Anna needs you, too. She needs your family. In many ways, she feels more like a Pipestone than a Whiting."

Ah, he thought. *Not Indian.*

"But your name is Pipestone, too," he observed, testing the waters cautiously.

"For now," she said as she rose from the bench. "Anna looks like a Pipestone. I don't. There are times when that makes a difference that I can't deal with without getting all . . ." Shoving her hands in her pockets, she drew a sharp, menacing breath through her teeth. "I hate it when they say things that—"

"Who's *they*?" he echoed with a knowing smile.

"Unfortunately, *they* are usually people who come from a background similar to mine, people who look like me, people Anna associates with me."

She looked to him for deliverance. He knew she wanted him to assure her that there was no reason for Annie to associate her mother with that particular kind of *they*. Clara knew as much about Indian history as he did. Okay, maybe more. But since he had the distinction of knowing more than she ever would about *being* an Indian, and since maybe he was feeling a little contrary, he stood silent, offering her no reprieve.

"I just hate it when they act *stupid* and say things out of ignorance, like . . ."

Silent until he tired of her beating around the bush.

"What did he say?" he asked. She questioned him with a look. "The math teacher," he clarified.

"He said . . ." She took a deep breath and backtracked. "Well, *I* said that I would certainly discipline her for talking back, that I'd had some problems with her lately, too, but nothing unusual for a thirteen-year-old, nothing we can't . . ."

With a look he appealed to her to get to the point.

She glanced away, barely able to control her emotions even in the retelling. "He said that if she continued to have trouble controlling her language, maybe I ought to take her back to the reservation, where she . . ."

"Belongs?" At her nod his blood pressure took a running leap. "You called the principal?"

"Yes. The principal said he found it hard to believe that Mr. Kraus would say something like that, but I reminded him that this was not a matter between a child and an adult now, this was . . ."

She looked to him again for deliverance, this time from her own fury and frustration, from the terrible feeling that she was actually helpless against the insidiousness of this particular threat to her child.

And he thought, yes. In this way she *does* know.

"I've never met the man face-to-face." She touched the sleeve of his jacket, tentatively at first, but as she spoke she slowly enclosed the fabric in a tight fist. "He said it to *me*, over the phone. I want to go to the school board. I want that man out of there, but—" She gave a shaky sigh. "I can't even talk about it without getting all emotional."

"I can."

"Oh, Ben, you'd never be able to control your temper over a thing like that. He'd make up some story, and you'd punch his lights out."

"So?" Grinning slowly, he covered her small fist with his hand. "If we didn't get his job, at least we'd get his lights."

She permitted only the flicker of a smile. "But the other thing is, I hate to subject Annie to any more stress."

He groaned.

"Don't you see, Ben? When it gets to be us against them, I look like one of *them* to her. I wish I could minimize all that somehow. I wish I could—"

"Turn her white?"

"No!"

"It would be a lot easier, wouldn't it?"

Wounded, she drew away from him and from his accusation.

He tried to shrug off her damned seriousness for both their sakes. "Maybe it's like one of those Mormon elders told me once when he was trying to get me into his church. When Indians go to heaven—after they get to be Mormons, mind you—they'll be turned white so they can see the face of God." He tipped his head slightly and offered a conspiratorial wink. "We'll be as pretty as you guys."

She pouted, which meant she was coming around. "That's a bunch of bullshit."

"Whoa. Clara-bow experiences a momentary loss of tongue control over the old 'mark of Cain' question." He laughed. "I always loved the way you handled those missionaries when they came knockin' at the door."

"You never turned them away."

"Well, they've got their job to do. Everybody wants to convert the Indians."

She smiled, slipping readily now into the remembrance. "And you'd holler out, 'Cla-ra. There's someone here to seee yooou.' Then you'd just let them in—especially the pretty ones, as I remember—and sit back as though you were tuning in to Monday night football."

"Yeah, but I was always rootin' for you, sweetheart. My woman with all the answers. It was fun to watch you fire them off at somebody besides me."

"Well, the older I get, the fewer I seem to have." Again, her heavy sigh. "For the important things."

Again, his easy shrug. "You *always* had 'em for me."

"Do you have any for me?"

Silence. Again, their impasse.

"I still don't understand why, Ben," she said softly, her tone resonant with a needy curiosity rather than the usual wrath. "That was the one question you never resolved for me."

"Even if I had an answer, what difference would it make?" He searched her eyes in pursuit of something more than simple truth. "It wouldn't change anything, would it? I can't explain it away. I did what I did."

She winced, and a wave of heartsickness engulfed him.

Gently he took her shoulders in his hands. "And God knows I'm sorry for it, Clara, but that doesn't change anything, either, does it?"

She closed her eyes and turned her face from his. "I shouldn't have brought it up. It only makes it worse."

He let another pain-filled moment pass before releasing her to step away. Away from the bench he'd built for her around the sacred tree. Away from her unholy husband.

She buried her hands in her blazer pockets and gave her head a quick toss, catching glimmers of autumn gold sunlight in her fine, straight hair. "There are some changes that have to be made. As soon as I—"

He clenched his teeth as he stared at her prim profile. "What about this weekend?"

"This weekend?"

"Would it be all right to have Annie . . ." He gestured vaguely south. "I could take her along now if she's got tomorrow off. You could come down to pick her up on Sunday, say hello to the ol' man." He gave a promising nod. "He'd like that."

She looked southward, and he knew she was imagining the drive beyond the city. She was thinking about following the meanderings of the Missouri River, crossing into his territory, into sweet-memory country. She lifted one padded shoulder. "I guess I could do that."

"Course, between the two of them hounding me over this ride . . ." Ben imagined them wearing him down, and he stubbornly shook his head.

"It might be good for her," she offered tentatively.

"You shittin' me? Like I said, she'll freeze her little toes off."

Clara smiled wistfully. "Her toes aren't that little anymore. Her feet are as big as mine now."

Ben whistled. "Man, that's . . ." Grinning, he wagged his forefinger. "See, she doesn't get that from the Pipestones. She's got your legs, too." His grin became a warm smile. "Which is nice."

But it was her eyes that held his attention now, because today they weren't so mad at him, even when they'd talked about—well, *touched on*—the hurtful things. God, she looked like a schoolgirl in her creamy stockings, her skirt and blazer. Maybe a bit too sad-eyed to be schoolgirl young, but at least those eyes weren't so mad at him today. And he wanted to remember the way they made him feel like smiling a little, even laughing some.

She lifted her shoulders in an exaggerated shrug. "If it got too cold, there's no rule that says she can't drop out, is there?"

He chuckled. "Try tellin' her that. You know how stubborn she is once she gets set on something. Besides, you said she couldn't go without you."

She challenged him with a tilt of her chin. "You don't think I could do it, either, do you?"

"You haven't been on a horse in years." But he wouldn't put it past her.

Squinting into the sun, she cocked her head to the side and smiled. "I might surprise you."

4

Ben wasn't worried about freezing his cowboy ass off riding horseback. He'd done that before, plenty of times. Once upon a time he'd told Clara that that was why he was so small and hard back there. Once upon a time she'd been impressed. Now she'd turned cold on him, and the weather had nothing to do with it, and *none* of that had anything to do with his reluctance to participate in the Big Foot Memorial Ride.

It was the old man, and that whole pipe-carrier thing. Ben Pipestone did not have the makings of a Lakota holy man. Not that Dewey had been talking it up much lately, but all the old man had to do was take out that red bundle. He always performed the unwrapping as though he were about to take his first look at his newborn child. Then he'd cradle the smooth red stone bowl in his palm, fit the wooden stem into place, and finally he'd look up at Ben. His dark eyes pierced the soul with an invitation to share the ancient beliefs and accept the hereditary commission.

Ben Pipestone made his living as a *mechanic*, for God's sake. All right, it was more like for his own sake, for his kid's sake, and if God needed a piece of that action, Ben could spare it. He'd gone to church with Clara, dropped some cash into the plate, even fixed the

Catholic Mission School's buses and jump-started the
Mormon elders' van. God had no shortage of repre-
sentatives on the rez.

Tunkasila, his father said, didn't need a car.

But Ben's wife was the one with the true Indian heart.
The ol' man had said so himself. She was dead serious
about the stories, getting the history right, and honoring
the artifacts in their glass cases.

Ben had an Indian face, a cowboy ass, and a cheatin'
heart. Underneath all that he had no idea what kind of
a soul the ol' man kept trying to chip away at with
his hawk-faced looks. Whatever kind of soul it was,
it was heavily tarnished. He'd all but sold it to the
low bidder, and it hadn't shown much sign of being
worth salvaging until just recently. Still undeveloped.
Still needed a hell of a lot of work. But at least it was
still his.

It had been fun to have Annie back with him for a
couple of days. It griped him a little that he'd had to call
Officer Turnbull before he took his daughter out of the
state, but he'd switched on the cowboy charm anyway.
The first thing he'd wanted to show Annie was his shop.
Not that cars held any appeal for her, but he wanted her
to see that her dad had a growing business, complete
with employee.

After the "grand tour" of Pipestone Auto Repair, he'd
taken her to the café for supper. Annie was just like
her mother; she loved to eat out. Besides the fact that
Ben wasn't much of a cook, he'd felt a little awkward
about the shabbiness of his living arrangements. He did
his cooking on a hotplate these days. Annie had never
seen a hotplate. And he'd had to laugh when she'd
marveled at his "antique" television set. "Wow, Dad,
a real black-and-white."

He decided to let her sleep over at his sister Tara
Jean's house, even though her family had plans to participate in the Big Foot Ride. The calculated risk turned

out worse than he'd expected. By the time Ben came
to pick Annie up mid Saturday morning, she and her
fifteen-year-old cousin Billie had it all planned. For
months Billie had been talking about being one of the
runners who would start the event off with a relay, but
now she wanted to ride instead. Because now "Uncle *had*
to ride." Because now Annie was dead set on riding. And
Billie had already spilled the beans about the little paint
horse he was giving Annie for Christmas.

Damn, he really knew how to get his ass in a sling.

They'd spent much of the weekend visiting out to his
dad's place, which was fifteen miles from Ben's little
hole-in-the-wall apartment in McLaughlin. The three of
them had swapped stories, shared meals, and they'd gone
riding together. It all felt pretty good. It felt almost right.
And when the one person they all missed finally showed
up at Dewey's door, Ben told himself to forget, at least
for another hour or so, that the three of them wouldn't
be going home together.

"Hey, I'm glad you're here." An understatement if
ever there was one. He was actually wishing for red
carpet as he shut the door behind Clara. "I need an ally.
They're gangin' up on me here."

She smiled. There sat the two conspirators, side by
side near the table that divided the little kitchen from
the all-purpose front room. A young head with memories
to make and an old head with memories to preserve,
both of one mind. Sometime over the weekend Anna's
single long, thick, black braid had become two, like her
grandfather's. But his were thinner. They were silver-
gray, and the tight red cloth wrappings made them lie
stiff against his shoulders, curved like two unstrung
bows.

"You're looking fit as ever, Dewey." Clara offered her
father-in-law a demure handshake.

Dewey, in turn, offered Clara a chair close to the
wood-burning stove. "I'm doin' okay. You must be

pretty fit yourself. Hear you're gonna go with us on the ride."

She slid a quizzical glance from Ben's face to Anna's as she draped her jacket on the back of the chair. "I am?"

"Annie's been talkin' like it's a done deal," Ben reported. He straddled a tattered kitchen chair and folded his arms on the backrest.

"And you said you'd have to go if I did," Anna reminded her mother. "You said you were gonna take some extra time off at Christmas anyway. It'll be a good time for a vacation."

"It would be a good time to go to Arizona for a vacation." With a smile Clara added, "I'd become a snowbird if I could afford to."

"See, that's my problem," Ben said. "I can't afford to take the time away from the shop."

Dewey lurched to his feet and headed for the stove. "Annie, you help me with the coffee."

"Sure, Lala."

Doggedly Ben passed a hand over his face and came up resting his chin in the crotch of his thumb. "Dad, people really need their vehicles in the winter, and that's when these rez runners break down the most. I hate to close up shop."

"You got a helper now," his father said tonelessly as he poured strong stove-top coffee into the first mug Anna handed him.

"Yeah, but he's not ready to take over for that long."

"And you're not ready to take over for me, so don't be thinkin' I'd step aside, either."

"Yeah, you *wish*." Ben chuckled ruefully, then cast Clara an incredulous look. "So, what, you've decided to go?"

Before she could answer, Anna handed her a cup of coffee. "Lala, can you take the pipe out again so my mom can see it?"

"She's seen it before."

"Yeah, but let her see it now. Anyway, I wanna see it again before we go home." She touched her mother's arm. "It's real old, Mom. You can just tell it's, like, an actual relic, and it's not even stuffed in a glass case or anything."

"And it won't be. Not as long as we have a pipe carrier." Dewey handed Anna a cup of coffee for her father, then took the red bundle down from the cupboard and claimed a cup for himself. "The pipe is only sacred if it is used for sacred purposes. Its age means nothing. Just look at me." Hands full, he squatted over his chair and lowered himself carefully. When the feat was accomplished, he nodded. "I'm pretty old myself."

"Glad you finally realized," Ben muttered.

But no one paid him any mind.

"Tell Mom about my great-great-grandfather, Lala. Tell her the story about Iron Hammer."

"Haven't I told you that one?" Dewey set his coffee on the yellowed linoleum floor and started loosening the ties on the red felt bundle. "About my grandfather bein' at Wounded Knee?"

"I think you might have, but it's been a long time."

Dewey nodded, his attention focused on old fingers and stubborn knots. "You always listen better than my son. Ben, he can't sit still for a story. Rather be out there messin' around with horses or cars."

"I've heard 'em all," Ben said. "And I don't forget 'em, so you don't have to keep—"

"That's the way it's supposed to be. You don't forget the stories, or we'll have other people remembering them for us. *Their* way." Lovingly he unrolled the long felt strip as he spoke. "But not your wife. She isn't like that. I read that paper she wrote when she was in school. It was a good one."

"Well, sure," Ben said with a smile. "It had Dewey Pipestone written all over it."

"How would you know, Ben?" Clara challenged. "You never read it."

"Yeah, I did. That's how I found out how smart you were. I had to get out the damn dictionary." Ben wrinkled his nose and gave a nod in Anna's direction, as though he had the final say. "It was pretty good, though."

"But did you know that Iron Hammer was there when Sitting Bull was murdered?" Anna took a cross-legged seat on the floor at her grandfather's feet. "He was at Sitting Bull's camp. He saw the whole thing. But back then people didn't say too much about what they saw, right, Lala? Because the army was saying Sitting Bull was like a criminal or something."

The old man nodded. "My grandfather was a young man that time," he said, putting the time into perspective by way of the generations of their relatives. "Early twenties, had a cabin not too far from here. My grandmother was young then, too, and she liked to go to the mission church they had over to Little Eagle. Back then, I think there was only one. But Iron Thunder had started in with the Ghost Dancing the summer before. People were gettin' together secretly, more and more all the time, sayin' they had a new religion now. They was all tryin' to dance back the buffalo and the dead relations, the way different ones were sayin' they learned to do in a dream."

"Turned out it didn't work," Ben flatly pointed out.

"No harm in tryin', they said." Dewey smoothed the felt strip across his knees and set the pipe atop it, laying the bowl in his palm. "They were supposed to try farming, and that sure wasn't workin'. That year it was so dry, they were eatin' mostly dust for every meal, they said.

"So Iron Hammer was out to Sitting Bull's camp that time with some of the Ghost Dancers. It was almost winter, but no snow yet, so they'd make this big circle and dance, shoulder to shoulder, and sing the songs. Sitting Bull, he wasn't one to stop nobody from dancin', even if he wasn't gonna take to it himself. And the truth was, he didn't put much stock in it. He'd had some powerful dreams himself, and lotta people looked up to him.

"But the Indian agent, Major James McLaughlin, he was tryin' to get the people to sign another agreement to give away most of the land they had left. Sitting Bull was talkin' against it, so McLaughlin wanted him dead. *Arrested* was what he said." Dewey shook his head. "*Dead* was what he meant.

"McLaughlin sent his Indian policemen out to Sitting Bull's camp really early that frosty morning. Most everyone was still asleep in their blankets, and the place was real quiet. The police had some troopers ready to back 'em up, just a couple miles away, so they went in the cabin, got the Old Bull up, and took him outside. They said he was their prisoner and they was gonna take him up to the agency at Fort Yates.

"But that quick, the Ghost Dancers were there, wantin' to know what was goin' on. Pretty soon somebody brought up a rifle and said they wasn't takin' the old man anywhere, and all hell broke loose. The two policemen who shot Sitting Bull, they got shot, too. And the police killed Sitting Bull's boy. The soldiers came ridin' in, saved what was left of their hand-picked Indian police, and the people camped there, they all scattered.

"After that, Iron Hammer and some of the other ones thought the army would come lookin' for them. My grandma was gonna have a baby, and that baby was my father. So she stayed with her missionary friend. A white woman, like your mother," he told Anna solemnly.

He looked at the pipe, turning it in his hands as he spoke quietly. "Grandma never went to Wounded Knee. She used to say that the way some tell it, havin' a baby could kill you, but it could save you, too. Her husband left her behind to have the baby, and he rode down to Cherry Creek to join up with Big Foot's camp." He raised his head, spoke to Anna first, then Clara. "We're gonna be ridin' to Cherry Creek, too. And we'll be meetin' up with the riders from Cheyenne River, and some from Pine Ridge."

"And cameras from the damn TV stations," Ben grumbled.

His father nodded. "We want those people to tell the story."

"So Iron Hammer was with Big Foot and the Minneconjou people on the journey to Wounded Knee," Clara said, tugging on the story's loose end.

Dewey nodded again. "The army was tryin' to break up the Ghost Dancing, and there were certain ones that were on the Indian Bureau's list of troublemakers, like Sitting Bull and Big Foot. Big Foot was old and sick, and he didn't know how he was gonna feed all these people, his own plus the cousins from Sitting Bull's camp. Some people believed the Ghost Dancing was really gonna bring everything back the way it used to be come spring, but they still had a lot of winter left to go. So then Big Foot was thinkin' if he could take his people down to Pine Ridge, to Red Cloud's camp, they could make it through the winter under Red Cloud's protection." He chuckled. "Eatin' ol' Red Cloud's rations."

"I'm sure Red Cloud would gladly have shared," Clara intoned, completely absorbed even though she knew every detail of the story.

Ben found himself taking some satisfaction in the fascination he saw in his wife's face. Damn, he must have been hard up for satisfaction. She'd always been one to lap up all that old Indian stuff, which was what he was fast becoming. Old Indian stuff.

So he came up with something an old Indian might say. "When people come, you feed them, even if all you can do is add water to the soup."

Dewey grunted in agreement. "But most of them didn't get there for any soup, because the army stopped them at Porcupine Creek, then took them to Chankpe Opi Wakpala."

"Wounded Knee Creek," Ben translated.

"They made camp there, with the soldiers camped just north of them," Dewey continued. "The major in charge posted guards and set up his Hotchkiss guns, aimed at the tipis. Iron Hammer put on his Ghost Dance shirt before he went to sleep that night. It was made of muslin, painted with moons and stars. He believed it could stop bullets, and for this reason he wondered whether the soldiers might try to take it from him. But then he said to himself, they probably didn't know about this medicine. He kinda didn't want them to know because that might make them wanna test it out. And he kiiin-da didn't want them to do that, 'cause he'd never tested it out himself.

"But the major had given them some food and put a nice stove in Big Foot's lodge to help the old man with his cough, so Iron Hammer thought maybe it would be okay." Dewey rubbed the smooth red pipe bowl with a leathery thumb. "But it wasn't okay. Because the next morning they made everybody gather in the camp circle. And they separated the men out. Right away Iron Hammer thought this was no good, because the women and children had no protection. And then they took all the knives and guns—even the sewing awls and tent stakes—put 'em all into a big pile.

"Then the soldiers wanted to make sure they had everything, so they started to search. Iron Hammer dropped his blanket and showed them he had nothing. But there was this one Minneconjou who was hard of hearing, and he had a new Winchester. And he *really* hated to give up that new Winchester. He wasn't gonna shoot nobody, but he'd paid plenty for that gun. He was pretty confused, too, because he couldn't hear everything that was goin' on. Everybody was gettin' nervous. Then one of the old men started singin' one of the Ghost Dance songs, tellin' about the sacred shirts. 'The bullets will not hit you,' he sang.

"My grandfather couldn't say whether it was the deaf man's Winchester that was fired when the soldiers spun him around, tryin' to get it away from him, or what. But after that one shot, the gunfire came crashing down on them, surrounding them like a thunderstorm. Some of the men were able to grab a weapon, but mostly everybody tried to run. Iron Hammer didn't have anything to fight with at first, so he took off toward the ravine. Then he felt a bolt of fire shoot through his leg, and he went down. But he got up again, didn't pay no attention to the pain. He was too scared. All around him, people droppin' like they was shootin' cattle in the stockyard pens. This man whose foot was shot clean off and he was bleeding bad—" Dewey touched his right eye "—from here, he gave my grandfather a rifle.

"Some women and little children were trying to get away, so Iron Hammer flopped on the ground to cover their retreat. He couldn't see nothin' but smoke, so he just fired the gun whenever he heard hoofbeats or got a glimpse of black boots.

"Hard to imagine the things my grandfather saw that day. So many women got killed. So many little children. When he got to be an old man, my grandfather still believed he saw more blood that day than he saw in all the rest of his days put together. And he wasn't talkin' about his own blood. He tried not to look at that, he said. He was shot again, here." Dewey touched his shoulder, then the side of his neck. "Here, too. But he remembered his wife and the baby she was havin' for him, and he fought hard to stay alive. So maybe his shirt protected him some way. Or maybe it was . . ." Tears stood in the old man's eyes as he ran his fingers along the wooden pipe stem. "He carried his pipe bag. He had the pipe with him the whole time."

The pipe drew three stares.

"The same one?" Anna wondered, childlike in her amazement.

"So they said."

"Did Iron Hammer tell you this himself?" Clara asked.

"I didn't get the pipe until long after he was gone. But I heard him tell about that day at Wounded Knee, many times." For Dewey, the connection was as true as blood. "We had to carry the pipe in secret all those years. We could have a pipe, but not the sacred way. Not with the ceremonies. No sacred dancing, no *inipi*, no *yuwipi*. The government said our religion was against their laws. But we kept it, some of us, in secret. It was hard for everyone after that day. Hard to live the Indian way, the way our fathers said it used to be." He looked at Ben. "The sacred way."

It was a legacy of grief. The old man always ended up getting tears in his eyes over it. Ben knew the story right up to the last word, which always had to do with sacred ways. Still, it sounded new to him as he watched its impact unfold in Clara's and Anna's eyes. Not because he grieved the way his father did. He couldn't bring himself to shed tears over the past. What was the use? What was done was done. It couldn't be changed. He'd never laid eyes on his great-grandfather, didn't have any strong feelings for him and couldn't bring himself to fake any.

But his women did. He could see it in their eyes. He didn't understand why or how, but somehow they knew Iron Hammer's sadness. And they were going to follow Dewey. And he himself could either take his place with them or stay behind and fix rattletrap cars.

"We're gonna need some really warm sleeping bags," he said, resigning himself to it once and for all.

Clara nodded. "Yes, I suppose so. *Really* warm."

Anna's face brightened. "I could tell she'd made up her mind. I could just see it in her eyes."

Ben sighed and shook his head, turning to Clara. "You wanna take the pickup?"

"How can I drive and ride at the same time?"

With a look he asked when she'd lost her mind.

She answered with a mindless shrug. "Well, if I'm going to do it, I'm going to do it right. Did you say you had an extra horse?"

"Aw, shit." Ben spun his chair aside as he got to his feet. "Now you're tryin' to make me look bad. No choice, I have to go along and watch out for you guys."

"Nobody said you had to ride with us." Dewey chuckled. "But we all know you got more pride on you than anything else, you get right down to it."

"You get right down to it, I'm probably the only one who can make it to the end. You're too old," Ben declared, raising an eyebrow his father's way. Then to Anna, "You're too young. And you're too—" He challenged his wife with an arrogant smile. "Let's say, too fragile."

"We'll see," Clara said smugly. "Maybe you're the one who should drive the pickup, Ben. Somebody has to haul our stuff. Unless we could take a packhorse. Should we do that?" She turned to Anna, her excitement growing. "Remember that trapper display we did with the mannequins? We learned all about loading a pack saddle with that little project, didn't we?"

"The thing kept coming off," Annie recalled, lifting her face toward her grandfather. "Course, that hairless horse was so slick. It was life-size, but no hide. It was like a Barbie doll horse. I was the one who figured out how to balance it so it wouldn't sag."

"I can just see you two, showin' up with your historically authentic packhorse," Ben predicted, getting into it now that the die had been cast. "Two days later, you've got your authentic saddle sores and your present-day frostbite, don't come cryin' to me."

Clara slid a glance between Anna and Ben. "You mean, you won't even let us warm up in your pickup?"

"Hell, no. You wanna play Indian, you stick to the rules." He wagged a finger under Clara's nose. "The rules that say the Indians go hungry, freeze their damn asses off, and end up losin' everything in the end."

"There's a difference between losin' it and throwin' it away," Dewey told his son.

"And anyway, we haven't lost everything," Anna said, touching the strip of red flannel that lay across her grandfather's knees.

Dewey chuckled. "You see, son? When the women have to turn to an old man like me—"

"Christ, here it comes."

"That's when the young men lose out. They think they have so many other things to worry about, while an old man has it narrowed down pretty good. We take what we need and leave the rest." With a nod he assured his granddaughter, "I can get enough horses."

"I've got my own horse now," she said proudly.

"I've got horses for both of them. And one for myself." Ben bristled at the sound of his father's dry chuckle. "I *said* I'd *ride*. I ain't gonna be drivin' no damn supply truck." He jerked his chin, signaling to Clara. "C'mon outside with me. I got something to show you."

To his surprise, she followed, the way she once had, without giving him any static.

The corrals were almost a quarter-mile hike east of the little house overlooking the Grand River. They were made of a motley assortment of weathered scrap lumber, posts collected along the river bottom, and splintering rails. The pens had been put up, torn down, and rearranged every summer since Ben could remember, depending on what kind of stock they'd picked up that year. It had never been more than a few head of anything, usually some animals to ride, some to ride herd on, a few to sell, and something to butcher in the fall. Before the ol' lady had flown the coop when Ben was ten, a variety of beasts had gotten the ax, but after she'd left, no one ever came up with any bright ideas about chickens or geese, pigs or goats. After Ben's mother had left the family for greener pastures, it was just cows and horses.

Part of the all-purpose chute Ben had framed out during the summer of his seventeenth year was still standing. He'd experimented with switch gates and makeshift latches, but it had never worked quite the way he'd wanted it to. Still, he and his sisters and their cousins had enjoyed some fine bucking action within the confines of those corrals. They'd roped calves, broke horses, even bucked out some lumbering cows.

As good as some of those times had been, he couldn't go out to the corrals anymore without remembering the best times, without dreaming of green and gold summer afternoons filled with meadowlarks singing in the grass. Every time he headed for the corrals, he could see himself saddling up not one horse, but two. He could feel his face catching a breeze down by the river. He could remember his hands and his mouth making chaste love with Clara in the shade of the big cottonwood. Horses had been as much of a turn-on for her as they were for him. Summer wind and horse sweat, damn! Ben and Clara. They'd get so close, 'til he'd thought it was do or die, and then she'd manage to hold him off at the very last. And he'd die a little.

They were close now, closer than they'd been in two years. The autumn-cool sunshine was not as brassy as that of young, green summer. It felt friendly and comfortable, and he liked watching their shadows travel across the pasture together. Their footfalls swished through the crisp buffalo grass. In the aftermath of unexpected decision making, the silence between them was strangely peaceful, as though for the first time in two years they were headed in a direction they could both accept because neither of them had dictated it.

He leaned on the top rail of the corral and braced a booted foot on the bottom one. She, in her tennis shoes, stepped up on the bottom rail and hooked her elbows over the top one. The three horses barely took notice.

"What do you think of the bay?" he asked.

"She . . ." She gave a quizzical look. "She?" He nodded, and she smiled. "She looks a lot like Misty."

"She still needs work, but I can have her ready in time. They're all gonna need conditioning for a ride like that." But he hoped she noticed how good they looked now. He'd given them his care, and they had carried him through his loneliness. "The little paint is Annie's."

"Perfect," Clara marveled. The black and white horse raised its head and pricked its ears as if on cue. "Oh, he's perfect. Has she ridden him?"

Beaming inside, Ben nodded once. "He was going to be her Christmas present."

"Well, he still can be, but I'm sure she won't be able to wait to tell her friends she has a horse of her own."

"We used to talk about it. Remember? Buyin' that piece of land behind the house so we could have a couple of horses." He reached for a cigarette, ignoring her glancing reproof. "Just one of my many pipe dreams."

"Anna will want to come down here more often now. We'll have to come up with some kind of a regular schedule."

"A regular schedule for seeing my daughter," he repeated, cigarette bouncing in the corner of his mouth. He struck a match and cupped his hand to shelter the flame, muttering dryly, "Ain't that the shits."

"As Dewey said, I'm sure you have lots of important demands on your time, but you only have one child—" she eyed him, affecting suspicion as she watched him suck up a lungful of smoke "—that I know of, anyway. And she still needs you. And yes, it might require a commitment on your part."

"Don't you know I'd give just about anything . . ." He closed his eyes, hung his head, and expelled a long, slow, smoky breath. "I've never done real well on a schedule, have I? But then, neither has Annie. Remember how you tried to get her on a nursing schedule?"

She rolled her eyes, recalling her determination.

He smiled, remembering the way the baby's persistence had melted Clara's resolve.

"When Annie wanted her mama, she wanted her right now."

"Much the same way you did."

His eyes widened, and she glanced away. Neither one could believe she'd said such a thing. Not now.

But he wasn't going to let it pass without an appreciative chuckle. "Yeah, but I was always willing to go to the trouble of coaxing Mama along until she wanted Papa pretty bad." He cocked his head, watching her closely as he touched her chin with the back of one restrained finger. "*Needed* . . . her Papa-bear . . ."

She closed her eyes, and for a moment she stopped breathing. "You can't do that to me anymore," she willed as she leaned away. "I've kicked the habit. I don't need your brand of heartache."

"Took the cure, huh?" He turned, rolling his shoulders against the rail as he took another long, deep pull on his cigarette. He spat a stream of smoke. "You wanna tell me your secret so I can get off these?"

"Knowing they're bad for you should be enough. And then . . ." She looked up at him, catching the sun in her eyes " . . . staying away."

"That's how it works with booze. I stay away. Can't trust myself to see it or smell it. It wouldn't take much more than a taste to get me started again." He studied the cigarette, the ash sheltered in his cupped hand. "I still think about it a lot, so I know I really have to stay away." Smiling, he lifted his gaze slowly to meet hers. "Course, if I didn't have a taste for it at all anymore, I wouldn't worry about staying away."

"You're about as subtle as a bulldozer, Ben Pipestone."

He chuckled. "Who was it said, it ain't over 'til it's over?"

"Some man." She folded her arms along the top of the rail, rested her chin on her sleeve, and watched the bay mare swat the big chestnut gelding with her tail. "I'm doing this for Anna."

"What? Going on the ride? So am I." He shook his head, still finding it hard to believe. "Turned the ol' man down flat. Told him there was no power on earth could make me do such a fool thing." He took a quick puff on his cigarette, then dropped it beneath his bootheel. "I hadn't counted on Annie."

"You wouldn't . . . take anyone else along, would you?"

She spared him a glance.

He hiked a brow, inviting a such-as.

"I mean, I know you *said* there wasn't anyone at the moment," she reminded him, trying to rush the notion headlong past her caring. "But who knows what opportunities might come your way between now and the middle of December?"

"Opportunities?"

"We've been separated for quite a while now." She stared hard at the bay. "And I'm not as naive as I once was. But since we're doing this for Anna . . ."

"Jesus, Clara." With a parched chuckle he shook his head. "I don't think it would go over too good, do you? Hey, baby, how about a winter getaway down to Wounded Knee, South Dakota? Where would we stay? Well, hell, I just thought we'd pitch a tent." He slid her a glance, saw that she wasn't amused, and shrugged. "I don't know anybody that damn desperate."

"I just think it might be awkward," she said stiffly.

"Awkward?" He laughed. "After a day or two in the saddle, I don't think 'awkward' is likely to be the first word that leaps to your proper little tongue. I'd say sooner or later this ride is bound to be a blue bitch. So when you finally give in and start cussin', just remember, this wasn't my idea."

She glared. "You'd be offended if my *proper little tongue* were to, for the sake of variety, direct a bit of profanity your way?"

He grinned. "Sweetheart, if the idea of offending me ever tempts you to talk dirty, then yeah." He gave her an insolent wink. "I'd be downright mortified."

5

Mid-December 1990

The Little Eagle Community Center smelled of cigarette smoke and boiled meat. Not much had changed in the many years since Clara had been there. Sheets of particleboard had replaced most of the windows, and the paint was peeling off the ceiling like curls of old paper. The Bingo apparatus was new. A sign above it read "Bingo on Last Call Only." Not being much of a bingo player, Clara had no idea what that meant. She had heard that all the districts on the reservation ran weekly bingo these days, partly to finance community improvements, partly to alleviate community boredom. There was so little employment available in the more isolated reservation districts like Little Eagle.

Whatever the doings at the center, there was always a crowd. There had been a good-sized crowd the day Tara Jean had given Clara's bridal shower in the same building, such a long, long time ago. She remembered the strands of purple crepe paper tacked to the wall where the "Last Call" sign now hung. She remembered the refreshments of Kool-Aid punch and sheet cake and the gifts of plastic refrigerator bowls and blankets. She'd been showered, literally, with thermal-weave blankets, a dozen or more, mostly from women she'd met for the first time that day.

From her side of the family, who stood firmly in opposition to the marriage, there had not even been good wishes.

After more than fourteen years, it didn't matter that plentiful measures of both the good wishes and the dire predictions had come true. What mattered was that it felt good to be back. Even though her marriage had failed, and even though every person who came and went through the ever-swinging front door probably knew that, she still felt welcome in her husband's hometown. It was December fourteenth, the eve of the anniversary of the death of Sitting Bull, and the people were gathering to honor the Big Foot Memorial riders. They might be surprised to see Clara among them, but no one would predict any dire consequences for her. No one would wish her ill.

"Hey, Mrs. Pipestone!" The greeting came from a young man in a fatigue jacket who was hauling a bass drum toward the singers' corner, dodging boisterous children as he made his way across the floor. "Where's the ol' man?"

Clara grinned and gave an exaggerated shrug. "How're you doing?" She recognized the man's smile, but his face had matured considerably, and the name she'd once had listed in her school attendance book was just beyond her memory's reach.

"Not too bad. Just finished a hitch in the army."

Clara nodded. The man—Howard, *that* was his name— Howard nodded as the children's commotion backfilled the space between them.

Ben apparently had not shown up. Not that Clara had any pressing desire to see him, particularly, but he had said he'd meet her here. She wasn't going to depend on him for anything but a horse. That was all she needed from him. She'd taken care of everything else. She had the tent, the subzero sleeping bags, the first aid kit, the silk long johns, the lamb's-wool earmuffs, and reams of tips from winter sporting experts who'd been coming out of the woodwork since she'd mentioned her plans to her colleagues at the museum.

So Clara had come prepared. As usual she derived considerable confidence from careful preparation. And if Ben didn't show up, she was prepared to find other means of transportation. Obviously she had friends here, people who remembered her well. She had her former students. She still had in-laws. And if she couldn't find a horse, she had a car. A promise with Clara Pipestone's name on it was a promise carved in stone, which was why Anna was counting on her. Not on Ben. Trusting her mother to take care of the remaining details, Anna had hooked up with a crew of cousins as soon as she'd gotten out of the car.

Clara hadn't seen Dewey yet. Not to worry; he'd be there. She didn't know about Ben, but she knew his father would soon be there. Like Clara, Dewey was as steadfast as the ancient buttes surrounding Little Eagle.

"Mrs. Pipestone?" A plump young woman with dark, smiling eyes touched Clara's arm. "Remember me? I was in your history class."

"Winona!" A spontaneous hug reminded Clara of the last time she'd seen the girl, wearing her maroon cap and gown. Clara had hugged her then, too. "Winona Taylor?"

"Still Taylor. Heard you moved up to Bismarck."

Clara nodded, suppressing the urge to elaborate, explain the move, as though she had deserted the reservation and she owed an apology.

"You had a baby that year I graduated," Winona said. "I remember those boys teasin' you about carrying a basketball under your dress."

"That's my baby, the one in the red sweater." Clara pointed to a girl-huddle she'd been keeping a casual eye on near the side door. "Her name is Anna."

"Eeez, has it been that long?" Winona shook her head in amazement. "How many kids you got now?"

"Just Anna."

"I've got three. This one is my youngest." She patted the unruly brown curls of a youngster who had just attached herself to her mother's sweatshirt. "She just turned five. Lisa, shake hands with my teacher."

The little girl responded shyly, left thumb in her mouth, right hand extended the way she'd been taught. Clara leaned down to take the small hand in hers.

"Did you get something to eat, Mrs. Pipestone? Some cold meat sandwiches, soup, fry bread, some *wojapi* over there, too." Winona nodded toward the tables laden with blue and white enamel kettles, square dish pans, and big plastic bowls full of food. A cardboard box was piled high with golden-brown fry bread. One of the kettles would serve up everyone's favorite *wojapi*, a traditional fruit sauce. Winona chuckled as she rubbed her little girl's round cheeks. "All this one wants is cake."

"Don't you like fry bread, Lisa?"

The little girl hooked a juicy finger over her tiny bottom teeth and set her head abobbing.

"Did you come to see the riders off?" Winona asked.

"I'm going to . . ." Clara cast a quick glance over her shoulder, as though she half expected someone to challenge her. Or laugh. "I'm going to go along."

Winona's eyes seemed to double in size. "All the way to Wounded Knee?"

"That's the plan," Clara confided with a sheepish smile. "Actually, Anna's had her heart set on it, and we had a contract. You remember my contracts?"

"So many points for an *A*, so many for a *C*. I used to go right down to the *D* line, see what I had to do to pass."

Clara laughed. "Well, you always met your goal, so I guess it worked. And it works for behavior sometimes, too, I've discovered. Anna must really want to go on this ride, because she's been making points right and left over the past two months."

Winona looked skeptical. "So you're gonna follow in a car or something?"

"I'm going to ride a horse."

"You?" The younger woman seemed genuinely impressed. "Jeez."

"Sounds a little crazy for an old teacher, doesn't it?"

"Ahhh, you're not old. Wish I could go, but . . . I've got these kids to watch."

Clara's gaze shifted to her own daughter, who had been coaxed into a chair so that her cousin Delia could reach her hair. Anna's long ponytail was turning into a French braid. "Maybe I should watch yours and let you watch mine."

"What about Ben? Isn't he going? He used to be the big rodeo cowboy."

"He was supposed to meet us here." Clara shrugged. "He says he's going. I don't know. I'm sure my father-in-law is going, though. Have you seen him?"

"I've been helpin' with the food." Winona scanned the big room. "He's around somewhere. Anytime they get something like this goin', Dewey's always right in the middle of it." With an invitational smile she nudged Clara toward the food tables. "You better get in line and eat, Mrs. Pipestone. Build up some muscle." She clamped her hand around Clara's slender arm and jiggled it, testing for substance. "You better eat a lot of that fry bread. And some meat."

You'd better eat was something between an invitation and a challenge. If you love us, you'll eat with us, was generally what it meant, so Clara moved into line. At work, people gave her advice and paid her money. Her mother still gave her advice and paid her obligatory visits. But here people fed her with fond recollections and fry bread.

A deep voice startled her as she reached into the cardboard box. "Take an extra one for the road."

"Ben!" She spun around, her face brightening, blushing, then shuttering as quickly as she could catch herself. She gripped the flimsy edges of her paper plate in both hands. "How do you still manage to creep up on me like that?"

"Easy." The black cowboy hat she'd given him years ago for Christmas shaded his broad grin from the fluorescent lights overhead. "You're always deep in thought. Did you think I wasn't coming?"

"My deepest thoughts are not about you."

"They're about fry bread." A smirk danced in his eyes, then played on his lips. "You wanna take an extra one?"

She shook her head innocently. "One's enough for me."

"Hey, you're holdin' up the line, cowboy!"

Ben turned, still grinning. "Hey, Howard." He stepped back and leaned over to shake hands with the same Howard who'd hauled the drum in. "You goin' on the ride?"

Howard gave a nod, then adjusted his glasses, grasping the wad of adhesive tape that held them together at one corner in place of a hinge. "You?"

"Looks that way. You remember my wife?"

"Sure." Howard stepped out of formation to shake Clara's hand. "She was my teacher once. Told us all about the Civil War."

"Among other things, Howard. How are you?"

"Doin' okay. Hear you're still workin' up in Bismarck. At that big museum, huh?"

"I wouldn't say it's that big." Clara took two pieces of fry bread, accepted a paper bowl full of soup from the girl who'd dished it up, then moved out of the way. "It's as big as we have in North Dakota, though. And, you know, we have a wonderful collection of . . ."

"Our stuff." Ben chuckled and tipped the brim of his hat in mock deference. "Clara's in charge of all the Indian stuff now."

"E'en it? Big cheese, now, huh?" Howard reclaimed his place in line. "Maybe I'll have to come up and visit. I might even ask you some questions, like you used to do to us. See if you know your beadwork."

"I know *your* beadwork," Clara said. "Do you still make belts?"

"I'm beading Reeboks now. Put in an order, I can have 'em ready . . ." He scooped up a spoonful of potato salad and plopped it on his plate. "Guess I'm tied up for the next couple weeks. You sure you wanna turn this ol' cowboy loose for that long, Mrs. Pipestone?" Howard claimed a cup of *wojapi* at the end of the line, balanced it on his plate, and came away grinning. "No tellin' what kinda trouble he can find between here and Pine Ridge. What've we got? We've got Timber Lake, we've got Lantry, we've got Bridger . . ."

"She's goin' along," Ben reported as he took a piece of fry bread from Clara's plate. Then, as an afterthought, he asked her permission with the arch of an eyebrow.

Howard winced, as if to say, so much for that idea.

"I'm not going *along*. I'm just going." Clara offered a sweet smile. "Ben's free to find whatever trouble tickles his fancy."

"I was just kidding. This ain't gonna be no joyride, right, Ben?"

"Right."

"No alcohol." Howard balanced his heavily laden plate in one splayed hand and dunked his fry bread in his soup with the other. "That's one of the rules. So I was just kidding about lookin' for trouble. Ain't gonna be none of that noise."

"But I'm serious about going on the ride, Howard. And I promise not to say a word about the Civil War."

Howard chuckled. "That's okay. You gotta talk about

something. Hey, maybe we'll teach you a little history, huh?" He bit off the soggy corner of densely textured bread, then talked around it. "I guess I don't know that much about Indian history, but Ben's dad really can tell the stories."

"I know."

Howard swallowed. "I guess that's not the same as history, like what you teach, but these old guys, you know, they could almost be *teachers* in a way. It's pretty interesting what they remember."

"Didn't we do the oral history project in your class? That was one of my standard assignments, where you were supposed to ask someone in your grandparents' generation about things they remembered."

"I probably got an *F* on that." Howard shrugged as he dunked his bread again. "Either that or I got my girlfriend to do it for me. She got me through high school." The bread hadn't quite reached his mouth when he paused to give Ben the male conspiracy look. "That's why I had to marry her. I had the diploma, but she had all my education."

The men chortled together.

Howard wandered off in search of coffee, and Ben directed Clara toward two vacant folding chairs. "Did Annie eat?" he asked between bites of fry bread.

"She had a plate, but whether she's eaten, I don't know."

"She's pretty excited, huh?" He took the cup of *wojapi* from the plate Clara had balanced on her knees, dipped his fry bread in it, then bit into the sauce-soaked corner as he put the cup back. He chewed, swallowed, then eyed her almost long enough to make her squirm before finally asking, "How 'bout you?"

"I'm a little worried about . . . details." Mainly *de tail* she was sitting on and whether it had any chance of holding up in a saddle for two weeks. But be damned if she'd tell Ben that. "I wasn't sure what we'd need."

"I told you what you'd need."

"I must have made a hundred lists, thinking, 'What if this happens? What if that happens?' "

He nodded. He knew her well. "So you're prepared for an avalanche, a tidal wave, whatever."

"I wouldn't say that. I'm definitely not prepared for making a fool of myself, and I have a feeling I'm about to."

"Don't worry about the mare," he said quietly. "I've got her handling like a dream, and her gaits are smooth as butter. She won't let you down."

She believed him. Ben had an eye for good horses and an extraordinarily patient hand. "I had intended to get a little more practice in, but I ran out of time."

"You'll be fine."

She nibbled gingerly at her fry bread, trying to think of something neutral to say. "The weather's just too good to be true, isn't it?" There it was. The obvious choice. "I've been watching the weather reports. There's no snow forecast for the next few days, anyway. Beyond that, who can tell?"

"You want my prediction?" Ben braced his hand on his knee and leaned back, winding up to deliver. "There's a good chance of snow. Excellent chance of cold. Guaranteed wind."

"I suppose that's a pretty safe—" Renewed activity beneath the "Last Call" sign drew Clara's attention. "Your father's here."

Ben straightened, turning slowly as though preparing to make some move. Maybe stand his ground. Maybe bolt. It was an old reflex in Ben, one he couldn't seem to shake. Watching him, Clara could almost hear him struggling to make a choice. As if he had any. Ben's loyalty to his father was embedded in his bone marrow, a place Ben could neither consciously discern nor purge.

"God, he looks old." Ben sighed, lowering his gaze to the fraction of fry bread he still held in his hand. "Ever since that day you were out to his place, the ol' man's really been acting funny."

She knew that around Ben's family, *acting funny* generally meant that two people had been shutting each other out, and if you asked, you'd hear two different versions of how it had gotten started. But Clara considered Ben's concerns as she watched Dewey move more slowly, more deliberately, than usual. He was putting his striped wool jacket over the back of a chair, setting his plaid Scotch cap on the seat, moving stiffly and taking pains with every move.

Was he *taking* pains or *feeling* pain?

"Ben, he looks so fragile."

"He's been . . . I don't know how to describe it. It's like he's living in the past. Talks about his grandparents like he just saw them last week." The old man put his hand to his mouth and turned away. His shoulders shook. "That damn cough's gettin' worse," Ben grumbled.

"Has he seen a doctor?"

"Says he has, but I doubt it." He sat back, tucked his thumb in his belt, and continued to watch his father. "I can't change his mind about going on this ride. I've tried. He just gets mad, like he thinks I'm trying to take something away from him."

"The pipe? I thought he wanted you to—"

"I'm not taking his damn pipe. He can take it with him to his grave, for all I care." He stared so hard, the old man sensed it. He looked up and stared back, for one pregnant moment. Then he went about his business beneath the "Last Call" sign with the other old men.

"I told him I'd do it for him this once if he'd stay behind and take it easy." Ben shook his head and turned to Clara, his eyes suddenly seeking sympathy from hers. "I thought he was gonna bite my damn head off when I said that."

"Anna's very touchy about it, too. Well, I *had* to make it clear that we couldn't go if she got into any more trouble," she explained. "She said I was holding it over her head, and I guess maybe I was. I'll admit, I've had more than a few second thoughts."

There had been times when she'd almost hoped Anna would break a rule so that she could call it off. She had also chided herself for that sorry sort of thinking. It was a kind of insincerity. It was a game her parents had played with her. Be especially good, Clara, and we will be especially nice. But Clara had seldom managed to make the grade, and she'd finally wised up. The definition of "especially good" was ever-changing. No matter what she did, she never quite hit the mark.

With Anna there would be no games. Clara was determined to be straight with her. She had to make up for all the losses, all the failures, all the unfairness of things. On top of all that, she had to deliver where Ben fell short. Anna had done her part over the last two months, and this adventure was her reward. In order to deliver on her promise, Clara would endure two difficult weeks in the company of Anna's father.

And surprisingly enough, it looked as though Ben might actually do the same, in the company of Anna's mother.

"I'm being summoned," Ben said as he rose from his chair. A subtle gesture from his father had been sufficient this time. "He probably forgot something, and I'll probably have to go lookin' for it. Wish they'd just get this part of it over with."

"What part?"

"All the damn ceremonial stuff." He grinned down at her, shoved one hand in his jeans pocket, and touched the brim of his hat with the other. "You know me. I just want 'em to open the gate and let me ride."

"Yes," she said quietly, watching him saunter across the dingy linoleum floor. "I know you."

The "ceremonial stuff" was launched, appropriately, by Alec Red Horse, who assumed the role of master of ceremonies by virtue of the fact that, of those who were "in the know," he was the first to claim the microphone. Alec spoke of Sitting Bull as his grandfather "in the Indian way," of Sitting Bull's family, of his own family, of the generations between them and how they all fit into the seven Lakota council fires, among them the Hunkpapa, the Minneconjou, the Oglala, which were the principle bands represented on the ride.

"I know most of you riders." Alec's dark, dispassionate gaze skimmed the room like a well-fed hawk cataloging the inhabitants of a prairie dog town for future reference. "And I know who your cousins are and your uncles and grandmothers. So we're all together in this.

"And even the ones who join us from other bands— the Germans and the Norwegians and the Japanese—" With a wave of his hand he included the blond heads, the down-filled parkas, the crepe-soled Oxfords, and the Nikon cameras. A few chuckles sounded in response, some a little nervously. Alec nodded, his stone face slowly cracking a smile. "They are our relations, too. That's why they're here. The ones who come to us and ask to join us on the ride, they must have come to realize that they are two-leggeds, just like us. So we say, come on along." He opened his hand in a welcoming gesture. "If you can say you're related to us, then come on along. Because a hundred years ago, when you broke faith with us, the sacred hoop was broken. And it's been hard for us to mend it. We haven't been able to do it yet. Maybe you can help us.

"But we don't want you to try to take it from us, that broken circle, and try to fix it for us. First of all, you've got your own fixing to do. So you come on along, and you do your mending. Let us do ours. Let each one of us take care of the little rips and tears we've made in the circle.

"Like fixing up our houses, where we live. You know, I look around our reservation here, and I see houses with broken screens, broken doors, junk all around, old cars full of boxes, and I say, 'Why do we live like this?' Loss of self-respect, that's why. We don't respect ourselves, we don't respect our women. We continue to use alcohol even if it kills us. Parents lose their children. We have to get our self-respect back. That's why we're making this ride.

"So come on," he invited with a smile in his eyes. "But bring your blankets with you. It's gonna get plenty cold. They talk about Indians goin' back to the blanket. Well, you guys with the cameras are sure gonna find out why."

Alec's remarks were followed by the traditional invitation to anyone else who felt called to "say a few words." First came Harriet Bone Club, who spoke proudly of her two grandsons who would be riding and of her hope that the community would take a hint from the young people and find ways to get along. "Like nobody should be lettin' their dogs run loose in another person's yard," she admonished seriously. She turned to offer the microphone to Alec, but she snatched it back before he could claim it, bowing her head over it to add one more remark. "I just might have to cook up a big pot of puppy soup pretty soon, so . . . I might have to put on a big feed. And that's all I have to say."

There were others who spoke, offering concerns, praise, reminiscences, and donations to the fund to help pay for meals for the riders and feed for the horses. Elliot Plume, one of the founders of the Big Foot Memorial Ride, recalled that he and his brother Eddie, who had been killed in a car accident six months ago, had conceived of the ride as a challenge, a test of endurance, a commitment to honor the past and restore hope for the future.

"What can we do for our people?" he asked rhetorically, remembering, as he'd explained, the night they had first come up with the idea in their mother's kitchen. "How can we make our lives better? What will be left for these little kids that are running around here? We came up with this ride for something we could do. It isn't easy. It isn't meant to be easy. If you've done it before, you know it makes you think about how you've been living your life, and how you want to live your life. It changes you.

"So if you want to stay just exactly the same person you are tonight, this ride isn't for you. But you're the only one who knows that. We don't exclude anybody, and we only have a few rules. First, take care of the horses. Second, no negative thoughts. And don't eat around those who are fasting." He paused, staring at the floor for a long moment. Finally he raised the microphone close to his mouth once more. "If you have any doubts about what you should do or how you should act, it's mostly a matter of respect."

Now it was time for taking vows. Dewey assumed his place at the front, and Ben, somewhat to Clara's surprise, stepped forward to hand him the willow staff, wrapped with red cloth and curved at the end to form a hoop, symbolizing the circle of life. Then he helped with the smudging, dispersing the fragrant smoke of burning sweet grass from a coffee can for purification. At the proper time he handed his father a leather tobacco pouch, anticipating Dewey like a seasoned, if reluctant, acolyte.

Clara had watched Ben assist his father before, but only on rare occasions. When he was a boy, he had readily taken part, or so she'd been told. But Clara had only witnessed Ben's occasional participation as an adult, his stiff, almost shy compliance and his occasional covert glances toward the exit door. Tonight he seemed more at ease with it, but he was also more than ready to step aside when Dewey called the riders forward, lining them up to receive a pinch of tobacco, touch the hoop, and shake hands with each other. Those who had earned eagle feathers on previous rides tied them to the hoop.

Clara held her breath when Dewey turned to Ben. He hesitated, and for a moment she thought he might back away from making his vow. He looked almost frightened, which seemed impossible. Ben had never shied away from a horse in his life. It was the vow, she realized. He'd made promises, and he'd broken them. It was the vow that scared him.

But he took the step, finally, lifted his hand to receive his tobacco, then touched the hoop gingerly, the way Clara had so often seen him use his hands when they were dirty from his work. He was always scrupulous about not letting his touch ruin anything.

But it was the vow itself that he was afraid to touch. The vow scared the hell out of him because it would require something of him. And she caught herself pulling for him, thinking maybe now he could. Maybe this time he would.

Then, quickly, she closed her eyes, shook her head, and sighed, cursing herself for a fool.

No negative thoughts. Oh, God, already she'd . . .

"C'mon, Mom." Anna tugged at Clara's arm. "We gotta take a vow."

"I made my vow." Clara's butt dragged, but she allowed herself to be drawn from the chair. "To you. That's the reason I'm here."

"Well, now you've gotta have a reason to go the distance. You're going, aren't you?"

"Yes, I'm going. But what if . . ." She hadn't entertained the prospect until now. "What if it turns out to be too much for me? I mean, I hate to make a promise and then not be able to keep it. What if I wimp out?"

Maybe some vows scared the hell out of her, too.

Anna laughed. "You're not gonna pull out halfway there and let me go the rest of the way on my own, are you?"

"No."

"I didn't think so. I'm taking a vow to go all the way. But you can promise whatever you want. Nobody's asking you to write it down and sign it in blood."

"All right." Clara smiled wistfully, touching the silky hair tucks that formed Anna's neat French braid. "I'll promise to do my best, how's that?"

"Usually pretty good."

Clara and Anna came before Dewey, shoulder to shoulder, and silently made their vows. There was no eye contact with the pipe carrier, for in the old way he respected their privacy in this moment. But Ben's eyes said, *We're in this together*. And Clara found that somehow that much of a promise brought true comfort.

The singers began their tonal song. Their leather-bound beaters rose and fell in unison, pounding out a steady, solemn cadence on the bass drum. They sat in a circle. Their thighs formed a circle around the inner circle, which was the drum itself, the heartbeat of the honor song.

The honor dance accompanying the song was a slow-moving circle, a somber, loose-kneed step-together-step, with community members following the riders, paying them respect, holding them up in esteem and physical, rhythm-phrased prayer. The men doffed hats of all shapes and sizes and carried them in hand. The cowboys shuffled along in pointed-toe boots, their bowed legs ill suited to any two-footed gait. The younger women gestured to the little ones, universal hand signals saying, *Come join me*, or *don't do that*, or *take care of your brother*. The mature women held their heads high and moved with assurance.

But the photographers fussed over their cameras or questioned each other with a look or a whisper. "Is it okay now?"

When the drumbeat faded to a soft echo, the riders gathered near the far wall. Dewey took the microphone in hand and addressed them. "You have come to make this ride. No one asked you to. You did it on your own. It has to mean something to you."

He turned to the crowd, addressing them. "Look at these riders who have come to make this sacrifice. Remember them in your prayers."

Now all in attendance filed past the riders, each well-wisher delivering a kind of communal respect for the whole undertaking with a handshake. There was a solemn formality in the way one line moved past the other. Few words were exchanged. Clara caught herself wondering what these people thought of her. What was behind this enigmatic pair of eyes, or that bit of a smile?

Who did she think she was, anyway? She'd taken the trouble to get herself on a horse twice in the last two months, and before that it had been, what? Three or four years? Did she expect special treatment? People probably assumed she did. Most of the riders were men. Most of them younger than she was. Almost all of them were Indians. Just who did Clara think she was?

Ben Pipestone's wife?

For now, yes. But didn't most people know the truth by now? That their marriage was a dismal failure. That they had split up. That because she had not been all the woman he wanted, Ben had not been a good husband. No one had said anything. Probably too polite to say anything. Or maybe they felt sorry for her. They knew what "the ol' cowboy" was like; they'd known it all along. Which meant that she really looked like a fool, coming back here like this.

And he—standing up front with a group of his buddies—looked every bit the cowboy hero he'd always been, even though he'd given up the rodeo long ago to become a family man. He was still tall and lean, dark and handsome. Such an imposing figure, he could have taken over and run this whole show. On a horse he was pure physical poetry. And he was the pipe carrier's son. This was his domain, and these were his people.

Clara watched him turn his head at the sound of a pretty woman's voice, calling his name. She watched him lean closer to hear what the woman wanted, or maybe what she offered. He nodded. Clara's stomach knotted up so tight so quickly, she had to turn away and scold herself for noticing, for questioning, for giving a damn.

"I don't wanna stay in that motel tonight, Mom," Anna told her as they headed for the chair where Clara had left her jacket and her purse. "Billie says it's haunted."

"Oh, Anna, don't be silly."

"I'm not kidding. Some woman caught her boyfriend steppin' out on her and shot them both."

Stepping out on her. Clara hated that expression. It sounded like a game.

Shooting them both, however, did not. She shook away the image that flitted through her mind. The faces were too familiar. "I'm sorry, Anna, but that's the only motel within—"

"I can stay with Billie. You can, too, if you want."

"I don't think they have room for me," Clara said, conscientiously replacing the ugly fantasy with a memory of the time she and Ben had stayed at his sister's home, putting three children out of their bed and adding to the stress on the already overtaxed bathroom. "But yes, you can stay with Billie."

"You're still gonna sleep in that haunted place? What if they give you the same room those guys died in?" Anna grimaced and shuddered dramatically.

Clara laughed. "If you don't believe in ghosts, they don't bother you."

"I believe in them. So does Dad."

"I don't. You'll need to get your overnight bag out of the car." She was fishing in her purse for her keys when, out of the corner of her eye, she saw Ben follow the woman out the side door.

It didn't matter, she told herself. All that mattered was

that her cousin Billie was dragging Anna away, giggling with her, distracting her so that *she* had not noticed. She located the keys in her jacket pocket and tossed them jauntily to her daughter. "Don't stay up all night, Anna. If you do, you'll regret it tomorrow."

"Excuse me, is that your daughter?" said a male voice.

For another moment Clara's attention belonged to Anna. Absently she gave a nonverbal answer, more a sound of appreciation than confirmation. She smiled when Anna and Billie playfully bumped hips on their way out the door, then she turned to find an attractive, silver-haired man waiting for his answer. She laughed. "That's my daughter."

"She's beautiful. How did you ever . . ." He waved his own question away with a sheepish gesture. "I'm sorry. You don't know me, and I'm about to ask you how you got your daughter. Cheeky of me, right?" He looked directly into her eyes, his smile filled with practiced charm. "Robert Cady."

Clara offered a handshake. "Clara Pipestone."

"Ah, *Pipestone*. I was about to make the rude assumption that your daughter was adopted. *My* wife and I—that is, my ex-wife—we tried to adopt an Indian child, but her tribe refused to let her go. Can't blame them, really, after all they've been through. But we had Mattie in our home for five years as a foster child, and we wanted to make her our own. But eventually we lost her."

"That must have been very difficult."

"It was. She'd be about your daughter's age. I lost touch with her." He fingered the buttons on the thirty-five-millimeter camera he had slung around his neck by a black strap. "My own fault. I run around a lot, looking for stories like this one." He plopped his hiking boot on the seat of a folding chair and gestured inclusively. "This is fascinating, isn't it?"

"Yes." Reflexively she glanced toward the side door, looking for Ben.

"You're a very brave woman." Robert Cady braced his forearm across his knee. "I mean, I noticed that you were among those taking the pledge, as it were. And I know how cold it gets here. I've been all over the world, and I can't think of too many places where the wind is any more relentless than here. It has no mercy."

"Are you riding with us?"

"I don't ride. But I'll be following you in old Harvey." He smiled, a little indulgently, she thought. "My pickup. Any friend as faithful as he is deserves a name, don't you think?"

Clara couldn't help giggling as she tried to imagine Ben christening his pickup. He'd called the old bomb by a lot of names, but none of them as cute as "Harvey."

"I know." Again the indulgent smile. "I sound a little off, but I'm really harmless."

"I'm sure you are. And I'm really quite a coward, but don't tell anyone."

"There's a difference between cowardice and fear. I doubt you have a cowardly bone in your body. But if you have a healthy fear of what may happen on a risky venture like this, then I would say you're human." This time his smile reached his blue-gray eyes and came across with more sincerity. "Since it's a secret, I won't tell anyone."

"You givin' away secrets, Clara?"

She nearly jumped out of her Keds, as though she'd been caught in the proverbial act of doing something she shouldn't. Which, of course, was absurd. She was still and always straight-arrow Clara.

And Ben was still Ben, still suspicious of men who approached her. Not *all* men. She'd never quite figured out the distinction between the men who didn't bother him and those who raised his hackles. But Robert Cady was suspect. She could see it in Ben's bearing. Like the dominant male in the herd sensing some intangible threat, his whole being—his stance and substance—suddenly overpowered the space he occupied and its perimeter.

Clara looked up at him, willing herself to appear anything but submissive.

Ben returned a shuttered look. Then he forced himself to smile. "You gotta be careful around these reporters."

"I'm not exactly a reporter." The interloper offered a handshake. "Robert Cady. This trip I'm a photographer, but I'm more of a jack-of-all-trades."

"Ben Pipestone. Master of none."

"Clara's husband, right?" Cady glanced from Ben's eyes to Clara's and back again.

"Let me give you a tip," Ben said as he withdrew his hand. "Watch where you point your camera. People get touchy when it's aimed at sacred things." And to Clara, softly, "Secrets are something else. We don't have many left."

"We were just sharing a few personal anxieties," Cady said. "I was telling Clara that I admire her courage. This is quite an undertaking."

Ben winced at the sound of his wife's name on the stranger's tongue. Then he shrugged, resurrecting his more customary, easy smile. "Something to keep us busy. Things kinda slow down around here in the winter."

"Your father's the shaman, I take it."

Ben chuckled. "The what?"

"The man who does the—"

"Pipe bearer," Ben said. "My father is the carrier of the sacred pipe."

"Do you use the term 'medicine man'?"

"We use the term *wicasa wakan*. Holy man, I guess you might say. Pipe bearer, that's what he is. But what he *does*—" the smile dropped away again, and Ben might have fried the camera with his eyes "—is what we'd rather not have you photograph."

"I understand perfectly. I feel a real kinship with

sha—" Cady caught himself and shrugged apologetical-ly. "I *think* of them as shamen, I guess, because they're a special breed the world over. And I think, maybe in another life, I might have been one, too."

"Talk to my dad," Ben suggested, his eyes brightening gradually with a spark of mischief. "Maybe you can get to be one in *this* life, and the world will be down one cameraman."

Cady laughed good-naturedly. "I think I'd better be careful what I photograph."

"Now you're gettin' the idea. Nice meeting you, Cady." Ben's handshake served as a cordial dismissal.

"What was that all about?" Clara asked after the man had gone his way.

"What?" Ben's tone was all innocence, but his eyes gleefully proclaimed his guilt.

"You're not usually that unfriendly."

"No?" He considered her assessment as he glanced over his shoulder at the retreating photographer, then shifted to another one who was packing up his video equipment. "Guess I don't like having my picture taken. These guys act like they own the place, getting right up in your face with their damn cameras."

"Robert wasn't in *my* face with his camera."

"Robert, huh?" Ben shoved his thumbs into the front pockets of his jeans. "He's really got cold hands. You notice that?"

"No, I didn't." He actually looked half-contrite, and she wanted to smile, chuckle a little, ease him off his self-made hook. But she didn't. "I thought you'd left."

He lifted one shoulder nonchalantly. "Somebody needed a boost. Ever since I opened the shop, you'd think I owned the only set of booster cables on the rez. I oughta start charging."

"Don't you?" Her challenge surprised him. She *tsk*ed him, but gently and with a smile. "It's your business. I had to pay a locksmith twenty dollars when I locked my keys in the car at the Kirkwood parking lot, and all he did was slip a blade thing through the window."

"Yeah, well, somebody calls me at the shop, then I charge."

"I didn't even *call* this man. He happened to overhear me grumbling when I was turning my purse inside out looking for my keys."

"Jesus, Clara." He scowled. "You're gonna get hurt one of these days, gettin' yourself stranded like that without—"

"The point is, when it's your business, people expect you to charge for your services."

"Don't give me any lectures about—"

"You just gave *me* one."

Now they both scowled. For a moment the waning activity around them—the winding down and packing up, the soft buzz of voices heading home—all of it blurred and faded around their standoff.

Finally Clara turned away, slipping her arm into her parka.

"Look, if you need a place to stay tonight, you can use mine," Ben offered. "It's not much, but there's a bed and a shower." He retrieved her purse from the chair and handed it to her. "I can stay at my sister's place."

"Anna's gone with . . . uh-oh, with Billie, and she has my . . ." She patted her jacket pockets, irrationally hoping she might hear a jingle.

But Ben produced the keys from his back pocket, grinning as he dangled them in front of her nose. "I saw her outside."

"Thanks. I . . ." She held out her hand. He dropped the keys in her palm. She shrugged, meekly smiling. "I almost forgot."

"*Almost* forgot," he echoed, crowing. "So Annie's gone with Billie, and you were gonna be locked out of your car, up shit creek without a paddle or a sleeping bag."

"I'm taking a room at the motel in McLaughlin."

"The Bunkhouse?" He groaned. "You don't wanna stay there, Clara."

"Because it's haunted?"

"Because it's a dump. My place is a dump, too, but it's free." They were ambling toward the door now, neither in a hurry. "I'm not in the business of renting rooms."

"I'd rather stay at the motel."

"Suit yourself."

She looked at him askance, unconsciously inviting more wheedling.

But he was finished. "If you change your mind, I'm stayin' in the upstairs room next door to the shop. Take the outside stairs behind the house."

He was right. The place was a dump. It was basically two long trailers, arranged in an *L* and cut up into small, dingy rooms with water-stained ceilings and dark, warped, eighth-inch paneling. The bathroom was a four-square-foot afterthought with a dribbling shower. The rusty porcelain sink had no stopper. The miserly faucet released water only as long as Clara held the handle. When she sat on the bed, the screechy springs sagged to the floor. Then the furnace kicked in, rattling like a freight train.

None of this was conducive to a good night's sleep. She turned the TV on in the hope that a late-night talk show would relax her, bore her, lull her to sleep. But the black-and white picture was snowy, and there was no sound.

Okay, bring on the ghosts.

It was a careless challenge, made under the shadowy glare of a bare light bulb. With a sigh Clara turned the light out and sank noisily into the deep pit of a lumpy mattress.

Then the walls closed tightly around the bed and began to taunt her.

6

He couldn't sleep for thinking of her staying in that goddamn motel. It griped him that she had chosen a dumpy motel over his dumpy apartment. Why would Clara, always looking for ways to save money, choose to *pay* for shabby accommodations when he'd offered her equally dumpy accommodations at no charge? The answer wouldn't have come as any surprise if he hadn't started letting himself believe that maybe she didn't hate his guts as bad as she used to.

He figured the Bunkhouse was probably booked full for the first time since the big rodeo last summer. Probably booked up with professional snoopers like Cady, that was the worst part.

No, it wasn't. The worst part was that Ben had stayed there himself once, but only for a few hours. Even though it had been a long time ago, he could still remember the smell of stale smoke and whiskey mixed with the stench of his sin.

God, he hoped they hadn't given Clara the same room.

He'd feel a lot better having her at his place, where he'd lived pure and sober for nineteen long, lonesome months. All that haunted his little one-room walk-up was his dream of her. He wanted her to know that. Maybe if she stayed there, somehow she would sense it. The work he'd done. The changes he was trying so damn hard to make.

Not much choice for the curiosity-seekers and the goddamn reporters. They'd all be staying at the Bunkhouse, lined up side by side in those shabby little boxes with paper-thin walls. Out-of-towners. Out-of-staters. Nosy bastards, mostly, out to spin some yarn about the vanishing race.

He wondered where Robert Cady bought his license plates. Some kind of sunshine state, most likely.

Maybe he ought to get dressed, take a walk, and find out, just for the hell of it.

Ben swung his legs over the side of the bed, sat up, and planted his bare feet on the cold linoleum. He located his cigarettes mechanically, struck a match, and lit up a smoke in the dark. One good thing about living alone was the freedom to have a cigarette whenever and wherever he damn well pleased. Some changes were harder to make than others. He still had a whole shitload of bad habits. Too many for a woman's love to cure. So his woman had taken hers back.

But who was she giving it up for now?

Maybe he ought to take a walk past the ol' Bunkhouse and find out. Ben took a long, slow drag on his cigarette, turning the ash into a small red demon, glowing in the shadows. Mean-lookin' little bastard, he thought as he dammed the smoke up inside his chest and held on to it until it gave him a nice sharp pain.

Christ, he was at it again, and he wasn't even drinking. He exhaled gradually, deflating, sinking like the damaged goods he was until his back touched the cool wall. Some fancy-talking white guy barely makes a little conversation with her, and inside his own thick head he's got them in bed together. He didn't know what she'd done for sex over the last two years. Didn't want to know. Didn't need the aggravation, so why play mind games? She'd refused to sleep in his bed tonight, even without him in it, so that pretty much told him where *he* stood. It was his own fault that he'd been hoping. With this ride coming up, and being with her, being with Annie, he'd been hoping . . .

The sound of footfalls on the wooden steps leading to his door straightened him up fast. He stuck his cigarette in the corner of his mouth and grabbed his jeans. He was sliding them over his naked butt when he heard the feet hit the landing.

"Hold on," he responded to the soft, bare-knuckled rapping on the door. No need to ask who it was. His thudding heart already knew, which made it a little tricky to zip his jeans. He tore open the door and let the reality of her, the sight and the sound of her, take what little breath he had away.

"I can't stay there," she said in a slight, tentative voice. Light from the streetlamp framed her in the doorway, turning her hair into a lustrous halo surrounding her shadowed face.

He felt like a half-wit when he stepped back, jerked the cigarette from his mouth, then couldn't find voice to invite her in.

"I'm sorry to wake you up in the middle of the night, Ben. I . . . Now that I'm here, I feel quite silly about it, actually, but I just couldn't—"

He followed her eyes as she noticed the cigarette in his hand. A dead giveaway. He hadn't been asleep, and there were no lights on. The streetlight shone through the shadeless window, dimly illuminating half the room.

Her eyes darted to the other half, the dark corner, where the bed was. "Am I . . . interrupting?"

"No," he said quickly, closing the door behind her. "Nothin' but . . . you caught me smokin' again. I'll get the light."

She sighed heavily. "You were right. It's really awful. So depressing, I couldn't—"

"Maybe I'd better *not* get the light."

"Oh, Ben, don't be silly. I've seen your socks on

the floor before. Your wet towels, your underwear, your . . ."

She shrugged out of her jacket, tugged on one end of her scarf like a bell cord, and went on explaining her unexpected visit as though her reputation were on the line. And he followed close behind, listening politely even though he didn't much care why she'd come, as long as she was there.

"Okay, maybe I *was* a little scared. The place reminded me of *Psycho*. That furnace took up half the room, and in the dark it kept kicking on, roaring like some kind of wild animal blowing its hot—" a quick pivot brought her up against the wall of his bare chest "—breath on me."

He wondered whether furnace breath smelled like smoke. He knew his did. Hers was warm and sweet and made him smile like a lovesick fool in the near-darkness.

"Must have been exciting."

"I tried sleeping with the light on, but . . ."

But, as he recalled, she never could. Light made her watchful, restive. In the dark she lost her inhibitions. She loved to be close in the dark, the way they were now, close enough to breathe each other's breath, sense the course of a shiver and gauge body heat without touching. In the dark she loved to be cuddled underneath the covers—at least a sheet, even in summer. She loved to be loved in the dark, in the night, when the air was damp and heavy, redoubling the intensity of every scent and sound.

Perhaps she remembered, too, for she hesitated to move away, and when he touched her cheek with a tentative thumb she closed her eyes, just for an instant.

But then, barely above a whisper she said, "Yes, Ben, please do turn the light on."

He leaned away from her to flip the switch, dodging his disappointment. He thought the light a rude awakening. The bare walls and shabby secondhand furnishings embarrassed him. But he deserved to be embarrassed. After the initial stab, he indulged himself in displaying for her the price he was paying. Let her look around and be satisfied, he thought. Good penance was hard to find these days.

"Besides, the chain on the door was missing," she said, wringing her hands. "And the other lock didn't seem too trustworthy. Such a flimsy door, and you think, gosh, anybody could just pull in off the highway, and they wouldn't even have to break—"

"It's okay." Cautiously he laid his hand on her arm, covered in soft wool, half expecting her to jump away like a green filly. When she didn't, he rubbed briefly, taking the rare opportunity to soothe her. "Really. Can I get you anything? I've got tea."

"All I really want is a little sleep, but I . . ." At a glance she took in the spartan furnishings, searching for a nesting place.

"You take the bed."

"The chair would be fine. At this point, I could sleep standing up."

"Yeah, right." He tossed a sleeping bag on the floor, followed by a couple of old blankets. He could feel her watching him. "I can fall sleep anywhere. You never could. 'The Princess and the Pea.' Remember?"

When he'd read the romantic fairy tale to Annie, he'd said, "Just like Mom." And, of course, little Annie had told on him. Clara had thought it a criticism at first because she liked to think of herself as a trooper. But he'd always treasured the fragility she tried so hard to hide, for it gave him the leverage to fancy himself needed.

The notion made him laugh as he shook off the pillow Clara offered him. It was the only one he had. "We've slept in some rough beds, haven't we?"

"I didn't complain, did I?" A fleeting smile reminded him of trooper Clara, from the days when she'd loved him no matter what, and he thought, yes, I treasured that, too.

Counted on it. Took it for granted.

She folded her arms around the pillow. "But things were different then."

"They sure were. We didn't have a damn thing then. We were two starry-eyed kids who could have come from different planets for all we had in common. But if my bed was the back of a pickup, that's where you slept."

"We had each other then. I was yours and you were mine." Then quietly, sadly hopeful, she asked, "Weren't you? For a while, at least?"

"I always have been, Clara." His claim rang with desolation, for no matter how deeply he believed it, he could not expect her to. He sighed. "Trouble is, there's always been a part of me you didn't wanna know."

"The part that didn't love me?"

"The part that can't love anything." Dispirited, he shook his head. "The ugly part. The part nobody wants to look at." The part he'd finally dug out and dissected when he'd run out of places to hide it. But she hadn't been there, and he didn't know how to describe it to her.

"The part you have to control," she said. For her it was that simple.

"It was easier to let you try to control it for me. Or deny it. Between us, I thought we had a good thing goin' there for a while. Thought I could be two people." He chuckled humorlessly. "The hell-raiser you fell in love with and the husband you expected to turn me into."

"I couldn't do it alone." She sat on the rumpled bed, flipping the blanket aside as she heel-toed her shoes off.

"You couldn't do it at all." He braced his hands on his thighs and lowered himself like a supplicant at her feet, landing his cracking knees on the pallet he'd made. "I was trying," he told her earnestly. "But only half-assed. Until the law took my driver's license away and I landed in treatment, and they showed me how close I was to losing my job, my home, my family, even my freedom. I was closer to prison than I realized. I was just lucky it didn't go that far. Pure dumb luck was all it was."

"I had no idea you were driving—"

"Come off it, Clara. How was I gettin' around?" He looked up, his eyes inviting hers to attend to their own blind spot.

She endured his provocation only briefly, then stubbornly turned the same old blue-blind eye.

Again he gave the mirthless chuckle. "I'd covered a lot of tracks, but I was gettin' pretty sloppy at it. Too damn cocky, I guess. Sure, I'd let you stop me sometimes. It made you feel good."

"It did not."

"Well, it seemed to make things easier."

With a disgusted *tsk* and a sigh she rolled her eyes toward the ceiling. "Didn't you know it was getting out of hand?"

"When I thought about it, yeah. I thought, one of these days I'm gonna wrap that pickup around a tree, or hit the ditch, slam into an approach, and go out in a blaze of glory. *Bam!*" He rammed the heel of one hand into the palm of the other. "You go from wasted to dead, you don't feel a thing. And you never think about takin' anybody with you. You never think about breakin' your neck and being left with nothin' but the brain you've been too lazy to use."

He rubbed his palms distractedly up and down the worn denim that covered his thighs. "Then you spend a couple days behind bars, and you stand before a judge who tells you you're one step away from being locked away for years." He lifted his eyes to meet hers. "*Years*, Clara. You know how close I came?"

"No, I—" She shook her head quickly, refusing to

entertain the notion that Clara Pipestone's husband could possibly have become a prison inmate. "I really don't. All I know is that—"

"All you know is that I fucked another woman."

She turned her face as though he'd struck her.

And in a very real way, he knew he had. He had added insult to injury. Sought to humiliate her by the same vehicle he'd used to defile himself.

"I'm sorry, Clara."

"For what?" She closed her eyes briefly, then shook it all off. The insult, the injury, maybe even the sixteen years. "It doesn't matter anymore."

"It matters to me."

"It's late, Ben."

"Too late?"

She ignored the question as she sought to make her nest by pounding the emaciated feather pillow into submission. "If we don't get some sleep, we'll both be sorry in the morning."

"I've sure been there before." He offered her a folded blanket, balanced on his right hand like a serving tray. "Here, you might need this. You're always gettin' cold at night."

She laid her hand on the army green wool in polite refusal, for he'd little enough for his bed. The gold band on her third finger flashed defiantly in his face. In answer, he put his hand next to hers. The wedding rings were a matched set. Remarkably, neither half had been put away.

She gazed wishfully at the two hands as though they belonged to mannequins in a shop window. "There's a promise engraved inside yours. Remember?" She looked up at him, and he nodded. The seam in her lips tightened. She stared into his eyes, letting him see and feel the fervor in hers cool. "There's nothing in mine."

"Your finger's still in it."

She lifted her chin a notch and claimed the blanket,

as though the action would somehow show him. Dumb-founded, he watched her unfurl it with a quick snap.

"You ordered the rings, Clara. I wish I'd thought of having yours engraved, but I didn't."

"I used to have this fantasy that you would—" the little laugh she permitted herself seemed to ease the stiffness from her shoulders "—steal mine sometime, and I'd look all over for it. And then you'd give it back, and I'd find a message engraved inside."

He'd never been good at guessing games. He always felt stupid asking for clues. But he did it anyway, because it seemed important to her.

"What message would you find?"

"I never decided. That part was up to you."

"I never knew you to take it off," he said, befuddled.

"I never did."

"So, in this *fantasy*, just how did I manage to steal the ring?"

"I don't know. I was asleep the whole time."

God, she was infuriating, but he had to laugh. He didn't know what else to do, since he'd be *damned* if he'd apologize for this one.

"If you wanted Prince Charming, why in the hell did you marry a cowboy?"

"Because for some strange reason I fell in love with a cowboy." She eyed him contemptuously, as though he'd forced it on her.

He draped his arm over his upraised knee and eyed her right back. "If you ever figure out what that strange reason was, could you clue me in? I know you loved me, Clara. I just don't know why."

He posted his chin on his arm and waited, watching her study her knees. Not only was she unable to come up with an answer, she didn't seem to know whether to take her jeans and sweater off and let herself be comfortable, even at the risk of letting him see more of the body he knew as well as he knew his own. Better, really. Loved infinitely better, which was why she was safe with him. Keeping her clothes on would make no difference.

"Do you ever take your ring off?" she asked quietly, without looking up.

"Sometimes, when I'm workin'." He wondered what kind of negligence he was inadvertently admitting to now.

"How about . . . when you're with someone else?" She glanced up, but her gaze ricocheted off his on the correction. "*Were* . . . with someone else."

He closed his eyes and turned his head, laying his cheek on his arm. His only answer was a soft sigh.

Determined to press him, she took a deep breath. "When you were having . . . *fucking* that other woman. Were you wearing your wedding ring?"

Now *she* was doing it again. Pressing him for details she neither wanted nor needed to hear. Backing him into the tight chute he'd erected for himself. It would always be there for her to herd him into with her questions. He could try to lie his way out, or he could tell it like it was. Either way, it was like bucking out a spinning bull. And his sweet Clara was no bull rider.

He lifted his head and looked her in the eye. "I didn't have anything to hide. She knew who I was. I was married." He uncurled his left hand and held it up for her. "I'm still married."

"What does that mean?"

"It means I still wear the ring. Is that okay?"

Fury flashed in her eyes, and he could tell that she was dying to say no. But she couldn't. Her shoulders jerked in a quick, spasmatic shrug. "I gave it to you. It's yours. I guess you can wear it to your grave."

"I'm gettin' cremated, remember? You can have it back then."

"Smart-ass," she grumbled as she lay back on the bed. "We can't go on like this indefinitely. It's only because of Anna that—"

"It's only because of her that we're goin' on this ride. Right? It only lasts two weeks. It doesn't go on indefinitely. We're gonna be together for two weeks. Can you handle that?"

"Yes." She stared at the ceiling, unmoving.

"Okay, then. It starts tonight. I'm gonna be right next to you, down here on the floor. Tryin' out for Prince Charming." He slid under the blanket, chuckling. "Protecting you from fire-breathing furnaces."

"I never said you couldn't be a hero when you wanted to be."

"At least I never kicked you out of bed. You've kicked me out of two now." He stuck his arms behind his head as he stretched out on his back. "But don't thank me. Just turn the damn light out and get to sleep."

She snapped the lamp off with a vengeance. Then she whipped her sweater over her head and dropped it on his face. "Use that for a pillow."

"Drop your jeans down here, too," he suggested tonelessly. "Add a new twist to my fantasies."

She tried to ignore him the way she ignored the remark, not dignifying it with a response. Except that in the dark he seemed to fill the room. Without touching him, she could feel his lean, hard presence. His sheets felt soft and smooth beneath her back. Smooth because he'd worn them smooth. She had missed the warm, masculine smell of him, the comforting sound of his breathing, the security of knowing he was there to defend her against obscure shadows and inexplicable noises in the night.

She had missed *him*, her husband, the man who wore the ring inscribed with her promise to love him. And she had done that. God help her, she had loved him, and she was very much afraid she loved him still. Hot tears scalded her eyes, escaped the eyelids she could not quite seal shut, slipped along her temples and into her hair.

"Clara?"

Oh, God, why couldn't she keep this humiliation to herself?

"Are you crying?"

When she didn't answer, he started to get up.

She gave a terrible, teary, tortured gasp. "Stay there, Ben, please."

"I just want to—"

"You can't." She closed her eyes and took a deep, ragged breath, struggling to steady herself inside. "If you touch me now, I'll fall apart," she confessed, instantly regretting the disclosure. She was leaving herself wide open again.

His voice closed in on her. "Just let me hold you until you fall asleep."

It was such a tempting offer. Some nights she'd missed that warm, safe feeling so desperately she'd called him, just to hear the sound of his voice. Then, of course, she'd hung up.

"I'm okay now," she whispered wretchedly. "Really. It's just that sometimes it still hurts a little . . . when I think about it."

"Aw, Jesus, Clara, don't think about it. I don't know why I said—" She shrank away when he reached for her. His hand fell to the edge of the bed and gripped a fistful of blanket. "—what I said about . . . you know, what I did. I never wanted to hurt you. Not now. Not then."

"But you must have known it would."

"I didn't think about it hurting you. Or Annie." He groaned miserably. "I know it sounds like a crock of shit, Clara, but I didn't think about what it would do to us."

It made no sense to her. It never had. "I think . . . if I just knew why."

"I wish I could give you a reason, but I still can't come up with anything but excuses." His low voice resonated in the darkness. She could feel his grip tighten, pulling the covers taut across her bare shoulders. "It was sick, Clara. I was sick. I was . . . I was so damn stupid. And a stupid man does stupid things."

"Oh, Ben . . ."

"Let me hold you." He touched her arm. "It's dark. You don't have to look at me. You can pretend—"

"There's no pretending anymore," she said evenly. "We're strictly on the level with each other now. Isn't that right?"

"That's right." His hand slid away.

He retreated, back to the cool floor, back to the pillow of his own arms. His gut was tied in tight knots, and he was exhausted. He'd have traded his winter jacket and the keys to his pickup for a double shot of whiskey. He wasn't particular about the brand. Anything strong enough to rot the knots in his gut would do him just fine. *If* he were a drinking man.

"Was it because you didn't want . . . didn't love me?"
Holy Jesus, would you tell her for me, please?
"Ben?"

"No. I swear, it wasn't that."

"I can't believe you still loved me then, Ben."

"I know."

But he knew he had. The decent part of him had always loved her. He'd screwed around with the other part, the part he didn't want touching her. The part that didn't love anything. She could never understand that, and he had no right to expect her to.

"Try to get some sleep, Clara."

Her first thought when she drifted into the light of morning was, *Did I actually sleep?* The whisperings and the soft footsteps at the edge of her drowsy consciousness roused her gently. Part of her wanted to ignore them and burrow deeper into the covers. But the other part pried her eyes open.

Steam from a blue mug advertising a Cenex station

misted Ben's smile. "We figured the best way to wake you up was to make you some coffee."

Clara braced herself on one elbow and accepted the offering. She was adjusting the blankets when Anna appeared at Ben's shoulder. "We've been loading the stuff into Auntie TJ's pickup. I brought your bag in from the car so you could get dressed." She gave a teasing grin. "Did the ghost run you out last night or what?"

Ben held up his hand. "I didn't say a word."

"You were both right. The place was a dump." She turned her wrist to get a look at her watch. "Are we running late? I'm sorry I slept so—"

"Relax," Ben said. "We're runnin' on Indian time today. It takes a while for people to gather up and hit the trail. If you wanna leave your car at the shop, I'll see it gets the tune-up it needs."

"Thanks." She glanced at the tattered overstuffed chair where her jacket and purse had ended up and noticed her sweater, neatly folded on top of them. "I think my keys are . . ."

Ben bounced them in his hand. "Always in your coat pocket, even though you thought you put them in your purse. How do you think we got your stuff out of the car?" A quick jerk of his chin directed her attention to the bag on the floor. He grabbed his black jacket off the hook by the door. "I'll pick up something for breakfast. Any requests?" He shot his arm into a sleeve, then raised a warning finger. "Keep it simple."

"Donuts," Anna said.

"Fruit," Clara added.

"Simple enough," Ben confirmed. "There might be three minutes' worth of hot shower in there for you, Clara. You kinda have to wash everything at once. Left you one dry towel. Only got two. See ya."

"How did I sleep through his shower?" Clara muttered to herself as he shut the door. Then she realized she was getting the cat-that-ate-the-canary look from her daughter, and she heaved a sigh. "Anna, it's not what you think. Dad slept on the floor last night. We're not . . ." She sat up, planting her feet on bare linoleum. Ben's pallet was gone.

"Jeez, Mom, I don't wanna know what you guys did last night. Puh-leeease. You're my *parents*."

"I just don't want you to be misled by the fact that we spent the night in the same . . ." The disclaimer faded into one of Clara's nonplussed *tsk*s.

"You know what?" Anna moved Clara's bag to the foot of the bed. "Sometimes I want to hate you. And sometimes I want to hate him. But most of the time, I just have to feel sorry for both of you for getting yourselves so messed up."

Clara groaned softly. "Out of the mouths of babes."

"What are you gonna wear today?" Anna asked as she flipped the top of the bag open. "Old jeans, new jeans, or the jeans you have on?"

"I have a wardrobe game plan. Change underwear and tops every day, bottoms when the horses start mistaking you for one of them."

"Sounds like a plan to me."

It seemed strange to use a shower that was just Ben's, not theirs. She wondered how he managed to stuff himself into such a small cabinet, even though he'd never been one to complain about accommodations or shortages. He'd taught her a lot about making do with less and appreciating more. But she knew he had to be too tall for this shower. She tried to imagine him scrunching down under the spray. She squealed when it turned cold and shuddered noisily with her rinsing. Then she used the dry towel on her hair and rubbed the damp one over her own skin. The towel he'd used to dry his body. Nothing personal, she told herself as she surveyed his bathroom, looking for nothing special.

He was all packed, so his toothbrush was gone. So

was his hairbrush. He always used a big brush. His hair was thick and coarse and so full-bodied that it was hard to resist touching it. She had rejoiced when Anna was born with her father's beautiful hair . . .

"The baby's crowning!" The freckle-faced nurse popped up smiling and peered over Clara's shackled foot, looking from Clara's dazed perspective like a woman just out of the shower—still wearing the cap—who'd dashed in to check on something in the oven and make a cheerful report. "So far, we know this one has black hair and lots of it."

"Oh, good," Clara gasped. The hair was good, but the pain was bad, bad, bad, even between contractions, when it was somewhat less bad but still awful.

She tipped her head back, searching for the handsome face of the man who'd caused all this. In the course of the last twenty-two hours she'd alternately proclaimed him an angel and damned him to the flames of hell for all eternity. But he'd stood by her side, held her hand, stroked her stomach and massaged her back, talked her through her pain and talked her out of her plan to kick the doctor into the river the next time he wanted to check the progress of her dilation.

"Ben?"

"I'm right here." His voice slid deeply, smoothly into her ear, fortifying her. "You're doin' great, honey."

"How can you tell?"

" 'Cause I'm shakin' in my boots, and you're cool as can be."

Her thready laugh turned into a sharp yelp. "Oh, Ben, make it stop!" She rolled her head to one side, panting, panting, pushing herself up on her elbows. She needed to sit up, to push down, to *get it out*. "Help me!"

"What can I do?"

Someone said, "Help her sit up so she can bear down better."

He slipped his arm beneath her shoulders and lifted her. "Better?"

"No, yes, oh no, not agaaain . . ."

He pressed his cheek against hers. "It'll be over soon, and we'll have our black-haired baby."

"It hurrrts!"

"I know. I'm sorry. Hang on, hang on, hang on."

Someone said, "Push, Clara."

"Give it all you got, Clara-bow," Ben urged.

Someone said, "Push, Clara."

"She's pushin', for crissake!"

"Here it comes!"

"Our baby, Clara! I see its whole head!"

She closed her eyes and pushed herself inside out. "Yeeeahhh!"

"It's a girl!"

For the moment it was absolute and unqualified relief.

"A girl, we have a girl, Clara! Look how . . . Jesus, I can't believe you could . . ." He lifted her a little more. "How did you do that?"

"What?" After the excruciating buildup she was still trying to catch up to the sudden explosion. Breathless, wrung out, she felt as though she had stepped outside herself.

"I can't believe it, Clara." He squeezed her shoulder. "She came out of you. Holy Jesus, I saw it with my own eyes."

She could feel the slippery little thing, warm and wet where the doctor had laid her on her mother's stomach, but all she could see was that beautiful black hair. First the baby's, thoroughly soggy, then the baby's dad's, damp around his face.

"Can I touch her?" Beaming, grinning, utterly awed, Ben looked to Clara for permission.

But somebody snatched the bawling baby away, and somebody else pressed hands on Clara's stomach. "We've got one more job to do, Clara."

The afterbirth was nothing compared to the real thing, and soon she had her baby back, wrapped in flannel and tucked in her arms this time. And the crying stopped.

"Oh, Ben, come see who's here."

He stepped closer, suddenly shy.

"Now you can touch her," Clara invited, for she was touching her, feathering a finger over the chubby red cheek.

"Nah, my hands are too . . ." He hid them behind his back and leaned closer. "Can I kiss her, maybe?"

"Oh, Ben . . ."

"Can I kiss you, maybe?" His eyes were bright with wonder, and by the looks of his smile he was positively intoxicated. "You won't hit me again, will you?"

"Just a love tap," she said, vaguely remembering the throes of an early contraction.

That part, amazingly, was all over now. His kiss made her drunk, too. Drunk enough to slur her words, but it didn't matter. They were in a world of their own, speaking a language no one else understood. They shared something like a mind-expanding drug or a winning sweepstakes ticket or a conversion experience, but more. It was all of those things, but it was also utterly brand-new.

They had a child together.

"Thank you for hanging in there with me," she said, speaking for more than just this day.

"The least I could do," he said, speaking for more than just this day.

"I'm embarrassed now, for putting up such a fuss."

He grinned. "Tell the truth, now. It wasn't as bad as it looked, was it?"

She groaned. "*You* get to have the next one."

His grin vanished. "I would if I could, Clara-bow. I don't ever want you to suffer like that again."

She looked up at him, blinked, blinked again, but it didn't go away. Ben Pipestone had tears in his eyes.

"Ben? Cowboys don't—"

"Shh." He swallowed hard, pressed his forehead against hers, and whispered, "Don't tell anyone, but that just scared the bejesus outta me."

She slid her free hand around the back of his neck and held him tight. "I couldn't have done it without you."

"Damn right, you couldn't." And then throatily he crooned in her ear, "It takes twoo, ba-by." His shoulders shook with laughter, and so did hers, both of them shaky, both euphoric as they softly harmonized, "Me and you."

Anna had tidied up while Clara was in the shower. It had undoubtedly been a labor of love for her, for, like most teenagers, Anna only cleaned her room when she couldn't find anything in it anymore. Now she was stretched out on her dad's bed. But she'd lost interest in the horse magazine that lay open in front of her, now that her mother was getting dressed.

"You think there's any point in putting on makeup?" Clara glanced up and smiled at her long-limbed, dark-haired, dark-eyed daughter. "I guess you must. You look wonderful."

"I didn't do anything extra." Anna swung her legs to the floor, planted her elbows on her knees and her chin in her hands. "You should wear the belt I gave you. It looks nice with jeans."

"Good idea." Clara brushed on a little blush, checked the results in the compact mirror, then added more before snapping the case shut. But Anna looked unsatisfied. "Too much?"

"No. But you've gotta wear some mascara. You *really* need mascara."

Clara took the magic eyelash-making wand from her purse and worked on her skimpy lashes. When she was done, she looked up for approval.

"Yeah. Makes your eyes look *really* big."

"I'd better hurry." She dropped the makeup into her purse. "Tell me when you hear Dad coming."

"He'll wait for you. 'Member when me and him used to sit on the bed and watch you get dressed?"

"Mmm-hmm. And make me flub up the eyeliner."

Anna smiled wistfully. "I still like watching you. It's fun to see how you turn out."

"It can't be much of a surprise. You know all my clothes." With splayed fingers she lifted her hair away from her temples, then flipped it back impatiently. "You know what this mop does."

"It's not a mop, and it makes you look like Mom. *My* mom. We like watching you get dressed because we know you're gonna turn out pretty, and we like watching it happen."

Clara returned the smile, which came prewarmed from deep inside her. "Even when you just want to hate me?"

"*Want* to," Anna made clear. "*Some*times. But I can't ever quite make it stick."

"That's a relief."

"*For very long.*" With a jaunty smile in her eyes she rose from the bed and started gathering Clara's few loose items. "I'm glad you decided to go on the ride. I never expected you to. And Grandpa never expected Dad to. So there must be some reason why it's happening this way."

"Please don't read anything into it other than the fact that—" She felt like a stingy-hearted killjoy when she looked up and saw Anna's sparkle start to fade. "We both love you very much."

"I know." Anna jerked the zipper tab on Clara's bag. "But, then, sometimes I think if you loved me, you wouldn't be split up."

"That has nothing to do with it." Clara gave a mother's sad-truth sigh. "I've explained all that, Anna."

"I know." Anna lifted her chin and flashed a defiant, self-assured smile that reminded Clara of her own former, younger, more idealistic self. "Anyway, I don't think you hate each other any more than I hate either one of you. But that's just me."

"Nobody said we *hated*—"

"And you look pretty. Your hair looks nice." She handed Clara her purse. "But you need lipstick in the worst way."

"I always forget."

"And I always remember for you. I don't know what you're gonna do when I go off to college."

"Neither do I."

Die a little, maybe. Ache a lot. Eat frozen dinners and let your dog sleep at the foot of my bed.

The door opened, and Ben stuck his head inside, his cheeks ruddy from the chill of mid-December. But his dark eyes were bright with anticipation. "Come on, girls. Let's git to gittin'."

Puffy white clouds drifted overhead like smoke signals, calling the riders to the meeting place on the banks of the Grand River. The gravel road turned to dirt, then to a set of parallel wheel ruts across the rolling sod. Clara and Anna bounced along, side by side on the pickup's big bench seat, with Ben at the wheel and the three hundred and sixty horses under the hood gobbling up South Dakota dust for breakfast. His sister would pull in later, horse trailer and four living, breathing mounts in tow.

Several miles back they had passed the relay runner, one of nine teenagers carrying the Big Foot staff from Sitting Bull's grave in Fort Yates to the campsite where the old *wicasa wakan* was murdered, a distance of almost fifty miles. A van decorated with a red, white, and blue banner followed along, flashing its lights. As the pickup pulled around them, giving the relay party wide berth, Anna recognized the runner as Billie's friend.

Ben tapped the horn, and everyone waved except the runner. The long-legged young woman dressed in royal blue sweats plodded along doggedly, her dark eyes trained purposefully on the road ahead as she carried the fur-wrapped crook toward the hand that waited somewhere down the road.

"She looks cold," Anna said, still rubbernecking.

"She's doin' fine," Ben said. "This time last year those kids were freezin' their tail feathers off. Wind chill was about fifty below."

"So far, it's really been mild this year," Clara observed hopefully. "Hasn't it? Really mild."

"Sure has. So far it's been an open winter."

"Winter hasn't officially started," Anna reminded them.

They drove on, past the stubbled hayfields, past the bread-loaf stacks, the round-bale stacks, the square-bale stacks, past the dugout stock dams, past the assortment of fence posts supporting boundless strands of barbed wire stuffed with masses of tumbleweeds, past the "No Hunting" sign painted on an old tire. Hereford and black whiteface cattle grazed alongside the occasional horse in a land where the signs of labor and its fruits were still dwarfed by the expanse of grass and sky. Autumn lingered on borrowed time, and prairie dwellers dreaded, waited, watched for signs of change.

Anna was right. It was only the cusp of winter.

As they neared the campsite the signs of man-made change all but disappeared. The tire path was nearly overgrown with tall buffalo grass, and there was a hallowed-ground feeling about the place. An aspect of beauty and desolation, a silent echo of timeless melancholy. The gray scrub oaks stood like gnarly old sentinels over clay washouts that were striated with God's own claw marks.

"Are we almost there?" Anna asked in a hushed voice.

" 'When are we gonna get there, Daddy?' " Grinning,

Ben indicated the road ahead with an expressive chin jerk. "Just over the hill, Annie-girl."

Just over several hills, Clara thought, but Indian miles were like Indian time. Close enough, soon enough. And sure enough, beyond the several hills they came to the river bottom, and the gathering of cars, pickups, horses, and people, all in rare attendance to a spot beneath the bare trees that had mercifully been left alone during most of the last hundred years.

But there was a monument, one that might be termed *permanent* by those who somehow failed to notice the river, the hills, and the sky. Clara thought it strange to find an official historical site marker so far from the beaten path. She wondered how many citizens of the state of South Dakota had ever seen it, nestled in the stand of little oak trees, only a few yards from the riverbank.

Inscribed on the stone tablet was the date—December 15, 1890—and an account of Sitting Bull's death. The original version of the Historical Society's authoritative chronicle alluded to "this unnecessary, tragic killing of a noble, if misguided, Sioux leader." The words "if misguided" had been removed, leaving behind a white imprint, which, ironically, stood out amid the raised letters like a neon sign.

One white mistake standing in testimony to another, Clara thought.

Greetings and introductions were exchanged as the gathering of riders and their supporters continued to grow. Horses were unloaded from their trailers, and saddles were hoisted on the animals' backs. Children begged to take their turns riding up and down the riverbank. Video cameras recorded the proceedings. Reporters pressed their questions on anyone who was willing to expound. All the while, preparations were being made for more ceremony.

Clara sat on the tailgate of Ben's pickup, watching him get ready several yards away, where Tara Jean had parked the horse trailer. She was going to have to get used to the idea that they were a family again, at least for the time being. She was going to have to harness all her mixed emotions and hold them in check. No more tears, she told herself. She simply had to face the fact that the attraction would always be there, but so would the betrayal. She had taken a chance on this man and lost. Nevertheless, he would always be Anna's father.

And he would always be her own first love. It was a fact of life she could not change. So she sat there, watching Ben adjust Anna's borrowed saddle to fit her seat, enjoying the excitement in her daughter's eyes. The paint horse had quickly become Anna's pride and joy. She had pictures of him on her bulletin board and a lock of his tail braided into a friendship bracelet. Anna "the good kid" had been reborn. She had been doing well at school, following all the terms of her probation and all the rules at home. They had been doing things together— talking, laughing, making plans for the ride. Clara wasn't sure which part of the gift was more important to the girl, the horse itself or the fact that her father had put so much of himself into choosing and preparing it for her.

Clara might have permitted herself similar musings about the bay mare, patiently waiting close by. Underneath the dense winter coat was a well-conditioned, well-disciplined animal, trained to the exacting specifications of a cowboy. More than just a trail mount, the mare had Ben's signature all over her, from selection to finished product. All for Clara. If she thought about that and nothing else, if she simply watched the way he fussed over the animals, the pains he discreetly took to show her what he'd accomplished for her in a short time, she couldn't help loving him for it.

Mixed emotions. God, what torment.

"It's a lovely spot, isn't it?"

Startled, Clara turned abruptly toward the sound of the voice. Robert Cady snapped her picture.

She laughed. "Oh, that's not fair."

He raised the camera again. "When you're ready, then."

"I won't be. Believe me. I'm anything but photogenic."

"That's for me to say. I'm the expert." He let the camera drop to the end of its neck strap and turned his attention to the activity around the monument. "Hard to imagine a murder happening in a place like this, isn't it?"

Clara shrugged. "Hard to imagine a murder happening anywhere."

"What do those colored markers signify, do you know?"

Clara shaded her eyes with her hand. "That's where the cabin was, the way it's remembered."

"Depending upon the rememberer's point of view, right? The camera remembers things exactly."

"I think the camera has a point of view. It's in the eye of the so-called expert." Turning to converse with Robert Cady, she put her back to her family. "Actually, there were photographs taken of the cabin when it was here, but obviously the surroundings have changed. Did you know that the cabin was removed and put on exhibition in Chicago at the World's Fair less than four years after Sitting Bull's death?"

"Everyone wants a piece of the action, don't they?" Cady wagged his head in dismay. "If you can't explain the source of the power, grab everything connected with it and pick it apart. Curiosity knows no bounds."

"Neither does bullshit," said a familiar voice.

They turned in unison. Ben stood close behind them, menacing the man with a cocky smile.

"That's probably another legitimate word for it," Cady said with an easy laugh. "Will you be taking part in the ceremony your father's setting up for?"

"You could say that."

"But no cameras?"

"You got it." He laid his gloved hand on Clara's shoulder. "It's that curiosity thing you were just talkin' about."

The photographer nodded. "And the releasing of spirits during this next ceremony, how is that accomplished?"

"I wouldn't wanna spoil it by givin' it away ahead of time." He gave Clara's shoulder a quick squeeze as he backed away, but his hard gaze held Cady's in wordless challenge. "Just keep your eyes and ears open, Cady. And your lens cap screwed on real tight."

"I'm not sure what I've done to offend your husband," Cady said quietly as they watched Ben take purposeful strides toward the monument. "But I have the distinct impression he doesn't like me."

"Whether Ben takes part or not, he's very protective." Clara smiled, remembering. "Once I saw him take the camera right out of a man's hands and smash it on a rock. He'd warned him twice, and the man kept pushing his luck."

"You think that's what it is? Defending his rights? Is that r-i-g-h-t-s, or r-i-t-e-s?" He smiled at Clara, as if they shared some commonality she should have known about. Perhaps knowledge of spelling. Or mainstream etiquette. "I'm not here to interfere," he assured her. "And I do take instruction in matters of decorum quite readily."

"I'm sure that's true. And Ben's generally pretty easygoing." At the first sound of the drumbeat she hopped off the tailgate and pointed at the pickup cab. "Why don't you leave your camera here? No one will bother it."

She didn't notice whether he followed her suggestion. That was Cady's business. Hers was attending to the ceremony.

A pole with red and black flags had been driven into the ground just a few steps east of the poles representing the corners of the cabin. This was the spot, according to the elders, where Sitting Bull had fallen when he was shot at daybreak a century before. While singers wailed and beat the drum, Dewey smudged the area to purify it by trailing smoke from the sweet grass and sage he had burning in the bottom of a large coffee can. He offered tobacco to the earth, then offered the pipe to the four directions. The river flowed to the west. The brown, barren hills stood to the east.

At the dawning of a new day a hundred years past, as the old man was taken from his cabin by force, he would have instinctively faced east, seeking the coming daylight as he emerged. Clara turned to the hills and imagined glimpsing the same horizon, hearing the blast, feeling her chest explode. More shots were fired, and more bodies fell to the ground. Policemen, Ghost Dancers, and the young Crow Foot, Sitting Bull's son, who begged his uncles among the *ceska maza*, the Indian police, to spare him. But by then hot tears mingled with hot blood, demanding more of the same.

The drums rolled. The singers' voices dipped and soared. Puffs of pipe smoke drifted above the official Historical Society marker.

And the spirits of the old ones were set free.

7

"You can sure tell some of these guys haven't been around horses much lately."

Ben lit a cigarette as he scanned the gathering of wanna-be cowboys and gotta-be Indians. Some new faces, some he'd known all his life. He guessed most of them had grown up with the same heroes, whether they'd had a television set in the living room and a dollar for a movie every Saturday or the kind of occasional access he'd had to screens, large and small. In one way or another he was sure they had all acted out the same fantasies, playing the Indian when it was the only way they could get into the game. Children knew all about winners and losers. Winners wore the straw hats with the chin cords. Winners had the Red Rider BB guns and got to decide who could come into the fort and who had to stay out. Winning added up to being one of the cowboys, even in Little Eagle, South Dakota, where the honest-to-God Indians lived.

Now, here came a truly motley crew to celebrate a lost cause in true lost-cause fashion. Catch as catch can. Sheila Bird had paid a local rancher $135 for the use of a one-trick pony. Its trick was crow-hopping. Dan Medicine's horse was doing its damnedest to put a dent in Cheppa Four Dog's pickup.

Some white woman with an Oklahoma drawl said she'd heard about the ride, loaded her saddle into her brother-in-law's eighteen-wheeler, gotten off his rig at the sale barn in Mobridge, and bid on every saddle horse they'd run through the ring until they'd stopped going over her price, which was $160. The mare she'd bought was hardmouthed as hell, and she wouldn't neck rein worth a damn.

Yessir, there were going to be some fandamntastic slapstick catastrophes on some of these begged, borrowed, and rented mounts. Ben could see it coming.

"Teachers, ambulance drivers, tribal councilmen," he mused on the tail of a stream of smoke. A pair of spurs caught his eye. They were almost as shiny as the silver toe caps on the owner's brand-new boots. "That guy probably hasn't been on a horse since he was a kid. We are definitely losin' touch with our roots."

"Is this the cowboy talking, or the Indian?" Clara wondered.

"One and the same, me."

Ben had his trappings, too, but at least they were all bought and paid for, and well broken-in to boot. In fact, the soles of his boots were nearly worn through. He dressed Western because he *was* Western. Always had been. Nobody ever challenged Ben's right to call himself a cowboy. He wore black leather chaps for brush-popping and windbreak, not for slick. He'd shaped his battered black hat for shade, not for cool. He wore a black jacket and black boots, not because they matched anything, but because they were what he had. No feathers. He'd never earned any. No beads. He'd given some as gifts in his time, but his own personal style tended toward austerity. Especially lately.

Besides his wedding band, the only bit of flash he wore was a turquoise and silver trophy buckle he'd won on the Indian rodeo circuit in 1976. He'd earned a chunk of turquoise, but not an eagle feather. A conservative Indian, Clara had called him once. Hey, he was a real cross-dresser, he'd told her, and proud of it. His heritage was written all over his face, so it didn't much matter what he wore when he ventured off the reservation.

"If your roots are potted in horses, then you're back in touch now," Clara said. She rubbed the mare's neck.

"I'd forgotten how much time they take. The ol' man doesn't mind if I turn 'em out on his grass, but you've gotta spend time with 'em. Otherwise, they won't be much good for anything."

"They're good for you. They're just what you needed."

Maybe, he thought. Wants and needs were two different things. It had taken a while, but he'd finally figured out the difference, and she was right. Without the horses, the time he'd done on his own lately would have been unbearably bleak.

"Look at that guy. He's gonna get—" Nipped in the butt. Ben shook his head, grinning. "Well, now he knows. It's gonna be a long ride." He turned to catch his wife smiling, too. "Ready?"

"I can't believe I'm doing this," she muttered, mostly to herself. "But I am. I really am." He stood by while she mounted. When she was settled, he took a marble-size red cloth bundle out of his pocket and tied it to her horse's halter.

"Thank you. Is that a tobacco tie?"

He gave a curt nod as he handed her the reins.

His deliberate concession to custom surprised her. She noticed that he'd added the same sacred symbol—a bit of cloth containing a pinch of tobacco—to his horse's halter and to Anna's. She might have expected the gesture from her father-in-law, but not from Ben. Not the Ben she knew, anyway.

He was quick to distract her from questioning the move or the meaning behind it, or the sentiment that might be attached to it somewhere in the back of his mind or in hers. "Stirrups look a little long." He stuck his cigarette in the corner of his cocky smile and squinted up at her, nudging her thigh aside so he could make the needed adjustment. "You shrinkin' or what?"

"Getting old."

"Nah. You're thinkin' young today." He patted her knee, signaling her to test the change. "Better?"

"That's perfect."

He savored one long final drag on his cigarette, then dropped the butt into the grave he'd dug with his bootheel. Clara watched him step into his stirrup and swing his long leg over the saddle in one smooth, fluid motion. *That* was perfect.

Shouts of *"Hopo!"* drew general attention to Dewey and Elliot, who were mounted now and waving arms in the air, signing for a circle.

"We'll start and end every day with a prayer circle," Ben explained. "We gotta pray real hard for all these tenderfeet. Okay?"

"I think that includes me." Clara smiled. "Okay?"

"How about me?" Suddenly he was as serious as she'd ever seen him, probing her with a disturbingly imperative stare. "You ever pray for me anymore, Clara?"

"Yes, I do." She said it quickly, avoiding his eyes. She wasn't sure why. Maybe because, like the tobacco ties, the question was such a wonder, coming from Ben. So simple, so straightforward, so unexpected, that it nailed her to the spot. It sounded raw. It felt intensely personal, startlingly intimate. It challenged her integrity, compelling her to add, "But not the way I used to."

"Why not?"

She remembered staring out the window, peering into the darkness, feverishly praying on headlights as though they were rosary beads. *Bring him home safely. I don't care what condition he's in, as long as it's one piece. I don't care what he's done, just bring him home.* It was a woman's prayer of last resort. She'd used it when he'd taken the car and left her with a sleeping baby. She'd used it when she'd run out of phone numbers, and there was not a damn thing left to do but wait. And because she couldn't accept waiting as a passive activity, she'd devised the prayer.

She'd always said it a few times before she remembered to add the word *please*. *Please bring him home.* Because without that, it sounded as though she expected her own will to be done. Her will, her way. Which, of course, would be pure vanity on her part.

But surely God's will was concurrent with her own in some instances, and surely this was one of them. *Please make him come home now, and everything will be fine.* But it wasn't fine. *Cancel the prayer of the foolish woman, God. Please, just make him stay away.*

She shrugged the whole notion off with a smile. "Because you're no tenderfoot, Ben Pipestone. You never were."

Twenty-three riders converged in a circle. Dewey took the feathered hoop into the center and offered a prayer in Lakota. Then in silence the riders formed a single file and headed for the fording place in the river.

Waiting her turn, Clara watched as one horse after another balked at the crossing. Some slipped as they broke through the thin crust of ice at the water's edge. Others churned and pawed or simply refused to take the plunge. Ben and Elliot Plume took turns leading the riders who needed help, while supporters stood on the bluff, the women trilling to lend encouragement in the traditional way.

When her mare met the first challenge without a fuss, Clara looked across the sparkling water at Ben, who had just led the woman from Oklahoma across. "I have a name for her," she announced as she rode triumphantly past him.

He tipped his chin, inviting her to elaborate.

"She's Misty Too."

He gave a brief nod, a pleasured smile, then turned his attention to another floundering rider. And it occurred to

Clara that it didn't matter who was in charge, where they were going, or what lay beyond the next hill. Ben was in his element now. She could trust him to handle the rough spots.

Clara followed Anna and Billie as the string of riders made its way through the river-bottom thicket and up the first ridge. When the leaders reached the high ground, she was struck by the breathtaking picture they made riding into the waning afternoon's western sky. The staff and the hoop were etched against the horizon, the sun's rays striking them on a slant, the eagle feathers fluttering in the breeze. Elliot Plume, the founder of the ride, carried the staff. Dewey, splendidly outfitted in a red and black blanket coat, carried the hoop. At the first campsite they would be met by the support vehicles carrying gear for many of the riders, pulling horse trailers, and leading the way for those journalists who were determined to follow. But for now there were only the riders and their horses crossing the brown and gold plains.

Ben had stationed himself at the rear of the procession after the river crossing. There were those beginner horsemen for whom the first few days were bound to be a trial by fire. The chubby little boy on the choppy-gaited Shetland was a good example. "Somebody trade horses with meee," the boy whined, his ruddy round cheeks bouncing along at the trot. "This horse wants to run. I don't wanna run yet."

It was a wonder the pony hadn't bucked the boy off, the way he was hauling on the reins. Ben rode up beside him and asked his name.

"Toby Two Bear."

"Mickey Two Bear's boy?"

"Yeah."

Ben braced his right hand on the cantle and swiveled in the saddle, checking the riders strung out behind them. He figured the boy to be about eleven or twelve. Too

young to be on his own. "Where's your dad? I didn't
see him when we started out."

"I haven't seen him for almost a year. My m-mom
brought me, but she's drivin' the pickup." The boy's
cheeks bounced like two rubber balls, marking the chop-
py rhythm for his singsong tale. He was pouring everything else he had into staying in the saddle. He couldn't
afford to spare Ben a glance. "Can you make this horse
stop running?"

"No, I can't. I'm not the one ridin' him."

"Yeah, b-but I can't either, and he's gonna m-make
me fall off."

"He's fightin' the bit, Toby. You would, too, if he was
pullin' on *your* mouth like that. You pull him up to stop
him, then you ease off. Tell you what, though, you're
gonna have to get used to that trot, or you're gonna get
left in the dust. Where'd you get the pony?"

"M-M-My cousin."

"When you get tired of bouncin' around like that,
stand up in your stirrups, like this." It wasn't going to
be easy. Toby's belly and his butt were just as round as
his cheeks. He tried to imitate Ben, but he had to grab
the saddle horn to pull himself up. He held the position
for a few seconds, then started bouncing again.

"Keep workin' on it, Toby."

"But I don't wanna run yet," Toby wailed. "I gotta
get used to walking first."

"Your pony's got other ideas. Looks like you're just
along for the ride."

Ben kept close tabs on the boy as they headed for the
first campsite. Clara and Anna seemed to be doing fine,
riding well ahead of him as he assumed the position of
drag rider. Apparently no one else saw the need. Either
that or they were just leaving it to him. When he swung
down to close a gate, Toby was the last one to pass by.
Once through, the boy dismounted. Gripping his reins,
clearly on the verge of tears, he glared up at Ben.

"Go ahead and do your business, Toby. I ain't lookin'."

Wordlessly Toby started walking, leading his pony. Ben followed, leading his big gelding. If they'd been closer to the campsite, or if the boy had been a little older or in better physical shape, Ben would have respected the fact that he hadn't asked for any help and just let him walk. But given the circumstances, he couldn't do that.

"How about if we ride double awhile?"

"Can't."

"Seat givin' out on you?"

"He still wants to run." The boy wasn't about to admit that his legs had turned to jelly, but it showed in his stumbling gait.

"I like the way you hung in there, Toby." The boy looked up, surprised. "I'd trade horses with you, but my feet would drag the ground on your mount."

Toby glanced at the pony, then at Ben's long legs. He gave a little guffaw.

Ben pulled them all up in their tracks and offered the boy a leg up. "You sit in my saddle, I'll sit right behind you and see you don't fall off."

By sunset all of Ben's soft spots—head, possibly heart, definitely upper and inner thighs—had developed the tender makings of hard-earned calluses. It was a relief to join the prayer circle at Ward Jackson's isolated little ranch. Ward was there to see that the horses had plenty of fresh water, grain, and hay. His wife helped the support crew put out the first evening meal. The balmy temperatures had dropped with the sun. Riders took care of their horses, then started heading for the campfire, which burned like a beacon in front of the big canvas tipi that had been set up near the shelter belt. They followed their noses toward the hot coffee and the tailgate supper that awaited them.

"Save me some coffee," Ben told Clara as he took charge of her mare.

"I can help you," she said. But it was dark, and she wasn't sure what to do, where to start.

"Help Toby find something to eat. He's had a hard time of it."

Toby relished the role of hard-time cowboy, especially since it meant a place at the head of the chow line. Clara took two cups of coffee, treasuring the simple warmth in each hand. Her nose was cold. Her legs were wobbly. Her bottom was sore. But hot coffee had never tasted better, nor had a fire ever been more inviting. She liked the notion that at day's end she was doing okay.

Anna complained of absolute starvation and a splinter in her thumb. Clara probed by firelight until Anna decided her hunger was more pressing than the pain. "Dad'll get it out later," she said. First aid had always been one of Ben's roles when he'd lived with them.

When he appeared out of the darkness Clara welcomed him with the coffee and a smile. Small thanks, she thought, because he'd had his share of roles today, and all she'd done was stay on the horse.

"Is that little boy going to make it?"

"He made it today." Ben shoved his gloves in his pockets and took the Styrofoam cup from her hand, sliding his fingers over hers. He smiled, then sipped, then shrugged. "If it had been me forkin' that damn Shetland, I'd 'a been on the ground walkin' before Toby was. I don't know why people always wanna put their kid on a pony."

"Because it's not as far to fall."

"How's the mare workin' for you?" He sipped his coffee, determined not to pin his next breath on her answer.

"Beautifully." Her smile was another small thanks.

Dewey joined them, carrying his bowl carefully, for it was full to the brim with soup. Meat and a few vegetables in a bland broth. "It's good," he said. "Better get some before it's gone. Got some hungry Indians crowdin' around the pot."

"Glad you got your appetite back," Ben said.

"The children have been fed now. Better eat while you can." Dewey plucked a chunk of neck bone from the bowl with his fingers. The broth dripped down his chin as he gnawed on the gristle. Eyeing Clara, he nodded toward the pickup parked at the edge of the circle of firelight, its tailgate serving as the buffet table. "Meat keeps us goin'. Your husband has an appetite, too."

Clara thought it a peculiar thing for her father-in-law to say, but since he'd spoken to her directly, she obliged without question, as though she were bound by a duty that was much older than she was. Ben took the soup from her without a word. Duty-bound as well, he ate in silence.

The wives, mothers, and friends of the riders who made up the support crew were in charge of food and shelter. After supper they cleaned up, put out water for washing, and made sure everyone had a place to sleep. The tipi would accommodate some of the men who were leading the expedition, along with those who'd brought nothing but a horse and a bedroll. Towering above the assortment of more contemporary-looking tents, the pine poles and pale canvas were reminiscent of many of the lodges Big Foot's people used as the nineteenth century drew to a close, when government-issue canvas had largely replaced scarce buffalo hide.

Tanya Beale, the adventurous woman from Oklahoma, made the claim that she wouldn't mind sleeping in a tipi, but Ben laughed and told her the snoring would drive her crazy. She accepted the offer of a piece of living room floor in the Jacksons' trailer, where the younger riders headed at the mention of rented videos.

It was a pleasant night to linger around the campfire. Not too cold. Not too windy. A good time to get acquainted, get reacquainted, share a few chuckles and a belly laugh or two in the warm glow of a good fire. The ground was frozen, but there were saddles and blankets and a few rickety old lawn chairs for seating.

"So where's all the shutterbugs?" Ben wondered aloud.

He and Clara shared a folded tarp. She was bundled up in the wool blanket they'd always kept in the car. He wished she'd open up one side and invite him to cuddle up next to her, the way old Marvin Cutler's wife had just done.

"Most of 'em went back to McLaughlin, where they could rent a bed," Marvin said.

"They'll quit following us pretty soon. Good stiff wind'll blow 'em back into their dens," Howard predicted, smiling.

" 'Til we get to Wounded Knee." Ben snapped a twig in two and fed a piece to the flames. "Then they'll be out in force again."

"We want them to take their pictures and get us our half a minute on the news," Marvin said. "Nobody wants to remember Wounded Knee. Too goddamned embarrassing."

Ben had always called Marvin's wife Auntie Mary, even though he didn't know exactly how the relationship worked. She wasn't his father's sister. For as much as he knew about his mother, she could have been hatched from an egg. But Auntie Mary was related to him somehow. As for Marvin, he didn't look much like an Indian, but he talked like one. Acted like one. Belonged to the family and always had, as far back as Ben could remember. Part of the never-ending system of relations. Marvin and Mary had always been a pair.

"I don't care if they forget what happened *then* if they'd just think about what's goin' on *now*," Sheila Bird contributed from the far side of the circle.

"You can't separate one from the other. It's cause and effect, man. Cause and effect," Howard said, punching a finger into the spark-salted night air. With the firelight reflected in the lens of his glasses, his face seemed to leap into flame as he turned to Clara. "Right, Mrs. Pipestone? Ain't that what history's all about? You told us that, remember?"

"What pleases me is that *you* remember."

"Eeez, she always used to say stuff like that." Howard chuckled. "Like she'd get all excited about that map stuff, if you could remember state capitols and all those little countries in South America and Africa, places that keep turning into new countries every other week."

"And, of course, that's the effect, so we learn by looking at the causes of the instability that led to—" she glanced at Ben "—the insurrection . . . or the overthr—" He smiled and shook his head, and she felt the fire in her own face. "Okay, okay. Sorry. I lost my head for a moment."

"How many years you guys been married?" Marvin asked Ben. "You must be a walking encyclopedia by now."

"I've learned a lot."

"So have I," Clara said softly. "I guess that's what marriage is all about."

Ben tossed the other half of the twig into the fire.

"How's your dad doin'?" Howard asked. "Did he hit the sack already?"

Ben nodded. "Jackson's wife offered him a bed in the house, but he wouldn't take it. He told her this was good sleepin' weather. So he goes in the tent, and I hear him singin' Indian, you know, real quiet, and then he's talkin' in Indian. Lot of times he prays like that, but lately it's Sitanka this and Maziyapa that. Like he thinks they're right there."

"Big Foot?"

"Sitanka, yeah. And Maziyapa was my great-grandfather, Iron Hammer." Staring into the fire, he blew a long breath, shook his head, and thought for a moment. "I don't know. I think he might be losin' it."

"He is not," Clara averred adamantly. "He's a very spiritual man. I wouldn't doubt that he *is* talking to those men."

"This from the woman who does not believe in ghosts," Ben told the group.

"Well, not in the usual sense, but from your father's perspective—"

"What does that mean? You don't believe in ghosts in the *usual* sense? What's the *usual* kind of ghost?"

"The kind that haunts houses."

"Or motels?" He cocked his eyebrow pointedly.

"The kind that most people mean when they talk about ghosts," she insisted, ignoring his reference. "I don't believe in the Hollywood kind of ghost."

"Who does? Me?" Ben laughed. "Hollywood ghosts, huh? What's my dad's kind of ghost then?"

"Well, Ben . . ." She gestured impatiently. "He's a spiritual man, which is pretty unusual in this day and age. I mean a *truly* spiritual man."

"And he ain't deaf!" Dewey shouted from his bed inside the tipi.

All eyes widened, some shifting left, some shifting right. Ben snickered and shook his head. "I'm in for it now," he said quietly.

"You think you'll take his place as pipe carrier?" Howard whispered.

Ben shook his head. He offered no explanation. He simply stared into the fire. For Howard, that was enough.

Ben turned to Clara. "You guys have everything you need?"

"Little camp cots, foam bedroll, space-age sleeping bags . . ."

"Make sure you check the mattress for peas." He raised his voice a notch and threw it toward the tipi. "If the ol' man gets to coughin', he's goin' in the house. I don't give a good goddamn how spiritual he is. I need some sleep if I'm gonna be herdin' greenhorns around all day tomorrow."

"Then quit your bullshittin'," came the suggestion from inside.

"I think it went pretty well today," Clara told Ben. She stretched her legs out in front of her, soles of her boots toward the fire. "I'm hardly sore at all. Our only crisis was a splinter in Anna's thumb, which—"

"I took care of it. I keep tellin' you, Clara, all you have to do is—"

Before he knew it, he'd taken her hand in his and started rubbing his thumb against hers to demonstrate his technique. But the friction soon begat aware-ness, and she looked up, her eyes silently ques-tioning his. The witnesses remained quiet. The fire crackled.

He laid her hand on her knee, then braced himself, hands on his own knees, and pushed to his feet. "It was a short day. Tomorrow's gonna be a hell of a lot longer. Thirty miles, and morning comes early." With an abrupt salute he took his leave. "See you all then."

The pale blond needlegrass and the darker bluestem were feathered with morning frost. The crisp air pumped the horses with enough sass to keep the riders busy in the corrals and cut the morning coffee short. Anna needed her father's help with her saddle, but Clara had hers under control. She'd slept surprisingly well in her cozy cocoon of a sleeping bag with Anna by her side. Getting dressed had been the challenging part, but she'd met the challenge within the warm confines of her sleeping bag. The Jacksons had offered the women the use of their bathroom, an opportunity not to be taken for granted for the next two weeks.

Something in the sound of Dewey's voice made Ben feel uneasy during the daybreak prayer. He turned his collar up, telling himself the chill that started in the back of his neck and shimmied down his spine had nothing to do with his father. The old man always sounded like somebody hanging his head in a barrel when he prayed first thing in the morning.

But he hadn't sounded too good last night, and it wasn't the cough so much as the way his breath seemed to get hung up in his chest. Ben hadn't said anything about it. Hadn't dared. Told himself maybe his ears were playing tricks on him, then and now. He was a great one for hearing things that weren't there. Maybe one of Clara's Hollywood ghosts, the kind she didn't believe in.

Dewey finally proclaimed, *"Mitakuye oyasin." All my relatives.* Ben echoed the words gratefully and wheeled his gelding toward the pasture gate.

Alta Two Bear was sitting opposite the gate in her green pickup, waiting for her son to ride through. Toby admitted to feeling pretty sore this morning, and he wasn't sure he wanted to ride that "dumb ol' pony" again. But when he saw his mother wave the eagle feather she'd brought for him, Toby squared his shoulders and trotted right up to her.

"I noticed yesterday that different ones had eagle feathers," she explained to Ben, who was ready to close the gate. She tied her gift to Toby's bridle. "You're probably supposed to give it at the end, but I thought my boy might need it sooner."

"He needed it yesterday," Ben allowed, giving the boy a conspiratorial wink. "Today's gonna be better. Right, Toby?"

"Hope so."

The way to Wounded Knee took the form of a snake-like gravel road that undulated over endless prairie. The morning sun spread its warmth like honey, and the leaders tried to hold a steady pace. But green horses and greener horsemen continued to disturb the peace. One of the younger riders let her horse's nose get too close to Howard White Calf's green-broke mount's tail.

Howard's bronky dun suddenly kicked its back hoofs at heaven, and Howard went flying.

He lay perfectly still, facedown in the grass. His scruffy dun sniffed at his shoulder. Several riders stopped, a few paused, but no one dropped to the ground right away. They approached him tentatively, like the dun horse.

"Howard?" Clara decided it was her move. But Ben's hold-off gesture forestalled her when the man on the ground stirred.

"Knocked you out of wind?" Ben asked.

Howard grunted and slowly pushed himself up.

"Ain't a cowboy can't be thrown," Ben quipped as he swung down in a leisurely dismount. He grabbed the loose mount's trailing reins, then leaned down and swept a pair of battered wire-rims out of the grass. "Well, the tape held," he observed, carefully straightening the bows. "How bad are your eyes, Howard? You still got one good lens here. You need to see out of more than one eye?"

Hands braced on his thighs, Howard poked his lips in his horse's direction. "Not if this guy would use his."

"Medic!" came the call from one of the half-dozen horsemen who'd gathered around.

"Medicine man!" someone echoed. "Warrior eatin' trail dust back here!"

Howard stood up, brushed himself off, and grinned. "Looks like that horse don't wanna go to Wounded Knee."

"Where'd you get him?" Ben asked.

"Borrowed him from my father-in-law."

Ben chuckled. "Looks like your ol' lady don't want *you* goin' to Wounded Knee."

"Somebody puttin' on a rodeo back here?" Elliot Plume asked, reining his horse in. "Thought you hung up your buckin' strap, Ben."

"Howard was trying to liven things up for us. Judge says he took a 'no time.' "

Elliot laughed. "Missed him out, Howard?"

"Hell, some of these kids . . ." Chagrined, Howard claimed his mount. "I know I've got a bronc here, but some of these kids need a little tuning up in the horse-manship department."

"I been thinkin' the same," Ben said.

"Hey, teacher," Howard said, recovering his easy smile. "We need you to discipline these kids."

"He's asking for it now," Clara told Ben.

But during the course of the morning it was Ben who gave the lessons. He wasn't much for disciplining other people's kids, but when two of the youngsters came galloping up from behind and went racing past Toby Two Bear, Ben helped Toby bring his Shetland under control, then caught up to the race jockeys and gave them a terse warning.

When bus driver Sheila Bird took a tumble, landing in the grass right next to her saddle, Ben told her that her horse was playing tricks on her. "Always check your cinch," he advised. He pulled the strap as tight as he could and buckled it. "Is that tight now?"

She showed him she couldn't wedge her gloved hand between the strap and the horse's belly.

"Lead him around once," Ben instructed, and Sheila obliged. "Now check it again," he said, and she discovered inches of slack. "He's holdin' his breath on you, just like an ornery kid. He'll do it every time now that he knows how good it works, so you need to remember every time you saddle up." He offered an artful wink as cushion for any hurt feelings he might cause. "Gotta be smarter than the horse you're ridin', Sheila."

Ben wasn't the only born-to-ride horseman on the journey, but there was none better. Elliot Plume did his share of troubleshooting, along with hefty, jovial Cheppa Four Dog. This was the first full day, and the leadership roles fell into the fittest hands as the mishaps continued to occur. Marvin Cutler and his big gelding both took a somersault when the horse stepped in a gopher hole. Cheppa caught the horse as Marvin emerged from the grass, rubbing his shiny forehead.

"Did he kick you?"

"Think I hit that fence post." Marvin laughed uneasily as he pointed out the culprit. "Guess I skinned up my old bald head."

"You get dizzy or anything, you let us know," Cheppa said.

"I ain't dizzy." He took a couple of experimental steps. "Nope. See any blood?"

From his elevated perspective Cheppa examined the top of Marvin's head. "Jeez. Never seen anything like it."

"What? Do I need stitches?" Marvin checked his hand for evidence.

"Hard to tell. The glare's blinding me." Cheppa grinned, his smooth round cheeks as shiny as any bald head. "Just a few scratches is all."

Despite mishaps, the main body of riders kept the pace, and those who fell back had to catch up. Ben was glad his wife and daughter were well mounted, because too many others were not. He'd started a mental list of riders to keep track of. Not that there weren't plenty of other eyes watching. As long as the route followed the gravel road, there were photographers waiting around every bend. Pesky, nosy, in-your-face camera jockeys. One of the few forms of life Ben regarded with contempt, and it wasn't only because there was one in particular who had a real penchant for snapping Clara's picture. Probably didn't think her husband would notice. Well, Cady the cagey shaman had another goddamn think coming.

"Ben? Hey, Ben?"

"What's up, Toby?"

The boy was bouncing easier at the trot, but his face looked seriously distressed. "My feather came off. The one my mom gave me this morning."

"Eagle feather?" Ben recalled. Toby nodded. "Got a cigarette on you?"

"Huh?"

"Never mind," Ben said with a smile as he wheeled his horse and started backtracking. He was glad for the distraction. "I got you covered on that score. We've gotta find it and ask Tunkasila to let you take it from the earth again."

"Will he let me?"

"Never know. He might take your feather back again if you don't take care of it."

"It wasn't my fault. My mom tied it onto the bridle, and this horse is bouncin' around so much."

Ben dismounted when he spotted the feather lying in the grass. Toby followed suit, but he didn't pick it up. He'd seen feathers fall off costumes at powwows, and he knew it wasn't that simple.

"I don't know why your mom gave you this, Toby, but she must have had a good reason." Ben took a cigarette from his pocket and broke it in half. Out of the corner of his eye he noticed the gathering of camera-faces. He pretended to ignore the clicks, but he kicked his lesson into high gear. "This is an honor for you. It came from the earth, and for some reason it went back to the earth. So now—" he took Toby's hands and formed them into a cup, which he filled with the tobacco from his cigarette "—you have to make a trade. This tobacco for the feather."

Cradling the offering, Toby looked up at his newfound mentor, eyes brimming with esteem.

With a quick chin jerk Ben redirected the boy's worshipful attention. "On the ground." Then an over-the-shoulder aside. "Hey, Cady, you lookin' to get kicked?"

"I was just . . ." Cady lowered his camera and blinked

his baby blues, perplexed. "You said when your father was doing a ceremony, or when the pipe was—"

"That's not a threat. It's a warning." Ben laughed. He nodded toward his big gelding, whose flank was inches from Cady's silver head. "This horse doesn't give a damn what you were in a past life. You stand behind him, he's liable to boot you into the next one."

"Oh." Cady moved quickly, then scowled. Toby had already made his offering. "Now I missed my shot."

Ben ignored the complaint. "Now you can pick up the feather and offer it to the four directions. *Mitakuye oyasin*," Ben said with a nod as Toby followed instructions. The camera clicked and whirred when the boy repeated in Lakota the prayerful acknowledgment, "All my relatives."

"Now, you tie it on there good, because if it comes off, we stop and do this again. Out of respect."

"How come you didn't do that when Howard fell?"

"Because Howard's got legs. Besides, the earth isn't ready to take him back." Chuckling, Ben remounted. "She'd probably give *us* tobacco just to keep him out of her hair a while longer."

"The earth *does* give us tobacco," Toby pointed out.

Ben grinned. "See, that must be why she does it. She's willin' to trade."

It was midday when the riders approached the Cheyenne River Reservation town of Timber Lake. It was more of a slough than a lake that stood between the town and State Highway 20, which were linked by a paved causeway. The driver of a black Blazer figured he owned the blacktop. He barreled past, blasting his horn. Several of the horses shied. One bolted, but the rider quickly brought it under control.

"Redneck asshole," one of the riders muttered.

Timber Lake was a "white town" situated smack-dab

in the middle of two adjacent Indian reservations. With the approach of the Wounded Knee Memorial Ride, it was vintage *High Noon*. The town seemed all but deserted. A loudspeaker on the roof of the motel piped Christmas music down the asphalt canyon that was Main Street. The clomping of nearly a hundred hoofs blended with the strains of "I Saw Three Ships A-Sailing." Two cowboys emerged from the liquor store, each carting a case of Budweiser, which they loaded into the black Blazer. One of them ceremoniously tipped his hat as Anna and Billie rode past.

Say something cute, jackass, Ben thought. There were two more buddies in the backseat making no secret of the fact that they were all half-shot. Ben figured he could take all four, easy. *Just make some rude redneck remark to my daughter.*

But the cowboys kept their remarks to themselves, and Ben had to give them credit for being able to count better than Custer.

Howard White Calf brought up the rear of the parade, his bronc trotting along with its ears laid back, saying it was ready to start bucking any time. Somebody stuck his head out the door of the bar and yelled, "You Indian! Get outta town!" then quickly ducked back inside.

Howard bounced along, smiling agreeably, clutching the reins as though they were handlebars. "Hell, I'd be glad to oblige," he muttered between his teeth.

A stretch of prairie grass at the end of the street provided a place for the riders to dismount and stretch their legs. Ben offered to stay with the horses while Clara and Anna went across the street to the gas station and convenience store. "Just be careful," he warned. "This is redneck heaven. While you're at it, bring me something cool and wet."

Clara headed straight for the bathroom and the closest of two stalls. Inside were toilet testimonials to several apparently devoted couples. Donita and Sly. Marilee and

Skip. Sam and Katie. And then the final word, the message from love betrayed, scrawled in red lipstick across the tableau of half a dozen sweetheart notes: "FUCK ALL OF YOU."

"Hey, Mom, guess what's written on the wall in here." Anna cleared her throat and read, " 'Clara loves Ben.' Jeez, Mom. Naughty, naughty."

"Are you serious?" Clara always gave initial credence, then followed up with a mental no-way. "You're putting me on, right?"

"When were you in here last?"

"I've never been in here before. I don't even know anybody in Timber Lake." She tried to imagine how her name might look on a stall door. Hers and Ben's. "You're kidding, right?"

"You wanna know what it *really* says in here?"

"I don't think so." Nor did she want Anna to see what her wall said, or to feel, ever, the sentiments of the poor lipstick artist. A sentiment Clara had put behind her. Truly kiboshed it. But she remembered what it was like, for a very short time, to hate love and curse all lovers. There were certainly better ways to express it. It seemed patently inappropriate to write the word *fuck* in lipstick.

Then again, she had to admit that some of the ways she'd thought of expressing her anger a year or two ago were even less appropriate, in thought, word, and certainly in deed. Fortunately, Clara Pipestone was never impulsive.

But, oh, she'd had some evil thoughts.

"But you'd never put it on the bathroom wall, right, Mom?"

"What?"

"Your name." Anna looked up from washing her hands in the rusty sink. "I can't ever see you doing that."

"No. No, never."

Clara stood silently near the cooler, absently reading the handbills taped to the plate glass window behind the cash register. Church potluck next week. High school basketball schedule; be there to support our team. No loitering. She could hear Anna and Billie in the back of the store, still chattering and giggling, taking their time deciding what they wanted. Finally Clara set her purchases on the counter. Three bottles of orange drink.

"Will this do it for you?" the blond woman asked, hand poised near the cash register.

"Plus whatever my daughter wants."

The hand came down, resting on the counter. The gray eyes shifted from the window to the candy rack that hid all but the top of Anna's head. "Wonder what all those Indians are doing here. Kinda spooky, huh, them ridin' in here like that?"

Spooky? "Actually, no. I rode in with them."

"Really? Powwow season's over, isn't it?" Clara's brow shot up, but the woman didn't seem to notice. She nodded toward the back of the store. "You know those two back there?"

"Yes." Pinning the woman with a cold stare, she shifted her shoulders and turned her head only slightly. "Anna, you and Billie find something quickly and let's go."

The girls brought candy, sunflower seeds, and gum to the counter.

The clerk eyed the pile of goodies as though the wrappers were grimy. "This is it?"

"This is definitely it."

It pleased Ben that she remembered his preference for orange. She'd also brought one for Dewey, who nodded his thanks.

"It's going well for you?" her father-in-law asked. "Not going too fast for you, are we?"

Clara shook her head, letting the breeze take her hair

away from her face. "I'm not about to let that hoop out of my sight." She eyed the gas station with growing distaste, then remembered her drink and took a quick sip, which helped. "It's nice when we're not following a road," she said, looking southward toward the unblemished blue horizon. "When we're out on the prairie, just following the hoop. Nobody else can get to us then. It's like a different world."

"No cameras and no rednecks." Ben tipped his head back, guzzled half the bottle of orange drink, then nodded, satisfied. "Different world, all right."

"Almost mystical," she said.

"I'd call it peaceful, and the sooner we get back to it, the better. Seems we're makin' the good citizens of Timber Lake a little nervous. The mayor's probably already put in a call to the governor, tellin' him he sees the makings of another Indian uprising right out here in his backyard."

"This is a reservation," Clara said. "You'd think these people hadn't seen Indians before."

"This is a white town on the rez, Clara-bow. The sad part is, they see you with us, you get less respect than we do."

She nodded. She remembered. She'd taught summer school in a town like this just before they were married. The people of McIntosh had all but run her out on a rail when they'd heard about her plans to marry Ben, and they'd gladly released her from her contract when she'd realized she couldn't live there.

"Real mystical, huh?" Ben tapped his father's shoulder with an amiable fist. "What do you say we round up the hostiles and get outta Dodge before they confiscate the ponies?"

No announcement was made. When the hoop and the staff were up, the rest of the riders took to their horses, and the journalists had to scramble to line up their next shots.

"Wonder how long they're gonna keep this up." The dance of the shutterbugs amused Ben almost as much as their presence irked him. He wanted Clara to wonder, too, but she wouldn't oblige. She didn't mind having her picture taken. Why should she? They'd never be able to record her bad side and put it on display for her daughter to see. Mostly because Clara didn't have any really bad sides. Damn her.

A small, dark-haired man snatched up his tripod and trotted alongside Howard White Calf, muttering something in Japanese as he lost ground.

"What's that?" Howard asked, slowing down to wait for Ben and Clara.

"I said to myself, better hurry," the man shouted, still running, pointing to the high ground up ahead.

Ben leaned toward Howard. "He was really saying, better get my ass in gear if I'm gonna catch that hill. It's goin' fast."

The two men laughed.

"Oh, Ben," Clara said. "Give the man a break. It's a good vantage point for a picture."

"This ain't my best side." Howard laughed again when the man shot a picture of him on the run. "You sure must have a lot of film."

"Plenty, yes."

"He came all the way from Japan for this, hey. You think he's gonna forget to bring film?" Ben shook his head as the man sprinted across the road, dodging horses as he went. "Jesus, he can run."

Clara was grateful when the riders pulled over to a copse of trees later that afternoon. They'd been holding to a steady trot, and her legs were beginning to turn rubbery. She could really feel it when she dismounted, and she hoped she'd be able to get back into the saddle without asking for a leg up.

She was following the crowd out of habit now, even on foot, just tagging along without thinking.

Ben stepped in to cut her off. "They're, uh—" he put his hands on her shoulders and turned her away from the trees, chuckling in her ear from behind "—takin' a pause for the cause over there."

"Oh."

"Elliot was just sayin' they haven't had too many women along before. Makes it kinda different." He leaned closer to her ear. "You okay?"

He was standing behind her. She couldn't see his face, but she could just picture that concerned-for-the-awkward-moment look in his eye. In his way, Ben was a sensitive man. It was sometimes hard for her to remember, with so many other things in her mind's way. But in his way, naturally and inadvertently, he reminded her.

And it made her smile when he wasn't looking. "I don't have cause to pause for, if that's what you mean."

"Just let me know. I'll stand guard."

Not far behind them there was a lot of water running. She giggled and whispered, "Sounds like the paddocks at the racetrack."

"It's a man thing. A contest."

"Historical reenactment?"

"Now, this," he intoned, tour-guide fashion, "is the way the Indians took a leak in their natural environment." Then louder, "Where the hell is the press corps?"

"Taking the long way around, fortunately."

His hand left her shoulder. "Don't turn around, now. I wanna see how many points I can rack up before they get here."

It sounded as though someone had turned on the garden hose. Clara couldn't resist taking a quick peek.

And Ben had to hold his sides to keep from splitting a gut as he proclaimed his gelding "the winner and still champion."

"Males can be so disgusting," Clara told her mare, loud enough for all the world to hear. Spotting Tara Jean's pickup parked at the side of the road, she headed

in that direction, leading Misty Too, seeking the pleas-
antries of woman things.

She discovered her sister-in-law behind the horse trailer, talking with an older man. He'd left his pickup running, parked on the other side of the road.

"What do you guys think you're doing?" Clara heard
the man say. "Having a big forty-nine out here?"

"Forty-nine?" TJ turned as Clara approached. "This
man wants to know if we're having a forty-nine. Do you
know what he's talking about?"

"Powwow or something," the man said.

The forty-nine was a circle dance, as Clara remembered, but she knew the powwow announcer would call
for it in Lakota. "*Hopo! Kahomni!* Everybody dance!"
And she would feel welcome in the circle when the
announcement was made. But she doubted the old rancher had ever been to a powwow.

"This is my land," he said. "I just wanna know what's
goin' on."

"This is the Big Foot Memorial Ride." TJ folded her
arms and squared her stance. "Maybe you read about it
in the newspaper."

"Don't get the newspaper. Mail don't come but three
times a week out here." He craned his neck, trying to
peer past Misty Too's flanks. He wanted to take his look,
but he was reluctant to be seen by anyone but the two
women. "So what's it all about?"

"We're going to Wounded Knee," TJ told him.

"Oh, Christ, not another protest."

"No, this is a memorial," Clara explained. "A peaceful
commemoration. It's the one hundredth anniversary of
the assassination of Sitting Bull and the massacre of the
people at Wounded Knee." She glanced down the road.
A local news van had joined the cavalcade, making it
look official. "Here come the reporters now. Reporters
from all over the U.S., Canada, Japan, Germany. You
just wouldn't believe what a story this is."

"Really?"

"And we *are* outside your fence," TJ pointed out. "We're on the right-of-way."

The man raised an appreciative eyebrow when he saw the cameras. "I didn't know it was such big news. Saw all these horses comin' down the road, thought maybe they was hunters or somethin'."

Clara and TJ exchanged doubtful glances.

"Nope," TJ assured him, suppressing a smile. "They're unarmed."

"I remember they had a ride or something last year. I think they were the ones broke my fence down."

"I don't know about that." TJ stepped away from Clara's horse and directed the man's attention toward the shady spot where some of the men had congregated to share a smoke. "You could ask my dad about it. He's the one in the black and red coat."

"Big chief, huh?" The rancher watched the press vehicles drive past. Then he took another look at the men, the horses, a group of women and children sitting in the grass closer by with more horses.

Then, finally, back to the two he'd started with. "Tell them they can let the fence down and water their horses in the creek. But they got to put it back up or I'll have cows from here to Texas."

"You want to relay that, Clara?"

"Maybe you should. You talk Indian better than I do." Clara turned a sunny smile on the dour old man. "But we will explain it to them. I'm sure they'll appreciate your generosity."

"You think there'll be something on the news tonight?"

Clara shrugged. "Might even make the network news."

"No kidding? That Tom Brokaw, he's a South Dakota boy, you know." He adjusted his stately high-crown cowboy hat. "You tell the chief to help himself to my water. It's gonna take some ridin' to get to Pine Ridge. Do they have winter gear and all?"

"Have you ever slept in a tipi?" TJ asked. The man shook his head. "It's almost like a house, really."

"Well, I 'spoze . . ." He hooked a gnarly forefinger over the brim of his hat as he backed away. "Nice meetin' you, ladies. You have a nice ride."

"What should we tell them?" Clara asked as she and TJ marched side by side toward the outdoor sanctum, the mare in tow.

"We'd better tell them if they don't cut it short, it's gonna be on the six-o'clock news, complete with that guy's account of how a bunch of Indians came and pissed in his creek." TJ's blue-black hair glistened in the sun as she shook her head ruefully. She imitated the gravelly voice. " 'Do they have winter gear?' " Then, in her own voice, "Why? Do you think it might get cold? Just a little bit *osni*? Jeez. They probably never thought of that."

Picking up the pace, TJ tipped her head back and laughed. The sun shone brightly in her face. "I used to say my brother sometimes acted too dumb to live, but even then he wasn't *that* dumb." She turned to Clara, and her smile faded. "What's wrong?"

They stopped walking. Clara shrugged and glanced away. "You know what? I almost asked him if he remembered to bring long johns."

TJ thought for a moment, then laughed. "You know how cold it gets in that shop of his sometimes?"

"It's not heated?"

"He's got a couple of space heaters, but it still gets cold. He's used to it, though. All we had growing up was a wood stove."

"I just . . ." Clara looked down at the toes of her boots. "You know, force of habit. It's not that I think he's dumb. Just . . . sometimes he doesn't take care of himself the way . . ." The way she would, damn it, so who was the stupid one?

"It's none of my business, Clara. I know my brother's no angel, and you've probably got good reason to divorce him, if that's what you have to do. Whatever he did . . ." TJ waited until Clara looked up.

She didn't expect Clara to tell her. The great thing about TJ was that she didn't have to know the details. She got the picture without them. "He's off the booze. I don't think he's fallen off the wagon once since he came back to the rez."

Staring into the trees, Clara nodded.

"I wouldn't lie for him, either, not to you. You're my sister."

"I know." Clara nodded again, staring hard, fighting tears, her voice giving her trouble. "I know."

"He's lonesome for you." Again TJ waited. Clara took a deep, cleansing breath and finally looked into those dark, deep-set eyes again. Eyes so much like Anna's. Eyes that reminded her of Ben. "I just thought you should know that, too," TJ said.

Clara pressed her lips together tight and nodded. She was okay. But she didn't dare try to speak just now.

A playful bark drew TJ's head around. "Annie! Billie! Get away from that dog."

The girls were trying to catch up to them, but a scrawny yellow mutt wanted to play. "He keeps following us," Billie said.

"Sssst! Go on!" TJ picked up a small rock and whizzed it over the dog's head. He jumped for it, missed, and went chasing after it.

Clara's laugh was a little shaky, but it was a laugh.

TJ shook her head. "Damn farmers'll be saying the Indians stole their dog next."

"You mean the dog-eatin' Sioux?" said a familiar male voice.

Clara groaned inwardly. Ben's favorite trick in the world was to creep up on people from behind. This time he'd used her horse as a blind. He'd brought Howard with him, sneaky as you please, and they were both grinning. Must have been a sight, women throwing rocks at innocent dogs.

"Hell, that's a sheepdog," Howard said. "They stink like sheep. We don't eat no damn sheepdog. Right, Ben?"

"Don't be bad-mouthin' sheepdogs," Ben warned. "I got one at home."

Over the top of her saddle he caught Clara's eye. "At the kennel," she said quietly. She gave a brief, wistful smile, then jammed the toe of her boot into the stirrup and hauled herself into the saddle without asking for a leg up.

And without asking exactly what Ben thought he meant by saying that he had a sheepdog at *home*.

8

"Hey there, pretty lady, where's the fire?"

Ben urged his gelding into a ground-eating lope. Clara was trotting well abreast of the hoop and the staff, but he could tell by the quizzical look she shot him when she turned toward the sound of his voice that he'd dragged her back from some dreamworld. He chuckled. "You don't wanna get ahead of the leaders."

She noted her advancing position, smiled bashfully, and reined in her mare. "I guess I was daydreaming."

"You'll be in the front row of the picture." He nodded toward the ubiquitous photographers who'd taken the high ground up ahead.

"Might be fun to make the evening news."

"Indians hire white scout. Details at ten." The laughter they shared came easily, just as it had earlier. His gaze drifted toward the western horizon. "Looked like you and TJ had your heads together back there at the creek. What did she tell you?"

"Maybe it was the other way around. Maybe I was telling her."

He turned, surprised by her challenging undertone. Hadn't they just enjoyed an inside joke? Hadn't his cleverness pleased her?

The hint of defiance in her eyes faded as she lifted one shoulder. "She was mostly grumbling about that rancher we told you about. Joking around, you know."

No, he didn't know. His sister and his wife. The two women in his life who knew him best, putting their heads together, combining what they knew into a composite picture that would probably scare the shit out of everybody, including him.

But Clara didn't look too scared. She even smiled a little. "She said . . . she just wanted me to know that you've been on the straight and narrow. That you've really quit drinking."

The corners of his mouth took an appreciative dip. "You believe her?"

"I believed you."

He nodded. He wanted to ask her when she'd believed him, but he just left it there. It was past tense, so it didn't matter now. No point in asking her to give it another shot, believe him one more time.

But he gave a lopsided smile. "I can balance a checkbook now. You believe that?"

"I never doubted that you *could*, if you ever decided you wanted to."

"Well, I still don't want to, but I have to. I've got a business to run. I even took a couple of courses at the tribal college. Got my columns in order, my debits and my credits. It used to scare me, you know?"

"Keeping books?"

"Seeing the whole thing laid out there in black and white." He stuck his left hand out and studied the palm of his split-cowhide glove like the page of a book. "My debts against my credits. The credit side always looked pretty skimpy. And I didn't wanna look at the debts in broad daylight." His saddle creaked as he shifted his weight. "They made me write 'em down when I was in treatment. All the debts."

As usual she chose to ignore the reference.

"How do you account for horses in your books?" He questioned her with a glance, and she clarified, "You said you took them in trade."

"Yeah." He shrugged. His system still had its weaknesses. "I've got a separate page for that. I think you have to make a place for it on your own time. I've got plenty of time on my hands these days, time and skill that I can trade for stuff. Cash isn't everything."

"And people can't always pay what they owe. That's just a fact of life."

"But they need to try." Total up your debts and try to make amends. Maybe it wouldn't be enough, he'd been warned. But you had to try. He chuckled. "Good ol' TJ, stickin' up for her wicked brother. That's kinda nice. I like it."

"It's not so unusual, is it? She's your sister."

"But she *isn't* my mother. She never could quite get that through her head."

"There's something about you, Ben, that just begs to be mothered."

"Not anymore." He watched her golden hair flutter away from her face, brightened by the cold air. Pink nose. Pink cheeks. Laughing eyes the color of late summer grass. She looked achingly like the girl he'd married. He grinned. "I ain't kiddin' you, Mama, I took the cure. Weaned off the bottle, gave up the breast."

"You're a big boy now, hmm?"

"Damn right. Motherless bastard and proud of it."

"Sounds like a line from Peter Pan, or a cowboy's twisted version of it." She gave him a pointed look. "Got news for you, cowboy, the Wendys of the world are wising up."

"That's okay. That's just fine with me. See if you can get TJ to join the movement, okay?" But his sister was the same kind of maverick he was. It was hard to imagine her taking up any cause, especially his. A wistful smile played across his face. "She really was stickin' up for me, huh?"

"That pleases you?"

"I guess it does." He was surprised. "She had to look after me a lot when we were kids, especially after the ol' lady took off. I've thought about it some lately, thought it was probably hard for her, being the responsible one. Our other sister—you know, Lila, the one who lives in Montana—she was always kind of a birdbrain."

"Ben!"

"Still is. She got herself hooked up with another loser now. She just can't learn. And then, you know, our brother that died, he was . . ." Hard to remember, harder to describe. "My dad's true son, him."

Our brother that died. That was the way Ben always referred to Richard, the Pipestone she'd never met. He'd been involved in some kind of a freak accident when he was a teenager. No one liked to talk about it. Out of a traditional respect for the dead—or fear, Clara was never quite sure—his name was seldom mentioned.

"But you were the baby," she acknowledged, smiling indulgently.

"Now, why do you wanna go usin' fightin' words on me when we're havin' such a nice talk here?"

"Sorry." Fighting was the last thing she wanted. They'd fallen back and drifted farther abreast of the group, and she wanted to pass the time in conversation with a man who had, it was true, never ceased to intrigue her. "You've never told me very much about your mother."

"There isn't much to tell. She ran off two days before my tenth birthday. TJ made me a pitiful cake, kinda thin and flat with sugary white frosting. I remember that cake, but my mother's face is a hazy gray blur in the back part of my mind."

"But you were her only child."

"You kiddin'?" He shook his head, chuckling humorlessly. "I've probably got more half brothers and sisters than you'd care to count. I just haven't heard about them."

"Then why would you think they exist?"

" 'Cause that's the way she was, all right?" Fury flashed in his eyes, then subsided just as quickly. He sighed. "That's just the way she was. She made my ol' man look like a fool, but he kept takin' her back. 'Til she finally stopped comin' back, and even then, he kept hopin' she would. No fool like an old fool." He offered a sad smile. "See, you did the right thing, Clara."

"What?"

"Kickin' me out. I was . . ." He glanced away, and his voice dropped to a place more within himself than without. "You did right. You did what he should'a done. He just couldn't."

"You never heard from her after she—"

He shook his head.

"Maybe she . . ."

He laughed, his eyes intent upon the herringbone clouds sliding over the edge of the horizon, straight ahead. "Maybe she got hit by a truck."

"Ben—"

"That would explain why she never . . ." He shrugged off whatever his mother had not done, for what she had done was quite enough. "You know, you gotta have a reason. I mean, you need to believe there was some kind of a reason."

"Yes."

"Not just plain selfishness."

She nodded.

He sought her with an anxious look. "I may be like her in some ways, but one thing's for sure, Clara. If my kid goes lookin' and can't find me, it's because I got hit by a truck."

"Is that the story you want me to tell her?"

"It'll be the God's honest truth. I'll always be her father." Then quietly he added, "As long as she wants to claim me."

They rode together without saying much for a while. Anna joined them, and the mood lightened. They played a word game Clara had invented years ago to entertain Anna on the long drives that were par for a life on the Great Plains, where there was no short distance between two points on the map. Then Anna rode off to join Billie, and Ben dropped back to check on the "bronc riders."

As the afternoon wore on, Clara's muscles started protesting the unusual demands she was placing on them. She started checking her watch, as if it might have something to say about wrapping up the day's ride. There were no mile markers, no signs, no familiar landmarks. Just more grass, more hills, more fence line, and an ever-distant horizon.

When Ben rode up beside her again, she hoped he'd come to deliver news of an end in sight. But no such luck.

"We've got riders strung out from here to the wide Missouri," he told her. She responded with a look that said she was well past caring. He smiled. "How're you doin', Clara-bow? You gonna make it?"

"How much farther?"

"Couple miles."

"Can't we take a break?"

"We don't wanna be ridin' too long after dark." He tugged at the brim of his black cowboy hat. The sinking sun was still bright. "You're doin' real good. You and Annie both."

"High praise, coming from a cowboy."

"Damn right." He nodded southward. "Just over that next hill."

She knew better, but she kept watching the top of that hill. By the time she crested it, she felt like blubber in a saucer. Ben knew what shape she was in, and she could feel him keeping an eye on her. But he was stingy with his pity. He caught up to her after they'd left "over the next hill" well behind them.

"How's it goin'?"

"I thought you said the next hill. The next hill is now the last hill, and all I see ahead of us is a stupid stock dam."

"No, I said just over *that* hill. I meant the *next* next hill." He pointed with a gloved hand. "You can't see it from here, but you see that one? It's just beyond that one."

Her lips were stiff with cold. "How far?"

"Two miles. It's just about two more miles."

Two more miles. He rode off again, and she tried to calculate fence posts per mile, hoofbeats per mile, butt bounces per mile. The sun slipped into the prairie's western pocket, spreading a bright blaze over deep purple buttes, and still the pack of horses trotted along, up one hill and down another. Her face was chill-set and her fingers were getting that way, too. Ben was pressing his luck, riding up beside her wearing a silly smile.

"We've gone over a bunch of hills, Ben Pipestone. When are we going to stop?"

"Pretty soon. Gettin' anxious?"

"I'm past anxious, past exhausted, and past that hill you said—"

"Honey, it's the *next* hill. Right up—" He stood tall in his stirrups and made a vain production of sighting along the rolling fence line. "Well, you can't see it yet, but it's just past those trees."

"Liar." She pouted. "I'm going to stop pretty soon. I'm just going to stop and get down and curl up in a little ball and . . ."

"And miss supper? There's a nice hot supper waitin' for you, just two miles ahead."

"You said that two miles ago."

"I didn't say supper. I was savin' that part."

"You said two miles!"

"So it must be less than that now. You never could judge distance, Clara-bow."

"Me!"

"You're gonna make it, Clara. I swear to God, we're almost there."

Almost there. Almost there. Almost there.

Just when she'd decided that come the next damn hill, she was going to slide out of the saddle like a sack of meal and get swallowed up in the ditch alongside the road, she saw a yard light.

And Ben was at her side immediately, claiming the credit. "You see that light, Clara-bow?"

"If you tell me that's not where we're going, Ben Pipestone, you are going to regret every dishonest word, every transparent promise, every flimsy—"

He grinned. "What are you gonna do to me?"

"I am going to take your lying lips in my two ice-cold hands and tie them together in a big, fat double knot."

"And then?"

Her lips were too stiff to do anything but sputter. "And then . . . and then . . ."

"C'mon, think of something good." He leaned closer. "Hell, I'm frozen stiff, and you're still givin' me one hell of a hard-on."

"I'd hit you, but you're not worth the effort."

"Go ahead, knock yourself out. Or off." With a deep chuckle, he offered her a hand. "I'll catch you."

She groaned miserably. "I can't go any farther."

"Can you make it to the light?"

"That's it?"

"That's it."

"Oh, thank God." She caught herself in the middle of a deep sigh of relief. "You wouldn't—"

"Uh-uh. Wouldn't lie. That's where we're gonna stop for the night." Then he added, "I know you, Clara-bow. You're never quite empty. You've always got something left in reserve."

The riders formed a circle within the circle of light that the big utility pole cast behind the small ranch house.

They could smell the promise of inner warmth. Soup and coffee. Dewey gave thanks for a day of safe travel, for the horses that had brought them to this place, and for Angus Barnes, the white rancher who had provided a place to stay. He'd offered the use of his corrals and stock tanks, the windbreak of his shelter belt, where the support crew had already set up camp, and all the hay and water the horses and riders might need.

They attended to the horses first. Two had pulled up lame, one with a rock wedged against the frog in its front hoof. If they weren't sound by morning, the riders would have to locate a spare mount or sit out a day. Taking care of the horses was the ride's foremost rule.

Some of the riders had pledged to fast during part of the ride. Those who would begin their fast tonight were escorted to a special tent, where Dewey, as spiritual advisor, would offer encouragement and help them renew their commitment. He would eat later, after the fasters had gone to sleep.

Angus Barnes and his two daughters helped Ben and some of the other riders feed the horses. Clara sought the warmth of the campfire, where the children had lined up to be fed first. TJ met her with a cup of soup, a piece of fry bread, and a smile when Clara sighed over the first hot sip of supper. More fires were built around the campsite. Riders and supporters gathered, ate, drank coffee, and shared in the warmth, both from the fire and the companionship. People drifted from fire to fire. There was little talk at first. Everyone was hungry and tired, content simply to stand or sit and stare and move sore muscles as little as possible.

Clara followed TJ to one of the camp stoves in search of more coffee. The blue enamel pot had been drained. TJ dipped in a little water. Clara dug the three-pound can of ground coffee out of the box of supplies that was sitting on the pickup's open tailgate.

"We were talking today, a little bit about . . ." Clara realized, having heard so little about the woman, that she wasn't sure how to refer to her. "Ben's mother. He's never told me much about her. I know it's been a long time, but—" She peeled the plastic lid off the coffee can. "He can't seem to remember anything specifically good about her. But your father must have loved her. I mean, there must have been something good . . ." She looked up, peering at her sister-in-law in the smoky shadows cast by a fire blazing several yards away. "Did you get along with her, TJ?"

"Sometimes." TJ rinsed the dregs of old grounds, flinging them into the grass with a quick snap of the wrist. "Stella ran hot and cold. Sometimes she'd make a big fuss over my brother, other times for days she'd act like she didn't even know he was there. She was bored living out in the country. She was a lot younger than my father. She was his second wife, you know."

"Yes, I knew that Ben was her only—"

"My mother died from some kind of an infection after my sister was born," TJ continued as she dipped more water into the pot. "A few years later, along comes Stella. She was pretty. My father was lonesome for a woman. But he's a real upstanding man, you know? He wouldn't just—" She shook her head, an unacceptable notion fluttering off like ash from the campfire.

"So he married her. And then she had Ben, which kinda slowed her down for a while. But then she got tired of staying at home, so she started steppin' out on our father about every other month. Sometimes he'd go find her, bring her back home. Other times he'd wait it out, and she'd come back when she ran out of whatever she'd found out there." She gestured vaguely at the line of trees that formed the shelter belt, the front row illuminated by firelight, the rest, like a tree farm, row on machine-planted row, retreating in darkness. "Then she started taking it out on Ben, so my dad finally just let her go."

Clara peered into the trees, disturbed by the unsettling image of a woman hurting the boy her husband had been. "Ben didn't say that she was mean to him or anything."

"She had a mean tongue, for one thing, but she didn't dare use it on me." TJ took the can from Clara's hands. "Don't tell him I said anything. He doesn't like to think it made any difference to him what she did. And maybe it didn't. He's a pretty tough cowboy." In the midst of measuring coffee grounds she glanced up at Clara. "Isn't he."

"Tough as they come, I'm sure. But I'm not." She shook off her growing concern for Ben as she followed TJ back to the camp stove, walking gingerly. "Oh, God, I am *so* sore."

"Why did you say you were doing all this?"

"For Anna."

"That's right. For Anna." TJ set the pot on the stove and brushed her hands together. "How's my father doing?"

"He stays right out there in front. It's like he has a mission. And Ben—" Clara marveled with a quick *tsk*. "You'd never know this wasn't his idea. It's like he's the wagon master or something."

"Wagon master?" TJ chuckled.

"You know what I mean. He's watching out for the kids and the stragglers, the people like me who were not prepared for this but insisted on doing it anyway." Clara laughed. "Wagon master isn't exactly the right term. *Akicita* might be better."

"*Akicita*, hmm? Warrior society. We don't have those anymore, but if we did . . . my brother?" TJ offered Clara a folding lawn chair, then pulled another one out of the back of the pickup for herself. "I don't know. He's always been a real renegade. My father and him—" She struck her fists together as she sat down in the frayed web of a seat. "Two rams. One old and stubborn, one young and even more stubborn."

"Do you think Ben likes what he's doing now? I mean, finally?" Clara shifted her weight into the half of her seat that still had most of its straps intact, ignoring the aluminum frame's squeaky protest. "You know, he made good money when he was working for the dealership in Bismarck, but he never liked it. It didn't suit him. He'd rather fix up some old wreck that was ready for the junk pile than work on a car that was still under warranty." She gave a small laugh. "He's always at his best when somebody says, 'Yeah, but can you do that blindfolded with your right arm tied behind your back?' "

"That's for sure."

"And he was always—" The memory had suddenly launched itself on her without warning, before she could nip the doleful image in the bud, the one of him looking out there, wishing. Her voice drifted as her mind's eye watched him "—gazing out the window at that little piece of land he wanted to buy someday so he could . . ." He'd mapped it out on a hundred scraps of paper. The little barn, the corral, the shop. She shook her head and sighed. "It was like he was in a cage. Maybe he wasn't cut out for marriage."

"I don't know if any man is cut out for marriage."

"Do you think women are?"

"Not all of them."

"Who does the cutting?" Clara looked at TJ, who had had a husband once but had dispensed with him after he'd wrecked her car one too many times. "I'd really like to know. I'd like to get over there and get one right off the cutting board. Because, you know, they don't label them, so you never know what you're getting."

"They don't label what?"

Both women turned toward the intruding voice. Tanya Beale, the cowgirl from Oklahoma, emerged from the darkness to join them.

"Men," TJ said. "So you never know what you're getting."

Tanya laughed as she squatted next to the camp stove. "Most of 'em are willing to drop their pants any time you say and show you exactly what you're getting."

"Drop his pants?" TJ leaned forward and gaped at the spindly-legged blond as though she weren't sure what species this one was. "As if that tells you anything about what kind of a husband he's gonna make."

"It oughta tell you *some*thing." Tanya turned to Clara for confirmation, gesturing graphically. "Huh? A guy drops his pants, and, I mean, there's his important credentials, right there."

"For marriage?"

"For whatever. Men don't need to hang a sign around their necks. They got it hangin' between their legs."

TJ gave an incredulous hoot. "Have you ever been married, hey?"

"I lived with a guy for three years. Same thing."

"I don't think so."

"Sure it is. It's the same thing. You sleep in the same bed, eat the same food, your money is his money, *his* money is his money." Laughing, Tanya straightened and shoved her hands into the pockets of her short-waisted parka. "It's just like marriage except that when you get tired of each other, splittin' up is easy. You just walk. Neat, clean, simple."

"What about children?" Clara wondered.

"Mine are with my mother. That was my mistake." Tanya studied the ground, then tapped a rock with her needle-toed cowboy boot. "I should'a never had kids. But I did, you know, so . . . what're you gonna do?"

TJ looked at Clara. "You never know what you're getting there, either, right?"

Tanya looked up. "You mean kids? Course, you get knocked up, you know what you're getting. You're getting a kid. But I figured out you don't have to put up with any guy who doesn't treat you right. I don't know about you, but any guy lays a fist on me once, he don't get no second chance. I mean, he's history." She jerked a thumb over her shoulder, which was presumably where the past lay. "And he don't sleep around when he's livin' with me. I've got my pride, you know? I've got house rules. No aces in the hole."

Tanya studied each woman in turn, trying to assess the impression she was making with her hard-line ethics. Interpreting wide-eyed stares as admiration, she smiled. "It's just the same as being married, except you've got your house rules instead of a marriage license. One piece of paper's as good as another."

"You've got this all in writing?"

"Not exactly." She tapped the dark roots at her temple. "Got it all up here."

"Mmmm." Clara had no words.

TJ nodded in agreement. "What exactly made you decide to come on the ride . . . It's Tanya, isn't it?"

"Tanya, yeah. I tell you, I read that story about all these guys goin' on this ride to remember the tragedy at Wounded Knee, like a tribute kind of thing, and my heart just pounded." She slapped her hand over her chest and tipped her head to the side. "I just thought, oh, this is so meaningful. You know, for healing and for kind of an awareness thing, and I thought, jeez, you know? I've gotta do this. I mean, I really felt *called* in a way."

"Really," Clara said, with TJ echoing a syllable behind her.

"For one thing, I'm interested in anything to do with horses. I love horses. Been around 'em all my life. Cowboys, horses . . ."

Tanya glanced over her shoulder, momentarily distracted by a chorus of male laughter at one of the campfires. But she missed only half a beat. "And the Indian people in this country got a real shitty deal, when you think about it. I mean, we've got Indians in Oklahoma, of course, and—" With a quick shrug she launched a small, half-apologetic laugh. "Lots of

Indians, right? I mean, obviously. Cherokee, mostly. Of course, some of them are pretty well off. I mean, they've got more money than I'll ever see, some of them, but what the hell? They got it comin'. If you think about it, they really got screwed by that Cherokee removal deal. That was bad news."

"Sure bothered me when I read it," TJ allowed, glancing at Clara.

"Course, it happened a long time ago, like this Wounded Knee deal. But we can't let it happen again. That's why—" Tanya hugged herself with genuine enthusiasm. "I feel like we're almost making history, don't you? With all those cameras following us?"

"Almost."

"Clara used to teach history," TJ said.

"A teacher?" Tanya sounded surprised. "You're married to Ben, right? He is a very nice—" Her eyes rounded appreciatively. "And what a hunk of cowboy. I mean, you can just tell . . ."

The laughter again drew Tanya's attention to the clutch of men with their faces burnished by firelight, and she drifted away like the proverbial moth drawn to the flame.

"Yes, ma'am, you sure can," Clara muttered.

"I don't think she's gonna last long." TJ shot Clara a conspiratorial smile. "Not if my father hears about her checking out anybody's credentials."

"Hmmm. You know what I think?" Clara reached for the coffeepot with her gloved hand. "I think a certain hunk of a cowboy might appreciate a cup of coffee."

Two cups in hand, she joined Ben at the campfire outside the tipi, where he was swapping tales with Howard, Elliot, and Cheppa. "There's fresh coffee on the camp stove, over by Ben's pickup," she announced as she handed Ben a cup. With his eyes he gave warm thanks.

She offered the second cup with a gesture at large. "I'd go back and bring the pot, but I'm so stiff and so sore, I don't think I can walk that far."

"Just park yourself," Howard said. "We'll help ourselves."

Ben made room for her beside him on the tarp he'd thrown on the ground. "You didn't think you could ride that far either, but you did. It's always the last two miles that seem the longest."

"Right." She used his shoulder for support as she eased herself down. "I may have no concept of distance, but if that's your idea of *two* miles . . ."

" 'Oh, Ben,' " he warbled, imitating her. His eyes sparkled with mischief. " 'I can't go on. I'm going to die. But I'm going to kill you first.' "

She was too tired to smack him, so she laughed. "I did make a fuss, didn't I?"

"I was gettin' worried there. That's exactly what you said when Annie was born. I had to do some fast talkin' then, too." He winked at her. "But she hung in there," he told Howard, seated nearby. "She's tougher than she looks."

"Hell, I know how tough Mrs. Pipestone is," Howard said. "She broke up a fight once, between me and Skunk High Eagle. Grabbed me by the collar." Howard hooked his arm over his shoulder and demonstrated the hold on his own jacket. "Scratched the back of my neck."

"I didn't mean to scratch you, Howard, and I did apologize for that, but as I remember, you were about to make mincemeat out of poor Sidney."

"*Skunk* meat." Howard laughed. "I had a hell of a time explaining those scratches to my girlfriend. She wouldn't believe I got 'em from Mrs. Pipestone."

"You didn't tell her that, did you?" Clara smiled. She enjoyed reminiscing about her teaching days, especially with reformed hellions, like Howard.

"Good thing there were witnesses."

"Oh, dear. Witnesses. Did I transform myself into Mrs. Hyde right before your very eyes?"

"I thought some raving *gigi* had come flyin' down the hall. Caught us off guard is what you did. Threw us off balance."

"The metamorphosis happens rarely, but when it does, I surprise even myself." A prim smile suggested untold potential. "As for my behavior during the last *hundred* miles today, I do feel a teeny weeny bit chagrined. Sort of the way I did the morning after Anna was born, looking back and remembering how—" she glanced at Ben "—vocal I'd been the night before."

"Cha-what?" Cheppa asked Elliot, chortling. "Does she mean she was moanin', moaaanin' the blues?"

"You were there?" Howard asked Ben, sounding genuinely interested. "You watched your kid get born?"

"Watched? Hell, I coached."

"While I did all the hard labor," Clara supplied.

"Damn, I just dropped my ol' lady off at the hospital and told her to call me when she needed a ride home." Howard paused, grinning, but nobody laughed this time. "Just kidding. I checked in later, found out we got a boy."

Ben raised his coffee cup in Howard's direction. "You should'a been there, man."

"I thought I'd just be in the way." Howard shrugged meekly. "She-it, nobody said anything about me stayin', so I beat feet outta there and just let her do her thing."

"I was told—" Ben cast his wife a pointed look "—that if I knew what was good for me, I'd damn sure better be right there for the whole show. Kinda surprised some of those IHS nurses, havin' me stick around. But it turned out to be one hell of a ride." He nodded. "Next time, Howard."

"Next time," he echoed distantly as the fire absorbed his attention. "If she lets me back in the house after this. She didn't really want me to come. She don't trust me as far as she can throw me." Still staring, he chuckled. "Can't imagine why."

Anna appeared in the dim margin of firelight, looking for her parents. Ben waved her over, and Clara made space for her between them.

"We were just trying to sneak a few chips, and Auntie TJ tried to put us on cleanup detail." Anna dropped to her knees, crawled into the wedge between her parents, and rested her head on her father's thigh. "Oh, Daddy, I'm so tired."

"What're you daddying me for, little girl? This was your idea." He smoothed errant locks back from her face and tugged tenderly at her scraggly braid. "You'd better hit the sack so you can get up early and do this all over again tomorrow."

Anna groaned.

Her dad patted her puffy parka. "You're not gettin' saddle sores already, are you?"

"I might be. You get used to it, though, don't you?"

"Some parts of you get used to it. It didn't take me long to get used to bein' *back in the saddle again.*" He sang the last part, and a couple of bass voices around the fire joined in on the last notes, ebbing into a round of chuckles.

"Your dad was one hell of a rodeo cowboy," Elliot said. "You remember that?"

"We've got some pictures," Anna said drowsily.

"You saw Dad ride lots of times, Anna. Don't you remember?" Clara was surprised when Anna rolled her head back and forth. "Has it been that long?"

Ben sighed. "Yeah, it's been a while."

"I remember playing 'pop stand' under the bleachers," Anna recalled dreamily. "I was playing with a girl named Crystal or Jewel or something like that, and we collected a bunch of cups and stuff under there and pretended we had a pop stand." She thought for a moment. "And I remember they had to shoot a horse one time."

"That was a bad scene. Real freak thing, like you hear about somebody fallin' some crazy way and ending up . . ." Ben turned to the men sitting across the fire. "It was that time in Fort Yates when one of the horses broke its back. They had to put him down right there."

"There was this boy who came and told us to come and see, but when I got up to the fence, Dad caught me." Anna sat up as the story flooded back to her. "You picked me up and carried me back toward the pickup, remember? I said, 'Don't let them do it,' and you said, 'He's hurting real bad.' Then I heard the shot. It felt like a crack of lightning slashing right through me, and you said, 'He's okay now.' "

"And you asked me how it felt to die," Ben recalled quietly.

"And you said, 'All the pain stops.' "

"You remember all that?" His eyes were warm with wonder, his smile spreading slowly across his face. "How come you don't remember seein' me ride?"

"I remember thinking, if it could happen to a horse, maybe it could happen to a cowboy, too."

"So you played pop stand. Smart girl." He patted her knee. "Well, Annie-girl, you'd better get to bed, 'cause we're gonna blow *this* pop stand pretty early in the morning. Okay with you?"

She nodded, gave her father a peck on the cheek, then—much to Clara's surprise, for it had been a long time—gave her mother one too. "Good night, parents of mine," she quipped saucily, and headed for the tent.

"Must be hard, with your family in Bismarck and you workin' on the rez," Elliot said. "Everybody's drivin' back and forth these days, one way or the other. You get home on weekends, or what?" No one answered, so he didn't press. "Hell, I didn't even see Bismarck until I was about thirteen."

Ben was uncomfortable with the brief silence that followed. "Indians didn't like to stray too far from home for a while there. They'd say, hell, look what happened to Big Foot's band. I'm stayin' right here." He gestured solicitously. "Bring on the commodity cheese and the chopped beef in a can."

"Hey, Mrs. Pipestone," Howard jumped in, poking his lips out at Clara. "You ever had an Indian fortune cookie?"

"What's that?"

"Piece of fry bread with a food stamp in the middle."

There was knee-slapping laughter, and a resonant *"Tuwale!"* from the other side of the fire. The laughter abated gradually, hanging on with a stray chuckle, then amiable quiet warmed by the sound of crackling wood.

"I never left the rez 'til they drafted me," Elliot said. "Some white guy says, 'You gotta fill out this paper.' " A dry leaf served as a prop, brandished by the storyteller. "I'm an Indian, hey. I'm used to fillin' out papers with form numbers on 'em, so I—" He made a flourishing scrawl in the night air. "Pretty soon I'm way the hell out in bum-fuck Egypt totin' an M-16 and shootin' at anything in the jungle that moves."

"In Egypt?" Clara asked innocently.

"He went to Vietnam," Ben interpreted for her amid the chuckles.

"Oh." She smiled. "That's close."

"Small world," Ben said affectionately. He'd always loved the way she took everything literally. She made it so easy to tell a good joke. "Why haven't you gone to bed yet, Clara-bow? Your eyes are at half-mast."

"Because I enjoy the stories." She sighed dramatically. "And because I don't think I can stand up." But with his help, she did. "Ohhh, I feel like I've aged fifty years in one day. I would give anything for a tub of hot water."

"I'm sure we could—"

"No." She waved Ben's offer away before he could finish it. "No, no. I'm good for another day. At least. Good night, all."

A chorus of good nights followed her, and so did Ben, still chatting. "It's kinda cozy if we all smell alike, you know. Horses, people. Keeps us all on friendly terms." She laughed, and he nodded back over his shoulder at the campfire circle. *"Mitakuye oyasin."*

"Yes," she said with a smile and translated, "All my relatives. They are, aren't they?"

"You fit right in. We couldn't ask for a better straight man." His smile was a little more suggestive than hers. "I could probably come up with enough water for a spit bath."

"You could, huh? Thanks, but I've already taken care of that."

"Damn," he clipped, snapping his fingers.

"You're flirting with me, Ben."

"Am I?"

"Shamelessly."

"I've done plenty of things I'm ashamed of, Clara-bow, but flirtin' with my wife ain't one of 'em." Her lips parted for a retort, but he touched them to forestall it. "Don't. Just let it lay. Wish me good night, okay? And you sleep well."

"Good night, Ben."

There was still plenty of activity around the campfires, but Ben decided to head for the tipi, hit the sack, close his eyes, and fancy himself rating a good-night kiss from his wife before the ride was over. A guy could dream.

Dewey was alone in the tipi, but he was having a hell of a conversation with somebody. Times like this, Ben didn't know whether to let the night shades have their way with the old man or wake him in hopes of driving them away.

Maybe Dewey didn't want them driven away.

On the other hand, maybe they would take him away.

The fires outside brightened the tipi's canvas walls. The interior was cast in shades of gray. Ben knelt beside his father's buffalo-hide pallet and shook him gently. "Are you okay, Dad? Bad dreams?"

The old man woke with a start.

"Look at you," Ben whispered, startled himself by an eerie sense that Dewey had been somewhere else just now, and it hadn't been easy for him to get back. "You're all out of breath. Jesus."

"It's nothing. I dream all the time." The old man settled back down with a sigh. "Even when I'm awake sometimes."

"Are you okay?" Ben adjusted the bedding and tucked the top blanket around his father's shoulders. "You warm enough?"

"I'm never warm enough anymore, *cinks*. I'm old," he closed his eyes. "But not too old to make this journey."

"It's not your age that concerns me. It's your health." Ben set about preparing his own bed, laying the tarp down first, then the foam pad.

"My health *is* what it *is*. It's important to keep going. It gets harder, you know."

"It doesn't have to. You can ride in the pickup with TJ any time."

"There wasn't much snow on the ground. Not at first. But it was cold, and it got colder. No pickups to ride in. Not many horses. Hardly any food." Dewey's voice drifted, becoming thin and hollow. "Be careful for the children, *cinks*. Make sure they get something to eat. And the women with small babies. Make sure—"

Ben unrolled his sleeping bag. "Dad, we don't have any women with babies."

"The most important thing is to keep going, every day. Don't let them catch us. Don't let anyone stop—"

"Nobody's chasin' us." He laid his hand on his father's shoulder, letting him know that it was his turn to be watchful now. He was good enough at least for that. "You need rest, *ate*. Sleep."

"The red roan," Dewey muttered.

"What red roan?" Then he remembered, and he smiled. "You tryin' to over on *my* dreams now, old man? Let it rest now. Let your old head rest."

Ben ducked outside for a cigarette. He'd had enough talk. He wanted solitude. He found it where the horses were penned. He took a seat on the corral rail, smoke wreathing his head, which was hazy on the inside, too. Full of smoky echoes and chilly doubts.

This had to be the worst kind of a fool's errand. Sore muscles, fingers and toes aching with the cold, kids who could hardly stay in the saddle, horses barely broke to ride, people setting out to push themselves way beyond their usual limits, and for what?

For him, it was a chance to be with his wife and daughter, which just showed how desperate a guy could get if he screwed up bad enough. A guy could get to the point where he'd have to turn himself inside out and stand the world on its head just to spend a few days with his family. He was willing to do that because he hoped he might find a way to make some repairs and get his world spinning on its axis again. Surely nobody else on this journey was as desperate as he was, but why would anyone ride all those days over all those miles of desolate, frozen prairie unless his life somehow hung in the balance? And why would anyone think pulling a wild stunt like this would change anything?

He decided the camp surrounding him had to be full of fools and saints. Nothing in between. The normal people were all home sleeping in their beds. They weren't running around in circles all the time, chasing and being chased, never quite certain whether they were getting close or getting away. Normal people weren't desperate. Desperate to catch some elusive pleasure, desperate to avoid getting caught by some shadowy threat. The worst of it was, they could be, as he well remembered, one and the same . . .

"Ben Pipestone?" The pale, beefy bartender tucked the telephone receiver into the pocket of his shoulder. "There's a woman asking for you. You here?"

Ben tugged at the dip in the brim of his hat, taking refuge. Damn, she was like a bloodhound. He'd just barely gotten a buzz on. He was just getting comfortable with the blue cloud that hung in the air, the boozy laughter, the whiskey voice gliding along a greasy steel guitar track, bewailing a loss of some kind.

"A woman or a wife?"

"If you got a wife, I'm bettin' this is her."

"Get your cowboy ass home, *right now*, Ben Pipestone," someone taunted.

"Like hell," Ben grumbled. "Nobody tells me when to go home."

"You sure? I hate to hang up on 'em when they sound like this."

"How does she sound?" He didn't know why he was asking. He wasn't interested.

The bartender shrugged. "Like she really wants you home."

"Like she's moaaanin', moanin' the blues," came the old favorite croon from somewhere down the barstool line.

"Shit." Ben leaned back and flashed a grin over his shoulder. "I used to wish I could sing, Jimmy. Now I wish you could sing." He turned to the bartender. "Tell her I just left."

"Tell her yourself." But when Ben shook his head, the bartender chose a line from his vast repertoire and bellowed it into the phone. "You just missed him." Pause. "Well, he'll probably be along pretty soon. Everything closes up here in about half an hour." Pause. "I wouldn't know that. Sorry."

Ben rapped his knuckles on the bar for another drink.

"She wanted to know if you were driving." The bartender shoved the phone under the counter and eyed Ben's empty glass. "*I* wanna know if you're driving."

"You can ride with us, Ben," came the offer from another barstool.

"Thanks, Jim."

"We're all ridin' with her." Jim White Hawk leaned back, peering past a row of shoulders hunched over their drinks, and gave Ben a nod. "The one at the table, drinkin' the pop and givin' you the eye."

Ben swiveled on his stool, locating the source of interest. The face was a blur. "You takin' me home, honey?"

"Well, sure, cowboy. Where's home?"

"Anywhere I hang my hat. Anywhere I damn well feel like . . ." He slapped his hand on the bar. The gold band on his third finger glared up at him. He made a fist. "I ordered a drink here."

"This is last call."

"Just for me?"

"For everybody."

Ben scowled at the pasty-faced bartender. "You married?"

"Yep."

"Guess that's okay for a bartender." Auto mechanics, too. After an argument with Clara that morning, Ben had admitted to himself, finally, that he was just another two-bit grease monkey. He was never going to fill his PRCA permit by winning enough money during a season to qualify for professional rodeo cowboy status.

He stared at the bottle in the bartender's hand as though it contained deliverance. "The only thing in this life I ever wanted to be was a rodeo cowboy. And I used to be pretty damn good at it. Then I got married."

"And?"

"And I've been married ever since. Come next spring, I'll still be married."

"Come the spring after that, he'll *still* be married," Jim White Hawk gibed good-naturedly.

"Workin' forty hours a week. Mowin' the goddamn grass for no good reason. Crissake, if you're not puttin' up hay, why cut the damn grass?" He watched the plastic beak on the upended bottle measure amber liquid into the shot glass next to his beer. "Tell you what, though, every goddamn time I wanna leave the house, she wants me to come up with some kind of a reason." He raised the shot glass, toasting the bartender. "I'm goin' on a drunk, hey. How's that for a reason? She's got her friends, goddamn, I got mine."

"Do yourself a favor, cowboy. Go on home."

"It'll still be there when I get there. So will she."

And that was true. They had since moved to another house, but it was still true. She was home. She was where his heart was. But he was no longer welcome there.

9

The third day of the ride was a true test of Clara's endurance. She started out sore. By noon every muscle in her body cried for mercy. The cold wind had coated her face with a layer of fine dust. She tasted it in the corners of her mouth. Talking became a gritty task. Simply staying on the horse required her continual effort. The only way to put an end to the torture was to give in to the demands of good common sense, quit the saddle and crawl into a pickup, as Toby Two Bear had done during a midmorning break. It was either that or embrace the misery by telling herself that quitting was not an option for her.

She couldn't stop, she kept telling herself. No stopping. If she stopped, the aching would only get worse. If she stopped, she would get left behind. If she stopped, she wouldn't be there for Anna. If she stopped, she would be a quitter. Nothing worse than a quitter. When the going gets tough, the tough get going. Only babies quit. Only girls quit. Only losers quit. Quitters never lose and losers never quit. She knew the whole routine. She'd been put on notice at an early age, and she was the consummate overachiever. She firmly believed that if she made it through today, it would be easier tomorrow. And she would make it through today.

There were fewer photographers with them now than

there had been when they'd started. There were a couple of video cameramen committed to taping the entire ride. Several foreign journalists were in for the long haul as well. There was, in fact, greater interest from foreign press than domestic. Robert Cady and his faithful truck, Harvey, were still with the program. The vehicles often traveled over a different route, but they had their copies of the itinerary, and they were never too far ahead or behind.

They stopped at the edge of a field for the noon meal. Clara smelled burning sweet grass, and her eyes followed her nose to the source. Dewey had taken the fasters aside for prayers. More and more she appreciated the sacrifice those five men were making. Bologna sandwiches and oranges seemed like a feast, even though every bite was peppered with grit. It was hard-earned grit, blown into her face across the hard-won miles. A little coffee washed it down easily.

The people from the support caravan, particularly the youngsters, were eager to relieve the riders of their horses during the break. Toby Two Bear was talking about "getting back in" soon. He'd been kicked in the foot by one of the other horses, he said, as evidenced by his limp. But he was okay, and he wasn't quitting. Just resting up a little.

"Hey, you know what, Mom? I think I'm developing my own saddle pad." Anna indicated her inner thighs. "It's gonna be like cowhide, no lie."

Ben was laughing when he came up behind them, just polishing off a sandwich. "I've been ridin' all my life, Annie-girl, and I'm here to tell you, it ain't gonna happen. You wearin' long johns?"

"Silk ones, like Mom's."

"Hmm." He raised an appreciative brow as he popped a corner of crust into his mouth. "Tight as those jeans are, I don't know how you'd be gettin' chapped. I've been meanin' to comment on the cut of those jeans, little girl." He gestured for a pirouette, shaking his head with fatherly disapproval as he watched her turn around. "I don't know. I thought the relaxed style was in these days."

"These *are* relaxed."

"Yeah, well, *I* won't be until we get you married off to some . . ." He puffed out his chest and flexed his left arm to illustrate the cut of a man he would require.

"Married off! Jeez, Dad, get with the twentieth century."

"What?" he protested guilelessly.

"Clue him in, Mom." Anna flipped her braid over her shoulder as she backed away, spotting Billie in the chow line. Somebody had just put out a cooler of pop. "Women don't get married off anymore, Dad. Just get me a German shepherd."

Ben shook his head as he watched her walk away. "I still think those jeans are too tight."

"Maybe I should try tighter ones," Clara muttered, absently rubbing the inside of her own thigh. She looked up to find him scowling at the prospect. "Mine are the matronly style, and they're chafing."

"You can take a break any time," he told her. "That's why TJ's followin' along with the trailer. You don't have to keep this up."

"After you," Clara said. She wasn't sure where such a notion had come from, or why she voiced it.

"Just what in the hell—" he adjusted the brim of his hat, then postured, thumbs hooked over the frayed slashes that were the front pockets of his jeans "—is that supposed to mean?"

"It means it's too soon for me to think about throwing in the towel."

"I'm not talking about throwin' in the towel completely. Just givin' it a rest."

"If you can hang in there, then so can I," she said,

deciding her criteria on the spot. "I'm tougher than I look, remember?"

"No doubt about it. Tough as nails. But there's no contest between you and me, Clara. I mean . . ."

"You mean, you're bigger and stronger, so this is easier for you than it is for me."

"Yeah." He shrugged. "Well, that's just the way it is. It's no big—"

"I can do this," she insisted calmly. "I'm not quitting."

"Nobody said—" Ben flapped his arms at his sides, exasperated. "What is with you guys? You and the ol' man both. So damn stubborn, you'd think this was life or death." He stepped back, making a quick cutoff gesture. "I'm just sayin' don't ride yourself into the ground. That's all I'm sayin'."

"Sound advice," she acknowledged. "Are you offering it around to everyone, or just your father and me?"

"I offered it to Toby, and *he* listened. There are maybe one or two people on this ride who think I might just know a little bit about . . ." He sighed, confessing with a candor she told herself not to take too seriously, "There are more than one or two people on this ride that I'm a little concerned about. I know nobody asked me to be. But, you know, Toby . . . he played out the first night. And last night you came pretty close."

"I made it last night, didn't I?" His assenting nod was surprisingly gratifying to her. "I've made a commitment. A vow. I'm sticking with it."

"All the way on horseback," he recounted for her.

"Yes. That's my plan." And she toasted it with the last of her coffee, then swallowed with a firm nod. "Right now, that's my thinking."

"If thinking would get you there, you'd have no problem. You're well-known for your thinking." He presented her the flat of his big hand with a flourish. "After you?"

* * *

The Indian community of Green Grass on the Cheyenne River Sioux Reservation was, in a sparsely populated state dotted with small towns, too small to be listed on most maps. But the cold, tired, famished riders were welcome there. After they held the circle for evening prayers, all they had to do was dismount, and the designated wranglers were there to assist with the horses.

Clara's body was as sore as it had ever been in its thirty-seven years, but she realized that she was not alone in her misery, which made it easier to bear and with less complaint than she would have voiced a week or even a day ago. She saw that her tent had been erected and that wood for the campfires had been gathered, and she silently thanked TJ and the rest of the supporters. At this moment, she valued the barest essentials and wished only for the simplest of pleasures. Like one of the bone-weary horses, she followed the others of her own kind, trusting them to lead her to a resting place, asking no questions, offering no opinions.

Ben caught up with her on the way to the small church with the open door and the lights blazing in every window. He pulled her aside.

"Did I hear somebody say she'd give anything for the use of a bathtub?" His smile flashed in the dim winter twilight. "I've found her one."

"Oh." Clara permitted the marvelous image to enter her mind. "Oh, a bathtub. Where? Wait, I need a towel."

"I have towels."

"And clean—"

"Clothes. Annie helped me out there. If you'll just follow—" he grabbed her arm, grinning as he resolutely set her behind him "—*after* me. Five paces behind."

She hesitated. This was the old joke between them, the test of how badly she wanted him to do something for her.

"For a bathtub?" he said, as if she needed a reminder. "Full of nice, hot water."

With a little whimper, she followed. It was the girlish, petulant sound she used to make in bed sometimes when he had her wanting and he withheld, just briefly, just to make her want even more. That sound alone made it worth his while to do her this service, even if he'd had to beg from door to door for the use of a tub. But it hadn't been that difficult. Members of the tiny community were more than willing to let hot water heaters be drained in behalf of the Wounded Knee riders.

"What about Anna?" she asked, skipping a step to catch up with him as their boots swished through the dry prairie grass toward a small trailer.

"Got her and Billie, TJ, and Dad all taken care of. This place belongs to an old rodeo buddy. Him and his wife are over at the house next door, helpin' get the food ready. Second wife. His first wife lives across the way."

She mounted the wooden steps behind him. She wasn't interested in first and second wives. "I don't care about food, but a bath would put me next door to heaven."

"Next door to heaven, and me with the keys." He set his duffel bag next to the door and tried three keys in the padlock, springing it open with the third one, then led the way inside and turned on the kitchen light. The quarters were cramped but clean and warm. Ben reached through the darkened doorway next to the stove and found another light switch.

Quickly shedding her parka, Clara glimpsed a small blue bathroom sink. She smiled.

Ben tossed his jacket over the back of a chair. "You wanna go after me, then?"

"That would be fine," she said tightly.

"Course, that won't leave much hot water. In fact, we'll probably have to use the same water. I'd say the tank is maybe ten, fifteen gallons." He grinned slowly. "Come to think of it, I wouldn't mind using your bathwater. Might be kinda sexy."

"Dirty bathwater?"

"Sweetened." He handed her the towel he'd pulled out of his bag. "It's all a matter of how you look at it. Sexiness is in the eye of the beholder."

"Pickin's pretty slim, are they?"

"I already picked." From his bag he produced a bra and a pair of lacy white panties. "I like these. I'm gonna enjoy bathing in the runoff from what goes in 'em."

She rolled her eyes incredulously. "Cowboy poetry at its finest. You go ahead. I'd feel as though I had to hurry."

"Not at all. I'll just sit outside the door, imagine you taking your clothes off, listen to you plunk your feet in, one at a time. Then you'll slide down slowly, and when I hear you say 'ahhhh . . . mmmmm . . . heaven . . . ' " He closed his eyes dramatically. "At that moment my own reward will come."

"Really."

"Oh, yeah. Believe me, it will be my pleasure to let you go first." His eyes were full of warm laughter. "After you?"

"If you insist."

He did. And he leaned against the kitchen wall and listened, just as he'd said he would. He listened to the water trickle back into the tub and imagined her soapy hand gliding over her silky skin. He closed his eyes and listened and remembered how it felt to slide a wet hand over her shoulder, breast, belly, and, ah, cleanse her deeply and thoroughly until she sighed for him. Ordinarily he preferred visual stimulation, but since all he could get was the audio, he let the dripping and soft splashing have its way with his head, for one head had a way of bringing out the ache in the other one. That insistent, throbbing, rock-hard ache was contained but hardly inconspicuous in his cowboy-cut jeans. After all the teasing he'd given her, if she came out now, she'd have the last laugh.

She did. She came out looking soft and satisfied, smelling damp and fresh as spring rain, smiling until she caught the hint of lust in his eyes. She glanced down, then away. She moistened her lips. Then her eyes, windows on her own need, sought his again. For one sad, silent moment they were both totally exposed, completely empathetic to each other's hunger.

She couldn't laugh. But she could, in the end, turn away.

The evening meal was served in a tiny church, where riders were given first chance at the food and the folding chairs. Most of the photographers had gone on to Bridger, where many more riders from the South Dakota Sioux reservations would join in the journey. But Robert Cady had stopped in Green Grass. He was particularly interested in the way the communities along the route responded to the ride, for, as he told Clara when they came together over a second cup of coffee, he thought the significance of the ride was reflected in the faces of the people it touched along the way.

Clara thought about the faces they'd met along the way so far, some skeptical or suspicious, some supportive, some even envious. She nodded. "That's a good way of putting it."

"Not that the faces of the riders themselves don't tell the story," he assured her. "They do, *you* do. Quite poignantly. But the difference between the reception in Timber Lake and this one in Green Grass . . ."

"Is like the difference between a wake and a wedding," she finished for him.

"And it isn't a matter of race," Cady said. "You and I are both white."

"Yes, and there are other non-Indians on the ride," Clara mused. "Several white ranchers have given us a place to stay. That reflection you're talking about, you can see it in their faces, too. You're quite right." She realized that it was a relief to talk with this man, not because he mattered to her, but because he did not. She had nothing to prove to him. Their conversation was simply an exchange of words.

"As for what you'll read in *this* rider's face, well, it's early yet," she confided. "The poignancy is liable to turn to pure pain, and then . . ." She sighed. "I'm not a quitter, but I don't suffer well, either."

"Who does?"

"It's a matter of keeping my commitment." She studied the black contents of her cup. "I didn't know what I was getting myself into, really. It's a different world out here." She looked into the eyes that were blue, which made them like hers, a rarity in the present context. And a rarity for them both, being in the minority. "I feel a bit like the robin who got her seasons mixed up or something."

"Ah, but you're not a snowbird, you're a prairie dweller, and the wise prairie dweller knows that winter is the time to hole up and stay warm." He smiled benevolently, knowingly. "And under ordinary circumstances I suspect you would do just that. Just as Big Foot and his band would have done, under ordinary circumstances. We know what drove them." He lifted his brow inquisitively. "Do we know what drives you?"

"I'm not driven." She banished the notion with a jerk of her head. "I'm not by nature much of a risk taker, either. But I will say that my circumstances have not been what I would call ordinary since the day I met Ben Pipestone." She glanced at the door, wondering why she'd bothered to notice when he left the building, probably to smoke a cigarette, and why she glanced reflexively toward the door every now and then, anticipating his return. "For better or for worse, it has never been ordinary."

"Then I envy you . . . and him." Cady took a piece of paper from his pocket and unfolded it, offering it to her. "They were showing me the route. They drew it out for me. After you leave here, you head for Cherry Creek, the area where the refugees from Standing Rock joined up with Big Foot's camp after Sitting Bull's murder. There's not much between here and there." He traced a penciled line with his finger. "You go to Bridger for another vows ceremony for the riders joining up down here. So that's another day's ride." His eyes met hers. "But, then, you must know all this."

"Actually, I'm just along for the ride." She laughed, a little ill at ease for having told him more than she'd intended. "This country is all quite new to me. Hardly the beaten path. I have to trust the people up front." Which was part of her challenge, letting someone else be completely in charge. "I know where we're supposed to end up, but I have absolutely no idea how we'll get there."

"Then it really is an adventure."

"Very much so. And a self-discovery in a way. I was just barely hanging on by the end of the day, but now that I've had a nice hot soak in a bathtub . . . all of a sudden I'm very easy to please." She included her coffee in her pleasures, gesturing with the cup.

"You appreciate the necessities more when they become scarce. But then it becomes easier to unload all the nonessentials. Harvey is big enough to carry everything that's important to me."

"Harvey, your pickup."

He smiled. "I'll bet your horse has a name."

"Yes," she said, responding to his reference with a smile. "Misty Too. Named after the first horse Ben gave me. We had to sell her, but she was such a beautiful—"

"See you found us again, Cady," Ben said, joining them. He carried the scent of woodsmoke, winter-cold air, and the freshly poured coffee he'd acquired along the way.

"From the looks of it, I'm about to lose you again," Cady said, flashing his map. "I probably won't catch up to you again until . . ."

"Bridger's easy enough to find. You wanna keep driving, I'd head down there if I were you." Ben looked at the map, then nodded toward the door. "We're on the Moreau River here. We're headin' for Cherry Creek. You're gonna need a horse if you wanna stick with us, 'cause we'll be ridin' through bum-fuck Egypt." He glanced at Clara, then smiled. "Ever been there, Cady? In your many travels?"

"Can't say that I have."

"You won't get there without a horse."

"Then I guess I won't get there." Cady folded his map and pocketed it. "I don't force any creature to submit to my will. It's not a crusade or anything. Just the way I like to handle that aspect of my life." With a gesture he hastened to add, "I make no judgments, you understand. Horses are a way of life for you people. In some ways, Harvey and I enjoy a similar relationship."

Ben looked confused. "Harvey's your boyfriend?"

"Harvey's my truck."

"Your pickup?" Ben shrugged as he took a sip of coffee. "I make no judgments, either, Cady. Hell, whatever works for you." He grinned mischievously. "Whatever turns ol' Harvey on."

"Just a simple key."

"The key to heaven? Or is it more like the one I've got?" Ben pulled the keys to his friend's trailer from his jacket pocket. "This'll get in right next door to heaven. But like I say, depends on what ol' Harvey likes. I'm pretty good with pickups myself. What is he, a Ford?"

Cady was laughing now. "A Ford, yes."

"I've got a thing for Chevys. But now, a Ford, you never force one o' those babies, either. You give 'em a little grease in a couple places most people don't know about . . ." Ben's eyes sparkled merrily. "Ah, but you do. I can tell, you're a sensitive man."

"You really crack me up, Ben. I've heard about Indian humor, that there's a special character to it."

Clara chuckled. "Actually, the special character is Ben Pipestone."

"I get kinda crazy when I've had a few drinks—" Ben tossed her a wink "—of Clara's bathwater. Damn, that stuff's potent." He folded his arms, balancing his coffee near his elbow, obviously feeling quite full of himself. "That wasn't really good Indian humor, Cady. That was more like cowboy humor. I'm bilingual, you know."

"I'd say you're way beyond bi," the photographer enjoined.

"Hey, good one, Cady." Ben nodded, slipping Clara another familiar look as he lifted his cup. "He *touché*d me pretty good, didn't he?"

"It went right over my head," Clara said, playing it coy.

"I'm sure you both have an appreciation for cowboy and Indian humor," Cady said. "You'll have to teach me the difference. I've always fancied myself a cowboy of sorts."

Ben nearly choked on his coffee. "What the hell's that? A cowboy *of sorts*?"

"Obviously not the kind who rides horses except maybe in some sort of—" Cady twirled his hand with an illustrative flourish "—mythical way."

"Ever worked on a ranch?"

"I'm speaking metaphorically."

"Meta . . . ?" Ben looked at Clara. "Must be a fancy word for bullshitting."

"Oh, Ben," she admonished. "He just means—"

"I don't give a damn how much bull you can throw, it ain't gonna make you no cowboy. Not even *of sorts*."

Cady drew back, wounded. "What have you got against me, Ben?"

"Not a goddamn thing. Just don't try to bullshit a bullshitter." Ben's smile did not touch his eyes. "Or a bullshitter's wife. She's heard it all."

"I'm sure that's good advice."

"Best piece of advice you're likely to come by around here. We don't go throwin' a lot of advice around." He shrugged. "Just bullshit."

Ben felt as though he'd just scored a knockout without even touching his rival. He'd always hated it when Clara got involved in a deep, heavy discussion with a man. She could discuss anything she wanted with another woman, but the sight and sound of his woman having a serious discussion with another man made his blood run hot with resentment. He had to work hard to keep his cool. He had to remind himself that discourse and intercourse were not the same, even though it sure seemed like infidelity—*of sorts*—to him. Especially when the guy was a philosophical smart-ass. The kind whose verbal sparring led to mind-fucking.

But not this time. Not with *this* cowboy's wife.

Clara was pissed at him over it, though, he could tell. She didn't realize what a coup he'd just scored. Hell, it was a man thing. It was the part that really *had* sailed right past her, which left her pretty pissed.

Ignoring the darts her eyes fired at him, he introduced her to Marty Thomas, the owner of the bathtub.

"That was a lifesaver," Clara declared, shaking Marty's callused hand. "Thank you."

Marty nodded. "I've got a girl your daughter's age. They've hit it off pretty good. They're all over to her mother's house." He puckered and pointed his lips at the window. "Just up the way."

"Annie asked me to ask you if you mind if she stays over there tonight," Ben told Clara.

"They're makin' a bunch of caramel rolls for breakfast," Marty said.

"Sounds very nice." Clara shrugged. "I don't mind."

"So you won't have any kids around tonight," Marty said, including both of them in his smile. "Give you a little elbow room, huh?"

Clara looked up at Ben after Marty walked away. "I take it you haven't seen that particular rodeo buddy in a while."

"No, I haven't. Even if I had . . ." Ben's eyes flitted nonchalantly over the heads of the gathering. "I don't discuss my private life with too many people. Everybody knows you're my wife, and until that changes—"

"That's always been part of your problem. You never really talk to people. Half the time you just smart off, like—"

He drilled her with an abrupt stare. "You mean like I did with your friend Cady? He can take a joke, can't he?"

"He's not *my friend*."

"You don't like him? Hell, I thought we were havin' a nice little talk there, like three *compadres*."

"I hardly know him." She returned his heated look. "But I know you, and I know exactly what you were thinking and what you were doing."

"Jesus, I wasn't thinkin' much, and I wasn't *doin'* a goddamn thing."

"Trying to make the poor man feel foolish."

"The *poor man* oughta feel foolish. He looks like a goddamn . . ." He stepped closer and lowered his voice. "I don't like the way he keeps tryin' to get next to you."

"Now you're being foolish." She spoke to him with that schoolmarm self-possession that always got to him when he felt his own confidence suddenly slipping. "You know, I've never understood this," she clipped. "*You're* the one who's always flirting around with other . . ."

"*I'm* the one," he echoed incredulously.

"I'm not like that, and I never have been. My interests are not . . . like that."

"And I've got no right to question anyone else's . . ." He didn't, and he knew it even though he'd yet to accept it.

"No *reason* to. Even if the man were my friend."

Settle down, he told himself. You're exposing your whole goddamn hand, and there's nothing in it but bluff. He folded his arms and eyed Cady across the room. "You think he's married?"

"Divorced."

"He told you that?" *Settle down, Jesus, just let it ride.* But he couldn't. "Hell, why shouldn't he? It's vital information for a guy who's interested in—"

"It holds no interest for *me*. He seems like a perfectly nice man, just to talk with."

Just out of idle curiosity . . . "You don't see the way he looks at you?"

"No, I don't." She laughed mirthlessly. "Oh, Ben, after all these years, you still don't know me."

"I know guys like that, and I know they flock to you like flies on honey." He shrugged. "And when I don't see you shoo 'em away, I figure I got a job to do."

"Really?" Her eyes widened. "Wait a minute," she said, seizing the upper hand. "Could this be the root of all our problems? I'm supposed to shoo away all those tacky little barflies who give you the eye, while you take cheap shots at the honey-sucking flies you seem to think are always hanging all over me? What a scintillating concept!"

A smile played at the corner of his mouth.

"The trouble is," she whispered, glancing askance, "we'd have to be running after each other all the time, wouldn't we? And I've already done my share of that. It did no good. I've learned my lesson." She eyed him pointedly as she backed away. "I'm quite finished."

"Where are you going?"

"Back to my own private little hive."

Ben didn't have much to contribute to the after-supper campfire tales. He watched the flames and brooded, deflecting the occasional attempt to draw him into a story with a laconic grunt. Mentally he was standing guard over Clara's little igloo-style tent, sitting off by itself behind a windbreak of chokecherry bushes. She was just being stubborn, he told himself, secluding herself for a "bout with a pout," as they used to say of Annie. Not that he wasn't a superb sulker in his own right, but since he'd quit drinking, he'd cut back.

Of course, Clara wouldn't know that. Damn, she was bundled up all alone in the little tent, probably shivering to beat hell and too proud to come out and share the best part of the day with the riders. She was one of them. She belonged in the circle. For all the sulky moods she'd coaxed him out of over the years, he figured he owed her one.

"Clara?" He said it just as softly and humbly as his deep voice would allow. "We got a fire goin' over by the tipi. Why don't you come over and sit with us for a while?"

"I'm sleeping," came the cool response from inside.

"Everybody's askin' for you. Auntie Mary, Marvin, Howard." He cleared his throat and dug deep. "Cady's over there, too."

"So?"

"I told him I was just, uh . . ."

"Just kidding?"

"Yeah. Just kidding." He shoved his hands in his jacket pockets and prodded the sod with the toe of his boot. "I told him I'd give him a hat and a pair of boots, a set of steer horns for ol' Harvey, put 'em right up there on the hood . . ."

"And he could play cowboys with the rest of the guys?"

"Yeah. Told him all he needed was the right outfit. He liked that all over." He tipped his head back and smiled into the jet-black night. Myriad stars twinkled as though they, too, were amused. "He laughed. We all laughed. So, you know . . . I apologized."

"What am I supposed to do? Give you a gold star?"

"I came to apologize to you, too." He waited, but silence was his only reward. He missed the warmth of the fire. "You gonna let me in? It's cold out here."

"You won't find it any warmer in here, Ben."

"What's happened to your manners, Clara-bow? I didn't keep you standin' outside when you came to my door the other night."

"Ben—"

He unzipped the door and ducked inside, muttering, "That's my name. It's probably as close as I'll get to a genuine invite."

Her cot creaked as she jerked her head up, the movement of a shadow amid shadows.

"I can't sleep with all that snoring," he said quickly, then chuckled. "It's almost as bad as a fire-breathing furnace." He knelt on the empty sleeping bag next to Clara's. "And ghosts. You listen to my ol' man, he's got all the ancestors in there with us. Place is gettin' pretty crowded."

"Did you arrange for Anna to spend the night elsewhere so that you could—"

"You think there might be ghosts on the ride?" He started pulling off his boots.

She sighed and drew herself back into her cocoon. "Ghost Riders?"

"Ghooost Rii-ders," he crooned softly, and she expelled a quick, soft laugh. "No, I'm serious. I know it's my dad who's the spiritual one, but I hear him talking . . ." He slipped into the envelope of Anna's sleeping bag and stretched out beside his wife as he spoke. "And I almost expect someone to answer. He'll say something like, 'What's to be done? What's to be done, that the people may live?' And then he'll stay real quiet, and I stay real quiet. I don't know if he hears an answer, or if he's still waiting." He chuckled dryly. "I keep hopin' some voice will say to him, 'Get your scrawny ass in that pickup and stay out of the wind, ol' man.' In Lakota, of course, otherwise he won't listen."

"This ride is very important to him."

"Yeah, but he doesn't have to risk . . ." He realized that he really wanted to talk with someone tonight, and God, yes, Clara was the one. "The way I see it now, this whole thing is about living. It's not about dying."

"That's why he asks what must be done that the people may live," she said softly in the respectful tone she always used in speaking of his father.

"Killing himself isn't the answer."

"He's an amazing man. Riding up front like that, sitting up straight and tall." She turned her face to him. In near darkness her words rustled like fine taffeta. "I've watched him, Ben. The way he carries that hoop. He must get tired, but you never see him falter at all. He sits a horse almost . . ." Her sigh was barely audible, but in his ear it sounded as rich as her whispered praise. " . . . almost as well as his son does."

"Almost that good, huh?" He felt his heart swell a little as he turned on his back. "Too bad we don't have a smoke hole in here. I made a nice little fire in the tipi. He said he was cold, and that was the best I could do for him." He chuckled. "He said I *could* go out and find him a hot-blooded woman, but hell, I'm no genie."

"You found me a bathtub."

"Maybe I am a genie, huh?" He rolled to his side again, edging his face closer to the dream-scented bundle that contained his sweet wife. "If you rub my belly, I bet I could grant you a wish."

"Oh, Ben." She let slip a dreamy sigh. "How can I be so mad at you one minute and so . . ."

"So what?"

"So sad. You make me laugh, and then you make me . . . you make me want things to be the way they were, and I have to remember that they can't be that way anymore."

"Things can be different," he ventured, having spent two years dreaming up the concept. And then, as long as he'd gone that far, he suggested quietly, "They can be better."

"I can't trust you, Ben. Not over the long haul. You broke the one promise that . . ." Her voice dropped to a whisper. "For a woman, it's the bottom-line promise. And it's broken. It's ruined. Nothing can fix—" the naming of it caught in her throat "—a thing like that."

"Then why haven't you divorced me?"

"Because of—"

"Don't say, because of Annie. That's not fair to her. It's between you and me." He reached for her, laying his hand lightly atop the sleeping bag and her shoulder within. "I want you to be happy, Clara."

She lay still and quiet. Then, in a small voice, "Maybe *you* should divorce *me*."

"I have no reason to." He moved his cold-stiffened fingers only slightly, wishing them beneath the insulated fabric. "You've got all the reason in the world."

"Yes, I do. I do."

Hearing only regret in her voice, he decided to take a chance. "Tell you what," he whispered as he located the zipper on her bag. "We'll both be a lot warmer if we zip these bags together."

She clutched hers to her chin, but the zipper was on its way down. "I can't sleep with you, Ben."

"Sure you can." He smiled in the dark, amazing even himself with his deft zipping. "You just can't have sex with me."

"As long as you understand that."

She didn't fight him, and that, too, amazed him. But, then, it was cold, and in the absence of a fire, sharing body heat made perfect sense. So he drew her into his arms.

She stiffened a little at first, but then she softened and filled in the contours of his body like melted wax, declaring on a sigh, "Your body's still so warm."

"Still alive and kickin'," he said with a deep chuckle. "I may be pinin' for you, honey, but I ain't no damn suicidal Romeo."

"I mean, your skin always felt so warm next to mine. *Compared* to mine."

"Dark colors soak up the heat, right? White reflects it. And you've got the whitest damn feet, Clara-bow. Like two snowballs."

Hers sought his in the bottom of the sack. She wiggled her toes. "I'm wearing three pairs of socks."

"I can still feel those snowballs." The low cot groaned like an old screen door as he shifted her within his embrace, turning her back to him so that he could curl around her. "It's good to hold you like this."

"Kind of awkward with these cots."

"Doesn't matter." He made one more adjustment so that she hardly touched the cot at all. He was her bed, his thigh supporting her lower body. And his lower body responded predictably.

"Ben?"

"Just ignore it. Maybe it'll go away." But it got worse when she shifted her hips. "Maybe not."

"Ben . . ."

"Have a heart, honey. Let the little guy sleep with us. He's got no place else to go."

She groaned, trying hard not to laugh. "He's not so little."

"Compared to what?" *Jesus, Pipestone, ruin it right away, why don't you?* "Forget I said that. I can make him behave. I swear. I put him through obedience training, and he listens real good now."

"But *you* don't. Ben, please . . ."

"I will," he whispered, flattening his hand over her collarbone, sliding his palm over the silk underwear that covered her from her ankles to her neck. "I'll make you feel good, Clara. Warm and sleepy and—"

"I don't want to." She lay still in his arms, hardly breathing, and he knew she was lying. But he also knew she felt compelled to say the words. "I don't want to feel good, Ben."

"Don't, then." He cupped her silk-covered breasts in his hands and simply held them. For a moment, that was all. For a moment they merely warmed to each other's touch, her breasts, his palms. He swept her hair away from the side of her neck with the side of his face and pressed his lips into the hollow behind her ear. His fingers stirred slowly, circling gradually, caressing gently, taking their time closing in on her nipples. Like a frightened doe she lay absolutely still in his arms. He sensitized her carefully, moving in on his target without rushing, anticipating the quick indrawn breath that was his signal to ply his thumbs provocatively.

"Don't feel anything when I do this," he whispered. "Don't tingle." He slipped his hands beneath her silk shirt. Her chest rose on a deep breath, drawing her breasts higher, dragging her nipples against his palms. "Uh-oh, honey, you're turning warm and tingly inside, I can tell."

She whimpered.

"Don't be feelin' good now. Don't—"

But he knew exactly what he'd started, exactly what she needed, and exactly how much it would take to satisfy her.

"I won't . . ."

"I know," he whispered close to her ear as he scissored her nipples gently between his fingers. "I won't ask you to. Just let me touch you, that's all I ask." He slid his hand over her softly rounded belly, remembering a time when it had been heavily round and hard like a melon. It had been like that because he had planted his seed inside her wondrous body.

His little finger strayed beneath the waistband of her long silk pants, leading the way for his other fingers. She moaned and muttered some words of exception as his fingertips crept into her crisp thatch of curls. He closed his eyes, tucked his face against her neck, and inhaled the fresh scent of her skin as he slid his middle finger along the damp cleft between her legs, carefully parting the sweet folds of her most intimate flesh. He loved the breathless way she said his name. He could feel her trembling deep inside.

"This is just for you, honey. I promise not to . . ."

"Not to stop." Her plea was fine and delicate, like the touch of crystal on crystal.

"Not to stop. Not to stop." His hand stilled. His heart was near bursting. "I love you, Clara. I can't stop that, either."

She stiffened. "Don't tell me that."

"It's true, I swear."

"You're a liar, Ben," she whispered desperately, her voice suddenly sodden and heavy with unshed tears. "You taunt and you tease, and you . . ."

"I love you," he whispered again. He knew her. He knew how to touch her and where and how much, holding her, cherishing even her curses because he could feel her fulfillment coming, coming hard and fast.

Her appeal became a reedy litany. "Ben, oh, don't. Don't do . . . this . . ." Her trembling quickened.

"Does it hurt?" He was suddenly frightened by the intensity of her response, shaken when she reached back and gripped his thigh. "Clara?"

"Yes, it hurts, it hurts, don't stop . . ."

He didn't. Not until she gasped and gave herself over to the pleasure. But she was crying, too.

"I'm sorry," he whispered, stroking her hair. "I'm sorry, Clara, I'm sorry."

"I hate you," she hissed. But she turned to him and held him tight, shuddering in his arms and weeping against his neck. "I hate you, Ben Pipestone, I hate you, I hate you so much."

The words cut him to the quick even though he only half believed them. Part of her hated part of him, yes, but there was more. Much more.

"Do you want me to go?"

"No!" She clung to him, her nails digging into his back. "Don't you dare."

"What can I do?" The fires of hell burned in his throat. It hurt to swallow, but that was the only way to get his offer out. "Anything, anything you ask. Just tell me, honey, what can I do?"

"Tell me it isn't true," she sobbed. "Tell me you didn't really . . ."

"Would you take me back then?"

She drew a wobbly breath. "I want you back. You know that."

"But you don't want any more lies, do you?"

"No." She gripped him hard, pulling on him as if to shake some sense into him. "I want you to make it not be a lie."

He sighed. "You lied when you said you hated me."

"No, I didn't."

"I know you, Clara." He stroked her hair. "You wouldn't let me touch you the way I just did if you hated me."

"Does it hurt to hear me say it?"

"Yes."

"Then I *hate* you." She rammed her head against his breastbone. "I wish you were dead. I wish I didn't have to look at you and think of you with . . . with someone . . . holding someone . . ." A terrible sob tore from her throat, chilling him to the marrow. "*Please*, Ben, tell me it didn't happen."

"I can't." And it was killing him, certainly deadening

him. He wished he could die, or cry, or do anything but hurt her more. "I won't lie to you anymore. All I can say is I'm sorry."

She lifted her head, and he felt the warm, damp breath of her question against his neck. "Why doesn't that help?"

"Because it doesn't make it go away. Only a genie could make it go away."

A long, desolate, hollow sigh seemed to purge her. She shivered, then settled quietly in his arms. "Or a shaman, maybe," she said softly. "Could a shaman?"

"You'll have to ask Cady. Maybe he can remember back. Get in touch with his primitive self." But there was no refuge for him in sarcasm. He closed his eyes. "I'm no shaman. I'm no genie. I'm just an ordinary man. I can't undo what I've done."

"You shouldn't have done it."

"I know. Believe me, I know." What he didn't know was how she could stand to hold his wretched body so tightly in her arms.

Neither did she, but at the moment, knowing meant nothing. Feeling was everything.

"It hurts worse now than it did the day you first told me," she confided, trusting him now with her pain.

"If you want me to go—"

"I don't." The embrace of the man who'd betrayed her seemed an improbable place for any self-respecting woman to find comfort, but there it was. "I don't want to hurt alone. And I don't want to hurt with anyone else."

"Jesus," he whispered, "we make a hell of a pair."

10

She had not permitted herself to grieve over the loss of her husband. One grieved for the dead, not for the living. Clara had lost her father when she was in her teens, and over a stiff upper lip, she'd shed the proper tears in the proper way. She'd also had a miscarriage, but that was something she found hard to think about. So she didn't. It was the child that never was, and so it was best left buried where it was, in a never-never land in the past. Before the ride, she had done just that, without vacillating.

Before the ride, she had taken that stiff-upper-lip approach and done a lot of things without vacillating.

After spending a rest day at Green Grass, the riders moved on. A few riders left the group to return to their jobs, but many more joined in. It was in the vicinity of Cherry Creek that the Hunkpapa from Standing Rock had sought refuge with Big Foot's Minneconjou band a century ago. Upon hearing of Sitting Bull's murder and of the troops that had been dispatched to hunt down the Ghost Dancers, Big Foot had decided to move his band of about four hundred south to Pine Ridge, where Red Cloud and his Oglala people would offer them sanctuary and much-needed food.

So, too, did the twentieth-century Standing Rock riders arrive near the old campsite. At the small commu-

232

nity of Bridger, South Dakota, they were joined by riders from Pine Ridge and Cheyenne River Reservations. There were also a few more non-Indians and a shuffling about of the media. More vows were made. More speeches were given. More people publicly took stock of who they were, where they were, and where they wanted to go.

Dewey spoke of seeking *wolakota*, which would manifest itself as an extraordinary peace that would be more than an absence of war or a wary truce. And, as always, he spoke of the importance of harmony, trust, and respect.

"This ride is a sacrifice. It is a prayer for *wolakota*. Each day, from now on, we pray for a special piece of *wolakota*. We dedicate tomorrow to the children. And not to ours only, but to children everywhere. We remember those who were cut down on the banks of Wounded Knee Creek a hundred years ago. But the same thing happens now, today, for lack of caring, for lack of respect, for lack of remembering. We pray for those who are cut down in the streets every day, here in this country."

He lifted his gnarled hands and made a circular gesture. "Everywhere, in all countries. The children who have no place to go, who have nothing to eat. We pray for them. The children who are betrayed by the ones they depend on to care for them. We pray for them. *Wolakota* for the children. This is what we ask. Tomorrow we ride for the children."

That night there was no camp. Some of the riders stayed with local families. Others, including the Pipestones, slept on the floor of the community building. The following morning was the coldest so far. It took the rising sun to edge the mercury above the zero mark. After breakfast the drum summoned the riders into the circle, where Dewey offered prayers. Some of the riders sang a strong-heart song, and many of the women trilled, "Li li li li!" The drum continued to sound the steady rhythm after the echo of the voices had faded, becoming the rhythm of the earth's heartbeat. Clara hugged her daughter, the child who would soon be a woman, then watched Anna saddle her own horse, kiss her father's cheek, mount up, and join her friends.

It was a cold, crisp day, but with little wind and sporadic flurries of small, harmless snowflakes. The call to pray for the children sent each rider into a quiet place that morning. Saddles creaked. Bridles clinked. Prairie sod muffled the hoofbeats. An occasional whinny was answered by a mist-making snort. Pressing on toward their destination, most of the riders had retreated to private places in their minds, places where they touched the lives of children . . .

Clara did not want to be pregnant again. Not now. Anna was nine years old, and Clara had begun to enjoy the fact that she no longer had a baby in the house. Anna was becoming less dependent on her parents for the little things. She dressed herself for school. She could get herself a bowl of cereal or a glass of juice without making a mess. She could walk to the sitter's house after school. She could read. She could write. She could use the telephone. Clara loved her job at the museum, and even though she believed that she was a good mother, certainly a responsible parent, she had to admit that she liked feeling less tied down. She wanted another child, but not right now. Ben wanted another child, but he wasn't in any hurry, either. Lots of people spaced their children further apart nowadays.

They had moved to Bismarck for better jobs. For Ben it meant a steady job with a regular paycheck, which was what he'd said he wanted. For Clara, it was a career goal come true. For both of them, it was a piece of the American dream. After years of reservation housing assignments, renting, moving, renting something else, they'd finally bought a house.

In some ways they were finally settled. In others, they were not. Even though Ben had initiated the move, there were times when Clara knew his whole heart wasn't in it. He'd get used to it, she told herself. He made friends easily—more easily than she did, in fact. She didn't mind if he went out with his buddies from work on occasion. She didn't mind if he went back to Little Eagle once in a while for a weekend. Sometimes she and Anna went along. Other times he didn't tell her he was going, and those . . . well, true, those were the bad times, but that didn't happen very often. It wasn't a regular habit. It wasn't a threat. After all, he was her husband; she was his wife. They both knew the full meaning of those words.

But another pregnancy, this one unplanned, this one not on Clara's master schedule. She wasn't *un*happy about it, but she wished—and she made the wish often—that it had not happened. Not now.

It couldn't be erased, but in the end it was undone.

She was in her fourth month. Nothing showed. Hardly anyone knew. And because the undoing was caused by a fall—an icy sidewalk, the turn of an ankle, a terrible tumble and a hard landing—she had a ready reason to be out of commission for a few days. She didn't have to discuss it with anyone. She didn't want to discuss it, and neither did Ben. It wasn't meant to be, she told herself. All for the best.

The fact that she'd been angry wasn't mentioned. Working late, waiting for him to pick her up at the museum, worried about Anna getting picked up late, too, pacing, pacing. The instant she'd seen the headlights, she'd headed out the door and down the steps. The slip, the fall, all of it had all happened so quickly. He was at her side immediately to help her, to lift her off the side-walk at the bottom of the steps and put her in the car. She didn't ask where he'd been—she could smell the smoke and the beer—but his balance was sure and steady.

And thank God it was, for she was in pain. She'd strained her back, and she was hurting deep inside her belly. Fear seized her, along with insidious guilt. She sat beside him in the car, suffering silently, trying to stem the tide of pain by sheer dint of her will. But there was blood seeping between her legs. God forgive her, she had caused this to happen. The careless blink of an eye, a misstep, a secret wish. This was her fault.

She came away from that night convinced she'd wished the baby away.

Ben rode flank much of the day, watching out for the newcomers, especially the younger ones. Toby Two Bear was back in action, bobbing along with more assurance at the trot. Another girl Annie's age had joined the ride. She showed Billie and Annie how to keep their legs warm the way the women had in the old days, simply by draping a wool blanket over the saddle and folding it back over their legs. Annie shared the trick with her mother, and they all rode together in a bunch. He watched them surreptitiously, taking fierce pride in their strength and beauty. His wife. His only child.

But this was the day to remember that there might have been another child. This was the day to confront one of his gut-gnawing demons . . .

Ben couldn't believe Clara was pregnant. He'd given up on the notion of having another child. He'd given up on a lot of notions. He'd never quite made it as a bronc rider. He'd been a big name in his own backyard, but he'd never turned pro. He earned his living as an auto mechanic. His wife worked fewer hours and earned more money than he did. She enjoyed her job more all the time. He liked his less.

Over the years he'd moved in and out, over and up, through the gate and down the road, but whatever he was trying to get away from kept following him. Whatever he was looking for kept eluding him. He felt boxed in. He wasn't sure who he was or who he wanted to be.

But he knew that whenever he got to drinking, nobody could touch him. When he was drinking hard, nobody wanted to, which was the whole idea. He was still a cowboy, and goddamn it, nobody could stop him from doing anything he damn well pleased.

The night Clara lost the baby, he'd damn well pleased to stop in at the Silver Dollar in Mandan for a beer. Clara was working late, so he had time to unwind a little bit before he picked her up. He was supposed to be working on his pickup so she could have the car back, but hell, he'd been working on other people's transmissions all week. His own could wait another day.

He also damn well pleased to shoot some pool with Marian Anders, who'd let him know on more than a few occasions that she would be available for a quick tumble if he were ever interested. She hadn't told him in so many words, but she had a way of pouring on the body language. Not that he planned to take her up on it, but it was nice to know he hadn't lost his appeal after being out of circulation for so long. That night they more or less ran into each other in the parking lot and ended up feeling each other out. Physically.

He was feeling pretty good when he left Mandan, but as soon as he crossed the bridge and saw the sign for the exit to the state capitol, he got hit in the face with a bad case of the guilts. To boot, he was late, but with a few beers under his belt and late autumn ice glazing the roads, he had to hold the speed down.

The minute Clara shoved the door open, he knew she was pissed. He could tell by the purposeful way she tossed her hair and shifted an armload of books from one hip to the other. He figured he'd better get his ass in gear and help her. He threw the car into park, sneaking a peek at himself in the rearview mirror as he stepped on the parking brake. His eyes glowed like a sonuvabitch, and pure wickedness was written all over his face. But at least it wasn't written in lipstick.

He didn't see Clara miss the first step, but he caught the motion of her fall out of the corner of his eye. *Holy Mother.* Instantly sober, he ejected himself out of the car on a prayer and a curse—the former for his wife and unborn child, the latter aimed at himself.

Punish me, not them.

He lifted her into his arms, put her in the car, and made up his mind to head for the emergency room only a few blocks away, all without saying a word. He couldn't speak, couldn't bring himself to ask, couldn't say what he was thinking.

Punish me, not them.

"Ben, I think I'm bleeding."

Oh, Jesus, God.

He ran a red light.

"Ben, I'mmmm—" Eyes shut tight, she dropped her head back against the neck rest.

"Clara?"

She clutched her middle with one hand and grabbed his thigh just above his knee with the other, squeezing the muscle until he thought his kneecap would pop off. But he had no objections. He had no *words*. No help, no comfort, nothing. He was afraid to take his eyes off the road or his hand off the wheel, afraid if he touched her, he'd make it worse.

"Take me to . . ."

"We're almost there."

But it was too late. He came away from that night convinced he'd caused Clara's fall as surely as if he had pushed her down the steps. They spoke little of the loss. Guilt oozed into the fissures in their marriage, festered and bloated, eroding the rift into a gulf between them.

And guilt begat more of the same.

Anna reclaimed her bed in the little tent that night. She and Clara zipped their sleeping bags together and heated the greater pocket with their bodies, which took some time. Time to huddle and shiver and whisper in the dark, like two friends at a slumber party. They shared Anna's remedy for chapped lips, giggled about how funny Cheppa Four Dog had looked when his saddle had slipped that afternoon, shared their concern for Dewey, and bemoaned the fact that Anna's period was due any day. It was the first time Anna had mentioned her period in such an easy, matter-of-fact way, at least to her mother. For Clara, it was a benchmark.

They had always been, would always be, mother and daughter. But *friends*, Clara marveled. Anna was growing up so fast. Maybe it wouldn't be so hard to lose her little girl if she was gaining a close woman friend.

"Mom?"

"Hmm?"

A long pause prefaced the change of subject. "How do you pray?"

"Well, you . . . you talk to God."

"No, I mean, how do *you* pray? Out loud, or inside your head?"

"Both," Clara said after a moment's consideration. "Probably more inside my head."

"I asked Dad, and he says sometimes he prays the way Lala does, out loud in Lakota. Like when they do a sweat, each one offers his own prayers. It's dark inside the lodge, so it feels private, but there's not much room, so you're close to the earth and close to the other people. So Dad says you share things more easily."

"Like now?" Clara asked.

"Yeah. But they've got steam." Anna snuggled against her mother's side. "That's what we need in here. Some steam."

"If we keep talking, between us we should be able to generate plenty of hot air, don't you think?"

"You, maybe, if you start lecturing."

"I won't," Clara promised. "Let's just talk." And she waited quietly for Anna to take the lead again.

There was a long silence. Then, "Is it all right to talk about Dad?"

"Behind his back?"

"About how we feel about him and how he's . . . how he's really doing now."

"We can try," Clara ventured. "But we have to remember that I'm not his daughter, and you're not his wife."

"Yeah, well, that's easy enough. But we both still talk to him." Pause. "Right?"

"Right." Clara patted Anna's arm. "Recently Dad and I have been talking. Honestly."

"And not just about me," Anna pointed out. "Right?"

"Right."

"That's good. Because there's other stuff you could talk about that's *almost* as important."

"Like what?"

"I can't think of anything myself, but . . ."

Clara laughed.

"I think Dad oughta be the next pipe carrier, don't you?"

"I think that's between him and your grandfather." And maybe Anna, too. In another life, Clara had hoped he would, but she had nothing to say about it now. Nothing.

"When I see Dad helping with the ceremonies and stuff, it's like he really wants to get into it, but he's holding back. Why do you think he does that?"

It was a child-woman's question about the man who lived inside her hero, asked of a woman who had lost touch with the hero who lived inside her man.

"I think it's called an approach-avoidance conflict."

Anna sighed. "Which means?"

"I think he believes more deeply than he's willing to admit. But he's afraid of commitments."

"Why?"

"I don't know." But she'd thought about it. Lately she'd thought about it a lot. "He hardly ever talks about his mother, but you know she deserted him when he was a little boy. I don't think he wants to admit how much that hurt him. Maybe it has something to do with that."

Anna took a moment to mull the theory over. "Why would that keep him from becoming the pipe bearer?"

"He always says that all he ever wanted to be was a cowboy." More than once Clara had told him that the claim sounded like a cop-out. In truth, he was that and more, but now she wondered whether he'd ever realized it. For her part, she couldn't remember whether she'd ever told him. "And a father, of course, a good one. He'll always be your father, Anna. He'll never—"

"I know that. I know he loves me." Tentatively Anna touched her mother's hand. "I know he loves you, too."

"In his way, I guess he does," Clara admitted with a shallow sigh.

"God, you *know* he does. You should see the way he looks at you sometimes when you're not looking."

Good try, Clara almost said, but she caught herself in time and asked instead, "How does he look at me when I'm not looking?"

"Like you're the ultimate grand prize."

"Really?" She chuckled. "Only when I'm not looking, huh?"

"I can just *imagine* how he must look at you when *I'm* not looking. Probably like you're the grand prize in a *Playboy* magazine sweepstakes, huh? But I'm not about to take that kind of imagining too far."

"Anna . . ."

"But there's one thing I wonder about sometimes, and today, when I was thinking a lot about children—I was thinking about other kids I know and the kids you're always reminding me about who are starving in Africa, and I was thinking, yeah, they really are, and I need to pray for them and stuff—but I kept coming back to this question I have about . . ."

She wound down to an abrupt halt and teetered there for a moment, as though she were trying to decide whether she wanted to take the plunge off the high dive. Then, quickly, "How come you only had one kid?"

Clara swallowed audibly.

"And don't give me that old line about how I filled your lives and you were just so blessed. I really wanna know. How come?"

"I lost one," Clara said quietly, her voice gone unexpectedly hoarse.

"Lost?"

In the dark she nodded once. "A baby. I had a miscarriage."

"How?"

"I had a bad fall. Slipped on the ice. Remember? I was in the hospital overnight."

"Oh, yeah," Anna recalled. "You said you hurt your back."

"I did. I hurt my back, too. But I was . . ." Her voice drifted. Pins and needles invaded her throat. "I was less than four months along. We thought we'd tell you we were having a baby about the time it started to show so you wouldn't have so long to wait. And then we . . ." Didn't think we should tell you. Didn't want you to be sad. Didn't want to think or talk or be sad ourselves, and so we avoided . . . *avoided approaching* . . .

"I kinda thought something bad had happened, but I wasn't sure what." Anna turned on her side and pillowed her head on her arm. "You guys both seemed sad, and then after that . . . different."

"It was a sad time, but maybe it was for the best in a way."

"What way?"

"Not that I didn't want the baby, or that it wouldn't've been . . ." Liar. *Liar.* " . . . welcome. It's just that . . ."

Just that it wasn't the right time? Just that Clara Pipestone's schedule has always been inviolate?

"Did it hurt? I mean, what's it like? Are there pains,
like with having a baby?"

"Not as bad, but yes, there are contractions. And
blood. And grief." *And guilt. Admit it. It won't kill you
to admit it.*

"And because you carry the baby in your body . . ."
Clara proceeded slowly, softly, treading lightly, speaking
carefully. "Because it was growing within you, you feel
responsible. You think, maybe I was being careless."
Yes, that's right. "Maybe . . . maybe I should have worn
different shoes. I shouldn't have been carrying those
books, I shouldn't have been working late, and I should
have watched my step, every single step."

It was good to get the words out. They sounded a little
foolish, uttered aloud, but it was good to have them out,
even though somewhere deep inside her they'd left a
tender, quivering little hollow behind them. It was a
place that needed filling, but she told herself not to rush
this time. Let it be what it was for a while. A sadness.
And it was okay to let it be.

"It wasn't your fault, Mom."

It took Clara a moment to find her voice. "How do
you know?"

"Because I know how you are. You worry about
everything." Within the now warm cocoon, daughter's
hand touched mother's again. "Accidents can happen to
anyone. Anytime, anywhere. That's just the way life is."

"That's true. When did you become so wise?"

Both at once they pressed their smiles against the
darkness.

Then Clara said, "It would be nice to have another
child. A brother or sister for you."

"You're not too old, are you? I mean, you're gettin'
there, I know, but you've got a few more good years
left, haven't you?"

"I hope so." Clara considered the question seriously. "No, I don't think thirty-seven is too old."

"Well, even if you got to work on it right now, you'd be thirty-eight. So what I think you oughta do is patch it up with Dad and get goin' on it."

"Anna . . ."

"Here it comes," the girl quipped, as yet well versed in few areas, but she could echo her mother's standard monologues perfectly. "*An-naa.* Your father and I are no longer *getting it going*, or getting it on, as it were."

The impression was impeccable, true to Clara's inflection and character, if not her exact wording. There was nothing she could do but laugh through the pain.

Encouraging Anna to go on.

"So you mustn't think the stork might still be dropping a little Pipestone bundle on our doorstep, Anna. You mustn't get your hopes up. You mustn't—" during the pause Anna's humorous tone vanished "—hope."

"Do I sound like that?"

"Sometimes."

"What a Scrooge, huh?"

"Sometimes." Anna's voice was all hers now, as were her hopes and fears. "I've seen the way you look at Dad, too. And I know there's something you're not telling me. Like you didn't wanna tell me about the baby."

"There are some things between Dad and me that are private." Clara chose her words carefully, remembering that Anna had many friends, but only one mother. "It's not a matter of keeping something from you. It's a matter of . . . of issues that really don't have anything to do with you or with anyone else."

That wasn't quite true, but close enough.

"You mean the kind of stuff they talk about on 'Geraldo'? Stuff that's nobody else's business but everybody wants to talk about?"

"It's nothing I would want to . . ." The ice was getting

thin here. "It's nothing *to* talk about, really. Our marriage simply isn't . . . viable."

"Come on, Mom. It's me, Anna. Not *viable*, for God's sake. I've seen you looking at all those old pictures in the albums." Her voice thickened. "And I've seen you cry sometimes when you look at them, which makes me get all choked up, too."

"Oh, sweetheart . . ."

Anna took a deep breath. "Some things Dad used to do really bothered me. Like when he'd get drunk and act stupid."

"He didn't do that very often, and he wasn't—"

"He wasn't mean, I know. But he'd take off, and I knew you were worried, so I was worried. I thought he might not come back. Or when he did, you'd argue. I remember finding him on the couch once and thinking there was something wrong 'cause I couldn't wake him up." There was a long pause. Then, in a voice that was a hush within a hush, "And there was this one time that I saw him on the news."

"On the news?"

"On TV. You never heard about it?"

Had to be a sports item, but Clara couldn't recall anything from his rodeo days. "What was he on the news for?"

"It was when he went to treatment, or right before. It was something about drunks getting picked up off the streets and people getting arrested for DUI, and they showed the cops making the arrests. Most of the people getting picked up happened to be Indians, of course. You'd think nobody else ever gets drunk around here." Anna paused. "One of them was Dad."

Clara was dumbfounded. "On television?"

"Yeah, it was pretty embarrassing."

"Does he know you saw it?"

"Yeah. I told him when I went to that counseling session with him for his treatment program."

"Why didn't you tell me?"

"Maybe for the same reason you didn't tell me about the baby."

Ah, yes, Clara thought. Protection.

"I never asked you because I was just hoping you hadn't seen it," Anna explained. "And I hoped no one would tell you. I couldn't imagine anyone coming up to you and saying, 'I saw your husband get arrested on the news,' but you never know. Did you know they print that stuff in the newspaper?"

"I never read that section." Feeling downright stupid, Clara sighed. "Another reason why the wife was the last to know."

"Yeah, well, some people read it. Then they ask their kids, 'Hey, don't you know somebody named Pipestone? Wonder if she's related to this guy who got charged with DUI.' "

"Oh, no."

"So there's no point in trying to keep secrets from kids. They find out."

"The hard way," Clara said, imagining what Anna must have seen, what she must have heard, what she had to have suffered in silence. "Just out of curiosity, Anna, whom were you trying to protect? Dad or me?"

"You were mad enough at him already."

"So—"

"But the thing is, now he's quit. He hasn't had a drink in two years. I think that's really good. Don't you?"

"Yes, I do."

"They oughta put something like *that* in the news once. Think anybody'd be interested?"

"We are," Clara said quietly. And saying it took her one step closer to believing in Ben's sobriety. That it was real and honest and, yes, good.

"Yeah." Ann rested her head on her mother's shoulder. "I'm sorry about the baby, Mom. Tomorrow I think I'm gonna pray some more for the children, and maybe for parents who've lost children. That must be hard. I don't know if I'd want to be a mother." She sighed. A deep, world-weary, thirteen-year-old sigh. "I don't even know if I wanna be a woman. God. All the stuff you gotta worry about."

"Be a girl a while longer, sweetheart. Let me do the worrying."

"Okay." Anna snuggled closer. "You're good at it."

"Kiktapo!" came the predawn announcement outside Clara's tent. The bass drum sounded ominous, like distant, early morning thunder. "Everybody up!"

"Oh, God." Clara poked her nose over the edge of the sleeping bag. "This body does not want to move." Or feel the cold outside her cocoon. Or put her feet into cold boots.

But her daughter dragged her up. Once the cocoon's seam was popped open, the butterflies couldn't flutter around fast enough, white breath puffing as they piled on the clothes. Clara made a mental note to dedicate at least one thankful prayer for the invention of central heat.

Dawn light faded in, filling the distant horizon, slowly supplanting misty gray. Dark shapes moved about the corrals, gray silhouettes against the sluggish brightening. Clara noticed the three horses—her bay mare, Anna's paint, and Ben's stout chestnut—already saddled and hitched side by side to a corral rail.

"Pejuta sapa," Ben said, greeting her with a steaming paper cup. Literally it meant "black medicine."

"Exactly what the doctor would order this morning," Clara said, letting the steam warm her nose before she took the first sip.

They stood together, side by side like the horses, close enough for the commingling of misty breaths and thoughts in the way of two who'd been one for a long time. After a night spent together, followed by a night in the same room and a night spent apart, they sensed each other's hangovers, unconsciously tuned in to the lingering daydreams and the haunting night musings. It was like old times. The *good* old times, before the guilt, before the loneliness.

"You okay?" he asked.

"Mmm-mm. You?"

"*Waste* Chicago."

He looked at her and smiled warmly. She'd once asked him to explain the expression, the connection between *waste*, which meant good, and Chicago. She was always questioning, always interested in the whys and wherefores of things he'd generally shrugged off. Who knew? Who the hell cared? *What's so good about Chicago? It ain't the rez.*

She smiled in return, remembering also. "Is that where you'd rather be now? Chicago?"

"Hell, no. What's in Chicago? I'm on my way to Wounded Knee."

"Me, too." She waved at Anna, who waved, then went back to untying her horse. "What were you thinking about yesterday, mostly?"

"Mostly about these kids." He scanned host Tom Scabbard's graveled yard. Billie, of late his favorite niece, was playing fetch with one of a pair of blue heelers, a breed popular with local ranchers, while Toby Two Bear, of late his ever-present tail, was trying to keep the other dog from stealing his breakfast.

"I was thinkin' about how they're goin' along on this ride, and it's harder than they thought, but they just keep on truckin'. About how they trust us." He looked at Clara. "About makin' the effort not to let 'em down."

She glanced away, looking toward sunrise. "Did you think about the baby?" No need to say which one.

"Yeah."

"I did, too." Her eyes met his again. "I never really took the time to be sad about it, so it was about time.

And I told Anna about it last night. It was about time for that, too."

She looked to him for affirmation. He gave it in a brief nod.

She smiled wistfully and confided, "I used to tell myself that God took that baby from me because I didn't deserve it. Didn't appreciate it. I know I can be very selfish sometimes."

"You?"

"What's hard to believe? That I'm selfish, or that I can admit it?"

"Is that a trick question?" He leaned close, touching his arm to her shoulder. "I refuse to answer on the grounds that anything I say may be used against me." He straightened, his smile fading, his eyes brimming with the need to unburden himself. "And on the grounds that I was the one who didn't deserve the baby. Or Annie. Or you. So guess who God was gettin' back at?" With a thumb he shoved his hat back, as if to expose the face of a sinner. "I was right smack in the middle of the whole grand scheme. Me and my big ego."

"Really?"

He nodded firmly. "That's right. So don't go tryin' to steal any of my miserable thunder."

She said nothing for a moment, then confessed softly into her coffee cup, "I should have been more careful that night."

And he, just as softly, "I should have been there on time to pick you up."

"But I wasn't," she argued, mostly with herself.

"Neither was I."

Out of respect for his father, Ben rode into the center of the morning circle to dedicate the day's ride to the elderly. He prayed for *wolakota* for those who had lived long and given much, who had endured and had shown the way. His voice rose strong and true as he ended with a song, sending a thrilling shiver through his astounded wife.

In sixteen years she'd heard him sing only snatches of country tunes. "Sing it again," she'd plead, but he'd claim not to know all the words. In church he would occasionally join in humbly on a hymn's refrain. But there was none of that reluctance now. On this cold December day, without backup, without accompaniment, without apology, he sang in Lakota. Clara had always admired his voice, but never more than she did on this day, the day they dedicated to the elders. The day Ben offered a song for his father.

The journey continued across desolate, windswept grassland. The better part of the morning had passed when a pickup suddenly shot away from a cattle guard gate near a crossroads, headed straight for the riders. Rather than slow down, as any knowledgeable stockman would, the driver speeded up, his pickup challenging the horses to a game of chicken.

"Heads up!" Cheppa Four Dog called out as he backed his horse away from the road.

"Hold on to your hats, folks!" someone called down the mounted line.

"Watch the kids!"

All they could see behind the rocking and rolling steering wheel was the bill of a cap and a gap-toothed grin as the big blue pickup headed for their side of the road, then veered away at the last moment, horn blasting all the way to high heaven. Several horses balked, reared, pranced. One bolted, and Ben was ready to lend a hand when he saw the hoop take a dip, then drop from his view.

"Jesus Christ," he muttered through his teeth. "Elliot, help that woman, huh?" he shouted as he wheeled his horse. At the jab of Ben's spurless heels the big chestnut gelding sprang off his powerful hindquarters and stretched into a full gallop. Ben searched for the hoop as he circled wide, conscientiously avoiding the other horses. Voices registered distantly.

"Ben!" Clara yelled.

"Hey, Ben, your . . ."

The lead horse recovered its legs, but the hoop lay on the ground alongside the red blanket coat.

"Dad!"

II

The old gray head bobbed up from the grass, then sank back down again as Ben knelt beside his father.

"He stepped on my leg. Don't think I can stand up."

"Just be still now." Ben took a quick look around and motioned to Howard White Calf. "Toss me your bedroll."

"Elliot's goin' for help," Howard reported, plucking his bedroll from behind the cantle as he swung down from his saddle. "Some of the vehicles are supposed to meet us this side of the river, so they should be close by."

"Put me in the wagon," Dewey mumbled in Lakota. "We must keep moving."

"We'll take care of you, *ate*." Ben's response came automatically in his native tongue. His father's face was drawn in pain, and it shook him, like a drill hitting a nerve, aggravating a long-forgotten but fundamental insecurity. "Where else is there pain?"

Dewey's gloved hand fluttered ineffectually. "My chest."

"Jesus," Ben breathed. Then, again in Lakota, "A rib, do you think?"

Dewey's hand went to his coat sash. "The pipe."

"It's here." Ben placed his father's hand on the leather

pouch he carried at his waist. "Lie still."

"When the people need meat, take my horse," Dewey said, his Lakota words couched in shallow gasps. "Be careful for the little ones. Stay close to the women."

"Do you feel dizzy?"

"I feel old," he said, switching back to English. His eyes rolled back, momentarily exposing only white orbs. Ben gripped a handful of his father's red wool sleeve, and the brown irises reappeared, searching. "Where is my granddaughter? Tell her to bring me water."

Ben looked up, locating Anna a few feet away. He banked his own fear, hoping his daughter wouldn't see it in his eyes. "Annie, there's some water . . ."

She snatched the canteen off her father's saddle before he could finish his sentence.

It wasn't long before a station wagon came flying down the road, plowing up dust wings. Rider Dan Medicine, who worked for the Indian Health Service as an ambulance driver, supervised Dewey's lifting and loading, then claimed the wheel. Ben and his sister rode with their father, trusting Clara and the rest of the riders to look after those they left behind. The closest Indian Health Clinic was at Eagle Butte, but the route required backtracking miles of gravel roads to get to the blacktop.

Dewey had been x-rayed, sedated, his torso bandaged, his lower leg plastered in a cast. Tara Jean was down the hall filling out papers. Ben sat beside Dewey's bed, waiting for some sign that the old man would return to the living rather than follow the way of those whose spirits seemed to reach out to more and more. The Old Ones, Dewey called them. The ancestors. It was as though he were fading into their world a little at a time. Soon he would complete the transition, but Ben wasn't ready for that to happen. Not yet. He knew that his own readiness had no bearing on eternity, but he couldn't seem to get his own head on any straighter than the old man's was.

Dewey stirred, searched the white room for his bearings, and found his son's vigilant eyes. "Why are you here? S'posed to be ridin' to Wounded Knee, aren't you?"

"I'm here because you're here, and the doctor says your leg is the least of your worries." Ben tucked his thumbs into his front pockets and leaned back in his chair, inwardly reassured, outwardly affronted. "You're old and sick, and you have no business being out there in all that wind and cold."

"Everywhere you look there are people living out in the cold. Who am I to be spared suffering?" Dewey sighed and stared at the ceiling. "And who are you?"

"Nobody. Nobody to be spared. And I haven't been spared."

"You've tried, and it hasn't worked." The old man glanced Ben's way. "So now what are you going to do?"

"I'm going to see that you let the doctors do their best work on you."

"How will you do that?"

Ben snorted. "You can't get up, old man. You've gone as far as you can go."

"Shoot me, then. Like an old horse. When I am dead, then I will have gone as far in this life as I can go."

Ben braced his hands on his knees and leaned forward. "What the hell do you want from me?" It was a challenge, barely controlled, barely audible. "You want me to stay, you want me to go? You want me to open a vein for you? What?"

"I want what your wife and daughter want. What your friends out there want. Your relations, your neighbors, what they all want." Dewey turned his head to the side and peered down his nose, the only way he could see his son's face. "We want for you what you want for us. *Wolakota*."

"I don't have a goddamn clue what that is."

"Yes, you do. You know. Everyone around you can see that you know. Everyone can see it but you."

"I don't know what the hell you're talkin' about, old man. You talkin' about the mistakes I've made, the failure I've been? You think I can't see that? I've lost my home and my family. You think I don't know that?"

"*Wolakota* is peace in the mind, *cinks*." The old man gingerly slid his hand up the middle of his torso to his chest and spoke in a strained voice. "*Wolakota* is peace in here. It does not come without sacrifice, and it does not come through separation."

"Separation is not my choice. I mean . . ." Ben sighed and slumped in his chair, searching for answers in the corners of the ceiling. "I brought it on, but it isn't the way I want to live. Christ, I've learned my lesson. She oughta be able to see that. I quit drinkin'. I changed my ways. Do you know how hard it's been?"

"Yes. You are doing a thing that is hard, *cinks*. But you are a strong man. That's why people look to you. They always have. Even when you were a boy, your cousins, all your friends, they would follow you for good or bad, wherever you wanted them to go." The leathery hand felt for the edge of the bed, groping to reach his son, who held himself back, tightly collected in his chair. "People have always turned to you, but you back away. There is a piece of you that you keep locked away, that you're afraid to take out and share because you know what it will require of you."

"You want me to carry the pipe. I said I would. I told you that I would do this for you on the ride because you shouldn't be—"

"You said you would carry the pipe on this ride to spare me. Because I am your father, and you are a good son. You want me to live another day, another season."

"What's wrong with that?"

"Nothing. But you cannot carry the pipe for me."

Ben's back stiffened. "Why the hell not? You say I'm your son. You don't think I can ever be as good as you? Huh? You think I can never be—" *A spiritual man.*

"What I think isn't important. What your wife thinks isn't important. It comes down to what you think. It's true you've changed your ways, how you act, what you put into your body, what you do with your hands." The old man paused to catch his breath. "Now there is this," he said, pointing to his temple. "And this," he added, touching the middle of his chest again. "Will you carry the pipe for yourself? Will you carry it for your family and your neighbors?"

Dewey closed his eyes, drawing deeply on reserves of strength for which he'd paid indisputable hardship dues. Then he looked Ben in the eye. "Will you carry it so that the people may live?"

Ben nodded once. "If you'll give it to me, I'll carry it."

With an affirming gesture Dewey called for the object he held dear to be brought forth from wherever his belongings had been placed. Ben took the pipe bag from the small closet and placed it in his father's hands.

Solemnly Dewey returned it to him. "Take it back to the people," he said.

Ben swallowed hard. The worn buckskin felt warm and soft, like a child's tender skin. He knew he was strong enough to carry it. He would guard it, keep it safe. But delivering it to the people in the way that his father had done, that *was* a charge for a spiritual man. Not a drunk. Not an adulterer. Not a man who had failed his own family so badly. But in his father's tired eyes he saw a spark of hope for himself. A promise of trust. Ben nodded once more.

Dewey lifted his hand toward the closet door, which still stood open, displaying a flash of red wool. "Take my coat."

"I don't need it. I have—"

"Tomorrow is Christmas. Give yours away." Dewey gestured insistently. "Some old women made that for the pipe carrier to wear on the ride. Take it. Wear it. Give yours to someone who needs it."

The riders continued their journey. Since there was no way to get word about their pipe carrier, Alta Two Bear came forward during the noon meal and offered to take Clara, Anna, and her cousin Billie to Eagle Butte. Sheila Bird and Cheppa Four Dog said they would take care of the horses.

Ben emerged from Dewey's room just as the rest of the family converged at the door. TJ took the girls in to see their grandfather, leaving Ben alone with his wife.

Clara pointedly noted the pipe bag and the coat in Ben's hands. "How is he?"

"He broke his leg. He's got a bronchial infection. He also has a spot on his lung."

"Pneumonia?" Clara asked fearfully, glancing at the closed door to Dewey's room, then back into her husband's dark eyes.

Ben shook his head. "They think there's more to it."

"He's known about this . . . spot?"

"We've all known there was something wrong, haven't we?" He sighed as he lowered himself wearily onto a bench sitting next to the long, bare hallway wall. "They're taking about transferring him to a bigger hospital, but he's turnin' a deaf ear. He wants us to go on with the ride. He wants me to wear this damn coat. He's gonna let me—" he lifted his burdens one at a time, the coat, then the bag "—carry the pipe, I guess."

"You can do it, Ben. This morning in the circle . . ." She sat beside him on the bench and laid her hand over his forearm. "I've never heard you sing like that."

His weary smile told her that he was grateful simply to have her at his side. "I sounded pretty good, huh?"

"I've always thought you had a wonderful voice, but whenever I tell you that, you always make a joke of it."

"How about spiritual? Did it sound like the voice of a real live *spiritual man*?"

"It gave me a spiritual feeling."

"That's not . . ." He shook his head, then leaned it back against the wall. "Hell, maybe that's what the job's all about, huh? Spread the feeling." He chuckled dryly. "I'm good at that."

"You're good at many things. More than you know, I suspect."

"You tell me, then. Tell me I've got the makings. If you say it's true, I'll believe it. My instincts are a little shaky yet."

Clara slid her hand over his rugged knuckles, deftly slipping her slender fingers between his beefier ones. He closed his eyes and pressed her fingertips into the center of his palm, grateful now for her touch, for some part of her to hold on to.

Anna stuck her head out the door, scouting the hall-way for her parents. When she saw them sitting on the bench holding hands, her eyes widened a little. She smiled. "Lala says he wants us to get back on the road. He wants us to tell everyone he's doing okay and to keep on going." She stepped into the hallway, followed by her aunt and her cousin. "He wants to see you, Mom."

Ben's hand slid away and fell behind as Clara rose instantly, favored by the summons.

She approached the chair close to the bed, taking quick, subtle survey of the white cast, the white blanket, the white plastic bracelet encircling the brown, weath-ered wrist. Hospital white made her uncomfortable, for she remembered seeing her father for the last time under similar circumstances.

Dewey's voice rustled like crisp parchment, and his eyes avoided hers as he spoke. "My son wants to take over for me, I guess. Wants to put me out to pasture. They turn an old stud out to pasture, I think they're supposed to put some fillies in there from time to time." He gave a dry cackle. "If they do, it's gonna be nice."

"You and I know he can do this, but Ben isn't so sure. So I wouldn't count on being retired to any pastures just yet."

"We can all count on it. To me it doesn't seem like a faraway place anymore. It's closer than Wounded Knee. Even closer than Little Eagle." He motioned, and she slid her chair closer to the bed. He lowered his voice, as though he were telling secrets. "It's very close. And I know the way. I am seeing where the road leads."

"But it's a circle, isn't it? I mean, it's not the end of the road, is it?"

"I want to tell you something about your husband." Dewey lifted an unsteady forefinger and managed to give her a wan smile. "When he was a boy he used to hear things about his mother. People said she was a loose woman. They said she traded her body for money and drinks, or even just to hitch a ride. They said she seduced the high school boys. They said she mocked me behind my back. When she left us, I thought the talk would stop, but it didn't. Not for a long while.

"Ben was a scrapper, and whenever anyone brought up the subject of his mother, he would fight them, as if that proved that none of it was true. And so the talk all but stopped. Until a girl that he was sparking asked him if he thought I was his real father. She said she'd heard I probably wasn't. I was just an old man who went goofy over a young, beautiful woman."

He rolled his gray head back and forth on the pillow and glanced at the ceiling in wonder. "I look back now, and it sure doesn't seem like I was that damn old. Not then. But goofy? I guess you could say that." His dry laugh rattled in his throat. "Anyway, when this girl started saying things, Ben couldn't very well punch her in the face, so he came after me."

"He hit you?"

"Only with questions. The same questions she had asked him. I told him I was his father. He asked, how did I know that? I told him he shouldn't have to ask. So he didn't. He never asked again."

Dewey paused. Clara could feel the heaviness in his silence as he considered the point he wanted to make to her. She offered him water, and he accepted a sip from the straw.

His tentative glance ricocheted off hers. Then he drew a shallow, painful breath. "I raised him. He's my son. If he doesn't believe that, then nothing I can say will change anything."

"I know what you mean. He has a blind spot."

"We all do. Every one of us." He held up two leathery hands, one before his face, one near the long gray braid behind his ear. "There are parts of ourselves that we can never see, not even with a mirror here, a mirror here."

"Can't we see those parts in other people's eyes?"

"If we're not afraid to look, but we don't always want to believe what we see."

"Maybe we shouldn't always believe what—"

"Daughter, you think too much!" His thin cackle cut off her philosophical ruminations. "No end to it, chewing the ideas to death. Jeez, you make me tired."

"I'm sorry, I didn't mean to—"

He wagged a finger. "A sick man can only be just so wise, and then has to sleep for a while."

"Of course." She rose to her feet. "I talk too much, too, don't I?"

"You sure talk a lot." His lips sketched a thin smile. "But you listen also. And you're easy on the eyes. Come back to see me, and I will give you more stories for your paper," he said, losing track of time and space again as he nodded off to sleep.

Clara closed the door softly behind her, glancing up as Ben approached. He looked so handsome in the red blanket coat, his black hair lying in rich contrast over the thick cowl collar. His demeanor literally took her breath away. Handsome and strong and fiercely independent. But the image of a boy taunted by treacherous rumors and a confusing mixture of emotions lingered in her mind as she put her arms around him and pressed her cheek to his.

The gesture surprised him, but he welcomed it without question, hugging her back. He'd take whatever he could get. "TJ says she'll stay here tonight if I can catch a ride with Alta," he told her. "I need to catch up to the riders."

"We do, too. Alta's waiting in the lobby."

"Tonight was gonna be kind of a special doings for Christmas Eve. But without him . . ."

"You'll do fine."

He squeezed her again, sucking up her solace for all he was worth. Of course he'd do fine. It was no big deal. Say a few prayers, sing a few songs, smoke the pipe.

The sacred pipe.

Okay, so he'd treat it with respect, which was a tall order, considering the most respectful thing he could do would be to keep his own evil hands off it.

He figured she'd read his thoughts when she drew away. He stepped back, lapped his father's red coat in front, tied the belt, adjusted the large fringed collar. He knew damn well he looked like a big red bird, but he returned the smile Clara offered as she admired the overall effect. Hardly the right style for the bronc buster she'd fallen for way back when, but he sure liked the way she was looking at him now as he settled the pipe bag at his hip.

He had to chuckle to himself as they headed outdoors. This would not have been a good outfit to wear if he'd been leading the way to Wounded Knee a hundred years ago. A big red bird would have been a sitting duck, and a holy man would have been a prime target. He thought about the pictures he'd seen of Jesus wearing a bright white robe parading into town on a donkey. Didn't he know there were soldiers just lying in wait for him, for crissake?

For Christ's sake. What, was he comparing himself to Jesus now, just because he was wearing his dad's coat? And on Christmas Eve, to boot. He damn well better get a grip and remember who he was, or he was liable to get struck by lightning in the middle of the winter. Trotting right up there in front—zap! Fried to a crisp by an angry God, right in front of friends, family, everybody he cared about.

He'd be expected to take the lead. Hell, as long as he was forkin' a horse, he could do that, easy. One thing he knew how to do was stay on a horse.

He'd be expected to carry the hoop.

The *sacred* hoop.

Well, so be it. But it wouldn't surprise him if the thing shattered in his hand.

The Christmas Eve camp was set up out in the middle of nowhere, at least from Clara's perspective. From Ben's it was on the north fork of the Bad River. Supper was served off pickup tailgates, shared around the campfires. The soup was meatier and thicker than usual, and the fry bread was filled with raisins. Simple treats combined with comfortable camaraderie made the occasion festive. The riders found satisfaction even in their fatigue, for it was hard-earned and evenly shared among them.

Swaddled in blankets and seated on saddles, tarps, and hay bales, the group gathered around the fire in front of the big canvas tipi. Ben offered prayers and conducted a pipe ceremony. After that the group sang traditional

Christmas music, taking turns introducing their favorites. Then Dan Medicine brought out a hand-held dance drum, and the celebration became a blending of traditions. The riders joined hands, formed a circle around the fire, and danced the *kahomni*, the loose-kneed side step that some called the forty-nine.

The Ghost Dancers had danced in the same formation, basically the same slow step. But a century ago they had danced until they were exhausted. They had danced because they were hungry and destitute, frightened and desperate. They had danced because their energy was all they had left to sacrifice. They would not believe that God had deserted them, but nothing made sense anymore.

"The whites hate everything that is good, and we do not understand why," Sitanka, the man who was called Big Foot, had said. In their unthinkable feeding frenzy, the white interlopers had slaughtered women, children, herds of buffalo whose numbers had once seemed infinite, even the very ground the people walked upon, slashing it open everywhere to take the gold they coveted, to plant their seeds, to make clouds of dust for the wind to carry away. And the Lakota could no longer fight them in this—had nothing left to fight with but their faith and their physical presence. Even that, the whites would try to take. Even that.

But they had not succeeded. For on the eve of Christmas, one hundred years after the hoop had been broken, a fire burned bright on the Dakota plains. A circle of survivors kept time with the rhythm of Earth's heartbeat, dancing to celebrate their faith and their perseverance.

And this time there were non-Indians among them. There was Paul Olsen, the white rancher who, like Angus Barnes at an earlier campsite, had offered the riders shelter in his home, his barn, his yard, wherever they could find room. There were the journalists who would tell the story, and there was the woman who had borne the pipe carrier's child. These were friends, witnesses to the occasion, sharers in the mending of sacred dreams.

The nights in December were dark and cold, and they were bound to get colder. The journey had already taken a toll. There was still a long road ahead. But they had come this far together, and there were many things to celebrate.

And Christmas was not the least among them.

Around the campfire circle they shared Christmas memories over cups of *pejuta sapa*, deliciously hot "black medicine." There were remembrances of Christmas feeds and communal giveaways and gift-bearing Santa Clauses whose booming voices had sent children scurrying under the chairs in the basement of many a mission church on the Sioux reservations across the Dakotas. The non-Indian fire-dreamers recalled their traditions, tinged with the same nostalgia whether they'd originated in the next county or halfway across the world. A German journalist taught the circle to sing "O Tannenbaum." A Japanese photographer spoke of the Shinto reverence for the ancestors, and his memories of visiting the temple as a small child and being delighted by the profusion of red.

And so they spoke of red holidays, red holy things, red people, and the red road. For the Lakota, the red road was a spiritual journey. Red represented the sun. Yes, the rising sun, the photographer from across the ocean said. The same sun shared by all the members of the circle. The same sun their ancestors had shared.

"How's your father, Ben?" Robert Cady asked.

"Still kickin'." The fire burnished Ben's wistful smile. "With one leg, anyway."

Howard laughed. "Hell, one's better than none."

But Cady persisted with a more sensitive approach. "Will he be okay?"

"I think he's okay now. He's an old man; he's lived a damn good life; he's done right by everybody, pretty much." Ben snapped a twig and tossed the pieces into the fire one by one. "He's hurtin' now, but that won't last."

"So you'll be the keeper of the sacred pipe now? How do you feel about that?"

Was this his first official interview? Ben wondered. If it was, a gritty feeling in his gut told him he wasn't going to be an easy mark. The question struck him as intrusive. He glanced up at Clara, perched on the bale he was using as a backrest, her eyes anticipating his answer. Damned if he'd admit to feeling anything about any of it at this point. Not before he'd sorted it out himself.

Since it was a Cady kind of snare, he turned it back on its author. "How do you feel about takin' pictures?"

"It's what I do," Cady said. "When I do it well, I feel good about it."

"There you go." Ben gave his old cocky cowboy smile. "I don't suppose your father and his father before him were photographers, too?"

"My father was a shop foreman."

"Really? Now, see, if I'd stuck with the job I had up in Bismarck, in another ten, fifteen years I could have been—" He gestured, weighing the possibilities, then turned his mouth down and shook his head. "Maybe a shift supervisor, but not a foreman. Not a manager. See, Indians are real good workers when they're not drinkin'. But sooner or later, they're bound to start missin' work or show up drunk. Everybody knows that, right? You see it on the streets, you read it in the paper." He gave Cady a nod. "Guys like you take pictures of it and publish them all over hell. How many sober Indians do you know, Cady?"

"All of the people here."

"Yeah, but what if next month you run into one of us at a bar? Right away he's a drunken Indian. A white man gets drunk, he's just a drunk. But an Indian gets drunk, hell, we're *all* drunks."

Cady shook his head. "I've shot at least a hundred rolls of film on this ride, Ben. The only drunks on any of those rolls were the bunch in the Blazer back in Timber Lake."

"And who's gonna publish that?"

"Probably nobody," the photographer had to admit. "But just for the record, I sure wish I'd gotten a picture of the guy who almost ran your father down."

"Me, too. We didn't even think to get his license plate number."

"I think it was one of those vanity plates," Howard put in. "If I remember right, it was R-E-D N-E-K."

A drawstring of laughter gathered the fabric of the circle firmly together.

"Hell, yeah," Dan Medicine said. "Did you see the tires on that thing?" His hands described whoppers. "Jacked up taller than ol' John Deere himself. Big ol' tape deck, speakers rigged up everywhere, woofers and tweeters bangin' out the 'Boot Scootin' Boogie.' "

"I didn't hear any music," Marvin Cutler said, chuckling. "All I heard was 'Yee-haa!' "

Firelight flashed in Howard's surviving glasses lens as he leaned into the conversation. "What worries me is the gun racks in those big four-wheelers. Specially when they've got more than one."

Ben laughed. "Loaded for bear, too."

"Damn straight." Teeth flashing in a grin, Howard pretended to take aim and shoot. "Pow! Oops. Was that one o' them redskin bears?"

"Just Lester Bobtail Bear."

Laughter danced buoyantly around the fire again.

"I got a gun rack, too, but mine's empty," Cheppa Four Dog reported. "Hocked my deer rifle. Sorry, Ben, but I ain't taken the cure yet."

"Eez, that guy," Ben said good-naturedly. "Hadda make us look bad."

"Still got my woofers and tweeters, though."

"Shit, Cheppa, the only woofers you've got are sleeping under your front step."

"Can you do that stuff? That Western dancing?" Cheppa took to his feet to demonstrate. "Jeez, you gotta keep count. Heel-toe, heel-toe, slide-two, three, four." Cheppa's hip swagger, part Texas Two-step, part *kahomni*, raised hoots and howls. "No, I've tried it, hey. Went to Spidey Leingang's wedding dance."

"Better stick to the ol' rez stomp, Cheppa."

"Whatever happened to Credence?"

"They're oldies, just like you, Dan."

"Whatever happened to good old-fashioned lyin', cheatin', ass-kickin' country?"

"It's still around," Ben said. "Always will be. Hell, you gotta have a lonesome song for every broken heart."

"For every lonesome cowboy who's moanin', moaanin' the blues," Cheppa crooned.

"Tomorrow we ride for those who are sick." Ben wagged a finger at the man on the opposite side of the fire. "And Cheppa, you sound like one sick puppy."

"Somebody throw him in the stew pot."

And so it went, until sleepiness settled in over merriment, and the riders stretched the circle as they drifted to their beds. After Clara said good night, Ben took time out in the privacy of a river-bottom grove. He leaned against a tree, lit a cigarette, thought about the days ahead, and recalled the time when he, too, had been one sick puppy.

He lifted his face toward the starry sky, rolled the smoke off his tongue, and tasted the bitter memory. Remembering was important. It had been two long, lonely years, and with no end to the loneliness in sight, remembering was as necessary as breathing. Times like today, when he'd left the hospital wearing the red coat, carrying the pipe bag. Without warning, the desire for a quick shot of fortification had popped into his mind like some naked woman stepping into his path.

Jesus, he had a sinning streak in his thick cowboy head that just wouldn't quit. The last time should have cured him . . .

He had nothing left to lose. Come clean, they'd told him. Get honest with yourself and the people you care about. So early on in the treatment program he'd told Clara the truth, and for one brief moment, he'd been relieved of a terrible weight. Ten tons of guilt had melted clean away. Moments later, double ten tons of debris had crashed down on his chest when Clara told him to get his lyin', cheatin' ass out of her life. Only she'd said it Clara-style. An eloquent condemnation of his wicked soul.

And that night he'd walked away from the treatment center. First thing he had to do was shed the damn hospital pajamas and find himself a pair of jeans. No problem. He had friends in Mandan. Mandan was a cowboy town on the west side of the river. *Where the West begins.* And Ben Pipestone was Hunkpapa Lakota. West-river Sioux. Damn if he'd get down on his belly and crawl for anybody, and damn if he'd let a white woman tell him how to run his life. Wife or no wife. If he wanted to get laid, he would, and DUI or no DUI, if he wanted to get bombed, he would.

He passed up the former and went straight to the latter. Big mistake, not taking a second pass. He'd forgotten about the Anabuse. He'd been warned that the drug was no cure, but it was meant to be a deterrent. And for anybody who used his head when he took the stuff, it worked. For the hard-ass who didn't think he could be touched, it taught him otherwise. All it took was one drink. Ben had never been so sick in his life. He spent some purging time in the men's room, but rather than come to his senses, he vowed that it would take more than a damn drug to cut his much-needed binge short. And he bought himself a bottle.

He tried as hard with that bottle as he'd ever tried with any fool thing he'd ever latched on to for distraction—cigarettes, booze, women, wild horses, the whole gamut. It nearly killed him. As if puking himself inside out wasn't bad enough, he got the shakes so bad, he could hardly push the buttons on the pay phone. He'd meant to call home. He figured he'd make it easy for Clara to come and get him, the way she always did—always would, hell, she wasn't fooling him—but he'd ended up babbling something obscene to a U.S. West operator.

When the police picked him up he was crawling on his belly for nobody but his sorry-ass self. He remembered puking bile on the trunk of the squad car when they cuffed him. For reasons he couldn't fathom, he'd ended up back at the treatment center. Why they hadn't shit-canned his ass after that stunt, he didn't know, but he remembered waking up with the worst hangover of his life, looking into counselor Bernie Tinker's pitiless eyes and asking how come hell was so damned cold.

"No colder than a morgue, Pipestone, which is gonna be your next stop."

"Yeah, well, let's just bypass the holding tank." He could hardly see for the blinding pain behind his eyes. "You said if I screwed up, I couldn't get back in. So what am I doing here?"

"You were wearing our pajamas under somebody else's jeans. Cops brought our property back with you in 'em."

Ben tried in vain to sit up.

"Restraints," Bernie explained. "You're about as bad off as they come, cowboy. You wanna live, or you wanna die?"

"I got a choice?"

"Sure, you got a choice. Sooner or later the booze is gonna kill you." He leaned closer and offered more gently, "But you can live without it."

"Maybe I wanna die."

"Why? Because you finally come clean, and your wife leaves you? That ain't fair, is it? It's not supposed to work that way. She's supposed to forgive you, like she always has before." Bernie sat back in his bedside chair and lit a cigarette. "You love your wife, cowboy?"

"Yes," Ben hissed fiercely, as though the question itself were an affront.

"The hell you do."

"I love Annie, too. My daughter, Annie."

"You don't love anybody but yourself. And this." He produced an airline bottle, miniature version of the same label Ben had acquired earlier. Warm brown, gut-steadying Seagram's whiskey.

Ben pressed his scummy, chapped lips together. He could almost taste the liquid fire, the only thing strong enough to purge the wickedness from his soul. Although Lysol might do it, too, if it ever came down to that. Lysol or Sterno just might do the trick. Do him in, once and for all.

He tried to stare a hole through his counselor. What did Bernie Tinker know about what it was like to be Ben Pipestone? Not a goddamn thing. Ben hated that bottle. If his hands were free, he'd grab it and break it.

Like hell. He'd open it and drink it.

He blinked furiously, hoping the damn thing would go away. Running low on voice, he croaked, "I don't wanna live without my wife and baby."

"Die then. There's a real good chance you can't have them back." The little bottle in Bernie's hand did a seductive jig. "But you can have this."

At this point Ben couldn't even swallow. The moisture that should have been in his swollen throat had gathered in his eyes.

"What's the matter?"

"I don't have anything left to puke up."

"So you can start all over. That's how it works, Ben." Bernie pushed the bottle closer. "Come on, drink up.

And up and up and up 'til nothing can touch you. The higher you go, the harder you fall, the sicker you get. Puke 'til you clean yourself out, then start all over." He twisted the little cap, breaking the seal. "This is enough to get you started again. I ain't shittin' you, Ben, I'll give it to you if it's what you want."

Ben squeezed his eyes shut and turned his head away. Something wet slid over the bridge of his nose, and he thought, Christ, the bastard's pouring it on me.

"How about this?"

"Fuck off," Ben growled, gritting his teeth.

"No, I think I'll stick around. Look at me, Ben."

"I said—"

"I've seen men cry before, Ben. I've been there myself. Turn over here."

The smell of smoke enticed him to turn his head. Bernie offered his cigarette and repeated quietly, "How about this?"

Ben's lips parted, and Bernie tucked the cigarette between them gently, as though he were feeding a sick child. Ben drew a long, deep, shaky drag.

"My wife left me, too," Bernie said quietly. "Same reason."

"Did she ever come back?" The question was tagged to a trail of smoke.

Bernie shook his head. "I never see my daughter, either." He withdrew the neck of the small bottle from his shirt pocket. "Change your mind on that happy note?"

Ben shook his head, then jerked his chin, soliciting another drag on the cigarette.

"So what'll it be? Should I fuck off, or should I hang around and light another cigarette?"

"Stay," Ben whispered. "Please."

"I'll light as many as you want. You hang in there."

And that was the first time he'd truly understood the sacredness of a shared smoke.

12

It was a Christmas unlike any Clara had ever experienced. She had known little real deprivation in her own life. She remembered her mother's annual notice that the family couldn't afford "to go overboard" at Christmas, and she'd probably said it herself once or twice since she had become the wife and mother, the cincher of the family purse strings. But during her childhood there had always been plenty of trappings, significant activity, and a profusion of booty. This year she and Anna had agreed to save the gift giving for the New Year. It might have seemed an austere holiday had the spirit of the ride not modified their outlook on ways to celebrate.

It was the best Christmas Ben had had in a long time. Even before he'd gotten himself kicked out, the holidays had often been spoiled by the strain of obligations, the kind that could easily send a guy out looking for a stiff belt. Like shopping. He had no problem with gift giving, but it was the "gift exchange" that seemed a little bogus. The necessity to buy more stuff than you could afford, usually the wrong stuff, which people then took back to the store so they could acquire the right stuff. In his world people didn't treat a gift that way. Visiting was different, too, and so was partying. But the holiday pressure cooker was good for an excuse to grab a drink on the way to the next obligation to socialize, make merry, hurry up or miss out.

Over the years Ben had come to dread this desperate season. He'd spent many a Christmas Eve church service wishing he could just belt out the songs, say the prayers, and look forward to the sack of hard candy and the one small toy with his name on it waiting under the tree in the church basement. It was hard to believe that there had been a time when it had taken so little to satisfy him.

But the time had come again, full circle. This year the season was simpler, but it was so much richer. For two blessed weeks he had his family back. He had his father's charge to finish the ride, carry the pipe, wear the coat and give his own away.

Before he signaled for the circle, he drew Howard White Calf aside and gave him his down-filled jacket. "My dad gave me his coat," Ben said with a wry smile. "Kinda like one of those red convoy flags, huh?"

There was no need to press for acceptance or voice any thanks. Howard was in need of a warmer jacket, and Ben had one to give him, one the giver had used and valued himself. It was a kind of giving ingrained even more deeply than the customary "Merry Christmas" the two men exchanged with a handshake.

Ben called for the morning circle. He belted out his Lakota song and prayed in the way his father had taught him. It was a clean, crisp, cold Christmas morning, and there were no doubts, no conflicts, no disappointments. On this morning, mounted on his chestnut gelding, resting the handle of the hoop on his thigh, he knew exactly what he was about.

"Looks like we might have a white Christmas yet," he announced, gazing at the circle of sky framed by the feathered hoop. "It sure is cold, and it's gettin' colder by the minute. We dedicate this day to the sick. We remember their suffering. But at the same time, we ought to appreciate and preserve our own health, so button up." With a quick chin jerk he puckered his lips out at Toby Two Bear, mounted on his pony. "Zip up your jackets and tie down your hats. You wanna give somebody a gift today, give something to chase away the cold. Bring someone a hot cup of coffee and offer a warm handshake.

"Also I ask you to remember my father today. You can be sure he's thinkin' about us. And remember the people who struggle with addiction, especially alcohol, which takes such a toll on us Indians. People like me. Maybe some of you."

His gelding pranced beneath him, blowing clouds of steam as Ben lifted the hoop toward the sky. "Today we ride for the sick."

There were close to two hundred riders now. During the course of the day the pack was strung out across prairie rangeland, which stood much the way it had a hundred years ago, taking its power from its vastness, the unbroken stretches of rolling grass and the boundless blue canopy of the sky. Ben carried the hoop and led the way. Each time he topped a rise and looked back at the riders, so many of them shivering in their saddles, he wondered how many of them were as uncertain as he was.

The one thing he didn't doubt was his horsemanship, and he felt a strong urge to pass the standard to someone else and ride back among the people. While he was sorely lacking in the qualities of a spiritual man, he did know when to shorten the chin strap on a bridle for better leverage or to offer a broken snaffle bit for better control of a bronky horse. He'd been shepherding some of these people along for days now, and he was uncomfortable with the fact that as long as he was stuck up front, he couldn't keep close track of them. He was glad when his apple-cheeked friend, Toby Two Bear, trotted up beside him.

"Guess what, Ben," Toby said, grinning. "I got a good

feeling today. Something tells me I'm really gonna make it all the way."

Ben grinned back. "You're sure, now."

"I'm sure. The ol' *onze* feels like a block of ice," he admitted, patting his own rump. "Purely numb. Can't feel a thing."

"It's just like part of the saddle, huh?"

"Wish I could leave it in the saddle at the end of the day. That's when I start feelin' it again. But heck, who cares? It'll take more than a sore butt to keep me awake after a day of riding this guy."

"Damn straight." Ben felt a surge of patronal pride in the boy. "When this is over, I'd say you've earned yourself a real horse."

"Oh, this one's not so bad. Short as his legs are, he's gotta work twice as hard as your horse. Your dad told me I should personally thank this pony every night for carrying me through the day, so I been doing that. And we've been gettin' along a lot better." Toby raked his gloved fingers through the pony's shaggy mane. "Your dad's a real smart man."

"Yeah, he is."

"What are we dedicating tomorrow for?"

Ben glanced down at the boy, arching an admonishing eyebrow. "Today's not over yet. You been prayin' for the sick today?"

"Yeah, sure." Toby's brown-eyed cherub face turned up anxiously. "Your dad's not really sick, is he? I mean, I know he got hurt, but they said it wasn't too bad."

"Who said?"

"Well, when Dan Medicine came back from driving you guys to the clinic . . ."

"My father's hurt, and he's sick, and he's old." Ben's gaze drifted across brown tabletop buttes. "Those are the facts we have to face."

Toby nodded solemnly, then eyed the buckskin bag dangling at Ben's hip. "You got the pipe now, huh?"

Ben nodded briefly.

"It's real old, ain't it?"

He nodded again. If he were Dewey, he would be jumping at the chance to tell the boy more about it. He knew the stories by heart. They lived in his soul, flowed in his blood. He'd tried, but he couldn't shake them. They wouldn't be hard to tell. Tell them straight from the heart that took its beat from their ancient rhythm. Tell the kid what was behind the pipe and the hoop and give him more reason to believe, both in himself and in the journey. From now on, Ben told himself, any time he had a young person's ear, he ought to launch right into one of the stories he'd inherited from his father instead of some yarn about bucking one out in Mobridge over the Fourth of July.

But if he couldn't bring himself to do that, he decided the least he could do was answer the kid's question.

"Tomorrow we ride for the people in prison."

"How come?" Toby's innocent eyes hardened. "They're gettin' what they deserve, ain't they? Gettin' punished for what they done wrong?"

"We all make mistakes. Sooner or later most of us manage to box ourselves into one kind of prison or another." There was a time when Ben might have said that marriage was one of those boxes, but now that he was boxed out, he had other ideas. He now knew isolation to be much worse. It was a prison with invisible walls.

"Did you know that my dad's in prison?"

"Mickey?" The surprising news pulled Ben out of his self-absorbed musings. "Since when?"

Toby shrugged, avoiding Ben's eyes as though he were confessing to his own crime. "Since he stole a car out in Wyoming."

"How come I never heard about it?"

"We didn't make no announcement." Toby's eyes narrowed as he stared between his pony's ears. "My mom says it's the dumbest thing he ever did."

"She's probably right about that," Ben offered quietly. "How do you feel about it?"

"Shitty."

"I know what you mean."

Toby looked up, dumbfounded. "Your dad never did nothin' like that, did he?"

"Nope. But I used to feel shitty about some of the stuff my mom did." Ben's wistful smile was dipped in sympathy and laden with regret. "Now I've lived long enough to feel shitty about stuff I've done myself. When you've done it yourself, you get to feel dumb and shitty both."

"You never got put in jail, did you?"

"Yeah, I did."

"For stealin'?"

"For drinkin' and drivin', which could've ended up a whole lot worse. Just pure dumb luck that I didn't kill somebody."

"Could've gotten killed yourself."

"I could have, easy." Ben sighed. "But I've done worse things, I guess."

"What's worse than that?"

"I broke a promise." He shook his head sadly. "Well, more'n one, but one real important one. And don't ask me what it was, because that's private. Just take my word, it was the most important promise I ever made, and I broke it."

"My dad breaks promises all the time."

"He's probably thinkin' about that a lot now, where he is. You can try to wish it away until you're blue in the face, and it doesn't do a damn bit of good. So you finally come to realize that the only thing you can do is try to be honest with yourself about it. You know, try to look at it with a clear head, see what you've done and look where it's got you. If there's a way to pay for the damage, you try to do that. And then you can

do what we're doing now." He would have laid a hand
on the boy's shoulder if he'd been within reach. This he
would have done in Mickey's stead. "I guess in a way
it's what your dad's doing, too. You make a sacrifice.
And you pray for . . ."

"Pray for what?"

"Help. Guidance. You can't make it on your own, no
matter how tough you think you are."

"We're pretty tough, hey." Toby's smile spread slowly, and his face reclaimed its rightful innocence. "Look
how far we've come."

"No kidding. We're a tough bunch of Sioux. We've
survived in spite of soldiers, missionaries, Indian agents,
the BIA, the FBI, the PHS, the IHS . . ." Ben chuckled.
"Hell, they've sicced the whole damn alphabet on us,
and we're still hangin' tough." Then he gave the boy a
sober look. "But we haven't done it on our own, Toby.
Tunkasila looks after us. I guess it's good that we're
makin' this ride, because we need to remember how we
survived, and who made the real sacrifices back in the
days when the going was a lot tougher."

Clara wasn't sure whether she was drawn to the mystical feathered hoop etched against the pale gray sky or
the tall, strong man who carried it, but she followed it,
followed him. Now that he carried the hoop, he couldn't
trot up and down the ranks as the spirit moved him. Poor
cowboy, she thought. Fated to be tied down, one way or
another.

But he wasn't without companionship. Elliot Plume,
who carried the staff, was usually close by. Young Toby
Two Bear rode with him for a while, as did Anna and
Billie and Howard White Calf, wearing the black jacket Ben had given him. Tanya Beale took a turn, too,
insinuating herself between Ben and Elliot. Her little
horse was almost as hot to trot as its rider.

Clara ordered herself to stop wondering what the

woman kept laughing about. What difference did it make? Ben had said something funny. Big deal. He could be wonderfully witty on occasion, and Clara was not about to interrupt. But when twangy Tanya finally dropped back, Clara decided to make her move. Actually, it wasn't exactly a decision, more of an impulse to catch up to him and ride by his side.

He welcomed her with a cowboy nod, two fingers touching the brim of his hat. "Did you come to scout for me?"

"I came to tell you that . . ." That what? She had an excuse just a moment ago. She stretched her stiff lips into a smile. "That coat looks like it was made for you."

"It was made for the keeper of the sacred pipe. For the moment, that's me."

"After Tara Jean comes back, it'll be my turn to go check on him. She and I can take turns so that you can stay with the ride." She sought his eyes. "That's what you need to do, isn't it?"

"What about your own vow? Your commitment?"

"We have a commitment to your father." It was an old habit, she realized, claiming an obligation for both of them. "I won't miss that much. If he's doing well, he'll probably tell me to get back where I belong."

"With your husband?"

"With the ride," she clarified carefully. "But I suppose I should tell you that I'm . . . very proud of you for taking this on."

"Ho, that was tough." He eyed her speculatively. "I suppose I should thank you."

"It's just awkward, Ben. I see you leading the way, and I feel this sense of pride in the fact that it's you, and I'm your . . ." She tore her gaze from his face. Her quick shake of the head was almost lost within the hood of her jacket. "And then I think, no, that's not quite right. We're not living together. But I can't help it. I'm impressed with the way you're handling all this."

"You wanna know the truth?" He looked up at the wooden banner he carried, its simple shape etched so compellingly against the prairie sky. "I feel like a big jerk, carrying this thing, riding up front like this, everybody looking at me like I'm some kind of—" he glanced at her, his slight smile suggesting bittersweet irony "—*very spiritual man*. I feel like a fake."

"You're not acting fakey at all."

"Really? That's comforting. Why do I feel like a fake?" He addressed his deliberations to the buttes underpinning the horizon ahead. "Especially when my own wife—who doesn't really wanna call herself my wife because we're not living together, but that's a technicality when all of a sudden she can't help being impressed, even though she's trying hard not to be—*my own wife* chokes out this compliment about my dad's coat and me sitting up here like some holy general. Christ!"

He looked to her in a silent plea for deliverance and found her eyes alight with amusement. He sighed and shook his head. "I'm not the right man for this, Clara. You know that better than anybody."

"I don't know that at all. And it's not for me to say, anyway. I'm not Lakota. But Anna is."

"Yeah, well, she thinks her dad could be king of the mountain and chief of the tribe."

"She knows you have your weaknesses. She told me about seeing you on TV the time—"

He did a double take. "You didn't know about that?"

She shook her head.

"Did she tell you what I did when she told me she saw that thing?" Again she shook her head. "I never saw it," he told her, his voice suddenly gone soft and husky, "but I remembered when they stuck the camera in my face, damn lights blazing in my eyes. I was so drunk I didn't give a damn what they did to me, but when she told me what it was like for her, seeing me like that . . ."

He turned away. A long silence ensued, and she thought that was it, that was all he could tell her. But finally he looked up at the hoop, then let the details of the memory spin off his tongue.

"It was hell bein' sober that day. No way I could run from it. No place to hide. My little Annie, her voice real quiet and trembling. It was god-awful bein' sober that day." He risked a glance at his wife. When he found no censure in her eyes, he risked even more. "I cried. Right in front of my daughter. Something I hadn't let myself do, not since I was a kid, you know? But I just couldn't hold back."

He wanted Clara to know what he felt. Not pity for himself, but real shame. Shame for what he'd done, and shame for the unmanly way he'd behaved later. And regret. His daughter should not have witnessed either spectacle. They'd never talked about it since, and he often worried about how it had really affected her.

And Clara, since he'd assumed . . . "She didn't tell you?"

"No." She squared her shoulders, adjusting her reins. "She was very angry with me because I wouldn't go to any of the family sessions at the end of your treatment program. But you know why I couldn't. The family session came after . . ."

"After I told you about—"

"Yes," she said quickly. "I almost didn't let Anna go, either. She was so young. But I talked to your counselor, and he said it was as important for her as it was for you." Her glance briefly touched his. "He tried to tell me it was important for me, too, but I told him to go to hell. He offered several suggestions that I ignored, like getting counseling myself or going to Al-Anon. I told him . . ."

"To go to hell," he finished for her, and he had to

smile, knowing that she could never have said such a thing easily or casually. He imagined her starching each word before she rolled it out.

But she shook her head. "That you were the one who needed counseling, not me. I hadn't done anything wrong, and I didn't have the time for that." She shrugged and added tentatively, "I may have been wrong about that. I've done some reading since, and I may have . . . needed some sort of . . ."

He smiled gently. "You should've come to the family sessions. I had to sit there and listen, not say a word. You could've cussed me out, dragged out every sin, every vice, every offense—"

"No, I couldn't. I couldn't admit that my mission had failed. I thought my love was strong enough to move mountains and change your ways. I thought my love had real power."

"Power over me?"

"Not *over* you."

"My little Clara-bow, trying to strong-arm me with love." He chuckled, then quickly turned serious again, searching her eyes for acceptance. "I've been workin' hard to change. I wanna be someone you can really like. Someone Annie can like. Mostly someone *I* can like." He shrugged his hopes off and stared at the hills. "I want people to like me, to look up to me. See, that's part of my problem. People are too damn fickle. One minute you're their hero, the next minute you're just some bum."

"Not with Anna. She's seen you at your worst, but she still thinks you're king of the mountain."

"I just don't want her to be ashamed to call me 'Dad.' "

"She and I were talking about how you take part in the ceremonies, how you talked with her about your beliefs, about the prayers and the circle." She turned to him and told him earnestly, "We don't think you're a fake."

He smiled. "You agree on that, huh?"

"All this humility is quite endearing, actually. When you were riding in rodeos, you were never this modest." She dropped her voice in an attempt to imitate him. "Hell, Ben Pipestone could scratch out anything on four legs, rope anything that moved—"

"I *could.*" He chuckled as he watched a jackrabbit zigzag through the grass and disappear into a hole. "Thought I could, anyway. Back in those days, that was what counted."

"Winning counted, and you did that, too."

"For a while."

"But I took that away from you, didn't I?"

"No. I made a choice." He looked up and found the hoop leaning, so he repositioned the stick against the swells of his saddle. "But I made it in kind of a halfhearted way, so I could always tell myself that I could have been a world champion if I hadn't gotten tied down. What I didn't tell myself was that there's a reason why there aren't too many world champions. You gotta really want it, and I guess I didn't want it all that bad. I kept kickin' myself because it gave me an excuse to feel sorry for myself, which gave me an excuse to get drunk."

"You didn't do it that often."

"Often enough." He looked at her and wondered why she persisted in that belief. "More often than you know."

"I refuse to believe I could have been that stupid. That *blind.*"

"I'm just tellin' you the way it was. You weren't stupid. But there were things you didn't wanna see."

She'd had her mind on other things. Her child, her home, her friends, certainly her work. All worthy of her attention. But her husband had had a problem that she really did not want to see.

"You know what, Clara, I think I'm doin' it again. I'm facing a choice here with this pipe-keeper thing, and I don't wanna do it in a half-assed way. The thing is—" He pressed his elbow against the bag, just as he had countless times during the course of the day, making sure it was still there. Really there. "I believe in the things my father taught me. I believe the Lakota ways are good. I know right from wrong, what's good and what's bad. But I've done so goddamn many bad things in my life. How can I do what's expected in a sacred way? How can I even have the nerve to carry a sacred thing in my hands?"

"You were never short on nerve, Ben," she assured him. He looked for mockery in her eyes, but he found nothing but kindness. Her smile shielded him from the cold. "Or courage," she said. "You have that, too."

Because she was sincere in her assurances, he gave himself a moment to try them on and see if they could possibly fit. Nerve? He could buy that much. But it wasn't enough to get by on. Not anymore. Courage? Now that was a little different. That one he'd have to ponder some more.

"It's good to be able to talk to you again. That's something I miss a lot. When we weren't fighting . . ." He grinned, suddenly feeling a surge of deep-inside warmth. "Hell, you get right down to it, Clara, there's nobody I'd rather talk with than you."

"Or fight with," she allowed with a smile.

"Or make love with."

Her smile faded.

He glanced away. "Sorry I brought that up."

"It's okay." Her voice turned small and shy, the way he remembered it sounding long ago. "I miss that, too."

"How about lettin' me give you a Christmas present, then?"

She looked at him, her eyes at once brimful of fear and wonder.

He spread an easy smile over his heartache. "Just kidding."

Just kidding. With Ben, "just kidding" often translated to "I meant it, but we're both uncomfortable with it, so don't take it seriously." And she *was* uncomfortable with it. She actually wanted to sleep with him, and she hated herself for it.

No self-respecting woman could possibly feel that way.

So that night when a snowfall broke up the evening campfire activity, Clara refused to let Anna spend the night with Billie. She insisted instead that Billie stay in their tent since her mother was still at the hospital with Dewey. Then she lay awake long after the girls had gone to sleep, remembering things she had tried hard to forget. The things she wouldn't talk about. The *one* thing in particular that was proof of her inadequacies. She hadn't been enough of a woman to satisfy the man she loved . . .

She'd believed him when he'd called and said that his father needed him, so he'd be in Little Eagle for a couple of days. She'd thought the background noise was curious, but he'd said he was calling from a gas station. She'd believed that, too, since her father-in-law had no telephone.

She found out later that he'd called from a police station. Three days later, when she'd been on her way out the door to head down to Dewey's place, Ben had called from Mandan. He had referred himself for treatment for alcoholism, he'd told her, and he'd been admitted to the inpatient program. He would be living at the treatment center for a month.

Clara didn't believe that Ben was a *true* alcoholic. Days later during her first interview with the counselor, she told him as much, and the man had the audacity to question her choice of words. Ben was not a drunk, she said, resolutely unfazed by Bernie Tinker's smug attitude. He had been known to drink too much on occasion, but he could easily go for months at a time without drinking at all, and he had always held a steady job. He had always been a good father. The DUI was a serious matter, yes, but it didn't necessarily mean that Ben was an alcoholic. And if Mr. Tinker had jumped to that conclusion because of Ben's race, then perhaps he ought to consider . . .

What *about* her own family background? Her family had nothing to do with this. No, they had not approved of her marriage, and no, she was not close to her mother, and no, her father had not had a drinking problem. He was a social drinker, according to her mother, and yes, he'd gone to an early grave, but none of this had anything to do with Ben.

Had he had any extramarital affairs? Ben? Of course not.

Tinker explained that it was not uncommon for people to be protective of their alcoholic spouses, that her so-called denial was normal. It all sounded quite condescending to Clara, but she agreed to participate in Ben's treatment program, and she agreed to a counseling session with him that day.

He appeared at Tinker's office door wearing hospital pajamas and scuffs, which was completely out of character. Ben didn't own any pajamas. He looked haggard. He stood there awkwardly, shifting his weight from one foot to the other and eyeing her nervously. Finally he cleared his throat. The first thing he said was that he was sorry for the mess he'd made of things, and the first thing she did was give him a hug. He put his arms around her and held on for dear life, as though he were a man awaiting execution.

"I want you to know that I am angry with you," she said, but she kept the anger from her voice. She prided herself on her control. "I just can't believe you got drunk and then got behind the wheel of that pickup."

"You can't?"

She drew back and looked him in the eye. "Ben, that's not like you."

"What do you mean, it's not like me? What do you know about me, Clara? I mean, really?" He let her arms slide through his grip, anchoring himself finally, fleetingly, squeezing her hands in his. "I've gotten caught before, remember? When you were away that time? You didn't find out until—"

"The insurance rates went up, but that was a long time ago."

"Why don't you both sit down?" the short, stout counselor suggested as he arranged two chairs a measured distance from each other. Then he sat in his desk chair and wheeled himself backward, withdrawing into the corner like a snail in a shell. The two men exchanged a look, as though they had concocted a plan in advance. Tinker gave a nod. Ben glanced toward the door, the window, finally the chair.

With a sigh he took the chair across from his wife. She waited. He watched. He braced his elbow on the arm of the chair and pressed the curled thumb of his fisted hand to his lips, still watching her. If he expected her to turn into a shrew, it just wasn't going to happen. Whatever he had to say, she was going to understand. He didn't need the drinking. He could count on her to help him quit.

"I've done things . . ." He stopped to clear his throat. "I've done things you don't know about, Clara. I referred myself for treatment because I don't wanna go to jail. But I got in here, I started right out lyin' about most things. I've been here for almost a week now, and I've thrown a lot of bull, like I usually do, and it's not workin'." He slid the counselor a glance, then stared at the toes of Clara's black flats. "Bernie's not buyin' it. But I don't much like the truth about myself. I like the bullshit a lot better. I always figured you did, too."

"That's not true. I love you for who you are, Ben. You know that."

"No, I don't know that." He curled his hands around the arms of his chair and lifted his gaze to meet hers. "Clara, if I don't know who I am anymore, how in the hell could you know?"

"Well, I . . . This drinking problem isn't all there is to Ben Pipestone. I mean—"

"I don't want to lose you," he ground out desperately. The tortured look in his eyes was beginning to scare her. "I've done some stuff . . . and I've been lyin' about it because I don't want to lose you."

"You won't. I'm your wife. Do you think I'm going to abandon you when you're in trouble?" She slid to the edge of her chair, reached out and touched the hard knobs of his knuckles, fingertips grazing his wedding ring. "We can beat this thing together."

"I need you. But I can't ask you to stick by me without tellin' you about something first." Like a man who feared drowning, he released the armrest and grabbed her hand before it got away. "Something you have a right to know."

An insidious chill slid over her body, and a voice in her head whispered, *You don't want to know. Tell him you don't want to know.*

But instead, she asked tonelessly, "What is it, Ben?"

"I've cheated on you, Clara."

"Cheated?" Her brain refused to process the word. *Cheated?* Cheated, how? Was this a game? Had he been burying aces somewhere?

"I had—" his low voice dropped further, approaching soundlessness "—an affair."

"You mean—" her voice weakened and fluttered ceilingward "—with another woman?"

"Yeah." He nodded once, cleared his throat, avoided her eyes. "With another woman. It's been over a year now since the last time I saw her. A year and a half at least. It didn't last long, and it wasn't anything . . ." He gave a quick shake of his head, his eyes approaching a connection with hers as he spoke, but taking the long way around her chair, her knees, her shoulders. "It was stupid, and I don't know why I did it. I knew it was wrong. I just wasn't—"

Numb everywhere, no feeling, no sense to the words. "You . . . had sex with this woman?"

"Yeah." He stared at the button in the middle of her chest. "Yeah, I did."

Eighteen months ago. When was that? Where was I?

"Who was she?"

"You don't wanna know that, Clara. And it doesn't matter. I mean, it was just—"

"Do you—" *No. Not possible.* "Did you love her?"

"No. God, no, it was just—" He dismissed it with a gesture. "It was just sex. That's all it—"

"*Just* sex?" Images formed. Awful, ugly images. Her pulse hammered in her ears. "*Just sex? What does that mean? You're married to me! That means you just have sex with me. No one else! How could you . . ."* She had her voice back now, full-strength and mortified. "How could you?"

"I don't know. All I know is, it's over. It was over a long time ago, and it'll never happen again." Their eyes met, his gaze latching firmly on to hers. "And I'm sorry."

"Who was she?" she demanded.

He shook his head dumbly.

"You're protecting her, aren't you?"

"No, I'm not. You're the only person I want to protect. You and Annie."

"Don't even *mention* Anna's name. You . . . you . . ." She felt as though she had run a long way, was still running, couldn't stop, couldn't catch her breath.

Don't run anymore. Don't ask.

"Who was she, Ben?"

Don't answer. Don't tell any more.

He glanced away. "Marian Anders."

"Marian Anders!" Clara stiffened. An acquaintance. Someone so different from Clara that she would never be more than an acquaintance.

But she needed someone to hate, someone besides the man she could no longer allow herself to love. She shook her head tightly. "You're right. It doesn't matter who the little slut was, but . . . but . . ." Her whole body steamed and melted, all happening at once, all turning to water. She swallowed furiously against the threat of a deluge. "She's not even . . . very pretty or anything. Did you . . ." His face blurred. *Deep breath. Steady.* "Did you meet her somewhere? Did you . . . Where did you do this . . . this *stuff* you did?"

"Why do you wanna know all this?" He loomed closer, a shape becoming less distinct, but his voice sounded tightly controlled. His eyes had always been the place to look for signs of his emotions, but they were smeared, like watercolors running together. "I wanna be honest with you, Clara. I don't wanna hide anything from you anymore, but I don't think it's good to—"

"What do you know about *good*?" She closed her eyes and gripped the front of the chair seat. "Ben, I don't understand this."

"I don't expect you to."

"I had no idea." Dashing the tears away with her knuckles, she turned, suddenly remembering the counselor's presence. Someone with some sense, maybe. She obviously had none. "Why didn't I know?"

"Because you trusted him, would be my guess. Ben is an alcoholic, Mrs. Pipestone. He's—"

"I don't care. That's not an excuse." She pounded her fists on the armrests and shouted at her husband. "That is no excuse for betraying your wife, your family, your marriage."

"I know."

"I wasn't offering it as an excuse." Tinker plucked a box of tissues off his desk and scooted across the floor on his wheeled chair. "But you asked me why you didn't know, and I'm offering a possible answer. Alcoholics are very good at covering up, and their spouses usually deny the disease in their own minds and very often enable the behavior by—"

"I didn't enable anything. I'm not the jealous type, not even suspicious. Ben's the one who gets jealous any time a man so much as talks to me. And I've always been—" she snatched a tissue from the box with a shaky hand "—absolutely faithful to him. Do you hear me, Ben? Completely and totally faithful. *How could you do this?*"

"It was a mistake. I knew it then, and I sure as hell know it now. I feel like shit."

"Good." Clutching the tissue, she drew a quavering breath. "Because that's exactly what you are."

Tinker touched her arm. "We'd like to have you join in our group sessions with—"

"Group sessions?" She drew away from the warm hand intruding on the cold storage locker she was frantically fashioning for her own refuge. "You don't actually think I'm going to discuss this with other people?"

"We can help you get through this," the counselor said gently, "but only if you want our help."

"I don't need help. I'm fine. I'll be fine." On that determined note she ejected herself from her chair and looked down her nose at her husband. "We're not going to tell Anna about this, of course. She's much too young. We'll just have to tell her . . . that we can't . . ."

He pushed himself up slowly, like an old man. "I'll tell her the truth if you want me to."

"No. That wouldn't be good." There was no goodness left except Anna. None. "I don't know where you're going to go when you leave here, Ben. I guess I really don't care, or at least I won't, by the time all this really sinks in." She drew a deep breath and faced him stalwartly. "You have no home with us anymore."

He swallowed audibly. "Clara, please . . ."

"If I have to get a court order, I will."

"You don't have to do that," he said quietly.

"Of course, anything that belongs to you . . ."

"Just throw my shit out in the garage if it's in your way."

"I'd appreciate it if you'd send someone else to pick it up." She turned to leave, then paused, thoughts and images swirling, swelling her brain, making her taste sourness, smell foulness. She felt a little dizzy. She didn't know if she could make it to the door. She closed her eyes briefly, trying to steady herself.

Say something. Somebody say something.

"I really don't know what to say to Anna," Clara heard her own voice say. "She . . . l-loves you s-so m-m . . ."

His hands were on her shoulders, his strong support so close, so close.

"Jesus, Clara, can't we talk—"

"I could have forgiven almost anything else, Ben, but not . . ." She looked up, her eyes pleading for an excuse to grant him a reprieve. "You gave your love to another—"

"There was no love," he said wretchedly. "It had nothing to do with love, Clara."

"You didn't like her?"

"Jesus Christ." He tipped his head back, searching for an answer from somewhere on high. "I liked her, yeah. I mean, I didn't *dis*like her. It had nothing to do with love. It's hard to explain."

"Of course it's hard to explain. It doesn't make any sense." She stepped away from him, away from his hands, away from his self-imposed turmoil. "And when things stop making sense, there's nothing else to say."

She'd been pleased with her exit. Much more so than she had been with her subsequent behavior. Not that she'd done anything untoward in front of any more witnesses. She declined the invitation to the treatment program's "family week." She wasn't interested in Al-Anon. She had no use for counselors or therapists. She'd told a few close friends that she and Ben were no longer living together, but she'd invited no questions and offered few details.

Privately, though, she had suffered in a way that she had never suffered before. The secure facade might well have been held together on the inside with staples and masking tape. She lay awake nights imagining Ben having sex with Marian Anders. She imagined the two of them in her own bed, in the back of Ben's pickup, in dark places and sunny places and all kinds of places that she had shared with him. She imagined him undressing himself, letting someone else undress him, undressing someone else, touching someone else, kissing someone else, and on and on and on until in the dark she had to cover her mouth with both hands so that no one would hear her terrible, throat-tearing scream.

She hated Marian Anders. The bitch. The home-wrecking whore. She hated Ben. The bastard. The lying, cheating, drunken . . . She couldn't come up with the right epithet. Cursing had never been her forte, but she was getting better at it. Mentally. She'd punished them mentally.

But she had punished herself more. The worst of it was that in all her imaginings and all her condemnations, she couldn't expunge Ben's face from her thoughts. And it wasn't monstrous. It wasn't ugly. Tearing his picture to shreds only filled her with regret. Remembrances of him—his scent, his touch, the sound of his voice—lingered in every corner of her life, still, in some foolish fragile female sense, cherished.

The worst of it was that she missed him.

The worst of it was that she still loved him.

The worst of it was that they had shared, *still* shared, big, beautiful chunks of their lives, and there was so much about him that she would always love.

13

Clara clamped her jaw to keep her teeth from chattering as she dressed in the dark. Remembering was hard, would probably always be hard, but the pain was not as acute as it had once been. It was late, but it was still Christmas, and she hadn't given Ben his gift. She hadn't given him one last year, either, but this Christmas was certainly different. The little joke he'd made about giving her a Christmas gift had thrown her off, but she'd been "off" for some time. Off balance, off schedule, off her usual track. She was going with the flow this Christmas. Against her own grain. Funny how the clichés came in battalions, even though this Christmas was anything but cliché.

Funny how eager she was to see him this time of night, and unlike a time not so long past, it wasn't because she had worked up the urge to scratch his eyes out. Figuratively, of course.

"Mom?"

"I'll be back in a few minutes, Anna. I just remembered that I have a gift for your father."

"You do?" The voice rose, gaining enthusiasm. "What'd you get him?"

"Long silk underwear, like ours, only men's."

Anna's giggle woke Billie, who groaned, then mumbled thickly, "Whas goin' on?"

"Guess what my mom got my dad for Christmas. *Silk long johns.*"

"Shhh," Clara warned. "He won't wear them if everybody knows. But they'll keep him warm, and they're—"

"They're great." Anna's bedding rustled as she settled back down, snuggling in newborn contentment. "Tell him they're from me, too. I was gonna give him a bottle of Obsession, but I decided not to."

"Why not?"

"Because I didn't pay for it."

"Oh."

"It was from before I got caught. I talked to Lala about it."

"What did he say?"

"He said that there were some customs we had to do away with a long time ago if we didn't wanna end up in jail or on the hangin' tree, and stealing horses was one of them. He figured it was probably the same with umbrellas and men's cologne." Anna sighed heavily. "So I've decided when I get home, I'm gonna give it back, along with some other stuff. That'll be my gift to you, Mom."

"Well . . . thank you."

After a pause, Anna came back in a smaller voice with, "Will you go with me?"

Clara tried to imagine trooping from store to store, introducing herself and her daughter to the managers and throwing themselves on their mercy. "Maybe we could just mail it back anonymously."

"Don't you want 'em to see our faces?"

"Mine would be forgotten immediately," she suspected, although her name probably would not. "I'm afraid yours would be remembered, and not for bringing the stuff back, but for taking it in the first place. But it's up to you. Since you've made the decision to return what you took, we'll do it your way."

"You wouldn't be embarrassed?"

Clara smiled in the dark. "I probably would, but I'd get over it. My admiration for you would get me over it quickly, I think."

"Maybe we should ask Mrs. Turnbull about the plan, huh? Give her one of those I've-got-this-friend scenarios. I'm not too anxious to go to the hangin' tree." Anna chuckled as she turned over. "You ever try shoplifting, Billie?"

"You kidding? My mom would kill me."

"Mine tried to lecture me to death. Right, Mom? Then the court sends us both to this probation lady, and then my dad gets his two cents in. It's not worth it, hey. Except I did get to come on the ride, and I did get this nice set of silk long johns."

"It wasn't *because* you got in trouble but *in spite of* the fact that—"

"No, no! Not the late-night lecture torture, Mom, *please*. I give up. I confess." She laughed, and Clara chuckled. "I hope Dad likes his Christmas present."

The snowfall had dwindled to a flurry of dancing flakes. With each footfall Clara's boots crunched grass and snow as she headed for the dark tipi silhouetted against the light gray night. The sky was overcast, but the snow whitened the night, and the brightness seemed comforting. She clutched the package to her breast. The closer she got to the tipi, the sillier she felt. She'd intended the gift to be practical, not funny. But Ben was bound to think she was trying to be funny and missing the mark. She should have given it to him casually. She should have done it earlier. Or she could do it tomorrow.

"Ben? Ben, are you awake?" What a dumb question, of course he wasn't awake. Somebody was snoring. Somebody else groaned. "Ben, may I talk to you for . . ."

A movement across the camp caught her eye. Someone else was stirring. Tanya Beale, if Clara wasn't mistaken. She stepped away from the tipi and watched the woman unzip a tent flap, then remove her jacket and her boots, presumably to avoid disturbing Sheila Bird, who had generously offered the Oklahoma pilgrim a place to sleep.

"What's up?"

Ben's whisper spun Clara around like a top. He was standing behind her, near the tipi door. She glanced back at Sheila's tent just as Tanya's derriere disappeared behind the flap. Besieged by unexpected suspicion, she turned back to Ben. "Where did you come from?"

He jerked his chin toward the tipi door. "My—" And then read her mind. "Not her, if that's what you're thinkin'."

"Well, no, I wasn't exactly thinking . . ."

"I heard you call my name," he told her softly, almost reverently, as though it had to be a miracle. "Thought I was dreamin' at first."

"No, I . . ."

"Then you asked if I was awake. You asked if we could talk," he recounted, seeking to assure her. "I haven't been tipi-creepin'. There's three other guys in there, Clara. I don't know what that lady's got goin', but she wasn't with me."

"She probably just had to go . . ."

He smiled. "You woke me up to be your lookout?"

"Oh, no, I just wanted to give you this." Suddenly angry with herself, she shoved the floppy paper package into his hands. "It's kind of mashed, but it's nothing breakable."

He spoke as though his hands were filled with wonder. "You got me a Christmas present?"

"Well, you gave me a wonderful . . . my Misty Too. She's such a good horse, thanks to your expert hand."

"Let's move away from—" He surveyed the sleeping camp. "Maybe we can find an empty pickup, huh?"

"I just wanted to give you that. It's from Anna, too."

She shoved her hands into her jacket pockets and stepped back.

"And I just wanna open it." He slipped his arm around her shoulders, coaxing her to walk with him. "And thank you properly."

"Well, wait 'til you see it before you start thanking me. You'll probably laugh."

"When have I ever laughed at any of your gifts?"

"There was that shirt with the colorful rooster and cactus motif," she recalled coyly. Something inside her wanted to believe, and that something was relieved and unexpectedly feeling a little playful.

"That was because the pink cactus looked just like—"

"I know." She laughed softly as they approached the motley collection of vehicles parked near a stand of skeletal cottonwoods. "I think we ended up calling it 'the sticker-with-cock shirt.' "

"You shortened it to that." He laughed, too. "And I wore it, didn't I?"

"To the teachers' Christmas party, as I recall. And told everybody—"

"Here." He tried a door after rejecting two vehicles with sleeping occupants. "Marvin's pickup is empty." She slid across the driver's seat, and he climbed in after her, quietly shutting the door. "Auntie Mary left the keys in it. She probably never takes them out. You want some heat?"

Clara shook her head. "I don't want to wake anyone up. Besides, I don't want to get spoiled with fancy gas heat."

He chuckled.

She stared pointedly at the package on his lap.

"Should I open it?" She nodded, and he tore into the paper, muttering anxiously, "Will it bite me, or will it shock me? Comin' from Clara-bow, I just never know."

"A bit of poetry," she said, smiling. He seemed so childlike in his excitement that she wished the package contained something really special.

He held up the lustrous pearl blue turtleneck shirt. The fabric glistened in the snow-bright night. "Jeez, it feels like silk."

"It is."

"Real silk?" He plucked the second item from its paper nest. "Pants, too?" He flashed her a grin. "You tellin' me I need to change my underwear?"

"They're very warm and lightweight. Skiers wear them all the time. *Male* skiers." She shrugged and quipped breezily, "But I can always send them back."

"No way. This coat isn't as warm as the down jacket I was wearin'. I'll wear anything warm. Even silk." Still grinning, he held the shirt up to his chest. "I ain't proud."

"Ben Pipestone, *proud*?" She laughed merrily.

"Kinda personal, isn't it? You givin' me underwear?"

"It's a practical gift. You know me." She tucked the turtleneck collar under his chin, admiring the soft blue sheen next to his dark skin. "Something to keep you warm."

"You could do that. Keep me warm." Regarding her uncertain expression, he laid his arm along the top of the backrest and put his hand around her shoulder, gently drawing her closer. "Come here. Let's keep each other warm." As her resistance melted, he jerked on his sash belt. "No, here," he said as he quickly unfastened three buttons. "You come inside the pipe carrier's coat." He opened it and enfolded her within the thick wool wrap.

She slipped her arms around his waist and snuggled against his shoulder, inhaling the woodsmoke and cold winter night scent of him. "It is warm in here."

"I didn't know if we'd ever spend another Christmas together, Clara." His embrace tightened. "Does it feel like Christmas to you?"

"Yes." She hugged him close, her gloved fingertips touching behind his back. "Very much so. I feel as though we've cleared away some of the trappings and discovered the basics of Christmas. The timeless journey. Following the hoop, sort of like a star. Finding shelter. Looking out for each other, praying for a better world." She tipped her chin up. "And Mary and Joseph had to flee with their child, much the way Big Foot's people did."

"Soldiers chasin' after them. God, that must be hell, gettin' chased by soldiers when you've got women and children, and you know it's not just the men they're after. Jesus, even babies."

"Yes, even Jesus. Even as a baby."

"Killing kids," Ben mused. "It's hard to figure, huh? How a guy could do something so awful and just walk away. Go home to his family, sit down to supper like nothin' happened." He tipped his head back and rested it against the cold window. "It eats at him, though. Like any sin, big or small, it has to eat at him until he either stops doin' it, or he stops caring. Or he stops living."

"What am I supposed to do?" Clara asked. "I know what you're talking about. I just don't know what I'm supposed to do." She closed her eyes and sighed. His heart beat close to her ear, and God help her, she cherished the sound. "I mean, you stopped drinking and whatever else, and presumably you feel better now. The only bad habit I had to give up was you, but having done that, I really don't feel any better. I can't stop caring, and I'm not about to stop living. So what am I supposed to—"

"Whoa, back up." He managed to shrink back enough to look down at her. "You can't stop caring about what?"

"About you." In close quarters and dim light her eyes unerringly met his. "I mean, I can't seem to stop caring about you *completely*, as much as I wanted to at first. But I can't love you anymore, Ben, because I can't trust you. I can't believe you. I don't know if I really believe that you weren't with that woman tonight."

"What woman?"

"Tanya Beale. I saw her going into the tent, and all of a sudden there you were."

"I told you—"

"I know. But instead of taking what you said at face value, I started thinking, okay, so I heard the snoring; I know there were other men in there, and I don't *think* you'd have a woman in there under those circumstances, and you *did* hear what I said. But maybe you weren't in the tipi. Maybe you were just close by. I didn't even hear you come up behind me."

"You never do."

"I didn't see you with her, but how do I know for sure? How will I ever know for sure?"

"How did you know for sure when you married me?"

"I knew you loved me." A wistful smile tugged at her lips. "I *knew* I loved you. I *believed* that you loved me."

"I did, but that didn't keep me from screwin' up, did it?" He slipped his glove off and touched her cheek with a warm thumb. "I still love you, Clara-bow. And I wanna *make* love to you in the worst way. No, in the best way, the most loving way I know how, but that still won't prove anything, will it?"

"No, it won't."

"And if you'd let me do that, what would that prove to me?" He threaded his fingers into her hair. "Hmm? What would it prove?"

"That I have no self-respect." She sighed, and their frosty breaths mingled. "That you can just walk all over me, and I'll still . . ."

"You'll still what?"

"I can't love you anymore, Ben." She closed her eyes, and her voice dropped to a sketchy whisper. "It hurts too much."

"Can you let me kiss you?" His lips grazed her cheek, his warm breath taunting her. "Just once," he whispered.

"A Christmas kiss. That can't hurt." He stroked her lips with the last words, then covered them with an openmouthed kiss. He stroked more, this time with his tongue, and when he finally dragged his mouth away, he had to take a deep breath before he could wonder hopefully, "How was that? All full of jingle bells?"

"Yes," she whispered on a sigh.

"How 'bout one for me? You can give me a 'Frosty the Snowman' one, huh?"

She sat up to kiss him, lightly at first, but he tipped his head to one side and recaptured the spirit of the last kiss, his lips coaxing a response from hers. And when she gave it, tongue tip to tongue tip, she took his breath away.

"Mmm, that wasn't frosty at all," he said on a puff of winter breath. "Kinda sets the ol' Yule log on fire."

"You're flirting with me again."

His lips skimmed her forehead. "Sparkin' you, as my dad would say." And he trailed kisses from her eyebrow to her eyelid to her nose, then seized her mouth again.

At the next opening she whispered against his lips, "That was a 'Rudolf the Red-Nosed Reindeer' kiss, I believe."

He touched his tongue to the tip of her nose and smiled. "No red nose on this cowboy, honey. I took the cure."

"Yes, so I've heard." She tucked her face beneath his chin and hugged him close. "I should have gone back for that family week of yours and really let you have it."

"You should have," he agreed, returning the hug and marveling at how good it felt just to hold her. How right. How comforting. To be able to hold her and talk. "I almost dropped out of the program after I—" he swallowed hard and held on tight "—told you what I'd done. Almost got myself kicked out, actually."

"How?"

"I walked out. Went to a bar, got so drunk I couldn't see, so sick I wanted to die." Eyes closed, he buried his nose in her soft hair and whispered, "But I decided not to."

"Not to die?"

"That's right." He leaned back and looked at her. There was so much he wanted to tell her, had long needed to tell her beyond his apology, which she'd never accepted. Making amends was a tall order, one he might never be able to adequately fill, but finding her willing to listen was the first step.

"I decided I couldn't live with myself the way I was, any more than you could. I always said I could quit any time, but it was a whole hell of a lot tougher than I thought it would be. Especially since I thought I'd lost everything that mattered to me, and no guarantee of getting any of it back. But love doesn't come with a guarantee. And marriage, you can't take that for granted, either, even when there's love. You've gotta work at it every day. And I didn't do that."

"I don't know whether—" She caught her lower lip between her teeth and glanced away. "I guess I didn't, either."

"But I believe in marriage more than I ever did. I don't much like livin' the way I'm livin' now."

"I don't either." She closed her eyes. "I wish it could be different, Ben."

"Well, it's different from the way it was." She started to shake her head, but he caught her chin and made her look at him again. "It is. I'll tell you something else I've found out. Other things matter. It matters that I started with nothing and got a business goin', even gave somebody else a job. Bein' Annie's father matters. My dad, my sisters, the rest of my family, they all matter." He watched her eyes, watched closely as it all sank in, and he smiled. She was listening, maybe even thinking it over, and that, he had to believe, was a beginning. "I'm comin' along, slow but sure, Clara-bow. Guess I'm kind of a late bloomer."

"Maybe in some ways." She smiled, too. "But in the area of 'sparking,' I'd say you probably got an early start."

"Want some more?" He nuzzled her temple and whispered, "How about another Christmas song to ring your chimes?"

Her sigh was more a sound of contentment than a breath. "Where is all this caroling going to lead us?"

"You think I'm gonna try to make love to you, don't you? You underestimate my self-control. I took a vow of celibacy."

"Celibacy?"

"It's kind of a one-day-at-a-time thing, too, like sobriety, but I'm doin' real good, other than the regular Saturday night date with my very own skilled laborer's hand."

"Ben!"

"So you can roast my chestnuts all you want, honey, I won't have any trouble keepin' a cool head."

"Really." Intrigued by the challenge, she nibbled his earlobe. "I wouldn't want to come between you and your date. It is Saturday night, isn't it?"

"I've lost track. No calendar." He slipped her glove off, kissed her hand, slid it down the path of his shirt buttons, over his belt to his lap. "If it is, would you mind filling in? Under the circumstances it's a little awkward for my usual date."

"It's more than a little awkward for . . ."

"Just hold me there while I kiss you again." And he kissed her gently, moving his lips against hers, whetting her taste for him. "Again," he pleaded. Deepening their kiss, he covered her hand with his and arched himself into her palm, quickening his desire for her. "Oh, Jesus, Clara."

"We can't . . ."

"Not here we can't." He closed his eyes and massaged himself with her hand. "We might as well be parked in your mother's driveway."

"Then it's safe for you to kiss me some more," she whispered, squeezing him gently as she nipped at his chin. "Let's see if we can fog up the windows when it's snowing out."

"Chest-nuuuts roaaasting—" He groaned pitifully, then touched his forehead to hers, grinning as he crooned softly, "And damn near on fire . . ."

Bitter cold was the order of the day that they rode for the people who were imprisoned. Slate skies hung low, promising to add another layer of snow to the light ground cover. TJ had returned from the clinic in Eagle Butte and reported to Clara, since Ben was busy making sure the riders were prepared for colder weather. He'd forsaken his trademark cowboy hat this morning in favor of his sheepskin helmet. He warned riders to monitor their horses carefully. As temperatures plummeted, an overexerted horse's lungs could freeze. The support vehicles would be on hand to take on riders and horses should trouble arise.

Shortly before noon they stopped for hot soup, sandwiches, and coffee. Clara fussed over Anna's loose scarf and reminded her to use her face mask when they got under way again. Ben held council with Elliot, Cheppa, and Howard. They were trailing through vast, desolate grasslands, and there were long stretches that were inaccessible except on horseback. The horses would be checked over carefully, and any marginal riders would be encouraged to hop in one of the pickups for the afternoon.

When the parley was over, Ben found windbreak behind a horse trailer, sat back against the wheel housing, and lit a cigarette. He smiled when Clara joined him with an extra cup of black coffee. "It's getting colder." He noted the clouds sliding briskly overhead as he sipped the coffee. "We're going to get more snow."

"And wind. You can feel it coming." He slid over, and she rested her bottom next to his, leaning more than sitting. "They want to move your father to Sioux Falls, but Tara Jean says he won't go."

Ben nodded. Smoke trailed from his lips and faded into the grayness overhead. "That's up to him."

"She says he's pretty weak. I thought I'd go see him this afternoon."

"In my place," he mused, half smiling. She had been known to appear occasionally in his stead when she'd thought he had a duty and he'd thought he had better things to do. He had once said that she should have been named Duty, and for weeks thereafter he'd gotten a kick out of quipping, *Well, howdy there, Duty.*

"In a way, I guess, if you feel you really need to be two people." She smiled, and the light in her eyes told him that she remembered, too.

He glanced away. "He's heavy on my mind right now."

"I know. But your place is also with the ride. You're his way of being in two places at once, and I can be that for you." She studied the toes of her boots. "It really is a circle, isn't it? We're together in it even if you and I aren't . . . together anymore."

"What about last night? Weren't we together?" She looked up quickly, and he smiled. "Or close?"

She shrugged, then nodded, but she was afraid to say what she was thinking. She'd felt closer to him in the last few days than she had for many years, but she was afraid to tell him that. Afraid of exposing herself any more than she already had. There was a void in her life that no one else could fill. There were places in her heart that no one else could touch. Only Ben. Only her husband.

But she was afraid.

"He'd rather see you anyway." Ben's smile turned

wistful. "As he would say, you're easy on his eyes. Easier than me, that's for sure." He sipped his coffee noisily. "How're you gettin' there?"

"Robert Cady offered to take me."

He eyed her speculatively. "Him and Henry?"

"Harvey," she amended. "Be nice, Ben. To him it's his trusty steed."

"His what?" He chuckled derisively. "His lusty seed?"

"Don't."

"Sorry," he muttered, as he braced his ankle on his knee and ground his cigarette against his bootheel. "Wind's pickin' up, and I'm hearing weird things like—"

"He's giving me a *ride*," Clara insisted. "This man does not interest me except as—"

He looked up at her, again with the speculative gaze. "Do I?"

"Unfortunately, yes. You still do." She'd shown it, surely, but it surprised her that she could admit it, surprised her even more that she could laugh about it. "Oh, God, I'm actually participating in a battle of wits with a man who thinks his ultimate weapon is in his pants."

His eyes sparked a quick grin. "You must be enjoying it. You're laughing."

"So are you."

"That's because you're funny. Also because I enjoy watching your face turn pink when you mention what I've got in my pants." He straightened and adjusted the overlap in his coat. "Enjoyin' it so much, it's beginning to show."

"Now *you're* turning red."

"It's just the coat." He draped his arm around her shoulders. "You know what? My dad told me once that if he'd'a been younger that time we first met, he'd'a fought me for you. But I'd'a beat him out, easy. And Cady, too, he's got no *taniga*," he averred, using the Lakota word for guts. "You belong with me."

"You're sure."

"Damn straight." And he gave her his charming, self-assured cowboy wink.

Cady dropped her off. He thought he would pick up a newspaper and have a cup of coffee at the café, and then he promised to wait for her in the lobby.

The clinic was quiet. Anyone who was able to go home for Christmas had done so. The few who occupied the hospital beds slept a lot, coughed some, left the bed rarely. Occasionally a quiet conversation drifted into the clean tiled hallway. There was a tree in the lobby, decorated with multicolored lights, and a "Season's Greetings" banner hung above the nurses' station, but there were no get-well flowers. Clara recalled the dry, wilting potted mums Ben had brought her when she'd given birth to Anna in a similar clinic. He didn't know much about flowers, he'd confessed, but he'd driven to Bismarck for them—150 miles round trip—because when he'd called her mother with the news of the baby's birth, she'd bemoaned the fact that she could find no flower delivery service to Fort Yates. So he'd figured the flowers must have been important, and he'd claimed they were from her mother, too, since it was her idea.

Dewey perked up when Clara entered his room. He pressed a button, and the bed jackknifed him gradually. He nodded approvingly when he saw that she'd brought him some magazines and a box of candy.

"All is going well," she reported. "As cold as it is, everyone still seems to be in good spirits."

He nodded again. "Today is dedicated to the ones in prison, and that's me. Glad they sent me a pretty visitor."

She pulled a chair close to the bed and seated herself. "How are you doing?"

"How do they say . . . as well as can be expected."

The bedding covered the hump of his cast. "Your leg will mend. It'll just take some time."

"Old bones are slow to heal. Like old wounds. When it cuts into the core, sometimes it doesn't heal right. Years later, you got all that scar tissue." He shook his head, giving a chuckle that converted to a brief cough. "Course, I don't have to worry. I got plenty of wrinkles to flop over the scars."

"Your wrinkles are very dear to us. People are asking about you, praying for you. Ben would have come, but he knows you want him to stay with the ride." She studied the old pipe keeper's timeworn hands, his crimped, tobacco-colored skin. "He's doing very well. The pipe is in good hands, and I think everyone knows that except . . ." She smiled sadly. "Except, perhaps, your son."

"He thinks he's got better things to do."

"A couple of weeks ago, I would have said that, too, and it would have been at least partly true." She drew a deep breath and boldly shook her head. After all, she was speaking to a man of considerable insight, daring to inform him about his own son. "Ben's unsure of himself in this role. People always look to you for wisdom and stories, for knowledge of the Lakota way. I think he's afraid to take on that responsibility, for one thing."

"You've studied all of that, daughter. You know a lot about Lakota ways."

"But I'm not Lakota. It's not in my blood. I wish it were." Brazenly she looked him directly in the eye and said quietly, "Sometimes I wish I really were your daughter."

After a quick bout with a deep, energy-sapping cough, he slid his hand across the white sheet, toward the edge of the bed where she sat. "You think you're not? Then you don't know as much as I thought."

"You've taught me more than my own father did. He was always distant."

"Maybe a respectful distance. That is the proper way when a daughter becomes a woman."

"I know, but my memories of him are so sketchy. He died before I was really grown. And my mother and I were never close. I tried to do things in a way that I thought would please them. I tried to be good at everything I did, to outshine everyone else so that my parents would finally say that I was the best daughter anyone could possibly have." She pressed her lips together tightly and gave her head a little shake. "They never did."

"What is the need to compare? There is nothing to compare with a daughter." He coughed and patted the mattress restlessly. "My daughters are all different. Better, best, what does that mean? They are all daughters." He thought about it for a moment, then chuckled. "If I say that you are the smartest one, in a way it would be true, but in a way not true. You and Tara Jean are both smart, but about different things."

"I admire her independence and her tough-mindedness."

"And she admires you. So it's not a question of being the best, is it? We Lakota love a good contest. A basketball game, a foot race, a rodeo, even a fancy dance. But not everything has to be a contest." He rested his head back against the pillow and stared contemplatively at the gray TV screen on the far wall. "Your people make learning a contest. How can it be? There is so much. Each one learns what they can, what they need, what they like. Learning is not a competitive sport, it's . . . it's living, same as breathing, same as praying to your god." He turned to her again. "Same as being a daughter. It's part of being a woman."

"I'm not sure I'm very good at that, either."

"Who told you this?" His head came away from the pillow. "Not my son."

"No," she said, too quickly. "Well, not in words, but . . ."

"But in the way he treats you?"

"He never raised a hand against me, even when he was drinking." She leaned closer, nodded and smiled encouragingly. "I want you to know that because I don't want you to think that he ever . . . hurt me in that way."

"It's too bad he had to hurt you at all. And it's too bad you had to hurt him." The turn of phrase surprised her, but he raised a finger to warn against contradiction. There was hurt on both sides. "Looks to me like you've both kept it up long enough."

"Maybe I'm just as unsure as he is, but one thing I do know is that I wasn't able to satisfy him. As a woman, a wife." She had told no one else, and she shouldn't be telling Dewey, not even a hint. But she had no one else, and this man was like . . . no, he *was* a father to her, even though she had failed his son. "I wasn't enough for him."

"Maybe you were too much for him."

She gave him an incredulous look.

"I don't mean too much sex. There's no such thing. I just mean too much woman. If I'd'a been just a few years younger . . ." He coughed, but the cough soon faded into a weak chuckle. "Now, you see. This is why, the Lakota way, a man does not speak directly to his son's wife."

"I know you didn't mean anything by that."

"Course I did. I meant something. I got a bad leg and bad lungs, but my eyes are still workin' pretty good." Again the long, thin hand patted the side of the bed. "I mean no disrespect, and I don't mean to be meddlin'. If my son wasn't satisfied, it was because he didn't know his own heart. He needs his family. He wants his freedom. He thinks he's a cowboy. He *knows* he's an Indian. He's not sure how all his parts fit together. He's been lookin' for answers here, there, everywhere." The old man bounced a clawlike finger against his own bumpy, scantily clad chest. "They're in his heart. You can tell him, I can tell him, he ain't gonna listen to us. Not until he listens to Tunkasila first."

"That's what he's doing now." Clara nodded vigorously. "I really think so."

"That's what we're all doing on the ride. It's a healing time, healing from the inside out." Again the coughing came, the sickness inside nagging the old man's breath away. Clara poured a glass of water, but Dewey waved it away in favor of finishing what he had to say. "Your husband has his scars. You have yours. Proud flesh, they call it on a horse. Like a callus, hard skin that covers the raw places on the inside. On this ride we open all that up and let the air heal it from the inside out."

She curled both hands around the glass, studying the clear contents. "But how can we keep it from happening again?"

"Well, you can die. Like I'm gonna do pretty soon. Like Sitanka did that day a hundred years ago. Him and most of his people. But not all, and the ones who lived, they still hurt after that day, and from time to time they probably got to thinkin', it hurts too much. Still they survived, and some lived a long time. Your husband is here because of that, and your daughter."

She looked up, her eyes pleading for promises. "Can I believe him when he says he loves me, when . . . when he hurt me in the worst possible way?"

"Can I believe you?" he asked gently. "Your people hurt my people in the worst possible way, but you are my daughter. Will you betray us again?"

"No. Never."

"How do you know that? How can I trust you?"

"Because I love you. I mean, you're more a family to me than . . ." She floundered, gesturing desperately. "I would rather die than to—" She stopped, drew a deep breath, then expelled it with a self-conscious laugh. "Boy, that sounds like a line from a bad movie, doesn't it? But I would never hurt you intentionally."

"My son shamed himself, and he hurt you. In two years I have watched him die a little. But what part of him still lives?" When she could not answer, he told her, "The part that loves."

She rolled her eyes ceilingward and sighed. "I want to believe that that part loves me."

"Your mind tells you what to think, and your heart tells you what to believe. They work together. Try to see the man as he is now." Dewey smiled knowingly. "He's like you. He wants to be the best, but the best what?"

"The best he can be?"

"Maybe. But that keeps changing. We get older, we do better at this, not so good at that. It's good that it keeps changing."

"Makes life more interesting?" She shook her head. "I like to know exactly where things stand."

"Then you get up in the morning and you look to the east. The sun will always be there, even if you can't see it. Each day that is exactly where things stand. The old day is gone. You put it behind you and start a new day. And you thank Tunkasila that people can change."

"But not always for the better," Clara insisted.

"No, not always. A man's promise is just the word of a man. Take it for what it is, and don't expect more. It may be a lie, or it may be the truth as he knows it." He lifted that instructive finger of his. "One thing you *can* count on. Tunkasila does not change. Be thankful for that."

She nodded, realizing that at least one more thing was certain. She couldn't go on living in limbo.

"If Ben continues to serve as the keeper of the pipe after the ride, where will he . . . I mean, is there a certain place he has to be?"

"You mean, like a Lakota Vatican or something?" Dewey's eyes lit up with the old familiar merriment. "My house don't look like St. Peter's too much, does it?"

"I was thinking his hesitancy might be . . ." Her voice dropped near a whisper. "I think he wants to come home."

"I think he wants to be with his wife and child. As for where he'd wanna be livin', we don't have no residency requirements. We're kinda nomadic at heart. But then you know that." Dewey's eyes glistened with a father's pride in all his children. "He could take the pipe to the North Pole if he wanted to, but he wouldn't find too many Lakota people there."

He chuckled, but when the merriment faded, the wisdom remained. "It's just a pipe. Like the ones you've got up in the museum. If it's used in a sacred way, it helps people find the spiritual part of their lives, the part that makes all those warring parts come together. *Wolakota.*" He shrugged. "It's just a pipe, and he's only the keeper."

"But he's needed here."

"Well, we all have choices to make."

She nodded. "And you've chosen not to go to the hospital in Sioux Falls."

"If they took me there, I would not come out. I want to go somewhere, but not Sioux Falls." He lifted his head from the pillow again and signaled for the water.

Clara held the glass for him, and he touched her hand to guide it to his mouth. His skin felt cold and dry. Like death, she thought fearfully, remembering when she'd touched her birth father's lifeless folded hands, bidding a diffident good-bye.

Dewey lowered his head back to the pillow and closed his eyes. "Tell my son that I want to be with the people at Wounded Knee."

Cady was waiting in the lobby, as promised. He jumped to his feet and put on his coat as soon as he saw her coming. "It's snowing out," he announced, nodding toward the expanse of glass near the door. "I'm for finding a hot meal and a room somewhere. How about you?"

"A room?" She scowled. Her thoughts were still down the hall with her father-in-law, but . . . *a room?*

"Well, rooms. A motel."

"Motels are as scarce as hen's teeth out here. Haven't you noticed?"

He shrugged. "We could drive to Rapid City."

She plunged an arm into her jacket sleeve as she peered out the window at the blustery, gray, waning afternoon. "It's not that bad out, is it?"

"It soon will be." He shrugged, half coaxing, half apologizing. "Look, I'm a journalist. My job is to notice when things are out of . . . alignment. I just thought maybe . . ."

Her stare turned hard, icy. She shook her head slowly.

"I did say *rooms* in the plural, so I wasn't . . ."

Her head was still turning back and forth.

"You're not even tempted to take one night off and spend it in a real bed?"

"No," she said lightly, but the look in her eyes had not changed. "Not even tempted. But if you are, I can probably find another ride." She smiled tightly. "Somehow."

"No need. I'm your driver." He drew on his gloves. "I just thought it was worth a shot."

"I suppose if you have shots to waste. But I made a vow." She headed out the door, casting a quick glance over her shoulder to see if he was coming. "Back in Little Eagle, remember? And long before that. Look, this is just a flurry."

It was blizzarding by the time they reached the Redwater Creek camp after stopping several times for directions and to clean off Harvey's windshield wiper blades. Cady did a little grumbling, but he finally admitted that he admired her resolve. And her commitment.

"Mom!" Anna came running as soon as Clara got out of the pickup. "Mom, what's wrong? How's Lala?"

"He's doing, in his words, as well as can be expected. And we had a heck of a time finding this place." She pulled her hood up and started tying it under her chin as she surveyed the camp. The riders must have just gotten here, she thought. A few were tending their horses in the corral, but many of them were still mounted. "Where's Dad?"

"He went out to find Toby."

Clara peered down the dirt road they'd just traveled. She couldn't see much for the swirling snow. "Out . . . where?"

"It was snowing pretty good by the time we got here, and when we made the circle and counted heads, Toby Two Bear was missing."

Clara's eyes widened. "Not out there in this!"

"Don't worry." Anna latched on to her mother's arm. "Dad's gonna find him."

14

Dancing helixes of snow teased Ben's sense of direction. The west wind was a fickle bitch, blowing into his left ear, then spinning around to the right side. He wore his face mask with his sheepskin helmet, but the Dakota wind would still have her way with him. He'd be lucky to get through with a few spots of frostbite.

"Toby! Toby Two Bear!"

Hollering was nearly wasted effort in this wind, but the visibility was deteriorating rapidly, even though it was still light. Gray-white light. He'd had tracks to follow at first, but those had disappeared. For his own safety he was following a fence line. His gelding snorted, then whinnied, wanting out of this part of the Wounded Knee expedition altogether. So did Ben, but fear for the boy overrode his reluctance and shouted down his doubts. It wasn't that far back that he'd run out of signs. Blowing snow had drifted over the tracks now. But there was a good chance Toby was clinging to the fence line, too, just beyond the next knoll.

The gelding snorted again, and an answering whinny drifted back in a whorl of snow. Ben's hopes climbed, then took a nosedive when the signal cut through the gale a second time. It was an equine challenge, not a distress signal. The caller appeared on the hill, first as an intangible ruddy shape, obscured by swirling white streamers. The phantom figure plunged from the hillcrest into a drift, sending up a snow splash. Profuse mane and tail rippled with the zigzag motion of the seemingly effortless descent. It was a feral stud, untamed, unruly, untroubled by the weather. A magnificent red roan mustang, undoubtedly looking for a fight.

"Shit."

Ben took up the slack in his reins and jerked on the half-hitch that secured the cowboy's requisite coiled hard-twist to his saddle. A territorial stud had no use for males, even if they were gelded. The rope was all Ben had with which to chase the mustang away, and he managed to whack him a good one on the first charge.

"Hee-yah! G'wan! Git!"

The gelding laid his ears back and stood his ground as the roan circled, prancing imperiously. Ben waved the hard-twist again, but the roan started bobbing and weaving like a boxer, lunging close, then bounding away.

"I ain't in no mood for games, you crazy sonuvabitch! Git!"

The roan circled again, taunting. He circled yet again, challenging. Easily dodging Ben's menacing coil of hard rope, the stud turned tail and gave a sassy snort, dancing just out of reach like a kid pressing to be chased.

"Yeah, you think you're hot shit, right? You been stealin' mares out here?"

The roan whinnied.

"Okay, we're impressed. Now beat it!"

The stud's nicker sounded too much like derision for Ben to resist taking after him with a whoop and a quick snap of the hard-twist. The roan pointed his nose into the wind and sprinted a few yards, then stopped short and circled again. Teasing. Testing.

Beckoning?

Now, there was a ridiculous idea.

Foolish enough to make him laugh out loud. "Hey, Red, you seen an Indian kid on a pony hereabouts?"

The roan pranced up a short slope, then turned and waited, mane and tail fluttering like pennants in the snow-strewing wind.

The pony. Ben hadn't paid much attention, having a personal disdain for ponies as mounts. Toby kept calling it *this guy*, but that shaggy little pony . . . just might have been a mare.

Ben glanced back at the fence line, stuffed with white-powdered tumbleweeds. Stick to what you know, Ben told himself. Even a cow generally had enough sense to follow the fence line. If he followed this fool stud, he'd end up wandering 'til he froze to death, and it would serve him right. So what if it was a red roan? A holy man would remember the dream. Any cowboy worth his salt would follow the fence line.

And Ben Pipestone didn't have a holy bone in his thick cowboy head.

The red roan whickered from the top of the rise.

He had to choose. He had bet on a red roan before and lost. He couldn't believe he was even *thinking* about making the same mistake again. He couldn't believe he was turning his face to the wind and tapping the geld-ing's flanks with the coiled rope. He *could not believe* he was taking a chance on a goddamn *dream*.

"You'd better not be shittin' me, Red, or there'll be down and dirty hell to pay!"

Like what hell? He imagined the tail he was following whacked off in the old way and hanging from his own burial scaffold. A fitting epitaph for a horse's ass, he told himself. "But it's not just me, it's that boy, too," he muttered into his turned-up collar. "Help me find the boy, Red!" he shouted, and then softly in Lakota, through quivering lips, "Tunkasila, please help me find that boy."

. The fence line was out of sight now, and out of mind. Haunted by the memory of the hill and the quest and the vividness of an old dream, Ben was determined to keep

the red roan in sight. The roan was not a vision. It was
a real horse. He'd struck the animal's scruffy hide with
his rope, and he'd felt the vibration of the blow. He was
following more than a hunch. A horse's brain didn't have
but one track, and if the stud's mind wasn't on the storm,
the scent of mare had to be somewhere in the air.

The horny bastard had to have a damn good nose on
him, too. Which, of course, he did; he depended on it.
So Ben had good reason to believe he was headed in the
right direction. The roan was king of these desolate hills.
If there was another horse around, be it potential rival
or mate, the roan made it his business to investigate. It
was a matter of instinct, a question of territory, a sound
survival tactic. Nothing to do with one boy's dream or
another's dread.

Tunkasila . . .

"Toby! Toby Two Bear!"

Tunkasila, that this boy might live . . .

"Toby! Answer me, Toby!"

Jesus, God, Tunkasila . . .

"Over here!"

The words sounded like distant bells on a stormy
Sunday morning.

"Over here!" The voice was strong but frantic. "Get
away, you!"

Mentally Ben blessed the sight of a cross fence and a
pony's rump, blanketed with snow.

And there was Toby, hunkering down on the side of
the fence opposite his pony, clutching the reins. "Ben!
That horse . . . trying to bite this guy."

"This ain't no guy, Toby, it's a she-horse." And the
roan was a horny savior, no doubt about it. Ben chased
him off with the wave of his hard twist, but he would
no more think of hitting the stud now than he would a
child. He had to believe the horse was *wakan.* Holy.

"Go on now, Red. I'd give her to you, but she ain't
mine to give. *Hiya, kola,*" he said, calling the roan his

friend. "I'll bring you a better one. You don't want her
'til spring, anyway. Go on, now."

The roan lingered briefly, eyeing the man as though
making sure he truly believed, truly understood, then
darted away and disappeared in a gust of wind, a whorl
of snow.

"You saw him, too, didn't you?" Ben asked tentatively
as he swung down from his saddle. "That stud. I didn't
imagine him, did I?"

"That was the meanest horse I ever saw. He chased
me." An ice-encrusted wool scarf drooped around Toby's
red, chapped face, which crumpled a bit as his bravery
melted around the edges. "Barely held on . . . crawled
under the fence . . . b-barely . . ."

Ben stepped the lower strands of fence wire down and
stretched the top one high enough for the boy to crawl
through. "You did fine, Toby."

Toby dove through the hole and hurled himself at
Ben like a football tackle, throwing his arms around the
man's waist. "Fr-Freeezing . . ."

Ben patted the boy's back, devoting one brief moment
to a show of mutual joy and relief. Then he directed
Toby to his own saddle. "I'm gonna ride behind you to
block the wind." He gave the boy a boost, then tied the
pony's reins to the gelding's tail.

"How'd you get separated?" Ben asked once they
were under way again. For direction Ben would have to
depend on the cross fence and have a little faith, which
seemed to be coming to him. Sure as hell, remarkable
as heaven, it seemed to be coming.

"Eagle feather came off. Blew away. Got it b-back." A
tearful Toby dragged his jacket zipper down a few inches
and carefully withdrew the sacred object. "See?"

"Jesus, Toby—"

"Didn't have any t-tobacco, so I left s-some—" he
sniffled noisily "—raisins. D-Does Tunkasila like raisins?"

"I believe so." Smiling stiffly beneath his face mask, Ben guided Toby's hand, tucking the feather back into its envelope. Then he zipped the boy's jacket back up. "Raisins and red roans and boys with more *toniga* than—"

More guts than brains, as some childhood hero had attributed to Ben long ago. Not a great compliment, now that he thought about it. He'd have risked anything for more praise from the older cowboy. And did, long after he'd forgotten the idol's name.

"Boys with a lot of heart," Ben amended. They would talk about using his head later. "Tie your hood down real tight over your cap, now," he said as he pulled his own scarf out of his coat. He used it to cover the boy's face, figuring on giving his new silk turtleneck a real field test.

They met a search party on the way back. A party of five on horseback, with some headlights bringing up the rear. Hard to believe they'd actually made their way back to the gravel road.

Hard to believe? Hell, at this point Ben was almost ready to say there wasn't a blessed thing on God's white earth that was hard for him to believe.

"Lookin' for us?" he joyfully bellowed into the wind.

Elliot Plume rode up next to them, grabbed Toby's shoulder, then Ben's, giving each a quick, robust squeeze. "We weren't sure which way you'd gone, but we rounded up all the four-wheel drives we could find."

"I'm not sure now, either. He was off that way," Ben reported, gesturing vaguely westward. "Couldn't've found him without a horse." He decided not to explain which horse.

Alta Two Bear came tumbling out of the passenger side of a red Blazer, clutching a blanket. Toby swung his leg over the gelding's neck and slid into his mother's waiting arms. She ducked to peer under the bill of his cap, just to make absolutely, gloriously sure it was really her child as she bundled him up in the blanket.

"You need to check for frostbite. He just got separated when his eagle feather blew off." Ben gently thumped the boy's blanketed, hooded head with a gloved hand. "We had us a scare, didn't we, Toby?"

"Yeah." All Ben could see in the upturned face was a pair of bright, appreciative eyes. "Thanks, Ben."

He was offered a ride, but he chose to stay with his horse for the short ride to Joe Bigger's place, where the storm seemed miraculously to dissipate in the windbreak of a thick shelter belt. Most of the horses had already been fed and watered, but a few of the riders were still bustling about the corrals and pens, tending to the last of the chores.

"Hey, Ben!" someone called out. "Still got your ears?" He couldn't see the face—looked like a walking snowman—so he just waved as he trotted alongside the railing toward the gate. He knew the campsite was situated in a sheltered coulee just over the hill from Joe's house, and supper would be waiting at the little community center another mile or so down the road. If his hands and feet didn't fall off before he got there, he was looking forward to pulling into the chow line and diving right into some hot soup.

Anna met him on the run as he dismounted, spun him around with an exuberant hug, and took charge of both horses. "I knew you'd be fine, but I think Mom's been doing her usual worry routine," she confided. "Personally, I think you oughta play it up for all it's worth."

Ben agreed with a wink and a smile. Then he turned and saw Clara, resolutely headed his way. Like Alta, she carried a blanket. Undoubtedly she planned to mother him with it, but he had other ideas. Somehow he was going to get himself loved up, not mothered up. When she enfolded him in her arms without the slightest hesitation, he figured it was a good start.

She'd been sitting in a warm pickup, and she could feel him shivering, but for one brief moment she held him hard and fast, then looked up, searching the eyes in the holes of his face mask as she furiously set about brushing the snow off his shoulders. "Are you okay?"

"Chilled to the bone, but . . ." He nodded.

She shook out the blanket and draped it over his shoulders. "Thank God. Where's . . . ?" She scanned the yard, located the vehicle, and escorted him in its direction. "Let's get in the pickup. TJ's helping the girls. I think we ought to have another prayer circle over at the community center, don't you? I mean, it has to be a miracle, finding him in this, and both of you coming back—"

He grabbed her arm and stopped her, midsentence, midthought, midway. She turned as he was tearing off the cumbersome helmet and face mask, his eyes seeking hers through the drifting, swirling snow. He looked pale, even a little disoriented, and that scared her. But he made her stop chattering and look at him, see that he was really there, that he'd been to hell and back and that if she wanted a miracle, she was looking it right in the face.

She threw her arms around his neck and pressed her warm cheek to his icy, badly chafed one. "I'll say the prayers this time, Ben, gladly. I'll sing glory alleluias if you'll let me."

"In Lakota?"

She stood on her toes and whispered hotly in his ear. "In bum-fuck Egyptian if there's such a language."

To his shivering delight she'd mixed the sacred with the profane, and he'd never been so glad to be alive. Laughing, he wrapped her with him in his blanket and headed them both toward the purring pickup.

She drove. He huddled in the blanket, clacking his teeth, shivering, and laughing perilously near the point of tears.

"What's so funny?" she demanded, but she was laughing, too, because the sound of it was infectious.

"Hell, I don't know. I was just thinking about what you said, and I imagined you singin' this crazy song all in cuss words, and me doin' this little teeth-chattering accompaniment." Which he kept demonstrating involuntarily between phrases. "I'd'a made one hell of an ice sculpture out there." His gesture indicated an imaginary tableau on the windshield, persistently being whapped by wipers. "*End of the Trail*. Frozen in time."

She giggled. "Now through April. See him before he melts."

"They could use a winter tourist attraction around here." He chuckled. "I can just see that bunch of movie stars who bought up half of Deadwood for casinos." He cupped a hand next to his mouth and faked a summons. " 'Hey, haul that frozen Indian up here. Put him up on the ridge there, overlooking the gold mines. Hell of a sunset shot.' "

"Oh, God, Ben, you have such a morbid sense of humor."

"Don't be bad-mouthin' my sense of humor, woman." He drew the blanket tight. "It's all I've got left."

"I don't think so," she said quietly as she parked the pickup in front of a small Quonset building. She shut the engine off and turned to him. "I think you have more going for you now than . . ."

He waited, hopeful.

She started to finish, then stopped herself and simply looked into his eyes, letting him see what she could not say. The silence was, for a change, not a cold one. It was replete with warm wishes and fragile possibilities.

He risked a bit of a smile.

She offered a surer one. "Turnabout is fair play. I found you a bathtub."

"I think I'd better eat something first. Haven't been eatin' much. It didn't bother me, but now . . ."

As if on command she flung the door open, hopped to the ground, hurried to the passenger's side, and offered him her arm. And arm in arm they went inside to share a hot meal with the rest of the Big Foot riders.

Anna had somehow beaten them to the center. She met her father with soup and fry bread in hand. "Eez, she's a good girl," he said wearily. "Thanks, An—"

"Here, Daddy, sit down." She kept glancing up at him anxiously as she led him to one of the tables, and he wondered whether he looked like someone who'd just stepped into his own grave. "You need fuel when it's this cold, Daddy. A little food and you'll be just fine. But I knew you'd find him. I told his mom she didn't have a thing to worry about."

"They said you hadn't been gone that long," Clara said, "but it seemed like forever."

"I didn't think he could've gotten too far. Had tracks to follow for a little way, but then it really started comin' down, and with the wind . . ." He shook his head as he took a seat at the end of a long table. "But we made it back." It already seemed like a dream, totally surrealistic, like something that couldn't have happened the way he remembered. There was only one indisputable reality for him now. "We made it back."

Clara touched his cheek with the back of her hand as though she were testing for fever. "Anna, would you bring Dad some orange juice? I think there was some over there."

"And coffee," he said between sips of soup.

"You need the juice. You look . . ." She studied his eyes. "What happened out there, Ben?"

"I'm not sure. Probably no big deal. I need to do some thinkin' about it and . . ." And talk it over with the one man who could help him sort it all out. "You saw my father?"

"We had a good talk," she told him, but clearly she wasn't sure how much more she ought to say. "He asked me to tell you that he . . ."

"He what?"

"He said to tell you that he wants to be with the people at Wounded Knee. I'm sure he means the riders, when we get there." Nothing more, although the apprehension in her eyes and her careful tone handed him all her misgivings on a guileless plate. "Crazy as it sounds, I think he wants us to go and get him or something."

He tore the thick square of fry bread in half. "You don't think he wants to be with the people who are waiting there for us? Who have been there for the last hundred years?"

She glanced away. "I'm sure he means he wants to be with us, after we arrive."

"How bad off is he?"

"He doesn't think . . ." She sighed heavily. "He feels that if he went into the hospital in Sioux Falls, he wouldn't come out."

"Alive," he added pointedly. "And he wants to go to Wounded Knee."

"That's what he asked me to tell—" she smiled gently, laying her hand on his coat sleeve "—his son. He's counting on you."

"To take him to a damn cemetery when I should be—" He tore a savage bite off the fry bread and chewed deliberately. "*His son* ought to go up there tonight and haul that old man's scrawny ass to a decent hospital, and the hell with all this—"

"I'll go with you if that's what you think you ought to do."

He stared at the broken bread. "I could make him go. I could just say, hell, he's out of his mind half the time anyway, he can't decide for himself." His gaze met hers, looking for his wife's sensible judgment, her reassurance. "I'm the damn pipe keeper now, right? I'm the so-called holy man. He's just . . ."

"He's your father." Her grip tightened on his arm. "Ben, you're shivering."

"I don't know what I'm doin' freezin' my ass off out here in this godforsaken . . ."

"Yes, you do," she said as Anna delivered the orange juice to her mother, as though Ben were, like his father, a patient. "Drink this. We need to get you into some warm water and soak the chill out of you."

"He's gonna die soon, Clara." She gave him that this-is-between-us grimace, but he ignored it. Anna's and Billie's chatter was drifting down the line of chairs as they served coffee to some of the other adults, and Ben needed to know what his wife had seen. "Isn't he?"

"After this is all over, maybe we can talk him into going into the hospital."

"He's always been real stubborn about going to the doctor, but he's always taken pretty good care of himself. Never drank or . . . Course, he uses the pipe, but no cigarettes. He hardly ever got sick." Saying it and believing it were two different things, but now the cold comprehension of his father's mortality shook him. "He just got old."

"And you've got a bad case of the chills," she said. "Stop talking and finish your food so I can get you into some nice warm water."

"You tryin' to mother me, woman?" He smiled and pushed his chair away from the table. "I really do like the sound of that last part."

Clara led the way out the side door, across a little alleyway, and through a waist-high wooden yard gate. Snowflakes danced in the circle of light cast by the lamp above the front porch. She took a key from her pocket and unlocked the door.

"Mrs. Whipple is a teacher at the school here," she explained as she flipped up the wall switch in the front room. "She's over at the community center, helping in the kitchen, but she offered anyone who needed it the use of her bathroom." She shrugged her jacket off, took his coat, and laid them both across the sofa, next to a pile of clothes she'd put there in advance. "I took her right up on it, brought our clothes over and got Anna taken care of. But I was waiting for you. Anna kept saying she wasn't worried at all, and I was sure you knew what you were doing, but I wanted to wait."

"Were you worried about me anyway?" He sat down to pull off his boots. "Annie said you were, but you know Annie. She jumps to conclusions." His smile invited her to try, just *try* to convince him otherwise.

"I was, a little." Her smile confessed to more than a little. She shrugged prettily. "Old habit, I guess. Shall I draw your bath, sir?"

"Takin' up a new hobby? You can draw me right in the bath if you want." Grinning, he followed her down the hall. "Full frontal nudity, exclusively for you, Clara-bow."

She'd already started running the water, and he wasn't sure she'd heard him until she looked up and he saw that coy twinkle in her eye. He smiled and watched her watch him unbutton his shirt. He peeled the second layer from the bottom up, unconsciously airing up his chest as he did so, but when he pulled the turtleneck over his head, she was adjusting the faucet with one hand and catching a handful of water with the other, missing his display. "There, that feels about right. I'm going in after you this time. We dug out a change of clothes for you, too. You need—"

Stripped down to his jeans, he was leaning back against the sink, balancing ankle over knee as he peeled off a sock. His toes were flame red.

With a murmur of sympathy Clara slid from the side of the tub to her knees and enclosed his toes between her warm, wet hands. She lifted her chin. "Are they frostbitten?"

He was surprised, moved by her tender gesture, shaken partly by her expression of concern, mostly by his unbidden fancy that an angel had suddenly floated down and landed at his feet. "No," he croaked. His throat had gone dry, and he had to swallow before he could say, "I think the red's actually a good sign."

"Then your hands and face must be in good shape, too."

He nodded as he reached for her shoulders and drew her to her feet, setting his own on the floor, pulling her into his arms for the kiss he'd craved since the moment he'd come in out of the cold. The deep, delicious kiss that would truly chase the chill away. His tongue darted into her mouth, searching for warmth and welcome. She greeted him with featherlight touches, tongue to tongue, her body melting against his. She needed to hold him in her arms and know for certain that he was safe and whole. And she was as eager for the kiss as he was.

The power and the joy of it unsettled them both. They drew back from it slowly, lips still parted, savoring the titillation and wordlessly seeking assurances, each from the other's eyes.

"I think I stopped shivering," he said.

"I think I'm starting to." Tenderly she touched his cheek. "You saved that boy's life, Ben."

"Kid gets lost, you go find him. Couldn't leave him out there. Ordinarily I'd say it was just a lucky find." His hands opened, then closed again on her shoulders as a veil of utter amazement settled over him. "But I have to say, it feels like more than luck."

"It was *you*," she insisted. "Your quick thinking, your cool head, and your willingness. Not everyone would take that risk. You've always had so much confidence in a crisis. More than I ever did. I'm just sort of a plodder."

"A plodder?"

"Day-to-day kind of dependable." As if to prove her point, she turned back to her task, tested the temperature, then added more hot water. "I never do anything remarkable. Neither remarkably bad nor remarkably good. I just plod along."

"It never looked like plodding to me. I mean, you know where you're goin', you take your time, you get there, get it done, get it done right." He unzipped his pants. "Which I personally think is pretty remarkable."

"No, you don't. It's dull and predictable, and you are neither of those things."

"Neither was Billy the Kid, but what did he ever accomplish?"

"I repeat, you saved a boy's life today." She smiled as he dropped his jeans atop the pile he was building on the toilet lid. "And you really do look great in silk underwear."

"Yeah, well, underneath, it's just the same ol' predictable—" he grinned as he gave the elastic waistband a quick shove "—ultimate weapon!"

"That's my cue," she said, sidling out the door. "Although you still . . ."

"What's that?" he shouted as he shut the water off.

" . . . look just fine without them."

Much later Clara emerged from her turn in the tub. An all-over bath had to be the finest of all luxuries, she'd decided. That and being under the same roof with the man whose presence in the world still in so many ways felt like her personal blessing.

Ben was standing at the window, a hulking shadow watching the night, his shoulder braced against the frame. Reflected light from the snow detailed the room in gradations of light and dark. "Snow's lettin' up," he said, his eyes fixed on some distant point beyond the glass. "Looks like most of the riders are stayin' in town. Tomorrow's a rest day."

"Anna and Billie are staying at the center."

He turned to her. "What about you?"

"I'll stay with the girls." She stepped closer. "You?"

"I kinda like sleepin' in the ol' man's buffalo skins."

"Is it warm?"

He hooked his right arm around her and drew her to his side. "When we build a fire inside, it's pretty warm. It has kind of a timeless feeling about it, you know? It helps me . . ." He rubbed his chin over her clean, damp, flower-scented hair. "At night I lay awake sometimes and try to make sense of things. When I make my bed in a tipi, it adds a little different shape to the sense of things."

"You know that tipi we have in the museum?" She slipped her arm around his waist. "I've gone in there and just sat a few times. The floor is covered with buffalo hides, and there's a willow backrest, a little fire ring, and that Indian mannequin. It's kind of cozy."

"But no earth, no sky, no fire burning."

"I imagine those. In a way it helps me make sense of my work, too. Preserving things under glass. Trying to keep them in perfect condition, exactly the way they once were."

"They don't stay the same if real people live with them and use them instead of mannequins." He smiled, imagining her checking to see that nobody was watching, then ducking inside the well-preserved tipi to keep company with a statue. "It's good to know that there's somebody like you watching over a few samples of our old stuff. Someone who cares about who we really were."

"And *are*."

Some of us, he thought.

Or seem to be, she thought.

He looked down at her, carefully smoothed her hair back from the side of her face and studied her, his smile turning melancholy. Light and shadow delineated his handsome, angular face, but his eyes were so dark, so hard to read. He'd won her heart long ago. Surely he did not doubt that, even though she'd said time and time again that she couldn't love him anymore. She'd also let him see that she couldn't *not* love him.

So there it was. The age-old enigma. The opposites who couldn't quit attracting.

"Are we finished here?" he asked. "I wanna check on Toby, say good night to Annie. And to you." He lowered his head, his lips seeking hers. At the last moment she turned hers away. "What's wrong? You kissed me in the bathroom."

"I know, but . . ."

He sighed, then planted a chaste kiss on her forehead. "Good night to you, Clara-bow."

The lights had been turned off at the center for the night, but there were still some murmurings in the sleeping bags and pallets scattered about the floor. The girls had gone to sleep, but Clara lay awake, still thinking of her husband. And suddenly he was there. She knew him by his shadowed shape, backlit and lingering in the doorway. And she knew he would come no closer than that. The rest was up to her. So she slipped from her bed and went to him.

He smiled, pulling her into the entry as soon as she came within reach. "You wanna spend the night in a real tipi?"

"Not with four men," she whispered.

"How about just one man? Everyone else has made other arrangements for tonight."

"At whose suggestion?"

"Guys just know these things. Between guys, they just know when it's time to make themselves scarce." He stepped closer, filling her senses with the proximity of a man just come in from the cold. "When somebody wants some time alone with his wife, who's never slept in a tipi before. I've got a nice fire goin'. The bed's all made the old way." His smile loomed scant inches from hers. "I'm wearin' fancy silk underwear."

"No breechclout?"

"I can get one. Whatever your heart desires."

Her heart desired him, even though her head knew better. They drove TJ's pickup to the campsite near the frozen creek, little more than a mile from the heart of the tiny community, but it felt as though they had traveled infinitely farther. The tipi rising from a snowy landscape seemed to touch night's low gray ceiling in another world, another time. Its walls glowed from the small fire inside, inviting them to come, warm themselves, spend the night together. Clara banished her doubts back to the world she'd left behind, much the same way she had done when she'd followed her young, bold cowboy so many years ago.

This time he'd made a furry bed for her beside a rock hearth. Smoke drifted toward the tip of the cone, where the lodgepole ribs poked past the canvas into the night.

"Take your coat, ma'am?"

She handed him her jacket, and he dropped it on the canvas floor along with his.

"You know, it's not easy, putting one of these things up in the winter, clearing a spot for it, pegging it down. We're kinda cheatin', havin' people prepare the campsite for us." He added wood to the fire as he spoke, and she hovered close, soaking up the heat along with his every word, exactly the way she had when she had first begun to love him.

"You think about Sitanka's people," he said. "They were runnin' for their lives, pushin' as hard as they could, lookin' for food along the way, while we've got people feeding us. But those guys long time ago, they still had to set up their own camp on ground frozen just as hard as this. They started out traveling at night, but later they marched in daylight. Sad part is, they were headed for disaster." He sat back on his haunches and poked at the burning logs with a stick, seeking just the right order. "What do you think they did at night, when they were camped like this?"

"Rested." She put her hands on his broad shoulders and knelt behind him, kneading the hard muscles she knew must be aching far more than hers did after the day he'd put in. "And sat around the campfires, the way we have been, talking and making plans."

"They couldn't have big campfires that would have attracted attention. Little ones like this were okay. I suppose the men got together for a while. The women tried to comfort their hungry children, rock them to sleep. God, that feels good."

"The rocking?"

"The comforting arms," he murmured. "Comforting hands." And he enjoyed them several moments longer before he reached up to his shoulder, took her hand in his, and pressed it gratefully to his lips. He turned to her, smiling. "Then I think they crawled into their beds and made love. I hope they did, because they weren't gonna get too many more chances." He took her by the hand and drew her to his own bed. "That's what I have in mind for us tonight."

"I know."

He took her boots off, then his. Between tender, almost shy kisses he draped them both in blankets and peeled away layers of clothing until only the silk remained. They slipped into the warm buffalo-hide nest, building the heat of their kisses, relishing one another like two devout pilgrims breaking a long fast. They were hungry, but more important, they were determined to savor, to appreciate, to memorize the taste of restoration.

And the touching was equally delectable, luxuriant silk abetting lips and hands with the tempting, the teasing, the plying of tingling, timeless magic on erogenous flesh. Every nerve was alerted. Legs wound around each other, thigh rubbing thigh, knee nudging groin. Her nipples tightened and strained, yearning for direct intercourse with his tongue. His nipples tightened and strained, yearning to be nibbled away by her harrowing teeth.

Just the feel of him threatened to liquify her senses and send them sluicing through her body's corridors.

Just the feel of her threatened to turn him into a human torch, incapable of resisting the impending flameover.

But first he would feel more, as would she. The silk finally fell by the wayside, and they touched skin to skin, lips to skin, tongues to skin, until neither could breathe anything but the air the other had warmed, neither could hear anything but the pleasured sound the other made, and neither could taste anything but the warm, erotic juices of the other's body.

"I need you, Ben," she gasped, choking back tears. "I need you now. I need you always."

He pressed his thigh between her legs, and she rubbed her mound against it, whimpering piteously.

"I can make you come," he whispered into the hollow of her neck. "With my hand, with my tongue. If you don't want my—"

"I do," she groaned, slipping her hand between his legs, seeking him. "I need this, too, and this needs me."

"Very much," he whispered, driving himself crazy just by pumping his aching rod against her palm. "Very, very much."

"Then let it love me."

"Then let yourself forgive me," he said as he rose above her on arms trembling with the need to do exactly what she asked. "Forgive me and take me inside you."

"I love you," she said breathlessly.

"Is that the same thing?"

She nodded, tears coursing into her hair.

"Can't you say the other?"

She closed her eyes and shook her head.

"Oh, God," he groaned. He didn't know if he could draw breath against the pain that pierced his chest. Neither could he draw back or move away or . . .

"I need you," she said softly. "I've always loved you, and I need you now."

"I need—" loving her with his eyes, he thrust his hips, probing gently "—to give you anything you need. Lay your hands on me, Clara. Touch me and heal me."

She slipped her arms around him, slid her palms down his warm, corded back, filled her hands with his hard buttocks and urged him to fill her deeply.

"Say you love me," she begged.

"I love you. I want you to love me."

"I do."

"Without hating me," he said, still holding back, still rubbing the tip of his penis against her moist portal. "Forgive my worthless body with your loving touch."

Trembling with want and love and free-flowing tears, she brought her hand up between them, tenderly touching his belly, his chest, his neck, his face, all the while opening her thighs and lifting her hips, arching herself to him.

"Tell me you belong to me tonight," she said, weeping.

"Tonight and always." He lowered his head and sipped her tears. "Sweet Jesus, I've been so lonesome for you, Clara . . . so damned miserable without . . ."

His body came home to hers.

He couldn't expect her to give him the solace he'd begged for. What he'd done was not forgivable. The very fact that she lay there in his arms, sated with lovemaking and watching the fire with him, was more than he had a right to expect. He watched her silky hair sift through his fingers, catching the firelight. "If we'd never met, Cady's the kind of guy that you might have married," he said, feeling a little sorry for himself out loud.

She looked at him curiously. "What kind of guy is that?"

His apology was couched in a warm smile. "The kind that's anything but a cowboy. The kind that might have made you happy."

"I'm happy right now. Tonight." She closed her eyes and nuzzled his bare shoulder. "With you."

"I'm happy, too." He kissed the top of her head. "I almost forgot what it was like."

"I don't want another man, Ben." She lifted her arm, propped her head on her hand, and looked into his eyes. "There's something I need to be able to tell you without you flying off the handle. Will you listen calmly?"

She was going to tell him she'd had to prove something to herself, and then she was going to tell him just what it was. He probably didn't want to know. It was a choice he hadn't given her when he'd made his unforgivable confession. He eyed her warily, but he nodded.

"Robert suggested that we stay in town tonight since the weather was getting bad. He suggested sticking to the highway, finding a motel."

His eyes glazed over. His throat went dry, and he couldn't swallow. His gut churned.

But he listened.

"The roads were bad," she reminded him. "It was probably a sensible suggestion."

"But you—" He willed himself to look only at her, think only of her, regard the look in her eyes and hear the clear, honest tone of her voice. She had her faults. She had her weaknesses. She wasn't perfect, and maybe she was just too damned stubborn or righteous to go along with such a proposition. But she was his Clara. And he didn't have to ask. He knew. "You wouldn't go along with it."

"No. I told him I'd find someone else to drive me back. I really didn't care whether it was sensible or not. I had to get back." She shrugged. "So he brought me back."

"He was just fishing to see how far he could get with you."

She nodded. "It surprised me. It was almost but not quite subtle. I'm not even sure he was actually suggesting anything really *specific*, but if he was, it was totally out of line, totally uncalled-for." She scowled suddenly. "Why would he do that?"

"To see what you'd do." God, she was beautiful. How could any man resist trying to catch her eye? He tucked a strand of hair behind her ear and smiled. "I oughta wrap his camera strap around his scrawny neck and give it one quick jerk."

"No need. I defended my own honor."

"How? Did you smack him?"

"I said no." She gave him a simple-as-that look. "I wasn't sure I should tell you, but I didn't want to feel like I was hiding something from you. I don't have anything to hide."

"I know."

"I don't want another man. Sometimes I wish I did. Or that I could just let you think I did, so you'd know how it feels." She laid her hand on his chest. "But I don't. And even if I did, I wouldn't."

"I know." He pulled her into his arms and wrapped his leg around both of hers. "I know all that in my head, Clara, but there's some part of my gut that's always in doubt when another guy comes around. 'She really doesn't think you're good enough for her,' it says. 'This guy's gonna take her away.' "

"Not if I don't want to go. How could anyone take me if I didn't want to—" She drew back. "How did that woman manage to take you? What kind of magic did she use?" In a quiet, somber tone, she wondered, "How was she better than I was, Ben?"

"It was more like she was as bad as I was. She was easy. And I was more worried about somebody makin' me *look* like a fool than about me actually being one. And that's what I was, a goddamn fool. I didn't believe . . ." He touched her bow-shaped lips with an adoring finger. "Nobody's better than you, Clara-bow. There may be some few things about you that I don't like sometimes, but there's nobody better."

She pouted. "What few things?"

"Right now I can't remember, but I know there were a few little things." He smiled. Talking about this stuff was getting easier, and that amazed him.

"There was a time when I thought you could do no wrong," she confided. "I fell in love with you first, you know. Way before you fell in love with me."

"Can you do it again?"

"That doesn't seem to be the problem, does it?" She rolled to her back. "The problem is trust. I no longer believe that you can do no wrong."

"And I no longer believe that what you don't know won't hurt you." He propped himself up and adjusted the bedding around her shoulders as he spoke. "Or that doin' wrong is just as easy as doin' right and more fun to boot. It's not fun." His gaze drifted to the dying fire. "It's not fun to wake up the next morning pukin' up everything but the guilt. The guilt stays with you. It poisons your blood and makes you go back, maybe a day later or a month later, but you go back because the poison hurts, and you figure your soul is already so black that one more time can't make it worse, and maybe you can get it out of your system this time, or maybe . . ." He closed his eyes and let the loathsome memory fill his head. "Maybe some miracle will happen and you can start over again, clean and new, good enough to be loved."

And maybe it finally had, because something told him now that he *was* good enough. It wasn't something new, either. Whatever it was, he was comfortable with it. It had been part of him all along. Buried under all the bullshit.

He laughed. He wasn't sure what he was laughing at. Himself, probably. But it felt good.

"Jesus, Clara, if you can't love me unless I can do no wrong, I guess I'm sunk."

"The loving isn't a problem. That's a given. I love you, and that seems to be irreversible." She lifted her head, touched her lips to the corner of his suddenly boyish grin, and whispered, "It's the trust."

"How can I earn your trust?" The grin vanished, replaced by the sincerity aglow in his eyes. "By being honest with you, right? Telling you the rock-bottom truth was the hardest thing I've ever had to do, but I gotta tell you, it taught me one thing. I can't live with my own lies. Lying is part of the sickness. I lied to myself first, then I lied to you. I built a wall out of lies, and when I tore that down—" he smoothed her hair back, as though he were uncovering treasure "—there you were, staring at this awful, ugly truth. Staring at the face of the sorry bastard that did you wrong."

"Oh, Ben . . ."

"Sinful, but honest. And I like the honest part because it gave me a new start. And I think I stand a chance of doing better. I can't live with my own lies, but I have reached the point where I can live with the truth. The question is, can you?"

She glanced away.

Softly he amended, "I guess the real question is, do you want to try?"

"I've lived with the truth for two years. I can't help caring about you. I can't help loving you. Obviously, I *can* have sex with you." She looked up at him. "The *real* question is, can I live with you?"

"Yeah. I guess that's the real question."

She touched his cheek. "It's not the only question, Ben. Can you live with me?"

He lowered his head, burying his face in her hair, averring huskily, "I don't wanna live without you."

"But you *can*. You've lived without me for two years, and you've been sober all that time. I didn't do that for you or with you. You did it yourself." She put her arms around his shoulders and held him close. "We're not the same two kids we were when we first got married. We're older. You're a lot wiser than I realized, and I'm finally wising up."

"We still fit together."

"Yes, but you also fit other—"

"No." He rose above her again, taking her chin in his hand, begging her to see the honesty in his eyes. "I don't, Clara, I don't. God, please don't think like that." He tore his gaze from hers, feeling powerless. He could do no more than ask.

Gently. "Please don't. All I know is, I love you. I can't explain it or dress it up to make it any prettier." He risked it again, looking into her eyes. And he exposed that fragile part of himself that had always been good enough. "It is what it is, Clara. A poor man's love. And it's all I have left to give you."

Her small arms enfolded him, pulling his head down, nesting his face close to her woman's heart. "I love you, too, Ben. God help me, I do."

15

Clara awoke to find herself alone in the pale light of early morning. The fire had been newly rekindled in the fire pit, and she wondered how she'd slept through it. Then she heard the pickup's approach. Quickly she pulled her long-sleeved undershirt on over her head and plunged her legs into the long, silky-cold bottoms.

Ben ducked under the tipi's door flap, frosty breath puffing through his smile. "I brought you some coffee." He lifted a Styrofoam cup in one hand, a small paper bag in the other. "And some breakfast. We had the morning circle already."

Clara yawned luxuriantly. "Why didn't you wake me up?"

"It's a day of rest, and you were resting beautifully." Squatting next to the pallet, he handed her his offerings, then pivoted and added several pieces of wood to his miniature tipi of a fire. "And this day is dedicated to the women. A good day all around."

She watched him while she snuggled into her warm nest and sipped her coffee. Indeed, it was. The sure way he moved his hands had always fascinated her, no matter what the task he'd set them to. Building a fire, changing spark plugs, saddling a horse. Touching her.

"You warm enough?" He'd taken his coat off, and now he was pulling off his boots.

"I put my underwear back on." The truth, it seemed, was that cold was easier to deal with once you got used to it, and warmth had become a truly valued pleasure. She smiled. "Without you cuddled up close to me, it wasn't quite as cozy."

He unbuckled his belt. "I'm about to remedy that."

"People will be looking for us."

"Not before noon." He stepped over her, giving her the fire side, and slid behind her, becoming her backrest. "I just want to hold you while you drink your coffee." He nuzzled the side of her neck. "Mmm, you smell like a woman's sweetness."

"And that's a sweet thing for you to say. I suspect I smell like an old buffalo hide."

"Truth is, you smell like woodsmoke and sweet sex."

She laughed. "Truth is, I'm going to *have* to get up soon."

"Just say when. I'll stand lookout for you." He pulled the sack closer and crooned temptingly, "I brought you something sweet."

She tipped her head back and looked up at him. "You know, when I was growing up and thinking about what it would be like to be married, about sharing so much time and space with another person, I remember thinking, gosh, if you go in the bathroom, he'll know what you're doing in there." Again she laughed, all her innocent delight suddenly replenished. "Imagine that. And after a while he will have seen everything, all your private parts and personal property, and he'll know all the stuff you go through, and I couldn't see how that would ever be anything but a daily embarrassment."

"Some things were touchy at first," he recalled, smiling. "Like the first time I had to buy those things for you because you were too sick to go to the store. I had to go back to that same aisle three times because people

I knew kept poppin' up every time I turned around, and I couldn't find the kind you wanted right away."

"As I remember, we were on a very tight budget, but you bought a bunch of paper towels and boxes of tissue that we didn't need."

"Had to bury that box under something." He chuckled. "Doesn't bother me anymore, though. I can walk right up to a stock boy and ask where they keep the kind without the applicator. Had one poor kid turning as red as his apron once."

"It doesn't bother me, either. It did at first, automatically picking the stuff you like off the store shelves." She closed her eyes and laid her head back on his shoulder. She hadn't known this kind of contentment in such a long time. Funny. The stupidest, littlest things had been impossibly difficult to deal with sometimes, and he was the only person she wanted to talk with about it. She gave a small laugh. "I clean with pine soap because you always thought that was the smell of a truly clean house. I still buy the kind of toothpaste you like, I guess because it's grown on me. I even have an old toothbrush of yours still in the bathroom."

"I don't have much of you," he said, his voice dropping so low, it felt sad and heavy in her ear. "A few pictures. Some things you gave me as gifts. A vest you made for me." He chuckled softly. "Remember that leather vest that was a little too small?"

"You wore it anyway," she recalled, staring wistfully at the flickering flames a few feet away as she finished her coffee and set the cup aside.

"You broke your sewing machine on it. Thought it was the least I could do." He paused, then stroked her silk-clothed arm. "After I first got my phone there were a couple nights when someone called but didn't say anything, just hung up. Not too many people had my number. I've wondered . . ."

"I was . . ."

She looked up. He looked down.

"Seeing who'd answer?"

"Worse." She felt so foolish, she hardly found voice to confess. "I wanted to hear your voice."

"Oh, Jesus, Clara. I'd'a talked all night. I'd'a called you back and paid the bill." His arms enfolded her tightly, and he rubbed his cheek against her hair, put his mouth close to her ear. "When I'd call to talk to Annie, most times you wouldn't say two words to me. I never thought—"

"The sound of your voice over the phone, speaking into my ear . . . even that is an intimacy because you speak to me differently from the way you talk to other people. A little quieter tone, maybe."

"And you have your special voice for me. For your husband. I am—" he paused, his voice slipping smoothly into a whisper "—still your husband."

"You are. And I guess I do." She curled her arms over his and pressed them to herself even tighter. "I can't think of letting another man come into my life that way, or of sharing myself. Not just in the sexual sense, but the intimate details of my life, the secret drawers, the . . . *personal* things."

She turned to him with a plaintive look, and he knew what was coming, knew it as surely as he knew he had no right to take such acute pleasure in the confidence she'd just shared.

"How did you . . . I mean . . ." She closed her eyes, gave her head a quick shake. "It's hard enough for me to think about you having sex with someone else, but the other things, sharing the same sheets, the cup in the bathroom, my hair mixed with yours in the hairbrush . . ." Her small, self-deprecating laugh pierced his heart. "It sounds really stupid when I say it out loud, but I begrudged her those pieces of you, too."

"Then don't bring her in here with us now, Clara, because I don't even remember the color of her . . ."

He caught her chin in his hand when she tried to turn away. "I wasn't interested. I never stayed with her. I don't—"

She was still unsure of him. He could see it in her eyes. He sighed and let her face slide over his open palm. "Clara, when I said the prayers this morning, I gave thanks for Toby Two Bear's restoration to us and to his mother after being lost yesterday. But I also gave thanks for my own restoration, because I was out there alone, too."

Her chin dipped to her chest, and she covered the back of his hand with hers.

He clutched her fingertips, acknowledging her gesture.

"I've been lost for a long time, Clara. You're my mooring. There were times when I used to think I didn't need a mooring. Sometimes I thought it was cool and breezy just to drift. Maybe it is, but only for an afternoon or so. I wanna put in at the same harbor every night."

"Some harbor," she said with a sigh. "I seem to be following you from pillar to post again, the way I used to when you were riding in rodeos. I'm really not the follower type, but I seem to be doing it again. Following you."

"Hey, this was our daughter's idea, and when you went along with it, no choice, I had to come along just to watch out for my . . ." She looked up at him, and he smiled. "For my girls."

"But there's more to it now. There's an added dimension to your journey, isn't there?" She glanced past the mound their knees made to the red coat at the foot of the bed, and to the buckskin bag on top of it. "One that's always been there in the corner of your mind, waiting for you to stop being afraid to touch it."

"Or take it from my father, who's as good a man as ever drew breath." He, too, studied the coat. "Treated like shit by a woman who wasn't fit to live in the same world with him."

"I've never heard you put it quite that way before."

"Pardon my French."

"No, I mean, you usually say something like, he should have known better than to let her make a fool of him. As though you were angry with him for not holding on to her or something."

He sighed. "He held on too long. She gave him nothing but heartache."

"And you."

"She didn't cause me any heartaches," he claimed a bit too lightly. "I thought I missed her 'cause the ol' man did, but—"

"I meant, she gave him more than heartaches. She gave him a son." She turned to him now, looking into his eyes, seeking to reassure him. "Whom he treasures."

"He never could be sure . . . I was really . . ."

"He has no doubt." She stroked his hair, watching him lose himself to some troublesome specter dancing in the fire. "It hurts him to know that you do."

"There was a lot of talk. People goin' back in their goddamn mental calendars, countin' the months and watchin' the way she—"

"You're very much like him, Ben, in ways you probably don't see. Gestures, facial expressions."

"I guess it doesn't matter." He shook his head, still staring. "We've spent a lot of time together over the years. He wouldn't let me go away to boarding school, said it was the government's way of stealin' Indian kids. So I went to the local schools, always figured I'd'a gotten more out of school if I'd'a gone someplace else. But I learned a lot from him, I know that. And I know I gave him a lot of grief."

"You look like him, too."

"Yeah?" He chuckled, allowing the notion to light a spark in his eyes. "Hell, we all look alike."

"No, no, no, this is me you're talking to. I know this face. Your eyes," she said, touching the spokes on an outside corner, then tracing the contour of his face with her fingertip. "Your chin. Ears, they're shaped a lot like your father's."

He laughed. "Who you been lookin' at? Him or me?"

"Both. But yours is the face I know so well." She smiled, watching her finger delineate the fullness of his lips. "Love so much."

He caught the fingertip in his teeth and flicked it with his tongue. She smiled slowly. He smiled, first with his eyes, then his mouth. And then they slid together under the buffalo covers, each drowning in the other's kiss.

Much later, they fed each other bites of a sticky caramel bun, and she teased him about his "something sweet."

Even after lunch was over, the community center was the place to hang out and take it easy. Somebody had brought a TV, and there were card games and checkers, a little guitar playing, and plenty of visiting. A beef supper was in the making in the kitchen, young children were chasing each other across the floor, and some of the older girls lingered near the long table where their mothers nursed cooling cups of coffee and a baby or two.

TJ had driven back to McLaughlin to pick up her younger daughter, Delia. They had stopped to check on Dewey and reported that he was "getting itchy feet." Pouty and irritable from the long drive, Delia whispered something to her mother.

"You have to wait, now," TJ told her. "If these little ones see you with it, they'll be wanting some, too. There will be food soon."

Clara thought of what Ben had said about Sitanka's camp and the mothers trying to comfort their children. This was different, of course. Delia had probably never known real hunger. Neither had Clara. But she knew that

TJ and Ben had known some lean and hungry times, even though he'd rarely spoken of it to her. Poverty had been a fact of life for most people in the world of his youth. Keeper of the Sacred Pipe had never been a paid position among the Lakota. Most of the ceremonies had been outlawed in the nineteenth and early twentieth centuries and continued to be illegal, even though they were practiced secretly, until the passage of the 1978 American Indian Religious Freedom Act. Consequently when Ben was growing up there had been less call for a Sioux holy man than there was now.

"It hasn't always been *in* to be Indian," Clara remembered Ben telling her. Dewey had kept a few cows and done odd jobs, but there had been times when there was no work, no money, and only the occasional gift from those who had kept the traditions.

But they had not suffered from lack of food on this journey, as Sitanka's band had done a century ago. During the ride Clara had given much thought to the problem of hunger. The aroma of coffee brewing in big percolators in the corner of the room stirred mouth and stomach alike. More than a week on the South Dakota trail had served to remind her of some of the things she took for granted, like easy access to a quick snack. But what would it be like to look into the half-starved face of her own child and have no food to give her? She hoped she would never have to experience that kind of heartbreak, but she needed to be aware that many women did, and it was the ride that had seeded the need. When it was over, she vowed to open her eyes and ears, to read and look and listen with her heart and to do what she could, to care at the very least.

Margie Bigger, Joe's wife, had spent most of the day in the kitchen. She announced that she was taking a break as she joined the women at the table. She'd heard them talking about raising teenage girls, the girls themselves taking exception to some of the claims, and she broached the subject again.

"How do you handle mixing the two backgrounds?" Margie asked Clara. Joe was white, but Margie was Oglala Sioux, from Pine Ridge Reservation. "My daughter is half-white, too. She has a lot of white friends, which is fine. I never knew too many white people growing up, and I think it's good. You have to get to know other people. Otherwise you believe all the stuff you hear, like white people are all stingy, or they think they know it all, or they smell like they've been eating broccoli."

Clara smiled. "Broccoli?"

"I don't even know what broccoli smells like. Joe likes to make sauerkraut, though." Margie pinched her nose and gave her head a tight shake. "But it's good the way he makes it. I never thought I'd like it after that first time I saw him skimming the mold off, but it turns out good." She deliberated a moment, concentrating on making a neat row of dents in the rim of her Styrofoam cup with her thumbnail. "I used to be pretty shy about being around white people, but since we've been married, well, being around his people helps me understand him better."

Clara chuckled. "You mean, like, it explains his bad habits?"

"Nah, we've both got bad habits." Margie looked up and tossed off a shrug. "But the differences, you know? Like, sometimes it's food or clothes or whether to let the dog in the house, or the way we treat company or the way we handle a death in the family. Or the way we raise kids. He wants to set down more rules for the kids, while I'm more likely to let them decide a lot of things for themselves." She leaned back in her chair and gestured expansively. "It's not that any one way is good or bad. Just different. The more I get around other people, the better I understand."

"I know what you mean," Clara said. "Where we live, the population is pretty homogeneous. You really have to go out of your way to meet a variety of people, and in this day and age, I think we'd better *start* going out of our way to get to know each other face-to-face, or we're all going to be in big trouble."

"Aren't we in big trouble already?" TJ said. "Kids shooting each other for a little pocket change."

"There's hope. There's always hope." Clara glanced from the older faces to the younger ones and smiled. "That's what being a woman is all about, I think. Building bridges for our children to cross."

"Yeah, just look at me." Anna thumped her fists on the table, then drew an arch in the air with her finger to illustrate. "There's Mom's world, there's Dad's world, and I'm the bridge."

"Not the kind people can walk on, however," Clara put in.

Anna laughed. "Just let 'em try."

"Your dad'll be right there to throw 'em off," TJ said.

"I can pretty much stick up for myself, but my mom—" She leaned over to give Clara's shoulder a quick squeeze. "Mom just hates it when people don't take us for mother and daughter right away, which they never do. Right, Mom?" Mother and daughter exchanged a shared-experience look. "I think it's funny sometimes, but sometimes I don't. They look at you funny, and they ask the dumbest things, like, is she your real mom? Was your dad married before?" Anna wagged her forefinger Clara's way. "Remember that nurse?"

"You mean, last winter when you had that sinus infection?" Clara nodded and picked up the story. "We were in the exam room, and this woman was taking down Anna's symptoms. Anna was sitting up there on the exam table, feeling miserable but patiently answering the questions, even though the woman kept trying to talk to me rather than to Anna. Finally she looked at me, and out of the clear blue she asked, 'Is she from the group home?' ''

"What gave her that idea?" TJ demanded.

"It wasn't an idea. It was ignorance."

But Anna laughed, demonstrating with splayed fingers. "You should have seen Mom's hackles just stand right up. She said in her crispiest voice, 'Anna is *my daughter*. I have the stretch marks to prove it.' God, you should've seen the red face on that lady. Did she look stupefied! She just went, 'Uh-uh-uh . . . ' ''

Emerging from the kitchen with a cup of coffee, Ben had gone unnoticed, but the story had put a grin on his face. "Mom's a she-bear when it comes to her cub."

Margie laughed. "I wonder if bears talk about being like a *she-human* when it comes to her child."

"I was thinking this morning about the women with Sitanka's band," Clara said. "And now, thinking back, I realize that I felt threatened by that nurse's remark, which was really nothing more than thoughtless. But Anna is my little girl, and when I think of the hostility there is out there . . . I mean, you'd think it would be safer now, after a hundred years, that there would be real understanding and tolerance, but . . ." She sighed, shaking her head. "Things haven't changed that much. It's the worst kind of fear, being afraid for your child."

"And that day there were men with guns all around, and no way to protect the children," Ben said quietly.

"To see those guns pointed at her," Clara said, watching Anna whisper something in Billie's ear. "I would want to swallow her whole. Put her back where she started, inside me, where I could—" She slid her hand over her flat stomach. "But when the test actually comes, we don't always come through for our children, do we? We think we would, but then—" She looked up at Ben. "Sometimes we're all caught up in other things."

"We're human," TJ said. "We can't always see the dangers. Even if we see them, we can't always run interference for someone else."

But when that someone else is inside you, Clara thought, when it's your baby . . . The memory burned, along with the regret. She watched a young mother shoulder her just-fed infant and pat his back. Then she looked at her own child, almost a woman, and thought, it wasn't that long ago that I fed her and held her the same way.

But I wasn't eager to have the second one, she reminded herself as she left the table for a coffee refill. Or maybe he wasn't eager to have me. Maybe he had an inkling about me, that I wasn't . . .

She'd always thought of the baby as *he*, probably because a boy had been next on her grand-scheme schedule. She'd often been ribbed about her fixation with clocks and calendars. Ben, Dewey, Anna, her students back in her teaching days.

Mrs. Pipestone's schedule had definitely gone awry.

But somehow it was beginning to seem okay. She was following somebody else's itinerary, and for once she wasn't questioning it. She was just going, from one marker in the middle of nowhere to another of the same. Just trying to stay warm, stay in the saddle, watch out for her daughter, keep an eye on the hoop. And think things over. Memories were the mile markers of this journey, but it wasn't enough simply to remember. This was a *journey*, not an exercise in dwelling on the past. She was being called upon to take the memory out and *do* something with it. Discover what it really was and move on.

The question was, move where? How far? How . . .

Ah, the question. Her questions always begat more questions, to which she always needed comfortingly, reassuringly precise answers. And suddenly she had none. She had only feelings. An uncontrollable flood of them, and it was the uncontrollable part that was scary.

A white ball bounced across the floor in her direction. She switched her coffee cup to the other hand and tried for a one-handed snatch. She missed, but someone made a solid catch right behind her. She turned as Ben tossed the ball back into the children's game. He plucked a cigarette from his mouth, pushing his fingers through his thick black hair as he spat the smoke away from her. His eyes seemed to read her mind, and his wistful smile seemed to sympathize.

But rather than give a reading, he asked, "Lost in your thoughts?"

"Second thoughts," she admitted.

"Hmmm." He took another pull on the cigarette, damming the smoke in his chest for a moment, then blowing it away speculatively. "Those old wish-I'd-taken-the-high-road kind of thoughts?"

"You'd never guess what was on that road, though. The one I've been wishing we'd taken." She sat down on a homemade bench, her eyes suddenly glued to the white ball as it passed from one small hand across the tiled floor to another. "We should have had more children. I mean, I wanted more children, but . . ."

"But you had me?" He put one booted foot on the bench and smiled knowingly. "A kid for a husband?"

"No. I had me." She stared sightlessly at the ball, which had gotten loose again. "I didn't want to take the time. This is a day of rest, and it's dedicated to women. A woman should take the time for her family. What kind of a woman doesn't want to take the time?"

"The kind who thinks everything she does has to be done perfectly. It doesn't, Clara. Give yourself a break." She looked up at him, surprised by the invitation. He shrugged. "Then maybe you'll be able to give the rest of us one, too."

"You're right. I'm much too demanding."

"I didn't say that. I said, give it a rest. You're a good woman. Not perfect, mind you, but basically pretty damn good. You finished with that?" With a jerk of his chin he indicated her nearly empty cup. She gave it to him, and he took a final drag on the cigarette before he doused the remains in the dregs of her coffee.

He sat down beside her. "Clara, you can drive yourself crazy with should-haves, but it doesn't change anything. You can't go back and do it over. Just ask me."

"I know. I mean, I really do know that, I just . . ." She laid her hand on his thigh. "You know what else I feel bad about? When you did something wrong, it made me feel all that much more right."

"I screwed up and you fixed it?" He found it easy to chuckle over it now, remembering how he'd come to expect it, depend on it, alternately loved her and hated her for it.

"But I really couldn't, could I? You're the one who's good at fixing things. You fix cars. You fix things that are really broken. Around the yard, around the house . . ." Her hand stirred on his thigh, an old comforting habit, but also a loving gesture. "You fix things that most people would throw away."

"Guess there's something to be said for growing up poor, although I wouldn't recommend it as a goal in life."

"But you would recommend repairing things rather than throwing them away?"

"If you can. If it's something you like and it's still got a few good years left in it." He shifted, angling toward her, looking into her eyes. "Maybe it'll become a collector's item, and you'll wanna keep it forever."

"Not the way it was." She flexed her hand, squeezing gently, urgently. "There are parts we'd both have to fix, Ben. You've made a good start. I'm still . . ."

"It's okay." He put his hand over hers. "I needed a head start. I was all messed up, Clara. In some ways I'm glad you dumped me, because if you hadn't . . ." It was his turn to do the squeezing. In response, she turned her palm to his, and they held hands and smiled at each other like a couple of lovesick kids. "So you fix your part, and let me fix mine."

"Then I'll let you play with mine if you let me play with yours?"

"I am shocked, Clara-bow." His smile turned sensual. "Besides, that's the easy part. Those parts seem to be workin' just fine."

"No, don't take that for granted, Ben. It's not easy. Not for a woman. Not for *me*." Her hand-holding tightened, became a frantic appeal. "You think your infidelity was a small mistake. I think it was a big one. Is that the difference between a man and a woman?"

"I might have said that then. I don't think so now."

"I want to believe that. I'm not sure broken dreams can be fixed."

"This ride is about people who died for dreams, Clara. And here we are, all of us, remembering their dreams, trying to build or rebuild our own and lookin' for some reason to believe some part of those dreams might come true. That's what this journey is all about. We're lookin' for a reason to believe."

She nodded, studying their hands. "What if we don't find it?"

"Go lookin' somewhere else, I guess." He sighed, his shoulders sagging as he turned his attention to the children playing a few feet away. "Tomorrow we ride for the next seven generations. We'll pray for them to find it, huh?"

The next day was deadly cold. It was too cold to talk. Too cold either to make or to take a joke. Definitely too cold to piss, which was why nobody drank much at breakfast. It was too cold to ride, but they had to ride. They were almost there. It was too cold to do anything but think. In fact, it was the kind of bitter cold that turned thoughts into prayers.

Please, God, turn off the wind.

Okay, Tunkasila, I can stand the wind, as long as you keep it to my back.

Please, God, let my toes stop aching.

Okay, Tunkasila, I don't mind if my toes ache, just don't let them fall off.

Please, God, make my nose stop running.

Okay, Tunkasila, I don't care if my nose runs, just don't let my bladder explode.

The eerie moonscape of the Badlands offered windbreak. Barren hills eroded into wondrous gray formations. The serpentine trail wound amid castle battlements and Gothic spires, topping a cold day with visual frosting.

That night it was too cold to sleep, but after making a prayer that the world might become a less frigid environment for the next seven generations, they were too tired to do anything else.

All the world was white the following day. Bitterly cold and blindingly white. Doggedly the riders pushed past their misery toward their destination. Bullet-ridden signs marked the road, including the one that said, "Site of Wounded Knee Massacre 4 Miles."

Four miles, and the curious would view the place of carnage.

Four miles, and the pilgrims would reach the site of martyrdom.

Four miles to the little church that had been the scene of the American Indian Movement's protest occupation in more recent times.

Four miles to the friends waiting, the families waiting, the eyes of the world waiting.

Four miles and the ride would be over.

Four miles didn't seem like much now that they'd come so far together. They'd skipped the planned midday stop and pressed on, realizing that if they stopped, it would be hard to move again. Skipping lunch would mean an earlier arrival, a change in the schedule, but such things were flexible in Indian country. Darkness came early this deep in December, and a cold sun was better than no sun at all.

The feathered hoop finally topped the rise overlooking Wounded Knee Creek. Ben looked down and gave a deep mental sigh. Physical deep breathing wasn't wise in this kind of cold. But the sight of the monument, the little white stones and crosses accosted by blowing and drifting snow, the winding road, the pickups and horse trailers, all of it was welcome. Even though he couldn't see them, he knew that all eyes were turned toward the hill.

It was Grand Entry time, he thought with a warm, deeply interior smile. He'd been chosen more than once to lead the Grand Entry at a rodeo, and he'd galloped around the arena, holding the flag high and lapping up the applause. Hero for a day, he thought. And why the hell not? He lifted the hoop aloft and gave out a piercing victory whoop as he dug his heel into his gelding's flanks and took off down the hill, fairly flying.

Why the hell not?

The riders behind him took the signal and sounded the cry as they crested the hill, bounding over the rise and plunging into the valley. The sacrifice was not made in vain. This day they rode for the ancestors. The men honored them with high-spirited whoops of victory, and the women chimed in with vivacious high-pitched trilling. This was the answer to the spent bullets and the guns of the past.

We have survived. We dwell in this land, and we know who we are, and we remember those who have gone before.

Hoka hey! The Lakota live!

Over two hundred riders poured over the ridge. Clara

lingered at the crest, drinking in the rare, timeless beauty of the moment. Tufts of red grass poked through the snow. Sun dogs, winter's rainbows, put on a cheerful display in the pale blue sky. On the windswept flat beyond the two-lane highway that was lined today with motorized vehicles, trailers, and spectators, there had once been an encampment. The women and children had outnumbered the men, and among the men were those who were too old and tired to fight anymore. They were all hungry. Most were poorly clothed, and their weapons were few. So many feet bled from the cold and from the long, desperate push southward. Some of the people were sick. They were all exhausted. And they were fearful of what the day might bring.

They were surrounded by another encampment, this one housing no women, no children, only men who were young and fit for duty, well equipped and armed to the teeth. Sitanka had surrendered, even though his people had not been fighting. Dancing and praying were their only crimes. Neither were they looking for a fight. They were looking for peace and succor, hoping to find refuge with their relatives.

Still they surrendered. They gave up their weapons, their knives, even their tools. But when one young man tried to conceal the rifle he said he'd paid dearly for, then objected to turning it over, a shot was fired, and the slaughter ensued.

From her vantage point Clara could see the draws and ravines, like wrinkles stretching away from the campsite, pockets and folds into which Mother Earth had tucked those she could reach and sheltered them as best she could from the hailstorm of bullets. Among those sheltered perhaps was Maziyapa, Iron Hammer, her own daughter's great-great-grandfather.

Clara watched, pulse pounding, as her husband led the riders, galloping in a circle around the little cemetery on the knoll below. He carried the hoop, eagle feathers fluttering, the heat of his triumphant outcry misting the air.

"Hey, Mom! We made it!"

Anna trotted up the hill on her frost-bellied paint. She caught up to her mother, shared a shivery hug, and together they plowed down the hill and into the valley below, trilling in the woman's way as they went.

The cameras clicked and whirred, recording the exultant arrival. They had to get all their pictures now, Alec Red Horse announced over a loudspeaker from the cab of a pickup. No photographs would be allowed during the graveside ceremony, which would be held "pretty soon, when the riders are ready."

But first they had the circle. One last circle for themselves and the spirit that had brought them this far. They were kinsmen in this venture. The ride had changed them both individually and as one. By becoming a circle they had accomplished a remarkable feat. They had carried one another to this place. Ben gave thanks for all this in a brief song. Then the riders and their friends and supporters saw to the horses' needs before they made their way to the fenced monument marking the century-old mass grave.

"We need to hurry right along," Alec said, his voice carrying across the sea of hats and blanketed heads. "It's pretty cold. If you have a camera, we'd like you to put it away now. Otherwise you might be asked to surrender it to our, uh, security people. Lately I been thinkin' about gettin' myself a new camera. Heh-heh-heh."

The journalists looked at one another, some conferring on the matter, others putting their gear away feverishly, just in case.

The loudspeaker came on again. "Okay, they want the family members, the descendants of those we mourn today, anyone who's a family member can go inside the fence. So, you know who you are."

The words echoed on the plain below, but movement of bundled bodies was slow.

"We need to hurry every chance we get," Alec intoned from inside the pickup. "It's pretty cold. There's gonna be a feed over in the Manderson school gym after we're finished here. That *papa* soup is gonna taste mighty good on a day like this."

People were still milling around, some seeking a good viewing spot outside the fence, some simply greeting one another with a gloved handshake. The holes of face masks and the edges of mouth-shielding mufflers were crusted with frost. At fifty below, only the eyes were visible on most of the walking bundles. It was hard to tell who was who. Most of the riders knew one another by the color of a jacket or a hat, but when TJ ran into Clara, she pulled the wool scarf off her nose and laughed. "Oh, of course. It's my *wasicun* sister. I'm goin' around exposing noses so I can tell who I'm looking at. You know you've got frosty eyelashes?"

"So do you." Clara adjusted her scarf, regretting the escape of a pool of her own warm breath. "TJ, we made it."

"I kinda thought so, the way you've been looking at each other."

"No, I mean—"

An impish spark danced in Tara Jean's eyes, made brighter by the blue cap and scarf closely framing them.

Clara stared, then burst out laughing. "We made it, and then we made it, and now, look here, we *made* it! *All* the *way*," she crooned gleefully.

"All the way," TJ echoed.

"Where's Ben? They want you guys inside the fence. And Anna and Billie . . ." Clara did a little rubbernecking, but it was useless in the meandering crowd.

"Ben's probably getting the stuff together," TJ said. "Don't worry, they can't start without the pipe keeper."

"Do you think he knows what to do? He's pretty new at this."

"No, he's not." TJ patted Clara's shoulder, her own sisterly pride beaming in her eyes. "Believe it or not, my brother was born to it. Whatever he does, it'll be the right thing."

And it was, for it was done, as their father would have had it, in a sacred way. While the drummer thumped a throbbing beat, Ben burned sweet grass in a simple coffee can and used an eagle feather to direct the fragrant smoke toward the mourners. He prayed quietly in Lakota, but when he lifted his voice in traditional song, timeless tears flowed freely all around him. Many heads were draped with star quilts, others with blankets, some colorfully striped, others emblazoned with a bird or a wolf. In the valley below a horse whinnied. The wind carried the echo of the pipe keeper's voice into the hills, while a crying baby spoke for the generations to come.

Clara's family was inside the fence. It felt a little strange, being on the outside looking in. It was a rare occurrence for one of her race, although not for one of her gender. And so she understood. She shared the sadness, and she wept for all the broken hoops and the shattered promises. For all the breaches in all the circles in all the universe, she wept.

And, for a moment in time, warm tears melted the frost that glazed the world's eternal pain.

The brief ceremony ended. The mourners began filing under the arch spanning the brick pillars to form the gateway to the concrete-edged mass grave. Clara turned away from the fence and found herself standing face-to-face with a woman draped Madonna-fashion in an old army blanket. Wisps of red-gold hair framed the blue-eyed face, ruddy from the cold. The angelic countenance seemed only vaguely familiar.

"Wasn't that somethin'?"

The voice, to Clara's amazement, was Tanya Beale's.

Clara nodded. "It certainly was."

The two women looked at one another for a moment, then shared a spontaneous embrace; both blubbering unintelligibly but communicating perfectly.

Tanya drew back and laughed. "Your mascara has made complete circles around both your eyes."

"Really?"

"Never seen anything like it. Must have something to do with how cold it is. We got circles everywhere." She looked around in absolute wonder. "It surely has been somethin', hasn't it, Clara?"

"Something very special, Tanya." Despite the cold, Clara's smile came easily. "I'm glad you came."

"Me, too." Tanya laughed as she pointed to herself, then Clara. "Me, too, you." Then something behind Clara's back caught Tanya's eye. "Looks like your husband's waitin' on ya."

Clara turned, barely hearing Tanya's soft "See ya" in her eagerness to join her husband and find some shelter from the cold.

But he had other plans. "TJ's gonna take you and Annie over to Manderson. I'll be there later. There's something I've gotta do."

"But they might need you for—"

"There will be people lined up from one side of the gym to the other to get at the microphone." He grinned as he backed away. "It's speech-makin' time. You know I'm no good at that."

"I don't know any such thing." A sudden flash of panic seized her. Instinctively she sought to stop him with a motherly "Besides, you haven't eaten anything."

"Save me a piece of fry bread, okay? Two pieces." Backpedaling, he showed her two heavy-gloved fingers. "I'll be back by eight at the latest."

"Tonight?"

"Tonight." Then he understood the real question, and he came back, took her shoulders in his hands, and told her solemnly, "I'll show you how good I am at keeping my word nowadays."

The word had gotten out. People were gathering for "the doings" at the Little Wound School gym. A set of bleachers had been pulled out on the side opposite a stage hung with blue curtains. The aroma of a feast in the making drifted through the kitchen doors into the center of the floor, where long tables and chairs covered basketball court lines. Painted geometric designs brightened the walls.

There was a lot of hand-shaking and shoulder-slapping going on as the riders were greeted by community members. The proceedings began with announcements. Somebody had left a gate open on one of the pens and some of the horses had gotten out. Most of them had already been rounded up, but horse owners might want to check. Riders who had borrowed equipment were to pile it in the corner of the gym so that the owners could claim it.

The formal speeches began with the introduction of the governor of South Dakota, who spoke of his admiration for the riders, of his commitment to recognizing the needs of the Indian people of the state, and of a "year of reconciliation" to end the long history of misunderstanding between non-Indians and the Lakota people.

Next, the local tribal chairman spoke of a bill recently passed in Congress which had originally contained a formal apology to the Lakota people for the massacre of their unarmed ancestors after they had surrendered to the U.S. Army in 1890. But the bill had been reworded by the South Dakota delegation, changing *apologize* to *express deep regret*. In addition, the request to rescind the Congressional Medals of Honor awarded to some of the soldiers for their actions at Wounded Knee had been denied. It would be impossible to go back and review the actions of each recipient so long after the fact, and it was unnecessary to humiliate their descendants at this point.

"Too bad they didn't feel the same way about taking Jim Thorpe's medals away after they found out somebody had paid him a few bucks to play a little baseball," TJ muttered to Clara as they listened together from their bleacher seats. "Finally they decide to give back the medals, way after he's dead. Interesting how these committees pick and choose who it's unnecessary to humiliate."

Clara recalled the old group photographs of the Seventh Cavalry taken after their so-called victory at Wounded Knee. Young men arranged row on row before the photographer, some standing, others sitting or kneeling so that every face would be recorded for posterity. With the uncompromising expression befitting a soldier, each displayed the weapon he'd presumably used during the recent campaign. Clara wondered what thoughts lurked behind each pair of eyes. She wondered if they'd gone back to the campsite days later when the frozen bodies shown in some of the other pictures were tossed into the trench by civilians hired to do the job.

When the air was filled with bullets and smoke and terror, maybe children were hard to see. If they had gone back, if they had seen the little bodies . . . But the old photographs said little of anyone's feelings. Feelings were left to the viewer, Clara realized. Along with those who would listen and connect the past with the present after so many years had passed.

After the dignitaries had their say, there were comments from some of the riders. They expressed their appreciation for the support they'd received from people along the way, from each other, from Tunkasila. Several of them told amusing anecdotes, stories about playing jokes on each other or having a run-in with a recalcitrant horse. It was difficult to express what the ride had meant to them. They knew it had changed them, but the experience was too fresh to evaluate. It was still hard to realize that it was over, that they had reached their destination.

Anna's turn came, and she took the microphone in hand and spoke with newfound confidence. "I'm really proud of my family. My mom and dad, my grandfather, my auntie, my cousins, we all got together on this, and we put aside everything else, and we just said we're gonna do it. But now I know I have even a bigger family than I ever realized I had. Whenever I had a problem, there was always someone to help me, and not just one of my parents. It was great. I think it's really helped me grow up a lot."

Clara's heart swelled with a mother's pride. The doubts and fears that had plagued her every waking moment in months past seemed like a bad dream now as she and Anna traded smiles past a crowd of jostling heads. But there was no distance between them. Not now. They'd shared the journey, and the circle would always connect them. Clara felt fat and full to overflowing. She wasn't sure she would be able to speak when her turn came. She listened to Elliot Plume speak of the pipe changing hands. He asked that people remember both the old pipe carrier and the young one in their prayers.

"Dewey carried the hoop for us, and then Ben carried it. It went from father to son, both good men. Both men we could trust to lead the way. So we followed the hoop throughout our journey. You learn to keep your eye on the hoop throughout your journey because you know it ain't gonna stop. It ain't gonna wait. But you stay with it, it's gonna keep you following the road in a sacred way. And that's how we got here." He scanned the line of riders before adding, "Ben Pipestone isn't here right now, but he'll be back with us soon, and I ask each and ever one of you to shake his hand when he gets here."

Clara took the microphone and cleared her throat as

she stole a glance at Anna. "I want to thank my daughter for inspiring my decision to come on the ride. And my husband, my father, my sister, my family . . . all of you for . . ." She swallowed hard and took a deep breath, seeking a steadier voice. " . . . for taking me in. I'm stronger than I thought I was. I think I have a better understanding of a woman's power. I want to keep going. And I believe I can."

She looked for her daughter as she handed the microphone back to Elliot. Anna was grinning ear to ear.

The riders received handshakes from a seemingly unending line of well-wishers, after which many community members came to the microphone and spoke of what had been accomplished. Much mention was made of the martyrs and survivors of Wounded Knee and of mending the shattered hoop. The people would mend the hoop themselves, many of them said.

One older man took exception to "all this talk of forgiveness." He pointed southward and said, "I go down to that cemetery, and I read the names on that monument, and I look around me at what's still goin' on, and I can't forgive," he declared, and there were some few *hou*s of agreement. "I won't forgive."

Won't forgive? Clara mused. Or won't forget. The man sounded bitter, and his bitterness had a familiar ring to it. She imagined herself aging in a vat of acrimony, unwilling to let go, unable to walk away. The image made her cringe inwardly.

TJ caught her shaking off the thought and gave her a puzzled look. "Chills?"

"Like somebody just walked on my grave," Clara said, using an expression of her mother's.

"What a thought. The girls want to stay at their cousins'."

"More cousins?"

TJ laughed and waved her hands. "They're everywhere, they're everywhere."

Alone again, Clara mused as she surveyed the crowded room. "Is it okay to sleep here, do you think? I mean, after this party breaks up."

"Sure, if that's what you want. But your husband might have other ideas."

Clara shook her head. "It's too cold to stay outside."

"Too cold for me, that's for sure. But you're the only one who can decide what's best for you."

"Do you know where he went?"

"I've got a pretty good idea, but he didn't tell me because he knew damn well I wouldn't approve." TJ folded her arms, glanced past Clara, and shook her head. "But you can't talk 'em out of it, you know. They're gonna do what they're gonna do."

Clara gave a sad nod. Obviously TJ assumed that she would welcome the man back with open arms no matter what. Clara wasn't going to comment. She wasn't going to ask *what* or speculate about *what*. He'd done what he'd been asked to do. He'd carried the pipe and the hoop to Wounded Knee. The rest was his business. She'd just about had herself believing he wouldn't backslide, and she decided to hang on to that possibility for a few more hours.

Supper had been set out, served, and put away. There was a giveaway going on, sponsored by the women of Manderson and Porcupine. It was getting close to nine, and Clara was beginning to worry. He wasn't drinking, she told herself. She couldn't imagine him doing that now. The weather was so cold, the roads so long and desolate, that anything could happen. Worse things than falling off the wagon.

Great. Either he's drunk or he's stuck somewhere, freezing to death. Could be both.

What was she thinking? They'd been on the road for two weeks in cold weather. They'd been living outside for two whole weeks. Ben could take care of himself.

Ben could, indeed, take care of himself.

Then the side door opened and Ben stepped inside, carrying his father in his arms. Howard White Calf followed with a wheelchair, which he quickly unfolded so that Ben could set the frail old man down.

"Shut the door," somebody shouted. "You're lettin' the cold air . . . Hey, it's Ben!"

Ben straightened the blankets over his father's lap, then turned, ignoring the greetings as he searched for his wife's face.

Clara rose slowly from her seat. She found herself trembling. She was relieved, overjoyed, and anxious, all at once. Ben was back. He was safe. He had, once again, done what he'd been asked to do. But Dewey was ill. He shouldn't have left his hospital bed, shouldn't have come out in the cold, shouldn't . . .

The old man's twinkling eyes met hers. He nodded, clearly pleased with himself for doing all those things he shouldn't have done. He waved her over. "You gave him my message," the old man said as she drew close.

"Yes, I did, but . . ." She knelt beside his blanketed knees. "How are you feeling?"

"On the outside, old," he said with a smile. "On the inside, young. If you could see me on the inside, you'd have a hard time choosin' between me and that husband of yours."

"I'm glad I don't have to choose." She leaned closer and whispered, "I love you both."

"Could you find me some decent food then, daughter? They've been feedin' me nothin' but baby food and pills."

After he'd eaten, Dewey demanded his chance at the microphone. Ben laughed, saying he should have known the old man wasn't about to miss his chance to tell a story. He pushed the wheelchair center stage. But before he had a chance to step away, Dewey caught his arm as he reached inside his shirt and withdrew an eagle feather. He motioned for his son to lean closer. Ben looked shaken. Slowly he lowered one knee beside his father's chair, bowed his head, and permitted the feather to be tied into his hair.

"I used to wonder what was gonna happen to us Indians," Dewey began, after Ben handed him the microphone. "Long time ago when they were taking all the children and putting them in boarding school, I used to think, when they come back, they won't be Indians no more. Then when they started all that relocation stuff, sending people to the cities for training and saying they were gonna terminate the reservations, I thought, pretty soon there won't be no more Indian country to come back to. And I knew how old Sitting Bull must've felt when the people were givin' in to the government, signing their papers, and he said he was the only Indian left.

"I saw a show on TV once about the buffalo, the lions, the wolves, and some of the other four-leggeds that they've been killin' off and killin' off, and pretty soon there was just a little bit left." He measured "a little bit" between a gnarled thumb and forefinger. "Somebody said, 'Wait now. These creatures are almost gone. We better save a *few*, anyway. Keep them in a place where they can't hurt nothin', so we can look at them and remember.' "

"In a way, that's what happened to us. After they got done at Wounded Knee, they said, 'Wait now, this don't look too good. Let them live, a *few* at least.' But it got so it was pretty hard to remember who we were, even for us, and some of the old ones got to thinkin', maybe I'm the last one. Maybe there won't be no seven more generations."

He searched the crowd until he found three of his granddaughters, and he smiled. "But there will be. I look around at these young faces, and I think, I'm gonna see that Old Bull pretty soon, and I'm gonna tell him he wasn't the only Indian left." He chuckled as he wagged a finger at nobody in particular. Nobody particularly *visible*, anyway. "And then we're gonna have some good laughs together, him and me."

As Dewey gave up the microphone, Robert Cady burst forth from the crowd with his camera. "I wonder if you'd mind if I took your picture, Mr. Pipestone."

Dewey nodded. "Take one of me and my son. The old pipe carrier, the new pipe carrier." He motioned to Ben to close in behind him.

"Try to look serious, now," Ben muttered, striking a square-shouldered pose. "Like two big Indians, can't crack a smile."

"Right." Dewey put his hand behind his own head and stuck up two fingers.

"Cut it out, now, you're makin' me laugh."

"One smilin', one serious," Dewey quipped. "We'll give you two for the price of one, if you'll promise to get the story right this time, Mr. News Man. This ain't no hostile uprising. Just tell what you saw, and don't put words in our mouths."

"Your words are better than any I could come up with," Cady said, lining up another shot. "This is the smiling one, now. What word would make you smile? Probably not cheese."

"Commodity cheese, hey," Howard White Calf put in.

"Just look at your wife's face, *cinks*," Dewey said to his son. Clara smiled and waved. Dewey grinned at Cady. "Now he's smilin', right?"

"He sure is." Cady smiled, too, and snapped the picture.

"We're checkin' him in at the clinic down here tonight," Ben told Clara later when, after all the hand-shaking, she finally coaxed him into the kitchen for a bite to eat. "We made a deal. He agreed to let them take him somewhere where they have the equipment to

check him over and see what they can do for him." He
tore a piece of cold fry bread in half and dipped it into
the soup she had pushed in front of him. "I agreed to
bring him here, and I promised I wouldn't let him die
in a hospital. If he has his way, he's gonna do it right
here before I can get him anywhere else. He's just gonna
wear himself out and die happy. There's stuff goin' on
tomorrow, and he wants to be here. Probably wants to
make sure I can offer a prayer without screwin' it up
too bad."

She watched him bite into the bread. "I'll be surprised if his heart doesn't burst with pride." As hers
was about to.

"What a way to go, huh?" He finished the fry bread
and half the soup, then looked up finally as he caught her
hand in his. "What are we gonna do, Clara-bow? Where
do we go from here?"

She glanced at the kitchen door. "I was wondering that
myself." Anywhere, she thought. "I was thinking it was
too cold to sleep in a tent tonight, but if that's where
you're going, I'm game."

"You are, huh?" He drew her hand to his lips, kissed
it, then looked up smiling. "You'll sleep with me anywhere?"

She nodded solemnly. "Anywhere at all."

"Will you take me back, Clara? You and Annie?
Not the way I was before. The way I am now, even
though . . ." He shook his head, his smile turning irre-
sistibly sad. "Honey, I ain't never gonna be perfect."

She smiled. "Maybe perfection isn't all it's cracked
up to be."

"A guy who's found himself a one-man woman, no
choice, he's gotta keep tryin'." He held her hand fast.
"I want you to trust me again. I want you to know that
Ben Pipestone really is a one-woman man."

"I believe you can be, Ben." She closed her eyes and
said the words. "I want you home."

"It's not just me," he warned, taking her in his arms. "It's me and this pipe. And whatever I have to do to keep the, uh . . ." He smiled softly at her. "The fire goin', I guess."

"Your home is with us," she told him, cupping his cheek in her hand. "But our place is with you. We'll work out the details. We always have, haven't we?"

"You'll sleep in a tent with me tonight?"

"I said I'd trust you. I guess . . ."

"Wait 'til you see." His eyes were full of boyish excitement. "Where's your jacket? Here." Quickly he wrapped her in the pipe carrier's coat.

"You can't go out . . ."

But the celebrational giveaways were still going strong, and he'd received a blanket, which he threw around his shoulders. "Courtin' robe," he said as he led her out the kitchen door and into the breath-stealing cold. "Remember when we were first married and we bought that little two-man tent to take along on the rodeo circuit?"

"We spent a whole month's pay on sleeping bags and a camp stove and all kinds of—" She had to practically run to keep up with him as he strode across the snow-packed street.

"Remember what we did that first night after we got all that stuff home?"

"We set it up in that dinky little living room and ended up—"

He hopped up on the front stoop of a similarly dinky little house and turned the front door knob. "An old rodeo buddy lives here."

"Another—"

"He said we could have the living room all to our-selves, but I think he's got three or four kids in each bed-room, so when we end up doin' what we did before . . ." He drew her inside, turned the switch on a lamp, and stepped aside to let her see that he'd taken the liberty of setting up her little tent. "Well, we'll just have to do it very quietly. None of that squealin' and buckin' you like to do."

"Ben!" She laughed, shaking her head in amazement as she eyed the tent. "So here we are. Back where we started."

"Not exactly. It's more like startin' all over. But only if . . ." He drew her into his arms, enfolding her with him in his blanket, holding her close. "You're never gonna be able to forget. I know that. But we've gotta find a way to put that behind us, Clara."

"By forgiving. It's not such a difficult thing to say once you understand how it works. It comes from faith and hope and the promise of healing." She looked into his eyes, just the way she had when they'd first exchanged vows. "I forgive your trespasses because I believe in you. And I hope you'll forgive mine."

He swallowed hard. "Woman, I'm gonna love you like you can't *believe*."

"Not a chance. Over the last two weeks I have increased my believing capacity by—"

Ben grinned. "Yeah, but I've been workin' on my lovin' capacity for *two years*, and you ain't even seen the tip of the iceberg."

"I'll take the tip, cowboy." Clara smiled saucily as she flipped his belt buckle open. "But no icebergs."

AUTHOR'S NOTE

꧁❧꧂

Summer is powwow time in Indian country. There's always plenty of food, games and contests, lots of music and dancing, and in the midst of it all there are "giveaways." People present gifts as a public show of appreciation, honor, respect. The giver calls a name, the recipient accepts a gift, and a simple handshake is shared. If this were a giveaway, I would have a table full of quilts and blankets on this page, and I would call the names of people who helped make it possible for Clyde and me to participate in the Big Foot Memorial Ride in 1990. First among them would be our nephew, Dwaine, his wife, Karen, and our brother, Glen. They shared their horses and gave their support. I would also honor Arvol Looking Horse, Carol Ann Hart, Ron McNeil, Isaac Dog Eagle, Howard Eagle Shield, and so many others whose influence helped shape the setting, the soul, and the integrity of this story.

Winter is storytelling, visiting, crafting, and pretty much staying-put time in Indian country. No one would consider walking or riding horseback across more than 250 miles of frozen Dakota prairie without good cause, which is what this story is all about. Although the 1990 Sitting Bull Memorial Run and Big Foot Memorial Ride were actual events, readers must bear in mind that the characters in *Reason to Believe* are fictitious, as is their story. I followed the itinerary of the ride fairly closely, and many scenes, such as the community celebrations and the ride through Timber Lake, parallel the experiences we had on the ride. So does the weather. Man, did it get cold! But this is a work of fiction. My intention was to weave the healing spirit of the ride into a story about mending broken relationships and to convey the ride's investment in understanding in a way that only fiction can. I do not presume to speak for Indian people, but only to reflect a piece of the experience of a sojourner in Indian Country.

In your letters many of you ask me for recommendations regarding charities that benefit Native Americans. I suggest you investigate any charity by contacting your state's attorney general's office. You might consider the American Indian College Fund for your donation. The address is 21 West 68 Street, Suite 1F, New York, New York 10023. This foundations helps support over twenty accredited tribal colleges located on or near Indian reservations.